the thousandth floor

ALSO BY
KATHARINE McGEE

The Dazzling Heights

the thousandth floor

KATHARINE McGEE

HARPER

An Imprint of HarperCollinsPublishers

HarperCollins
PUBLISHERS
Since 1817

The Thousandth Floor
Copyright © 2016 by Alloy Entertainment and Katharine McGee

alloyentertainment

Produced by Alloy Entertainment
1325 Avenue of the Americas
New York, NY 10019
www.alloyentertainment.com

Library of Congress Control Number: 2016938974

ISBN 978-0-06-241860-9

Typography by Liz Dresner

18 19 20 21   PC/LSCC   10 9 8 7 6 5 4
❖
First paperback edition, 2017

For Lizzy

PROLOGUE

November 2118

THE SOUNDS OF laughter and music were dying down on the thousandth floor, the party breaking up by bits and pieces as even the rowdiest guests finally stumbled into the elevators and down to their homes. The floor-to-ceiling windows were squares of velvety darkness, though in the distance the sun was quietly rising, the skyline turning ocher and pale pink and a soft, shimmering gold.

And then a scream cut abruptly through the silence as a girl fell toward the ground, her body falling ever faster through the cool predawn air.

In just three minutes, the girl would collide with the unforgiving cement of East Avenue. But now—her hair whipped up like a banner, the silk dress snapping around the curves of her body, her bright red mouth frozen in a perfect *O* of shock—now, in this instant, she was more beautiful than she had ever been.

They say that before death, people's lives flash before their eyes. But as the ground rushed ever faster toward her, the girl could think only of the past few hours, the path she'd taken that ended here. If only she hadn't talked to him. If only she hadn't been so foolish. If only she hadn't gone up there in the first place.

When the dock monitor found what remained of her body and shakily pinged in a report of the incident, all he knew was that the girl was the first person to fall from the Tower in its twenty-five years. He didn't know who she was, or how she'd gotten outside.

He didn't know whether she'd fallen, or been pushed, or whether—crushed by the weight of unspoken secrets—she'd decided to jump.

AVERY

Two months earlier

"I HAD A great time tonight," Zay Wagner said as he walked Avery Fuller to the door of her family's penthouse. They'd been down at the New York Aquarium on the 830th floor, dancing in the soft glow of the fish tanks and familiar faces. Not that Avery cared much about the aquarium. But as her friend Eris always said, a party was a party, right?

"Me too." Avery tilted her bright blond head toward the retinal scanner, and the door unlocked. She offered Zay a smile. "Night."

He reached for her hand. "I was thinking maybe I could come in? Since your parents are away and everything . . ."

"I'm sorry," Avery mumbled, hiding her annoyance with a fake yawn. He'd been finding excuses to touch her all night; she should have seen this coming. "I'm exhausted."

"Avery." Zay dropped her hand and took a step back, running his fingers through his hair. "We've been doing this for weeks now. Do you even *like* me?"

Avery opened her mouth, then fell silent. She had no idea what to say.

Something flickered over Zay's expression—irritation? confusion? "Got it. I'll see you later." He retreated to the elevator, then turned back, his eyes traveling over her once more. "You looked really beautiful tonight," he added. The elevator doors closed behind him with a click.

Avery sighed and stepped into the grand entryway of her apartment. Back before she was born, when the Tower was under construction, her parents had bid aggressively to get this place—the entire top floor, with the only two-story foyer in the entire structure. They were so proud of this entryway, but Avery hated it: the hollow way it made her footsteps echo, the glinting mirrors on every surface. She couldn't look anywhere without seeing her reflection.

She kicked off her heels and walked barefoot toward her room, leaving the shoes in the middle of the hallway. Someone would pick them up tomorrow, one of the bots, or Sarah, if she actually showed up on time.

Poor Zay. Avery did like him: he was funny in a loud, fizzy way that made her laugh. But she just didn't feel anything when they kissed.

But the only boy Avery *did* want to kiss was the one she never, ever could.

She stepped into her room and heard the soft hum as the room comp whizzed to life, scanning her vitals and adjusting the temperature accordingly. An ice water appeared on the table next to her antique four-poster bed—probably because of the champagne still turning in her empty stomach, though Avery didn't bother asking. After Atlas skipped town, she'd disabled the voice function on the comp. He'd been the one to set it on the British accent and name it Jenkins. Talking to Jenkins without him was too depressing.

Zay's words echoed in her head. *You looked really beautiful tonight.* He was just trying to give her a compliment, of course; he couldn't have known how much Avery hated that word. All her life she'd been hearing how beautiful she was—from teachers, boys, her parents. By now the phrase had lost all meaning. Atlas, her adopted brother, was the only one who knew better than to compliment her.

The Fullers had spent years and a great deal of money conceiving Avery. She wasn't sure how expensive she'd actually been to make, though she guessed her value at slightly below that of their apartment. Her parents, who were both of middling height with ordinary looks and thinning brown hair, had flown in the world's leading researcher from Switzerland to help mine their genetic material. Somewhere in the million combinations of their very average DNA, they found the single possibility that led to Avery.

She wondered, sometimes, how she would've turned out if her parents had made her naturally, or just screened for diseases like most people on the upper floors. Would she have inherited her mom's skinny shoulders, or her father's big teeth? Not that it mattered. Pierson and Elizabeth Fuller had paid for *this* daughter, with honey-colored hair and long legs and deep blue eyes, her dad's intelligence, and her mom's quick wit. Atlas always joked that stubbornness was her one imperfection.

Avery wished that was the only thing wrong with her.

She shook out her hair, yanked it into a loose bun, and walked purposefully from her room. In the kitchen she swung open the pantry door, already reaching for the hidden handle to the mech panel. She'd found it years ago during a game of hide-and-seek with Atlas. She wasn't even sure whether her parents knew about it; it wasn't as if they ever set foot in here.

Avery pushed the metal panel inward, and a ladder swung

down into the narrow pantry space. Clutching the skirts of her ivory silk gown with both hands, she folded herself into the crawl space and started up, counting the rungs instinctively in Italian as she did, *uno, due, tre*. She wondered if Atlas had spent any time in Italy this year, if he'd even gone to Europe at all.

Balancing on the top rung, she reached to release the trapdoor and stepped eagerly into the wind-whipped darkness.

Beneath the deafening roar of the wind, Avery heard the rumbling of various machines on the roof around her, huddled under their weatherproof boxes or photovoltaic panels. Her bare feet were cold on the metal slabs of the platform. Steel supports arced from each corner, joining overhead to form the Tower's iconic spire.

It was a clear night, no clouds in the air to dampen her eyelashes or bead into moisture on her skin. The stars glittered like crushed glass against the dark vastness of the night sky. If anyone knew she was up here, she'd be grounded for life. Exterior access over the 150th floor was forbidden; all the terraces above that level were protected from the high-speed winds by heavy panes of polyethylene glass.

Avery wondered if anyone had ever set foot up here besides her. There were safety railings along one side of the roof, presumably in case maintenance workers came up, but to her knowledge, no one ever had.

She'd never told Atlas. It was one of only two secrets she had kept from him. If he found out, he would make sure she didn't come back, and Avery couldn't bear the thought of giving this up. She loved it here—loved the wind battering her face and tangling her hair, bringing tears to her eyes, howling so loud that it drowned out her own wild thoughts.

She stepped closer to the edge, relishing the twist of vertigo in her stomach as she gazed out over the city, the monorails curving through the air below like fluorescent snakes. The horizon seemed impossibly far. She could see from the lights of New Jersey in the west to the streets of the Sprawl in the south, to Brooklyn in the east, and farther, the pewter gleam of the Atlantic.

And beneath her bare feet lay the biggest structure on earth, a whole world unto itself. How strange that there were millions of people below her at this very moment, eating, sleeping, dreaming, touching. Avery blinked, feeling suddenly and acutely alone. They were strangers, all of them, even the ones she knew. What did she care about them, or about herself, or about anything, really?

She leaned her elbows on the railing and shivered. One wrong move could send her over. Not for the first time, she wondered how it would feel, falling two and a half miles. She imagined it would be strangely peaceful, the feeling of weightlessness as she reached terminal velocity. And she'd be dead of a heart attack long before she hit the ground. Closing her eyes, she tilted forward, curling her silver-painted toes over the edge—just as the back of her eyelids lit up, her contacts registering an incoming ping.

She hesitated, a wave of guilty excitement crashing over her at the sight of his name. She'd done so well avoiding this all summer, distracting herself with the study abroad program in Florence, and more recently with Zay. But after a moment, Avery turned and clattered quickly back down the ladder.

"Hey," she said breathlessly when she was back in the pantry, whispering even though there was no one around to hear. "You haven't called for a while. Where are you?"

"Somewhere new. You'd love it here." His voice in her ear sounded the same, warm and rich as always. "How're things, Aves?"

And there it was: the reason Avery had to climb into a windstorm to escape her thoughts, the part of her engineering that had gone horribly wrong.

On the other end of the call was Atlas, her brother—and the reason she never wanted to kiss anyone else.

LEDA

AS THE COPTER crossed the East River into Manhattan, Leda Cole leaned forward, pressing her face against the flexiglass for a better look.

There was always something magical about this first glimpse of the city, especially now, with the windows of the upper floors blazing in the afternoon sun. Beneath the neochrome surface Leda caught flashes of color where the elevators shot past, the veins of the city pumping its lifeblood up and down. It was the same as ever, she thought, utterly modern and yet somehow timeless. Leda had seen countless pics of the old New York skyline, the one people always romanticized. But compared to the Tower she thought it looked jagged and ugly.

"Glad to be home?" her mom asked carefully, glancing at her from across the aisle. Leda gave a curt nod, not bothering to answer. She'd barely spoken to her parents since they'd picked her up from rehab earlier this morning. Or really, since the incident back in July that had sent her there.

"Can we order Miatza tonight? I've been craving a dodo burger for weeks," her brother, Jamie, said, in a clear attempt to cheer her up. Leda ignored him. Jamie was only eleven months older, about to start his senior year, but he and Leda weren't all that close. Probably because they were nothing alike.

With Jamie everything was simple and straightforward, and he never seemed to worry that much at all. He and Leda didn't even *look* alike—where Leda was dark and spritely like their mom, Jamie's skin was almost as pale as their dad's, and despite Leda's best efforts he always looked sloppy. Right now he was sporting a wiry beard that he'd apparently spent the summer growing.

"Whatever Leda wants," Leda's dad replied. Sure, because letting her choose their takeout would make up for everything.

"I don't care." Leda glanced down at her wrist. Two tiny puncture wounds, remnants of the monitor bracelet that had clung to her all summer, were the only evidence of her time at Silver Cove. Which had been located perversely far from the ocean, in central Nevada.

Not that Leda could really blame her parents. If she'd walked in on the scene they'd witnessed back in July, she would have sent her to rehab too. She'd been an utter mess when she arrived there: vicious and angry, hyped up on xenperheidren and who knew what else. It had taken a full day of what the other girls at Silver Cove called "happy juice"—a potent IV drip of sedatives and dopamine—before she even agreed to speak with the doctors.

As the drugs seeped slowly from Leda's system, though, the acrid taste of her resentment had begun to fade. Shame flushed over her instead: a sticky, uncomfortable shame. She'd always promised herself that she would remain in control, that she wouldn't be one of those pathetic addicts they showed in the health class holos at school. Yet there she was, with an IV drip taped into her vein.

"You okay?" one of the nurses had said, watching her expression.

Never let them see you cry, Leda had reminded herself, blinking back tears. "Of course," she managed, her voice steady.

Eventually Leda did find a sort of peace at rehab: not with her worthless psych doctor, but in meditation. She spent almost every morning there, sitting cross-legged and repeating the mantras that Guru Vashmi intoned. *May my actions be purposeful. I am my own greatest ally. I am enough in myself.* Occasionally Leda would open her eyes and glance around through the lavender smoke at the other girls in the yoga tepee. They all had a haunted, hunted look about them, as if they'd been chased here and were too afraid to leave. *I'm not like them,* Leda had told herself, squaring her shoulders and closing her eyes again. She didn't need the drugs, not the way those girls did.

Now they were only a few minutes from the Tower. Sudden anxiety twisted in Leda's stomach. Was she ready for this—ready to come back here and face everything that had sent her into a tailspin in the first place?

Not everything. Atlas was still gone.

Closing her eyes, Leda muttered a few words signaling her contacts to open her inbox, which she'd been checking nonstop since she left rehab this morning and got service again. Three thousand accumulated messages instantly pinged in her ears, invitations and vid-alerts cascading over one another like musical notes. The rumble of attention was oddly soothing.

At the top of the queue was a new message from Avery. *When are you back?*

Every summer, Leda's family forced her to come on their annual visit "home" to Podunk, middle-of-nowhere Illinois. "Home is New York," Leda would always protest, but her parents ignored her. Leda honestly didn't even understand why her parents *wanted* to keep visiting year after year. If she'd done what they did—moved from Danville to New York as newlyweds, right when the Tower was built, and slowly worked their way up until they could afford to live in the coveted upper floors—she wouldn't have looked back.

Yet her parents were determined to return to their hometown every year and stay with Leda and Jamie's grandparents, in a tech-dark house stocked with nothing but soy butter and frozen meal packets. Leda had actually enjoyed it back when she was a kid and it felt like an adventure. As she got older, though, she started begging to stay behind. She dreaded being around her cousins, with their tacky mass-produced clothing and eerie contactless pupils. But no matter how much she protested, she never could worm her way out of going. Until this year.

I'm back now! Leda replied, saying the message aloud and nodding to send it. Part of her knew she should tell Avery about Silver Cove: they'd talked a lot in rehab about accountability, and asking friends for help. But the thought of telling Avery made Leda clutch at the seat beneath her until her knuckles were white. She couldn't do it; couldn't reveal that kind of weakness to her perfect best friend. Avery would be polite about it, of course, but Leda knew that on some level she would judge her, would always look at Leda differently. And Leda couldn't handle that.

Avery knew a little of the truth: that Leda had started taking xenperheidren occasionally, before exams, to sharpen her thinking . . . and that a few times she'd taken some stronger stuff, with Cord and Rick and the rest of that crowd. But Avery had no idea how bad it had gotten toward the end of last year, after the Andes—and she definitely didn't know the truth about this summer.

They pulled up to the Tower. The copter swayed drunkenly for a moment at the entrance to the seven-hundredth-floor helipad; even with stabilizers, it still faltered in the gale-force winds that whipped around the Tower. Then it made a final push and came to a rest inside the hangar. Leda unfolded herself from her seat and clattered down the staircase after her parents. Her mom was already on a call, probably muttering about a deal gone bad.

"Leda!" A blond whirlwind hurtled forward to engulf her in a hug.

"Avery." Leda smiled into her friend's hair, gently disentangling herself. She took a step back and looked up—and faltered momentarily, her old insecurities rushing back. Seeing Avery again was always a shock to the system. Leda tried not to let it bother her, but sometimes she couldn't help thinking how unfair it was. Avery already had the perfect life, up in the thousandth-floor penthouse. Did she really have to *be* perfect too? Seeing Avery next to the Fullers, Leda could never quite believe that she'd been created from their DNA.

It sucked sometimes, being best friends with the girl too flawless to come from nature. Leda, on the other hand, probably came from a night of tequila shots on her parents' anniversary.

"Want to get out of here?" Avery asked, pleading.

"Yes," Leda said. She would do anything for Avery, although this time she didn't really need to be coaxed.

Avery turned to embrace Leda's parents. "Mr. Cole! Mrs. Cole! Welcome home." Leda watched as they laughed and hugged her back, opening up like flowers in sunlight. No one was immune to Avery's spell.

"Can I steal your daughter?" Avery asked, and they nodded.

"Thanks. I'll have her home by dinner!" Avery called out, her arm already in Leda's, tugging her insistently toward the seven-hundredth-floor thoroughfare.

"Wait a sec." Next to Avery's crisp red skirt and cropped shirt, Leda's end-of-rehab outfit—a plain gray T-shirt and jeans—looked positively drab. "I want to change if we're going out."

"I was thinking we'd just go to the park?" Avery blinked rapidly, her pupils darting back and forth as she summoned a hover. "A bunch of the girls are hanging out there, and everyone wants to see you. Is that okay?"

"Of course," Leda said automatically, shoving aside the prickle of annoyance she felt that they weren't hanging out one-on-one.

They walked out the helipad's double doors and into the thoroughfare, a massive transportation hub that spanned several city blocks. The ceilings overhead glowed a bright cerulean. To Leda, they seemed just as beautiful as anything she'd seen on her afternoon hikes at Silver Cove. But Leda wasn't the type to look for beauty in nature. *Beauty* was a word she reserved for expensive jewelry, and dresses, and Avery's face.

"So tell me about it," Avery said in that direct way of hers, as they stepped onto the carbon-composite sidewalks that lined the silver hover paths. Cylindrical snackbots hummed past on enormous wheels, selling dehydrated fruit and coffee pods.

"What?" Leda tried to snap to attention. Hovers streamed down the street to her left, their movements darting and coordinated like a school of fish, colored green or red depending on whether they were free. She instinctively moved a little closer to Avery.

"Illinois. Was it as bad as usual?" Avery's eyes went distant. "Hover call," she said under her breath, and one of the vehicles darted out of the pack.

"You want to hover all the way to the park?" Leda asked,

dodging the question, trying to sound normal. She'd forgotten the sheer volume of *people* here—parents dragging their children, businesspeople talking loudly into their contacts, couples holding hands. It felt overwhelming after the curated calm of rehab.

"You're back, it's a special occasion!" Avery exclaimed.

Leda took a deep breath and smiled just as their hover pulled up. It was a narrow two-seater with a plush eggshell interior, floating several centimeters above the ground thanks to the magnetic propulsion bars in its floor. Avery took the seat across from Leda and keyed in their destination, sending the hover on its way.

"Maybe next year they'll let you miss it. And then you and I can travel together," Avery went on as the hover dropped into one of the Tower's vertical corridors. The yellow track lighting on the tunnel walls danced in strange patterns across her cheekbones.

"Maybe." Leda shrugged. She wanted to change the subject. "You're insanely tan, by the way. That's from Florence?"

"Monaco. Best beaches in the world."

"Not better than your grandmother's house in Maine." They'd spent a week there after freshman year, lying outside in the sun and sneaking sips of Grandma Lasserre's port wine.

"True. There weren't even any cute lifeguards in Monaco," Avery said with a laugh.

Their hover slowed, then began to move horizontally as it turned onto 307. Normally coming to a floor so low would count as serious downsliding, but visits to Central Park were an exception. As they pulled to a stop at the north-northeast park entrance, Avery turned to Leda, her deep blue eyes suddenly serious. "I'm glad you're back, Leda. I missed you this summer."

"Me too," Leda said quietly.

She followed Avery through the park entrance, past the famous cherry tree that had been reclaimed from the original

Central Park. A few tourists were leaning on the fence that surrounded it, taking snaps and reading the tree's history on the interactive touch screen alongside it. There was nothing else left of the original park, which lay beneath the Tower's foundations, far below their feet.

They turned toward the hill where Leda already knew their friends would be. Avery and Leda had discovered this spot together in seventh grade; after a great deal of experimentation, they'd concluded it was the best place to soak in the UV-free rays of the solar lamp. As they walked, the spectragrass along the path shifted from mint green to a soft lavender. A holographic cartoon gnome ran through a park on their left, followed by a line of squealing children.

"Avery!" Risha was the first to catch sight of them. The other girls, all reclining on brightly colored beach towels, glanced up and waved. "And Leda! When did you get back?"

Avery plopped in the center of the group, tucking a strand of flaxen hair behind one ear, and Leda settled down next to her. "Just now. I'm straight from the copter," she said, pulling her mom's vintage sunglasses out of her bag. She could have put her contacts on light-blocking mode, of course, but the glasses were sort of her signature. She'd always liked how they made her expression unreadable.

"Where's Eris?" she wondered aloud, not that she particularly missed her. But you could usually count on Eris to show up for tanning.

"Probably shopping. Or with Cord," said Ming Jiaozu, a suppressed bitterness in her tone.

Leda said nothing, feeling caught off guard. She hadn't seen anything about Eris and Cord on the feeds when she checked this morning. Then again, she could never really keep up with Eris, who'd dated—or at least messed around with—nearly half the boys and girls in their class, some of them more than once. But Eris was Avery's oldest friend, and came from old family money, and because of that she got away with pretty much anything.

"How was your summer, Leda?" Ming went on. "You were with your family in Illinois, right?"

"Yeah."

"That must have been *awful*, being in the middle of nowhere like that." Ming's tone was sickly sweet.

"Well, I survived," Leda said lightly, refusing to let the other girl provoke her. Ming knew how much Leda hated talking about her parents' background. It was a reminder that she wasn't from this world the way the rest of them were, that she'd moved up in seventh grade from midTower suburbia.

"What about you?" Leda asked. "How was Spain? Did you hang out with any of the locals?"

"Not really."

"Funny. From the feeds, it looked like you made some really *close* friends." In her mass-download on the plane earlier, Leda had seen a few snaps of Ming with a Spanish boy, and she could tell that something had happened between them—from their body language, the lack of captions under the snaps, most of all from the flush that was now creeping up Ming's neck.

Ming fell silent. Leda allowed herself a small smile. When people pushed her buttons, she pushed back.

"Avery," Jess McClane said, leaning forward. "Did you end things with Zay? I ran into him earlier, and he seemed down."

"Yeah," Avery said slowly. "I mean, I think so? I do like him, but . . ." she trailed off halfheartedly.

"Oh my god, Avery. You really should just *do* it, and get it over with!" Jess exclaimed. The gold bangles on her wrists glimmered in the solar panel's light. "What are you waiting for, exactly? Or maybe I should say, *who* are you waiting for?"

"Give it a rest, Jess. You can't exactly talk," Leda snapped. People always made comments like that to Avery, because there was nothing else to really criticize her about. But it made even less sense coming from Jess, who was a virgin too.

"As a matter of fact, I can," Jess said meaningfully.

A chorus of squeals erupted at that—"Wait, you and Patrick?" "When?" "Where?"—and Jess grinned, clearly eager to share the details. Leda leaned back, pretending to listen. As far as the girls all knew, she was a virgin too. She hadn't told anyone the truth, not even Avery. And she never would.

It had happened in January, on the annual ski trip to Catyan. Their families had been going for years: at first just the Fullers and the Andertons, and then once Leda and Avery became such good friends, the Coles too. The Andes were the best skiing left on earth; even Colorado and the Alps relied almost exclusively on snow machines these days. Only in Chile, on the highest peaks in the Andes, was there enough natural snow for true skiing anymore.

The second day of the trip, they were all out drone-skiing— Avery, Leda, Atlas, Jamie, Cord, even Cord's older brother, Brice—falling from the jump seats of their individual ski-drones to land on the powder, cut a line through the trees, and reach back up to grab their drones before the drop-off at the glacier's edge. Leda wasn't as strong a skier as the others, but she'd swallowed an adrenaline drop on the ride up and was feeling good, almost as good as when she stole the *really* good stuff from her mom. She followed Atlas through the trees, trying her best to keep up, loving the way the wind clawed at the contours of her polydown suit. She could hear nothing but the swish of her skis through the snow, and, beneath it, the deep, hollow sound of emptiness. It struck her that they were tempting fate, hurtling through the paper-thin air up there on a glacier, at the very edge of the sky.

That was when Avery had screamed.

Everything afterward was a blur. Leda fumbled in her glove to push the red emergency button that would summon her ski-drone, but Avery was already being scooped up a few meters away. Her leg jutted out at a garish angle.

By the time they got back to the hotel's penthouse suite, Avery was already on a jet home. She would be fine, Mr. Fuller assured them; she just needed her knee re-fused, and he wanted her to see experts in New York. Leda knew what that meant. Avery would visit Everett Radson afterward to have the surgery microlasered. God forbid there be the slightest trace of a scar on her perfect body.

Later that night the kids were all in the hot tub on the deck, passing around frosted bottles of whiskeycream, toasting to Avery, the Andes, the snow that had started falling. As it started to come down ever faster, the others eventually grumbled in protest and retreated to bed. But Leda, who was sitting next to Atlas, stayed behind. He hadn't moved yet either.

She'd wanted Atlas for years, ever since she and Avery became friends, since the moment she first met him at Avery's apartment, when he walked in on them singing Disney songs and she turned bright red with embarrassment. But Leda had never really thought she had a chance with him. He was two years older, and besides, he was Avery's brother. Until now, as everyone was clambering out of the hot tub and she hesitated, wondering if maybe, possibly . . . She felt hyperaware of where her knee brushed Atlas's under the water, sending tingles up her entire left side.

"Want some?" he murmured, passing her the bottle.

"Thanks." Leda forced herself to look away from his eyelashes, where snowflakes were clumping like tiny liquid stars.

She took a long sip of the whiskeycream. It was smooth, sweet like a dessert, with an aftertaste that burned in her throat. She felt light-headed, dizzy from the heat of the hot tub, of Atlas so close to her. Maybe the adrenaline drop hadn't worn off yet, or maybe it was just her own raw excitement that made her feel strangely reckless.

"Atlas," she said softly. When he turned to her, an eyebrow raised, she leaned forward and kissed him.

After a moment's hesitation he kissed her back, his hands reaching up into the heavy curls of her hair, dusted with snow. Leda lost all sense of time. At some point her bikini top came off, and her bottoms too—well, it wasn't like she was wearing much clothing to begin with—and Atlas was whispering "Are you sure?" Leda nodded, her heart hammering. Of course she was sure. She'd never been so sure of anything.

The next morning she nearly skipped into the kitchen, her hair still damp from the hot tub's steam, the memory of Atlas's touch carved indelibly on her skin, like an inktat. But he was gone.

He'd taken the first jet back to New York. To check on Avery, his dad said. Leda nodded coolly, but inside she felt sick. She knew the truth, why Atlas had really left. He was avoiding her. *Fine*, she thought, anger swirling in to cover the pang of loss; she would show him. She wouldn't care either.

Except that Leda never got a chance to confront Atlas. He went missing later that week, before classes resumed, even though it should have been the spring semester of his senior year. There was a brief and frantic search for him, limited only to Avery's family. It ended within hours, when his parents learned he was okay.

Now, almost a year later, Atlas's disappearance was old news. His parents publicly laughed it off as a youthful indulgence: Leda had heard them at countless cocktail parties, claiming that he was traveling the world on a gap year, that it had been their idea all along. That was their story and they were sticking to it, but Avery had told Leda the truth. The Fullers had no idea where Atlas was, and when—or if—he would ever come back. He called Avery periodically to check in, but always with the location heavily encrypted, and by then he was about to move on anyway.

Leda never told Avery about that night in the Andes. She didn't know how to bring it up in the wake of Atlas's disappearance, and the longer she kept it to herself, the more of a secret it became. It ached like a bruise, the realization that the only boy she'd ever cared about had literally *run away* after sleeping with her. Leda tried to stay angry; feeling angry seemed safer than letting herself feel hurt. But even the anger wasn't enough to quiet the pain that pounded dully through her at the thought of him.

Which was how she'd ended up in rehab.

"Leda, will you come with me?" Avery's voice broke into her thoughts. Leda blinked. "To my dad's office, to pick something up," Avery repeated. Her eyes were wide with meaning; Avery's dad's office was the excuse they'd been using for years, when one of them wanted to ditch whoever they were with.

"Doesn't your dad have messenger bots for that?" Ming asked.

Leda ignored her. "Of course," she said to Avery, standing up and brushing bits of grass off her jeans. "Let's go."

They waved good-bye and started on the path toward the nearest transport station, where the clear vertical column of the express C line shot upward. The sides were startlingly transparent; Leda could see inside to a group of elderly women whose heads were tipped together in conversation, and a toddler picking his nose.

"Atlas pinged me last night," Avery whispered as they moved to stand on the upTower platform.

Leda stiffened. She knew that Avery had stopped telling her parents about Atlas's calls. She said it only upset them. But there was something weird about the fact that Avery didn't share this with anyone except Leda.

Then again, Avery had always been oddly protective of Atlas. Whenever he dated anyone, she invariably acted polite, but a little aloof—as if she didn't quite approve, or thought that Atlas had made a mistake. Leda wondered if it had to do with Atlas being adopted, if Avery worried he was somehow more vulnerable, because of the life he'd come from, and felt an impulse to protect him as a result.

"Really?" she asked, keeping her voice steady. "Could you tell where he was?"

"I heard a lot of loud voices in the background. Probably a bar somewhere." Avery shrugged. "You know how Atlas is."

No, I really don't. Maybe if she understood Atlas, Leda would be able to make sense of her own confused feelings. She gave her friend's arm a squeeze.

"Anyway," Avery said with forced brightness, "he'll come home soon, when he's ready. Right?"

She looked at Leda with a question in her eyes. For a moment, Leda was struck by how much Avery reminded her of Atlas. They weren't related by blood, and yet they had the same white-hot intensity. When they turned the full force of their attention on you, it was as blinding as looking into the sun.

Leda shifted uncomfortably. "Of course," she said. "He'll come back soon."

She prayed it wasn't true, and at the same time, she couldn't help hoping it was.

RYLIN

THE NEXT EVENING, Rylin Myers stood at the door to her apartment, struggling to wave her ID ring over the scanner while balancing a bag of groceries in one arm and a half-full energy drink in the other. Of course, she thought as she kicked shamelessly at the door, this wouldn't be a problem if they had a retinal scanner, or those glitzy computerized lenses that the highlier kids all wore. But no one could afford anything like that where Rylin lived, here on 32.

Just as she was drawing back her leg to kick again, the door opened. "Finally," Rylin muttered, shoving past her fourteen-year-old sister.

"If you got your ID ring fixed like I keep telling you to, this wouldn't happen," Chrissa quipped. "Then again, what would you say? 'Sorry, officers, I keep using my ID ring to open beer bottles, and now it's stopped working'?"

Rylin ignored her. Taking a long sip of her energy drink, she heaved the grocery bag onto the counter and tossed her sister a box of veggie-rice. "Can you put this stuff away? I'm running late." The Ifty—Intra Floor Transit system—was down again, so she'd been forced to walk all twenty blocks from the lift stop to their apartment.

Chrissa looked up. "You're going out *tonight?*" She'd inherited their mom's soft Korean features, her delicate nose and high arched brow, while Rylin looked much more like their square-jawed dad. But they'd both somehow gotten their mom's bright green eyes, which glowed against their skin like beryls.

"Um, yeah. It's Saturday," Rylin answered, purposefully ignoring her sister's meaning. She didn't want to talk about what had happened on this day a year ago—the day their mom died and their entire world fell apart. She would never forget how Child Services came to their house that very night, while the girls were still holding each other crying, to tell them about the foster system.

Rylin had listened to them for a while, Chrissa's head turned into her shoulder as she kept on sobbing. Her sister was smart, really smart, and good enough at volleyball to have a serious shot at a college scholarship. But Rylin knew enough about foster care to know what it would do to them. Especially to Chrissa.

She would do anything to keep this family together, no matter what it cost her.

The very next day she'd gone to the nearest family court and declared legal adulthood, so that she could start working her terrible job at the monorail stop full-time. What other choice did she have? Even now, they were barely keeping up—Rylin had just gotten yet another warning notice from their landlord; they were always at least a month behind on rent. Not to mention all their mom's hospital bills. Rylin had been trying to pay those down for the last year, but at this interest rate the mountain of debt was actually starting to *grow*. Sometimes Rylin felt like she'd never be free of it.

This was their life now, and it wasn't changing anytime soon.

"Rylin. Please?"

"I'm already late," Rylin said, retreating into her roped-off section of their tiny bedroom; thinking about what she would wear, about the fact that she didn't have to go into work for a whole thirty-six hours, about anything but the reproachful look in her sister's green eyes, which looked so painfully like their mom's.

Rylin and her boyfriend, Hiral, clattered down the steps of the Tower's Exit 12. "There they are," Rylin muttered, raising a hand against the glare of the sun. Their friends were gathered at the usual meeting place, a hot metal bench across the street at 127th and Morningside.

She glanced at Hiral. "Are you sure you don't have *anything* with you?" she asked again. She wasn't exactly thrilled about the fact that Hiral had started selling—at first just to their friends, then on an even bigger level—but it had been a long week, and she was still on edge after her conversation with Chrissa. She could really use a hit, of relaxants or halluci-lighter, anything to silence the thoughts that were cycling endlessly through her brain.

Hiral shook his head. "Sorry. Cleared my whole inventory this week." He glanced at her. "Everything okay?"

Rylin was quiet. Hiral reached for her hand, and she let him take it. His palms were rough with work, and there were black circles of grease underneath his fingernails. Hiral had dropped out of school last year to work as a liftie, repairing the Tower's massive elevators from the inside. He spent his days suspended hundreds of meters in the air like a human spider.

"Ry!" her best friend, Lux, exclaimed, rushing over. Her hair, cut in jagged bangs, was ash-blond this week. "You made it! I was worried you weren't going to come."

"Sorry. Got caught up," Rylin apologized.

Andrés snorted. "Had to get a little *transmission* in before the concert?" He made a crude gesture with his hands.

Lux rolled her eyes and pulled Rylin into a hug. "How are you holding up?" she murmured.

"Fine." Rylin didn't know what else to say. She felt a confused pang of gratefulness that Lux had remembered what day it was, mingled with irritation at the reminder. She caught herself toying with her mom's old necklace and quickly let go of it. Hadn't she come out precisely to *avoid* thinking about her mom?

Shaking her head, Rylin let her gaze roam over the rest of the group. Andrés was leaning back on the bench, stubbornly wearing a leather jacket in spite of the heat. Hiral stood next to him, his deeply bronzed skin gleaming in the setting sun. And on the far side of the bench was Indigo, wearing a shirt that she'd barely managed to turn into a dress, and sky-high boots.

"Where's V?" Rylin asked.

"Providing the fun. Unless *you* were planning on bringing today?" Indigo said sarcastically.

"Just partaking, thanks," Rylin replied. Indigo rolled her eyes and went back to messaging on her tablet.

Rylin took plenty of illegal drugs, of course—they all did—but she drew the line at buying or selling. No one cared much about a few smoking teenagers, but the laws were harsher on dealers. If she ended up in jail, Chrissa would go straight to foster care. Rylin couldn't risk that.

Andrés glanced up from his tablet. "V's meeting us there. Let's go."

A blistering wind tossed a few stray pieces of trash along the sidewalk. Rylin stepped over them, taking a deep, bracing breath. The air out here might be hot, but at least it wasn't the recycled, oxygen-heavy air of the Tower.

Across the street, Hiral was already crouched at the side of the Tower, sliding a blade beneath the edge of a steel panel and peeling it back. "All clear," he murmured. Their hands brushed as Rylin stepped into the opening, and they exchanged a look; then Rylin was stepping into the steel forest.

The sounds of outside instantly vanished, replaced by the low hum of voices and drugged-out laughter, and the whoosh of air cycling from the bottom of the Tower. They were in the underworld beneath the first floor; a strange, dark space of pipes and steel columns. Rylin and Lux walked softly through the shadows, nodding at the other groups as they passed. One cluster was gathered around the dim pink glow of a halluci-lighter. Another, half clothed and sprawled out on a pile of pillows, was clearly about to start an Oxytose orgy. Rylin saw the telltale gleam of the machine room door ahead, and started to walk a little faster.

"You can all go ahead and thank me now," came a voice from the shadows, and she almost jumped. *V.*

He wasn't as tall as Andrés, but V had to weigh at least twenty kilos more, and it was all muscle. His broad shoulders and arms were covered entirely in inktats, which danced across his body in a swirling chaos; shapes forming, breaking apart, and reforming elsewhere. Rylin winced at the thought of inking that much skin.

"Okay, guys." V reached into his bag and produced a stack of bright gold patches, each the size of Rylin's thumbnail. "Who's in for communals?"

"Holy shit," Lux exclaimed, laughing. "How did you score these?"

"Hell, yes!" Hiral high-fived Andrés.

"Seriously?" Rylin asked, her voice cutting through the cele-brations. She didn't like communals. They induced a shared group high, which felt somehow invasive, like having sex with a bunch of strangers. The worst part was being unable to con-trol the high, putting herself entirely in someone else's hands. "I thought we were smoking tonight," she said. She'd even brought her halluci-lighter, the tiny compact pipe that could be used for almost anything—darklights, crispies, and of course the halluci-nogenic weed it had been created for.

"Scared, Myers?" V challenged, after a moment.

"I'm not *scared*." Rylin drew herself up to her full height and stared at V. "I just wanted to do something else."

Her tablet vibrated with an incoming message. She looked down to see a text from Chrissa. *I made Mom's baked apple bites*, she'd written. *In case you want to come home!*

V was watching her, an open challenge in his gaze. "What-ever," Rylin said under her breath. "Why the hell not?" She reached out to grab the patches in V's hand and slapped one on her inner arm, right by the elbow where her vein was close to the surface.

"That's what I thought," V said as the others began eagerly reaching for the patches.

They stepped into the machine room, and suddenly all Rylin could hear was the electronic music. It slammed angrily into her skull, obliterating any other thought. Lux grabbed her arm and began jumping hysterically, shouting something unintelligible.

"Who's ready to *party*?!" the DJ exclaimed from where he stood perched on a coolant tank, an amplifier spreading his voice throughout the room. The space, hot and close with cramped bodies, erupted in screams. "All right," he went on. "If you've got a gold, put it on now. Because I'm DJ Lowy, and I'm about to take you on the most insane ride of your life." The dim light reflected off the sea of communal patches. Almost everyone here was patched up, Rylin realized. This would be intense.

"Three—" Lowy shouted, counting down. Lux gave an eager laugh and jumped higher on her tiptoes, trying to see over the crowd. Rylin glanced at V; his inktats were swirling even wilder than usual in the space surrounding his patch, as if his very skin knew what was about to happen.

"Two—" Most of the crowd had joined in the count. Hiral came to stand behind Rylin and wrapped his arms around her waist, resting his chin on her head. She leaned back into him and closed her eyes, bracing herself for the communals' activation.

"One!" The scream reverberated through the room. Lowy reached for the tablet hovering before him and flicked on the electromagnetic pulse, tuned to the frequency of the communals. Instantly all the patches in the room released waves of stimulants into the bloodstream of everyone wearing them. The ultimate synchronized high.

The music turned up and Rylin threw her hands into the air, joining the loud, seemingly endless scream. She could already feel the communal taking over her system. The world had realigned to the music, everything—the flashing of the lights overhead, her breathing, her heartbeat, *everyone's* heartbeats—timed perfectly with the deep, insistent pulse of the bass.

Don't you love this? Lux mouthed, or at least that's what it seemed like she said, though Rylin couldn't be sure. Already she was losing her grip on her thoughts. Chrissa and her text messages didn't matter, her job and her asshole boss didn't matter. Nothing mattered except this moment. She felt invincible, untouchable, like she would be this way forever: young and dancing and electric and alive.

Lights. A flask of something strong being passed to her. She

took a sip without tasting what it was. A touch on her hip—
Hiral, she thought, pulling his hand closer in invitation. But then
she saw Hiral a few rows forward, jumping and punching at the
sky with Andrés. She spun around only to see V's face whirl up
out of the darkness. He held up another gold patch, an eyebrow
raised suggestively. Rylin shook her head. She wasn't even sure
how she'd pay him back for the one she'd already taken.

But V was already peeling back the adhesive on the back side.
"No charge," he whispered, as if reading her thoughts, or had she
spoken them aloud? He reached down to sweep her hair back
from her neck. "A little secret: The closer it is to your brain, the
faster it kicks in."

Rylin closed her eyes, dazed, as the second wave of drugs
snapped through her. It was a razor-sharp rush, setting all her
nerves afire. She was dancing and somehow also floating when
she sensed a vibration in her front pocket. She ignored it and kept
jumping, but there it was again, drawing her painstakingly back
into her awkward, physical body. Fumbling, she managed to grab
her tablet. "Hello?" Rylin said, gasping as her breathing became
irregular, no longer in time with the music.

"Rylin Myers?"

"What the—who is this?" She couldn't hear. The crowd was
still buffeting her back and forth.

There was a pause, as if the speaker couldn't believe the
question. "Cord Anderton," he said finally, and Rylin blinked in
shock. Her mom had worked as a maid for the Andertons, back
before she got sick. Dimly Rylin realized that she did recognize
the voice, from the few times she'd been up there. But why the
hell was Cord Anderton calling *her*?

"So, can you come work my party?"

"I don't . . . what are you talking about?" She tried to shout
over the music, but it came out more like a rasp.

"I sent you a message. I'm throwing a party tonight." His voice was fast, impatient. "I need someone here—to keep everything clean, help with the caterers, all the stuff your mom used to do." Rylin flinched at the mention of her mom, but of course he couldn't see. "My usual help bailed last minute, but then I remembered you and looked you up. Do you want the job or not?"

Rylin wiped a bead of sweat from her brow. Who did Cord Anderton think he was, *summoning* her on a Saturday night? She opened her mouth to tell this rich, entitled asshole to shove the job right up his—

"I forgot," he added, "it pays two hundred nanos."

Rylin choked back her words. Two hundred nanodollars for just one night of dealing with drunk rich kids? "How soon do you need me there?"

"Oh, half an hour ago."

"I'm on my way," she said, the room still spinning. "But—"

"Great." Cord ended the ping.

With a herculean effort, Rylin pulled the patch from her arm, and then, wincing, ripped off the one on her neck. She glanced back at the others—Hiral was dancing, oblivious; Lux was wrapped around a stranger with her tongue down his throat; Indigo was sitting on Andrés's shoulders. She turned to go. V was still watching her, but Rylin didn't say good-bye. She just stepped out into the hot stickiness of the night, letting the used gold patches flutter slowly to the ground behind her.

ERIS

ERIS DODD-RADSON BURROWED deeper under her fluffy silk pillow, angry at the ringing that was playing incessantly in her eartennas. "Five more minutes," she mumbled. The ringing didn't stop. "I said snooze!" she snapped, before realizing that this wasn't her alarm. It was Avery's ringtone, which Eris had long ago set on full override, so that it would wake her up even when she was sleeping. "Accept ping," she mumbled.

"Are you on your way?" Avery's voice sounded in her ear, pitched louder than usual over the clamor of the party. Eris glanced at the time, illuminated in bright pink numbers in her lower left field of vision. Cord's party had started half an hour ago and she was still lying in bed, with no idea what to wear.

"Obviously." She was already halfway to her closet, shimmying out of her oversized T-shirt as she picked her way through discarded clothes and stray pillows. "I just—*ow!*" she yelped, clutching a stubbed toe.

"Oh my god. You're still home," Avery accused, but she was laughing. "What happened? Oversleep your beauty nap again?"

"I just like making everyone wait so they'll be that much more excited to see me," Eris answered.

"And by 'everyone,' you mean Cord."

"No, I mean everyone. Especially you, Avery," Eris said. "Don't go having too much fun without me, 'kay?"

"I promise. Flick me when you're on your way?" Avery said, and ended the ping.

Eris blamed her dad for this one. Her eighteenth birthday was in a few weeks, and today she'd had to visit the family attorney to start her trust fund paperwork. It was all excessively boring, signing countless documents with an official witness present, taking drug and DNA tests. She hadn't even understood all of it, except that if she signed everything, she'd be rich someday.

Eris's dad came from old money—his family had invented the magnetic repulsion technology that kept hovercrafts aloft. And Everett had only added to the already-massive fortune, by becoming the world's premier plastisurgeon. The only mistakes he'd ever made were two expensive divorces before he finally met Eris's mom, when he was forty and she was a twenty-five-year-old model. He didn't ever talk about those previous marriages, and since there were no children from either, Eris never asked about them. She didn't really like thinking about it, to be honest.

Stepping into her closet, she drew a circle on the mirrored wall, and it turned into a touch screen that lit up with her closet's full inventory. Every year Cord threw this back-to-school costume party, and every year there was a fierce and unspoken competition for best costume. She sighed and began sorting through her various options: the gold flapper dress, the faux-fur hood her mom had given her, a hot pink sequinned gown from last Halloween. None of it seemed right.

Screw it, she decided. Why was she trying to find a costume anyway? Wouldn't she stand out more without one?

"The black Alicia top," she announced to her closet, which spit the item into the output chute at the bottom. Eris pulled the top on over her lace bra and stepped into her favorite suede pants, which she knew made her ass look fantastic. She snapped a set of silver cuffs on her elbows and reached up to yank out her ponytail, letting her strawberry-blond hair fall around her shoulders in a wild tangle.

Biting her lip, she plopped down at her vanity and placed her hands on the hairstyler's two electropulsers. "Straight," she ordered, closing her eyes and bracing herself.

A tingle spread from her palms, up her arms, and into her scalp as the machine jolted her with a wave of electricity. The other girls at school always complained about the styler, but Eris secretly enjoyed the feeling: the hot, clean way it set all her nerves afire, almost like pain. When she looked up, her hair had fallen into straight layers around her face. She tapped at the screen of her vanity and closed her eyes as a fine spray of makeup misted over her. When she looked up again, eyeliner now brought out the strange and arresting amber flecks in her irises, and a blush softened her cheekbones, highlighting the smattering of freckles along her nose. But something was still missing.

Before she could second-guess herself, Eris was moving through the darkness of her parents' room and into her mom's closet. She felt for the jewelry safe and typed the passcode, which she'd figured out at age ten. Nestled inside, next to a colorful array of gemstones and a rope of thick black pearls, were her mom's stained glass earrings. The rare, old-fashioned kind of glass—not flexiglass, but the kind of glass that could actually break.

The earrings were exorbitantly expensive, hand-blown from the panes of an old church window. Eris's dad had bought them at an auction, as a twentieth-anniversary present. Pushing aside her twinge of guilt, Eris reached up and screwed the delicate droplets into her ears.

She was almost at the front door when her dad called out from the living room. "Eris? Where are you headed?"

"Hey, Dad." She turned around, keeping one heeled bootie in the hallway so she could make a quick exit. Her dad was sitting in his favorite corner of the brown leather couch, reading something on his tablet, probably a medical journal or patient record. His thick hair was almost entirely gray, and his eyes were creased with worry lines, which he refused to surge away like most of Eris's friends' parents did. He said that patients found the lines reassuring. Eris secretly thought it was kind of cool of her dad, to insist on aging naturally.

"I'm going to a friend's party," she explained. Her dad glanced over her outfit, and Eris realized a second too late that she hadn't concealed the earrings. She discreetly tried to pull her hair forward to hide them, but Everett was already shaking his head. "Eris, you can't wear those," he said, sounding a little amused. "They're the most expensive thing in this apartment."

"That's an exaggeration, and you know it." Eris's mom sailed in from the kitchen wearing a scarlet evening dress, her hair piled atop her head in a cascade of curls. "Hey, sweetie," Caroline Dodd said, turning to her daughter. "Want some bubbly before you go? I'm about to open a bottle of that Montès rosé you like."

"The one from the vineyard where we swam in the pool?"

"The one with the 'Pool Closed' sign, you mean." A smile lifted up the corners of her dad's mouth. That had been a particularly ridiculous family trip. Eris's parents had let her drink the wine pairings at lunch, and it was so hot out that Eris and her mom kept trying to fan each other with their napkins the whole meal, then ended up sneaking, giggling, into a gated-off hotel pool and jumping in fully clothed.

"We never saw that sign!" Caroline laughed in protest and popped the bottle. The sound reverberated through the apartment. Eris took the outstretched glass with a shrug. It *was* her favorite.

"So whose party is it?" Caroline prompted.

"Cord's. And I'm already late . . ." Eris still hadn't told her mom about her and Cord. She shared almost everything with her mom, but never the hookup stuff.

"I believe it's called fashionably late," her dad added. "And you'll only be a minute later and just as fashionable once you put the earrings back."

"Oh, come on, Everett. What harm can she do?"

Eris's dad shook his head, giving in, as Eris had known he would. "All right, Caroline. If you aren't upset, then Eris can wear them."

"Outvoted again," Eris teased, and exchanged a knowing smile with her dad. He always joked about being the least powerful person in the apartment, outnumbered as he was by two highly opinionated women.

"Every time." Everett laughed.

"How could I say no when they look so gorgeous on you?" Caroline put her hands on Eris's shoulders and turned her around to face the massive antique mirror on the wall.

Eris looked like a younger version of her mom. The only tiny differences, aside from age, were the slight modifications Eris's dad had agreed to give her this spring—nothing major, just the insertion of the gold flecks in her eyes and the lasering on of a few freckles for texture. There was nothing else to be done for her, really. Eris's features were all her own, her full mouth and cute upturned nose and most of all her hair, a lustrous riot of color, copper and honey and strawberry and sunrise. Eris's hair was her greatest beauty, but then, there was nothing about her that wasn't beautiful, as she was well aware.

She gave her head an impatient toss and the earrings danced, catching all the glorious colors of her hair as if lit from within.

"Have fun tonight," Eris's mom said. Eris met her eyes in the mirror and smiled.

"Thanks. I'll take good care of these." She finished her champagne and set it on the table. "Love you," she said to both her parents on her way out. The earrings glowed against her hair like twin stars.

———

The downTower C lift was pulling up right as she walked into the station, which Eris considered a good sign. Maybe it was because she was named after a Greek goddess, but she'd always attributed an omen-like significance to even the smallest things. Last year there had been a smudge on her window that looked like a heart. She never reported it to outside maintenance, so it stayed that way for weeks, until the next rain day finally washed it away. She liked to imagine that it had brought her good luck.

Eris followed the crowds on board and edged toward the side of the lift. Normally she might have taken a hover, but she was running late and this was faster; and anyway, the C line had always been her favorite, with its transparent view panels. She loved watching the floors shoot past, light and shadow alternating with the heavy metal framework that separated each level, the crowds waiting for the local lifts blurring together into an indistinguishable stream of color.

Mere seconds later, the elevator pulled to a stop. Eris pushed past the swirl of activity around the express station, the waiting hovers and the newsfeed salesbots, and turned onto the main avenue. Like her, Cord lived on the expensive north-facing side of the Tower, with a view uncluttered by the buildings of midtown, or the Sprawl. His floor was slightly larger—the Tower narrowed as it got higher, ending in Avery's apartment, which was the only thing on the top level—but she could feel the difference even in those sixteen floors. The streets were just as wide, lined with tiny grass plots and real trees, fed by discreetly hidden misters. The solar lamps overhead had dimmed to match the real sun, which was only visible from the outward-facing apartments. But the energy down here was somehow different, louder and a little more vibrant. Maybe it was thanks to the commercial space that lined the center avenue, even if it was only a coffee shop and a Brooks Brothers fitting room.

Eris reached Cord's street—really just the shadowed cul-de-sac that ended in the Andertons' front steps; no one else lived on this block. A dramatic *1A* was inscribed over the doorway, as if anyone needed reminding whose home this was. Like the rest of the world, Eris wondered why Cord had continued to live here after his parents died and his older brother, Brice, moved out. It was way too much space for one person.

Inside, the apartment was already crammed wall-to-wall with people, and growing warmer despite the ventilation system. Eris saw Maxton Feld in the enclosed greenhouse, trying to reprogram the hydration system to make it rain beer. She paused at the dining room, where someone had propped the table on hovercoasters for a game of floating pong, but didn't see Cord's telltale dark head in there either. And there was no one in the kitchen except a girl Eris didn't recognize, in a dark ponytail and formfitting jeans. Eris wondered idly who she was, just as the girl began stacking dishes and carrying them away. So Cord had a new maid—a maid who was already out of uniform. Eris still didn't understand why he paid for a maid; only people like the Fullers, or Eris's grandmother, had them anymore. Everyone else just bought all the various cleaning bots on the market and set them loose whenever things seemed dirty. But maybe that was the point: to pay for the human, un-automated-ness of it all.

What are you supposed to be? "Too cool for costumes"? "Over-sleeper"? Avery flickered her.

I prefer "professional attention-getter," Eris replied, smiling as she glanced around the room.

Avery was at the living room windows, dressed in a simple white shift with a pair of holo-wings and a halo floating above her head. On anyone else it would look like a lame last-minute angel costume, but Avery was, of course, ethereal. Next to her stood Leda, in a black feathery thing, and Ming, who was wearing a stupid devil costume. She'd probably heard that Avery was being an angel and wanted to seem like they were a set. How pathetic. Eris didn't feel like talking to either girl, so she flickered Avery that she would be back and kept on looking for Cord.

They'd started hooking up this summer, when they had both been stuck in town. Eris had been a little worried at first—everyone else was jetting off to Europe or the Hamptons or the beaches in Maine, while she'd be stranded here in the city, interning at her dad's medical practice. It was the trade he'd insisted on in exchange for the surges he did last spring. "You need work experience," he'd said. As if she planned on working a day in her life. Still, Eris had agreed. She wanted the surges that badly.

And it was all just as boring as she'd expected, until the night she ran into Cord at Lightning Lounge. One thing led to another, and soon they were taking atomic shots, and walking out onto the enclosed balcony. It was there, pressed up against the enforced flexiglass, that they had kissed for the first time.

Now Eris could only wonder why it hadn't happened sooner. God knows she'd been around Cord for years, ever since her family moved back to New York when she was eight. They'd spent several years in Switzerland so her dad could study all the latest European surge techniques. Eris had attended first and second grades at the American School of Lausanne, but when she came back—speaking a strange polyglot of French and English, with no understanding of a multiplication table—Berkeley Academy had gently suggested she repeat second grade.

She would never forget that first day back, when she'd walked into the lunchroom not knowing anyone in her new class. It was Cord who had slid into the seat beside her at her empty table. "Wanna see a cool zombie game?" he'd asked, and showed her how to set her contacts so the cafeteria food looked like brains. Eris had laughed so hard she'd almost snorted into her spaghetti.

That was two years before his parents died.

She found Cord in the game room, seated around the massive antique table with Drew Lawton and Joaquin Suarez, all of them holding real paper playing cards in their hands. It was one of Cord's weird quirks, how he insisted on playing Idleness with that old card set. He claimed that everyone looked too vacant when they played on contacts, sitting around a table but staring away from one another, into space.

Eris stood there a moment, admiring him. He was so insanely gorgeous. Not in the smoothly perfect way that Avery was, but in a swarthy, rugged sort of way; his features a perfect mix of his mom's Brazilian sensuality and the classic Anderton jaw and nose. Eris took a step forward, and Cord glanced up. She was gratified by the flash of appreciation in his ice-blue eyes.

"Hey there," he said as she pulled up an empty chair. She leaned on her elbows so that the neckline of her top skimmed lower over her breasts, and studied him across the table. There was something shockingly intimate in his gaze. It felt like he could reach over and touch her with nothing but his eyes.

"Want to play?" Cord swept a pile of cards toward her.

"I don't know. I might go dance." It was so quiet in here. She wanted to go back to the loud chaos of the party.

"Come on, one hand. Right now it's just me against these two. And it hasn't been that fun, playing with myself," Cord quipped.

"Fine. But I'm with Joaquin," Eris said, for no real reason except that she wanted to push him a little. "And you know I always win."

"Maybe not this time." Cord laughed.

Sure enough, fifteen minutes later, the pile of chips in front of her and Joaquin had tripled in size. Eris stretched her arms overhead and pushed her chair back from the table. "I'm getting a drink," she said meaningfully. "Anyone want one?"

"Why not?" Cord met her eyes. "I'll come with you."

They stumbled into the coatroom, their bodies pressed close together. "You look fantastic tonight," Cord whispered.

"No more talking." Eris yanked his head down and kissed him, hard.

Cord leaned forward in response, his mouth hot on hers. He snaked his hand around her waist, playing with the hem of her shirt. Eris could feel his pulse quickening where his wrist touched her bare skin. The kiss deepened, became more insistent.

She pulled away and stepped back, leaving Cord to stumble forward. "What?" he gasped.

"I'm going to dance," she said simply, reaching up to straighten her bra and smooth her hair; her motions brisk, neat, practiced. This was her favorite part, reminding Cord that he wanted her. Making him just a little bit desperate. "See you later."

As she started down the hallway, Eris could feel the weight of Cord's gaze tracing the long lines of her body. She didn't let herself look back. But the corner of her mouth, her red paintstick just a little bit smudged, turned up in a triumphant smirk.

WATT

"**REMIND ME WHY** we're here again?" Watzahn Bakradi—Watt to everyone but his teachers—comm-linked his best friend, Derrick Rawls.

"I told you, this place makes girls go crazy," Derrick said. His voice filtered through Watt's eartennas, which were playing a drowsy jazz beat, blocking out all the other noise of the club. "Some of us need all the help we can get," he added, without resentment.

Watt didn't argue. In the past hour alone he'd received seven flick-link requests, while Derrick was yet to get a single one. "Fine," he conceded. "I'm getting a drink."

"Grab me a beer while you're there?" Derrick asked, unable to look away from a brunette who was swaying near them, her eyes closed, arms moving in no apparent rhythm.

"I would, except I'm not buying." Watt laughed. At the bar, he switched off his music and turned to stare out over the club, listening as the shuffling feet and chorus of whispers echoed eerily in the quiet.

They'd come to Pulse, the midTower silent disco, where music was blasted directly into each person's eartennas instead of coming from external speakers. But the strange thing about Pulse was that each eartenna feed differed: no two guests were hearing the same song at the same time. Watt supposed it was fun for most people, trying to guess what others were listening to, laughing at the fact that they were streaming a slow song while their date had EDM. But to him it just meant everyone awkwardly stumbled over one another on the dance floor.

He leaned back carelessly on his elbows and met the gaze of a girl across the bar. She was gorgeous, tall and willowy with wide-set eyes, definitely out of Watt's league. But he had a secret weapon, and knew exactly how long to make eye contact before looking away. According to Nadia's estimates the girl would come over in three, two—

His eartennas sounded with the double beep that indicated a ping request. He nodded his acceptance and the girl's voice sounded in his ear, the wireless link allowing them to speak directly to each other over their individual music, though of course Watt's was already off. "Buy me a drink," she said, sidling up next to him at the bar. It was a command, not a question. This girl knew how much hotter she was than him.

"What are you drinking?" Watt tapped the bar's surface, and it lit up into a touch screen menu.

The girl shrugged and began drawing circles on the menu pad, scrolling through brightly colored bubbles representing the drink categories. There was a small inktat on the inside of her wrist, a rosebud that kept opening into a blossom and then furling back. "Guess."

Watt put his hand over hers to still it. She glanced up at him, an eyebrow raised. "If I guess right, you're buying," he challenged.

"Sure. But you'll never guess."

"I think . . ." He flipped through the categories for a moment as if weighing the various options. But he already knew what she really wanted, and it wasn't on the menu. "Something special," he concluded, pushing OTHER, and pulling up a keypad to type *squid ink martini.*

The girl tossed her head back in laughter. "You cheated somehow," she accused, her eyes roving over Watt with new interest. She leaned forward to order their drinks from the bot-tender.

Watt grinned. He felt attention shifting toward them, everyone clearly wondering what he'd said to attract a girl like that. Watt couldn't help it; he loved this part, loved feeling like he'd won some unspoken contest.

"Thanks," he said as the girl slid him a dark beer.

"How did you know what I wanted?" she asked.

"I figured, an unusual drink for an unusually beautiful girl." *Thank you, Nadia,* he added silently.

I wouldn't waste your time with this one. Girls 2 and 6 were more interesting, Nadia—Watt's quantum computer—answered, flashing the words across his contacts. When they were alone Nadia spoke directly into his ears, but she defaulted to text whenever Watt was with someone else. He found it too disorienting, trying to carry on two conversations at once.

Well, this one is prettier, Watt replied, smiling in amusement as he sent the sentence directly to Nadia. She couldn't read his every thought, only the ones he intended for her.

Re-rank selection criteria for potential romantic partners appeared in his to-do list, alongside buying a present for his brother and sister's birthday, and his summer reading.

Sometimes I wish I hadn't programmed you to be so snarky. Watt had constructed Nadia's mental architecture to favor oblique and associative thinking over strictly logical if-then. In other words, to be an interesting conversationalist, instead of just a powerful calculator. But these days her speech pattern bordered on what could only be called sarcasm.

Nadia had been with Watt for almost five years now, ever since he had created her as a thirteen-year-old scholarship student at an MIT summer program. He'd known, of course, that it was technically illegal: the creation of any quantum computer with a Robbens quotient of over 3.0 had been banned worldwide since the AI incident of 2093. But he'd been so lonely on that college campus, surrounded by older students who pointedly ignored him, and it hadn't seemed like it would do any harm. . . . He'd started tinkering with a few spare parts, and soon, bit by qubit, he was building a quantum supercomp.

Until the professor in charge of their program caught him working on Nadia, late one night in the engineering lab.

"You need to destroy that—that *thing*," she'd said, a note of hysteria in her tone. She took several steps back in fear. They both knew that if Watt was caught with a quant, he'd go to prison for life—and she would probably be arrested too, simply for failing to stop him. "I swear, if you don't, I'll report you!"

Watt nodded and promised to do as she said, cursing his own stupidity; he should have known better than to work in a nonsecure space. The moment the professor left, he frantically transferred Nadia onto a smaller piece of hardware, then smashed the box he'd first housed her in and delivered it silently to his professor. He had no desire to go to prison. And he needed a nice recommendation from her so that he could get into MIT in a few years.

By the time Watt's summer program was over, Nadia consisted of a qubic core the size of his fist. He wedged her in his suitcase, in the toe of a shoe, and snuck her back to the Tower.

Thus began Watt's—and Nadia's—hacking career.

They started small, mainly messing around with Watt's friends and classmates, reading their private flickers or hacking their feeds to post funny, incriminating inside jokes. But as time went on and Watt discovered what a truly powerful computer he had on his hands, he got bolder. Nadia could do so much more than crack teenagers' passwords; she could scan thousands of lines of code in less than a millisecond and find the single weak sequence, the break in a security system, that might let them inside. Armed with Nadia, he could access all kinds of restricted data. He could make money off it too, if he was careful enough. For years Watt kept Nadia safe in his bedroom, periodically upgrading her into smaller, easier-to-hide pieces of hardware.

And then, two summers ago, Watt took what had seemed like a normal hacking job, a request for removal of a criminal record. When it came time for payment, though, the messages got strangely threatening—in a way that made Watt suspect the client somehow knew about Nadia.

Watt was suddenly and powerfully afraid. He usually tried not to think about what would happen if he got caught, but he realized now how foolish that had been. He was in possession of an illegal quant, and he needed to hide her somewhere she could never be found.

He'd tucked Nadia in his pocket and taken the next monorail downtown.

He got off at South Station and stepped into another world, a cluttered maze of alleys and unmarked doorways and pushcarts selling hot, greasy cones of fried wheatchips. The steel form of the Tower loomed overhead, casting most of the Sprawl—the neighborhood south of Houston Street—in shadow.

Watt turned toward the water, blinking at the sudden onslaught of the wind. Green and yellow buoys bobbed in the aquaculture pens over the long-submerged Battery Park. They were supposed to be farming kelp and krill, but Watt knew many of them also grew ocea-pharms, the highly addictive drugs cultured in jellyfish. Keeping his head down, he found the doorway he was looking for and stepped inside.

"What can I do for you?" A burly man stepped forward. His hair was clipped close to his scalp, and he was wearing a gray plastic jacket and surgical gloves.

Dr. Smith, as he called himself, had a reputation for performing illegal surgeries like drug wipes, fingerprint replacements, even retina transfers. They said there was nothing he couldn't do. But when Watt explained what he wanted, the doctor shook his head. "Impossible," he muttered.

"Are you sure?" Watt challenged, reaching into his pocket to hold Nadia out for inspection. Her hardware burned hot on his palm.

Smith took an involuntary step closer and gasped. "You're telling me *that's* a quant?"

"Yeah." Watt felt a surge of satisfaction. Nadia was pretty damn impressive.

"All right," Smith said reluctantly. "I can try." He peeled off one of his surgical gloves and held out his hand. It had six fingers. "Dexterity boost," he boasted, noticing Watt's gaze. "Helps in surgery. Did it myself, with the left one."

Watt shook the doctor's six-fingered hand and gave Nadia to him, praying this crazy idea would work.

———

Leaning against the bar at Pulse, Watt brushed his fingers over the slight bump above his right ear, the only evidence left from that day. Sometimes he still couldn't believe the surgery had succeeded. Now Nadia was always with him—at the edge of his temporal lobe, where Smith had embedded her, drawing her power from the piezoelectric pulse of Watt's own blood flow. The authorities hadn't ended up tracking them down, but still, Watt felt safer this way. If anything bad ever did happen, no one would think to look for a computer in Watt's own brain.

"Do you come here a lot?" Squid Ink Martini Girl asked. She took a small sip of her martini, its purplish liquid swirling in the glass like a gathering storm.

Several lines of text instantly flashed across Watt's contacts. She was a year older, a student at the local college majoring in art studies.

"I like coming here to observe," Watt said. "It helps me with my art."

"You're an artist? What kind of art?"

He sighed. "Well, I used to work primarily in 3-D sculpture installations, but lately I worry they're a little overdone. I'm thinking of incorporating more audio into my work. That's part of why I'm here, to read everyone's responses to the music." He turned to look the girl in the eye; she blinked under the force of his gaze. "What do *you* think?" he asked.

"I totally agree," she whispered, though he hadn't really stated an opinion at all. "It's like you read my mind."

This was the side effect of having Nadia in his brain that Watt hadn't anticipated—that she'd become his secret weapon for getting girls. Before the procedure, Watt's batting average had been exactly that: average. He wasn't unattractive, with his olive-gold skin and dark eyes, but he wasn't particularly tall, or confident. Having Nadia changed all that.

Of course, up here in midTower—almost a mile higher than where he and Derrick *actually* lived—everyone could afford pretty decent contacts. You could look things up on your contacts while talking to someone, if you wanted, but you'd have to speak the question aloud. Aside from a few preprogrammed commands like nodding to accept an incoming call or blinking repeatedly to take a snap, contacts were still voice-operated. And while it was normal to mumble while you were on the Ifty or at home, it was definitely uncool to give contact commands mid-conversation.

Nadia was different. Because she was in Watt's head, they could communicate through what Watt had dubbed "transcranial telepathy mode," meaning that he could *think* questions and Nadia would answer him. And when he talked to girls, she could follow the conversation, instantly feeding him any relevant information.

In the case of Squid Ink Martini Girl, for instance, Nadia had made a complete study of the girl in under ten milliseconds. She'd hacked the girl's flickers, found every place she'd checked into and who her friends were; she even read all twelve thousand pages of the girl's feeds history, and calculated what Watt should do in order to keep the conversation going. Now Watt was self-assured, even smooth, because he always knew the exact right thing to say.

Martini Girl studied him as she idly twirled the stem of her glass. Watt stayed silent, knowing that she didn't like overly aggressive guys, that she wanted to feel like she was making the first move. Sure enough—

"Wanna get out of here?"

She was gorgeous. Yet Watt didn't even feel excited as he automatically said, "Sure. Let's go."

He slid a hand low around the girl's waist, walking with her toward the entrance, noticing the envious stares of all the other guys. He usually felt a thrill of victory at times like this, his stubbornly competitive streak coming out. Now he couldn't bring himself to care. It all felt too easy, and predictable. He'd already forgotten this girl's name and she'd told him twice.

"Winner's curse," Nadia whispered into his eartennas, and he could swear he heard amusement in her tone. "Where the victor gets exactly what he wants, only to find that it isn't quite as he expected."

AVERY

"ZAY'S TALKING TO Daniela Leon." Leda's eyes narrowed at the other girl, who stood below them wearing some kind of black flouncy dress. Daniela tipped her head back and rested a hand lightly on Zay's forearm, laughing uproariously at whatever he'd just said.

Avery followed Leda's gaze, though she didn't particularly care who Zay talked to. "It's fine."

"What's she supposed to be, anyway, in that weird dress? A matador?" Leda snapped, turning to Avery.

"I think it's a French maid costume?" Avery volunteered, trying to keep from laughing as she reached for her drink, which floated on a hovercoaster near her elbow.

But Leda wasn't listening. She'd turned her attention inward and was muttering to herself, probably planning revenge on Daniela. That was typical Leda, though; when she thought Avery had been slighted, her reaction was swift and uncompromising. It was just her brand of friendship, and Avery accepted it, because she knew what love and fierce loyalty were behind it. *I hope I never piss you off*, she always joked, and Leda would just laugh and roll her eyes as if the very idea was ludicrous.

The two friends were standing on Cord's second-floor landing, right at the top of the stairs. Avery's eyes scanned the crowded room below. It had been overwhelming down there earlier, with guy after guy telling her how amazing she looked tonight. She leaned forward on the railing and the halo above her head followed, its tiny microhovers programmed to track her movements.

Everyone was here. There was Kemball Brown, wearing intricate Viking armor that looked fantastic against his dark, muscled shoulders. Laura Saunders, the light catching all the sequins of her low-cut pirate bodice. And in a liftie uniform was Leda's older brother, Jamie, covered in a tangle of facial hair.

"What's up with Jamie's beard?" Avery asked Leda, amused.

"I *know*," Leda agreed as her eyes returned to regular focus. "When I first saw it the other day, I was grossed out too."

"The other day?" Avery repeated, confused. "Wasn't Jamie with you all summer?"

Leda wavered for a moment, so quick that Avery might have imagined it. "He was, of course. I meant when I saw the whole thing together, with the uniform. You know it's a real one—he bought it off an actual liftie."

Leda's words were normal enough. Avery had to be imagining the weirdness in her voice, right? "I need a refill," she decided, sending her drink back toward the bar. "Want one?"

"I'm okay," Leda protested. Her glass was still mostly full. Come to think of it, Avery realized, Leda hadn't been drinking much at all tonight. "Looks like you need to catch up," she teased.

There was that hesitation again. The sounds drifting up from below seemed suddenly amplified. "Guess I'm not back in party shape yet," Leda answered, but her laughter was hollow.

Avery watched her best friend, the way she shifted back and forth, studying the tiny bows on her black heels. She was lying about something.

The realization made Avery's chest hurt a little. She'd thought she and Leda told each other everything. "You can talk to me, you know."

"I know," Leda said quickly, though she didn't sound like she believed it.

"Where were you this summer, really?" Avery pressed.

"Just let it go, okay?"

"I promise I won't—"

Leda's mouth formed a hard line, and her next words came out cold and formal. "Seriously. I said let it go."

Avery recoiled, a little stung. "I just don't understand why you won't talk to me."

"Yeah, well, sometimes it's not *about* you, Avery."

Avery started to reply just as a commotion sounded from downstairs, voices rising up in greeting. She glanced down in curiosity—and saw the figure at the center of all the turmoil.

Everything came to a halt, the room suddenly devoid of air. Avery struggled to think. Next to her she felt Leda stiffen in surprise, but she couldn't tear her eyes away long enough to look at her friend.

He was back.

"Atlas," she whispered, though of course he couldn't hear.

She ran blindly down the stairs, the crowds parting to let her pass, hundreds of eyes on her, probably taking snaps and loading them straight to the feeds. None of it mattered. Atlas was home.

The next thing she knew, Avery was in his arms, burrowing her face in his shoulder, inhaling his familiar scent for a single precious moment before the rules of normal behavior forced her away.

"You're back," she said stupidly, her eyes drinking in every inch of him. He was wearing rumpled khakis and a navy sweater. He looked a little stronger than she remembered, and his light brown hair was longer, curling around his ears like it used to when he was little. But everything else was the same: his chocolate eyes framed by thick lashes, almost too thick to be masculine; the sprinkling of freckles across his nose; the way one of his bottom teeth was slightly turned, a reminder that he wasn't perfect. That was one of the things she'd loved about Atlas when her parents brought him home twelve years ago—the fact that he had actual, visible flaws.

"I'm back," he repeated. There was a shadow of rough stubble along his jaw. Avery's hands itched to reach out and touch it. "How's it going?"

"Where *were* you?" She winced at the sound of her own voice and lowered her tone. No one but Leda knew that Atlas hadn't told his family where he was this whole time.

"All over the place."

"Oh," was all she could think to say. It was hard to form coherent thoughts with Atlas so close. She wanted to run back into his arms and hold him so tight he could never leave again; to run her hands over his shoulders and assure herself he was really here, really *real*. She'd made so much progress this summer, and yet here she was, fighting the familiar need to reach out and touch him.

"Well, I'm glad you're home," she managed.

"You'd better be." His face broke out into a broad, easy smile, as if it were the most natural thing in the world for him to show up at a party unannounced after being gone for ten months.

"Atlas . . ." She hesitated, unsure what she wanted to say.

She'd been so worried. For his safety, sure, but even worse had been the worry at the back of her mind—the terrible, persistent fear that he might never come back.

"Yeah?" he said softly.

Avery took a step forward. Her body was reacting instinctively to his nearness, like a plant that had been too long in the dark and was finally exposed to sunlight.

"Fuller!" Ty Rodrick barreled over and slapped Atlas on the back. The rest of the hockey guys appeared, pulling him forward, their voices loud.

Avery bit back a protest and stepped away. *Act normal*, she reminded herself. Over the chaos she locked eyes with Atlas, and he winked at her. *Later*, he mouthed.

She nodded, breaking every promise to herself, loving him.

LEDA

LEDA DROPPED HER clutch on the marble countertop of Cord's bathroom and blinked at her reflection. Her hair was pulled into a bun and adorned with feathers, and her black ballerina costume clung to her in all the right places, even managing to create the illusion of cleavage. Real, illegal peacock feathers dusted the hem of her tutu. She reached down to run her fingers along them. Totally worth the import bribes.

Leda had long ago accepted that she wasn't beautiful. She was too severe, all sharp edges and narrow angles, and her chest was painfully small. Still, she had her mother's rich brown skin and her father's full mouth. And there was something interesting in her face—a bright, hard intelligence that made people look twice.

She took a deep breath, trying to ignore the sense of uneasiness prickling over her. It almost didn't seem possible, yet after all these months, it had finally happened.

Atlas was back.

Music played suddenly in her eartennas, the upbeat melody of a pop song she and Avery had been obsessed with last spring. Avery's ringtone, again. Leda shook her head to decline the ping. She knew Avery was looking for her, but she couldn't face her best friend yet, not after the way Leda had blown up at her earlier. She hadn't meant to; she was just on edge and defensive about the rehab stuff. Why couldn't Avery just stop pushing and give her some space? Leda didn't want to talk about it.

Especially not now, when the whole reason she'd broken down in the first place was back again, and as gorgeous as ever.

Snap out of it, Leda told herself. Reflexively she reached into her bag for her lip gloss and reapplied, then stepped back out into the party, her head held high. She wouldn't let Atlas get to her. She couldn't afford to, not again.

"Leda." Cord fell into step alongside her, wearing a dark costume with a sash slung across his chest. "Long time, no see."

"Hey," Leda said cautiously. She'd always been a little unsure of herself around Cord. Unlike Avery and Eris, she hadn't known him since childhood, and ever since she had asked him for help getting xenperheidren a few years ago, it felt somehow like he had the upper hand.

"How was your summer?" he asked, reaching for a pair of atomic shots from a passing tray and handing her one. "Cheers," he added before tossing his back.

Leda's fingers curled around the glass of clear liquid. She'd promised her mom she wouldn't drink tonight. Cord watched her, reading her hesitation, missing nothing. He raised an eyebrow in sardonic amusement.

Then she heard a familiar burst of laughter from behind them—Atlas was walking past. *Why not?* Leda thought suddenly; it wasn't like one atomic would send her back to popping xenperheidren. She raised the shot to her lips and took it in a single gulp. It burned her throat, not unpleasantly.

"Now I remember why I like you," Leda said, setting the shot glass down.

He laughed in approval. "I missed you this summer, Cole. I could have really used my smoke buddy."

"Please. You have plenty of other people to get high with."

"None as interesting as you," Cord insisted. "Everyone else just gets dumber the more stuff they take."

Leda shifted uncomfortably at the reminder. *I'm sharp enough without xenperheidren*, she told herself, but the words didn't ring as true as they had just a few days ago. Mumbling an excuse, she turned and moved farther into the party. The feathers on her ballerina skirt had started falling off, leaving a little trail on the floor.

Hey, where are you? she flickered to Avery. Avery didn't know about how she used to smoke occasionally with Cord—and Leda didn't want to tell her—but seeing her might help calm Leda down.

"Leda?"

She turned slowly, trying to seem like she didn't care, though of course she did.

Atlas was standing in a group of his old hockey friends. Leda waited, unmoving, as he mumbled something to the guys and came over toward her. "Hey," he said simply.

Leda's temper flared. That was all he had to say, when the last time they'd seen each other was naked in a hot tub, halfway across the world?

"So where were you?"

Atlas blinked. "I took a gap year, traveled around."

"Don't give me that bullshit." She crossed her arms. "I know the truth, okay?"

"I don't . . ."

"It was a pretty shitty thing to do, leaving like that. Especially after—you know." Her mind flashed to that night, to the way he'd touched her and the snow that had fallen over both of them, melting wherever it met the heat of their skin. She felt herself flush at the memory.

"Fuller!" Henry Strittmayer yelled out. "We're starting Spinners! Get your ass over here."

"In a minute." Atlas's eyes were locked on hers. "I'm glad you said something, Leda. I was thinking about you a lot while I was gone."

"Oh?" she said cautiously, trying not to get her hopes up.

"I owe you an apology."

Leda felt like she'd been slapped. "You don't owe me anything," she said quickly, defensive. *Stupid*, she chided herself, thinking that Atlas might have missed her, when all he apparently felt was that he *owed* her. God, she hated that word. It was about as far from romantic as you could get.

They looked at each other in layered silence. "Want to play Spinners?" he asked after a moment.

"No." The last thing she wanted was to sit next to Atlas like everything was normal, and play a game that might end with them being forced to kiss. "I'm going to find Avery," she amended. "She seemed a little drunk earlier."

"I'll come with you," Atlas offered, but she was already pushing past him.

"It's okay," she said quickly, heading into the hall. "I've got it."

The pull she felt toward him was as insistent and powerful as it had been in Catyan, when their bodies were so intertwined that he'd felt like a part of her. Yet she didn't understand him any better now than she had then. Maybe she never would.

Leda's stomach gave a sudden twist, her head pounding angrily. It felt like something was pressing at her from within, the way she used to feel when she came down too abruptly from a high—

She needed to get out of here. Now.

She elbowed through the hot, teeming crowd that filled Cord's apartment, a mechanical smile pasted on her face, and slipped into the first hover she could find.

By the time she got home Leda was nearly frantic. She raced down the hall to her room and flung open the door, reaching for her lavender-scented aromatherapy pillow and burying her face in it, taking several deep, desperate breaths. Hot tears pricked at the corners of her eyes. God, she was an idiot. She couldn't believe how easily seeing Atlas had sent her veering toward the edge.

Finally Leda plopped into the chair at her vanity. She began wiping the makeup—and the tears—from her face with brusque, angry movements. Her body was so tense it was almost shaking.

A tentative knock sounded at her door. "Leda?" Ilara Cole appeared in her daughter's doorway. "How was the party?"

"You didn't need to stay up." Leda didn't turn, just met her mom's gaze in the mirror. Ilara never used to wait up for her before.

Her mom ignored the comment. "I saw some of the snaps, from the feeds," she persisted, in a clear attempt to be upbeat. "All the costumes looked fantastic. Especially you and Avery together!"

Leda spun around on the vanity chair and stood up, her hands clenching into sudden fists. "You're *spying* on me now? I thought you said you would trust me this year!"

"And *you* said that if I let you go to the party, you wouldn't drink!"

Leda recoiled, and her mom's tone softened. "I'm sorry," Ilara went on. "But, Leda, I'm not stupid. I can smell the atomic from here. What am I supposed to think?"

"It was just one drink," Leda said tersely. "That's not exactly going on a xenperheidren bender last I checked."

Ilara started to put a hand on her shoulder, but Leda brushed it away, and she lowered her hand in defeat. "Leda, please," she said softly. "I'm trying here. I *want* to trust you again. But trust has to be earned. And so far I'm not seeing any effort from you, to—"

"Fine," Leda said woodenly, interrupting her mom. "The party was great. Thank you for letting me go. I promise I won't drink at the next one."

They stared at each other, neither of them sure what to say next. There was affection on both their faces, but wariness too. They weren't sure how to act around each other anymore.

Finally Ilara sighed and turned away. "I'm glad you had fun. See you in the morning." The door clicked shut behind her.

Leda yanked off her dress and shimmied into her mono-grammed pajamas. She sent a quick flicker to Avery, apologizing for her earlier outburst and saying that she'd left the party early. Then she crawled into bed, her mind spinning.

She wondered if Avery and Atlas were still at the party. Was it weird of her, to have left early? Was Avery upset with her about earlier? Why couldn't Avery just accept that some things in Leda's life were private? And now, as if she didn't have enough to deal with, her stupid mom had started monitoring her every move on the feeds. Leda hadn't even realized Ilara knew how to look that stuff up.

At the thought of the feeds, she decided to pull up Atlas's, though she already knew what she would find. Sure enough, it was as vague as it had always been. While most of the guys she knew lived their entire lives on the feeds, Atlas's profile had nothing but an old picture of him at his grandparents' beach house and a few favorite quotes. He was so maddeningly opaque.

If only Leda could see past the public profile, to his messages and hidden check-ins and everything else he wasn't sharing with the world. If only she knew what he was *thinking*, maybe she could put all this behind her and finally move on.

Or maybe she could get him back, part of her whispered; the part she couldn't seem to ignore.

Leda rolled onto her stomach, tangling her fists in her sheets in frustration—and had an idea so simple that it must either be brilliant, or stupid.

Atlas might be hard to read, but maybe there was another way to figure him out.

AVERY

SEVERAL HOURS INTO the party, Avery found herself in the liquor closet off Cord's kitchen. She wasn't quite sure why she'd come in here: maybe for some of the gold-leafed bourbon lined up on the top shelf, or the stash of illegal retros. She paused, swirling the ice chips in her empty cup. Her *two* empty cups, she realized; she had one in each hand.

Atlas was back. The look on his face when he saw her—and that word, *later*—kept replaying in her head. She'd been desperate for him to come home for so long, and yet now that he was finally here she didn't know what it meant. So she'd decided the best course of action was to get as drunk as possible. Evidently she'd succeeded.

A shaft of light sliced through the darkness as the door was pushed open. "Avery?"

Cord. She sighed, wanting to just be alone with her thoughts right now. "Hey. Great party," she murmured.

"Here's to your guy," he said, and reached over her to grab a handle of the bourbon. He took a long, slow sip, his eyes glittering in the dim light.

"Who?" she asked sharply. Did Cord somehow know? If anyone could figure it out, she thought darkly, it would be him. He'd known her forever. And he was screwed up enough himself to guess the crazy, twisted truth.

"Whoever got you so hot and bothered, and brought out Double-Fisting Fuller. Because it isn't Zay Wagner. Even I can tell that."

"You're a real asshole sometimes, you know," Avery said without thinking.

He barked out a laugh. "I do know. But I throw such great parties people forgive me for it. Kind of like they forgive you for being prudish and unreadable, because you're the best-looking person on earth."

Avery wanted to be angry with him, but for some reason she wasn't. Maybe because she knew what Cord was really like, under all the layers of sarcasm.

"Remember when we were kids?" she said suddenly. "When you dared me to climb into the trash chute, and I got stuck inside? You waited with me the whole time until the safety bots came so I wouldn't be in there alone."

The lights in the liquor closet flickered off. They must have been standing very still to turn off the motion sensors. Cord was nothing but a shadow.

"Yeah," he said quietly. "So?"

"We're all very different now, aren't we?" Shaking her head, Avery pushed out the door and into the hallway.

She looped idly around the party for a while, saying hi to everyone she hadn't seen since the end of last spring, drinking steadily from her two different cups. She couldn't stop thinking about Atlas—or Leda. Where had Leda been all summer, that she refused to tell Avery about it? Whatever was going on, Avery felt terrible for the way she'd pressed the issue and clearly upset Leda. It wasn't like her to leave a party early. Avery knew she should go to the Coles' and check on her, yet she couldn't bear the thought of leaving while Atlas was still here. After all those months apart, she just wanted to stay close to him.

I'm sorry about earlier. See you tomorrow? she sent to Leda, pushing aside her guilt.

Eventually she found Atlas in the downstairs library, playing a game of Spinners, and paused near the doorway to watch. He was leaning over the table as he Spun, his lashes casting subtle shadows on his cheekbones. Avery hadn't played Spinners in years, since that time when she was fourteen—at another of Cord's parties, in this very room. If she closed her eyes, it almost felt like it had happened yesterday, not three years ago.

She'd been so nervous to play. It was her first time drinking, and though she hadn't told anyone, it was her first time at Spinners. She'd never even been kissed. What if they could all tell?

"Hurry up, Fuller!" Marc Rojas, a senior, had groaned at her hesitation. "Spin!"

"Spin! Spin!" the rest of the room took up the chant. Biting her lip, Avery reached up to swipe the holographic dial projected in the middle of the table.

The arrow whipped around the room in a blur. Everyone leaned forward to watch its progress. Finally it began to slow, and paused in front of Breccan Doyle. Avery braced herself, on the edge of her seat.

With its very last bit of momentum, the arrow shifted onto Atlas.

The game console immediately cast a privacy cone where they sat, refracting the light to hide them from the rest of the room, and deflecting all sound waves. Beyond the shimmering wall of photons—which rippled and bent like the surface of water in a pond—Avery could see the others, though they couldn't see her. They were shouting and waving at the gaming console, probably trying to reset the game and make her spin again. Nothing fun about having siblings together in the cone, right?

"You okay?" Atlas asked quietly. He had a half-full bottle of atomic in his hand, and tried to pass it to her, but she shook her head. She was already confused, and the alcohol was stirring up her feelings for Atlas in a dangerous way.

"I've never kissed anyone before. I'm going to be terrible at it," she blurted out, and cringed. What had made her say that?

Atlas took a long pull of the atomic, then set it down carefully. To his credit, he didn't laugh. "Don't worry," he finally said. "I'm sure you'll be a great kisser."

"I don't even know what to do!" Outside the cone, Avery saw Tracy Ellison, who had a huge crush on Atlas, gesturing angrily.

"You just need practice." Atlas smiled and shrugged. "Sorry it's me in here instead of Breccan."

"Are you kidding? I'd rather—" Avery halted. She couldn't let herself finish that sentence.

Atlas looked at her curiously. His brow furrowed in an expression she couldn't quite read. "Aves," he said, but it came out more like a question. He leaned closer. Avery held her breath. . . .

The invisibility cone dissolved, letting reality back in.

Avery had never been sure whether that almost kiss was real, or whether she'd just imagined it. As the memory washed over her now, she looked at Atlas, who glanced up, seeming to feel her gaze. But if he was thinking of that night too, he didn't give any indication. He just studied her for a moment, then seemed to come to a decision. "I'm out this round," he said, disengaging from the game and walking over to where she stood.

"Hey." He gently pulled the drinks from her hands and set them on a table. Avery had forgotten she was holding them. She tripped forward a little.

"Want me to take you home?" Atlas reached out to steady her. It was just like always; Atlas knowing what she wanted without her even having to say it. Except, of course, for the one thing he could never know.

"Yes," Avery said, a little too quickly.

He nodded. "Let's go, then."

They walked out onto Cord's doorstep and took the hover that Atlas had called. Avery leaned back on the seat and closed her eyes, letting the familiar hum of the magnetic propulsion system wash over her. She listened for the rise and fall of Atlas's breathing. He really was here, she kept telling herself. It wasn't just another one of her dreams.

When they reached the thousandth-floor penthouse Avery fell backward onto her bed, still in her dress. Everything was a little dizzy. "You okay?" Atlas asked, settling onto the corner of her enormous cream-colored comforter.

"Mmm-hmm," she murmured. She was better than she'd been in months, here, alone, with Atlas, in the semidarkness. He scooted over a little. She closed her eyes. Right now, with him sitting on her bed, Avery could almost pretend he was just a boy she'd met and brought home. Not someone her parents adopted when she was five years old, because she was lonely and they didn't have time for her.

"Remember when you first came here?" she asked. She'd been sitting on the playroom floor brushing her doll's hair, and the front door had opened to reveal her mom, holding the hand of a hopeful, lost-looking boy. "This is Atlas," her mom had said, and the boy had given a tentative smile. From that moment on Avery adored him.

"Of course I remember," Atlas teased. "You demanded that I go straight to the park with you, and drag you along on your hoverboard so you could pretend it was a pirate ship."

"I did not!" Avery propped herself up on her elbows to glare at him in mock anger.

"It's okay. I didn't mind," he said softly.

Avery leaned back on her pillows. How strange that there had ever been a time in her life before Atlas. It didn't seem possible anymore.

"Aves?" she heard Atlas say. "If there was something I needed to know, you would tell me, right?"

She opened her eyes and looked at his face, so clear and guileless. He wasn't suggesting the truth—was he? He couldn't be. He didn't know what it was like, wanting something you could never have; how impossible it was to un-want it once you'd let the feeling in.

"I'm glad you're back. I missed you," she told him.

"Me too."

The silence stretched between them. Avery fought to stay awake, to drink in Atlas's presence, but sleep was dragging her down. After a moment he stood and walked to the hallway.

"I love you," he said, and pulled the door quietly shut behind him.

I love you too, her heart whispered, curling around the phrase like a prayer.

ERIS

I'M HEADING HOME, Eris flickered Cord, not bothering to wait for his response. His apartment was emptying as the party began to slowly disintegrate, people stumbling home alone or in pairs. Everywhere she looked Eris saw the debris of an epic night, scattered cups and lost costume pieces and broken hallucilighters.

She hadn't meant to stay this long. She'd been flitting from group to group and lost all sense of time. She wasn't sure where Cord was and she felt too exhausted, suddenly, to go looking for him. All she wanted was a cleansteam shower and her thousand-thread-count sheets.

Eris started toward the door, scrolling idly through her messages, and realized with a start that she had several missed pings from home. They were timestamped from a couple of hours ago— she'd been on the dance floor; she remembered tossing her head back and forth, ignoring them—but she hadn't registered at the time that they were from her parents. She wondered what was going on.

When she reached her apartment on 985, Eris opened the door as slowly as she could, her black shoes in one hand and her clutch in the other. She knew the moment she stepped inside that something was wrong. The lights were on their brightest setting, and an awful strangled sound came from the living room. *Oh god.* It was her mom, crying.

Eris dropped her shoes on the floor with a loud clatter.

"Eris?" Caroline lifted her head from where she lay curled on the couch. She was still wearing her evening gown, a beautiful scarlet question mark against the white cushions.

Eris ran forward to throw her arms around her mom, pulling her close. She thought suddenly of when she was little and her parents would come home from parties. Eris would hear her mom's heels clacking in the hallway—a sound she'd always found strangely reassuring—and no matter how late it was, Caroline had always come to brush Eris's hair and tell her about all the wonderful, magical, grown-up things she'd seen that night. How many times had Eris fallen asleep listening to the sound of her mom's voice?

"It's okay," Eris said softly, though clearly it wasn't. Her eyes darted nervously around the apartment. Where was her dad?

"No, it's not okay." Caroline took a deep breath, and pulled back to look Eris squarely in the eye. Mascara-filled tears etched black rivers down her face. "I'm so sorry."

"What happened?" Eris scooted back from her mom to sit upright, the movement brusquer than she'd intended. "Where's Dad?"

"He . . . left." Caroline looked down, studying the hands clasped tight in her lap, the crumpled folds of her magnificent crimson dress.

"What do you mean, he *left*?"

"Remember that DNA test you took today?"

Eris nodded impatiently. Of course she remembered; she'd taken countless tests, given a cheek swab and peed on a stick, and signed so many old-fashioned paper documents with a real ink pen that her hand had cramped with the unfamiliar movement.

Wordlessly Eris's mom tapped the coffee table, which, like all the surfaces in their apartment, had touch-screen capabilities. A few quick swipes and she'd pulled an attachment from her message queue. Eris leaned forward to look.

Her DNA was mapped there in all its glory, its strands an unrealistic bubblegum pink, but Eris's eyes were already skimming past that, to the jumble of medical words and bar charts below. She knew they'd run her DNA against her dad's, which was already on file, yet she couldn't process what she was seeing now. What did it all have to do with her?

Her eyes caught on a single line at the bottom—percentage match: 0.00%—and she reached out a hand to steady herself. An ugly, sticky realization was closing around her throat.

"I don't believe this." She sat up straighter, her voice gaining volume. "The lab messed up the sequencing. We need to ping them back, get them to redo it."

"They did redo it. It's not wrong." It seemed as if her mom was talking from very far away, as if Eris were underwater, or buried under a mountain of sand.

"No," Eris repeated blindly.

"It's true, Eris."

The finality in Caroline's tone made Eris cold all over. And then she understood why her DNA wasn't a match, why her mom wasn't acting more surprised. Because Eris wasn't her father's daughter, after all.

Her mom had cheated on her dad, and kept it a secret for the past eighteen years.

Eris shut her eyes. This wasn't happening. It couldn't be. If she kept her eyes closed it would go away, like a bad dream.

Her mom reached out a hand and Eris shot to her feet, knocking over the coffee table as she did. Neither of them looked at it. They just stared at each other, mother and daughter, so painfully alike—and yet to Eris they had never felt more like strangers.

"Why?" she asked, because it was the only word her mind could process. "Why did you *lie* to me all those years?"

"Oh, Eris. I didn't mean—it wasn't about you—"

"Are you serious? Of *course* it's about me!"

Caroline winced. "That's not what I meant. It's just . . . whatever happens between me and Everett—it's not your fault."

"I know, because it's *your* fault!"

Neither of them spoke. The silence scraped at Eris's eardrums.

"Where did Dad go? When is he coming back?" she asked finally.

"I'm not sure." Her mom sighed. "I'm sorry, Eris."

"Stop saying that!" By now Eris was screaming. She couldn't help it; she didn't want to hear another apology from her mom. Apologies meant nothing when the person you trusted the most had been lying to you your whole life.

Her mom was utterly still. "I know this is really hard on you, and you must have a lot of questions. I'm here to answer—"

"Fuck you and your *fucking* explanations," Eris interrupted, enunciating each word.

Her mom drew back in wounded shock, but Eris ignored it. Her mind was shuffling through all her memories of her mom: of when Caroline would come wake her up for elementary school, only to snuggle into Eris's bed with her and fall back asleep, forcing Eris's dad to come wake them both up, laughing about what sleeping beauties his girls were. Of the Christmases they had baked cookies to put under the tree for Santa, made almost entirely from raw dough, and then Dad would go eat them in the middle of the night even long after Eris knew Santa wasn't real. Of every year before her birthday, when Caroline would make up a fake doctor's appointment and pull Eris out of school to go shopping so they could pick out her presents and then go to Bergdorf's for tea. "Your mom is so cool," the other girls always said, because none of their moms ever let them out of school just for fun, and Eris would laugh and say, "Yeah, I know, she's the best."

It all felt fake now. Every gesture, every *I love you*; all of it was tinted by the great ugly lie underpinning her life. Eris blinked in confusion at her mom's familiar face. "So you've known my entire life," she said bitterly.

"No. I wasn't sure." Her mom's eyes brimmed with unshed tears, but she managed to hold them back. "I always thought— hoped—that you were Everett's. But I never knew for certain until now."

"Why the hell did you let me take that DNA test, then?"

"You think if I knew there was a test I would've let you go?" her mom cried out.

Eris didn't know what to say. She didn't understand how her mom could have done this to her, to her dad, to their *family*.

"Please, Eris. I want to make this right," Caroline began, but Eris shook her head.

"Don't talk to me," she said slowly, and turned away.

Somehow Eris stumbled to her round bed, nestled to one side of her enormous circular room. Shock and fear were swirling dangerously in her chest. She couldn't breathe. She clawed suddenly at the neck of her shirt, still damp with her mom's tears, and yanked it brutally over her head, then took a desperate, ragged breath. She was pretty sure she'd heard one of the seams rip out.

Can I be of assistance? her contacts prompted, sensing that she was almost crying. "Shut up!" she muttered, and they obediently powered down.

Everett Radson wasn't her father. The truth of it kept ricocheting painfully against her skull like gunfire. Her poor dad—she wondered what he'd said when he got the lab results. Where was he now? A hotel, the hospital? She wanted to go talk to him, yet at the same time she wasn't quite ready to face him. She knew that when she saw him—when she truly came face-to-face with it all—that everything would be different, for good.

Eris closed her eyes, but the world kept spinning around her. She wasn't even drunk tonight. This must be the feeling, she thought bitterly, of her life coming untethered.

She sat up and studied her room with an odd sense of detachment. Everywhere she looked were expensive things—the crystal vase with its ever-young roses, the closet filled with delicate, colorful dresses, the custom-made vanity cluttered with gleaming pieces of tech. All the trappings of her life, everything that made her Eris Dodd-Radson.

She started to lean back onto her pillows and cursed aloud as something sharp dug into her ear. Her mom's earrings. She'd forgotten all about them.

Eris unscrewed the right earring and held it out on her palm. It was so beautiful; a glass sphere glowing with whorls of color, like the eye of a coming storm. A beautiful, rare, expensive present from her dad to her mom. Suddenly the earring and everything it stood for struck Eris as unbearably false.

She pulled back her arm and hurled the earring against the wall with all the strength she had. It exploded into a million pieces, which scattered over the floor like shards of glittering tears.

RYLIN

AS THE LAST guests stumbled from Cord's party into a waiting hover, Rylin heaved a sigh of relief. The night had felt endless—cleaning up all those drunk kids' messes, pretending not to notice how some of the guys looked at her. She was exhausted, and her head still pounded from being yanked out of the communal. But thank god she was finally done.

Stretching her arms overhead, she wandered to the windows in Cord's living room and gazed hungrily at the horizon line in the distance. The view screens in her apartment were so old that they didn't even look like windows anymore, more like garish cartoons of a fake view, with a too-bright sun and overly green trees. There was a window along the side of her monorail stop at work—Rylin's snack stand was at the Crayne Boulevard stop, between Manhattan and Jersey—but even that was too close to see anything except the Tower, squatting like a giant steel toad that blocked out the sky. Impulsively she pressed her face to the glass. It felt blissfully cool on her aching forehead.

Finally Rylin peeled herself away and started upstairs, to check in with Cord and get the hell out of there. As she walked, the lights behind her turned off and the ones ahead of her clicked on, illuminating a hallway lined with antique paintings. She passed an enormous bathroom, filled with plush hand towels and touch screens on every surface. Hell, the *floor* was probably even a touch screen: Rylin was willing to bet that it could read your weight, or heat up on voice command. Everything here was the best, the newest, the most expensive—everywhere she looked, she saw money. She walked a little faster.

When she reached the holoden, Rylin hesitated. Projected on the wall wasn't the action immersion or dumb comedy she had expected. It was old family vids.

"Oh, no! Don't you dare!" Cord's mom exclaimed, in vibrant 3-D.

A four-year-old Cord grinned, holding a garden hose. *Where was this*, Rylin wondered, *on vacation somewhere?*

"Oops!" he proclaimed, without an ounce of contrition, as he turned the hose on his mom. She laughed, throwing up her tanned arms, her dark hair streaming with water like a mermaid's. Rylin had forgotten how pretty she was.

Cord leaned forward eagerly, sitting almost on the edge of his leather armchair. A smile played on his lips as he watched his dad chase his younger self around the yard.

Rylin retreated a step. She would just—

The floor creaked under her feet, and Cord's head shot up. Instantly the vid cut off.

"I—I'm sorry," she stammered. "I just wanted to let you know I'm finished. So I'm heading out."

Cord's eyes traveled slowly over her outfit, her tight jeans and low-cut shirt and the tangle of neon bracelets at her wrists.

"I didn't have time to go home and change," she added, not sure why she was explaining herself to him. "You didn't give me much notice."

Cord just stared at her, saying nothing. Rylin realized with a start that he hadn't recognized her. Then again, why should he? They hadn't seen each other in years, since that Christmas his parents had invited her family over for presents and cookies. Rylin remembered how magical it had seemed to her and Chrissa, playing in the snow in the enclosed greenhouse, like a real-life version of the snow-globe toy her mom always got out for the holidays. Cord had spent the whole time in some holo-game, oblivious.

"Rylin Myers," Cord said at last, as if she had stumbled into his party by chance rather than been paid to work it. "How the hell are you?" He gestured to the seat next to him, and Rylin surprised herself by sinking into it, pulling her legs up to sit cross-legged.

"Aside from being groped by your friends, just great," she said without thinking. "Sorry," she added quickly, "it's been a long night." She wondered where Hiral and the gang were, if they'd finally noticed her disappearance.

"Well, most of them aren't my friends," Cord said matter-of-factly. He shifted his weight, and Rylin couldn't help noticing the way his shoulders rippled under his button-down shirt. She sensed suddenly that his carelessness was deceptive, that beneath it all he was watching her intently.

For a moment they both stared at the dark screen. It was funny, Rylin thought; if you'd told her earlier that her night would end here, hanging out with Cord Anderton, she would have laughed.

"What is that?" Cord asked, and Rylin realized she was playing with her necklace again. She dropped her hands to her lap.

"It was my mom's," she said shortly, hoping that would end

it. She'd given the necklace to her mom as a birthday present one year, and after that her mom never took it off. Rylin remembered the pang she'd felt when the hospital sent it back to her, folded in plastiwrap and labeled with a cheerful orange tag. Her mom's death hadn't felt real until that moment.

"Why the Eiffel Tower?" Cord pressed, sounding interested.

Why the hell do you *care*, Rylin wanted to snap back, but caught herself. "It was an inside joke of ours," she said simply. "We used to always say that if we ever had the money, we would take the train to Paris, eat at a fancy 'Café Paris.'" She didn't bother explaining how she and Chrissa used to turn their kitchen into a snooty French café. They would make paper berets and draw mustaches on their faces with their mom's paintstick, and adopt terrible French accents as they served her the "chef's special"—whatever frozen food packet had been on sale that week. It always made their mom smile after a long day's work.

"Did you ever end up going?" Cord asked.

Rylin almost laughed at the stupidity of the question. "I've barely left the Tower."

The room sounded with sudden shouting and water spraying, as the screen lit back up with the holovid. Cord quickly shut it off. His parents had died years ago, Rylin remembered, in a commercial airline crash.

"It's nice that you have those vids," she said into the silence. She understood why he would be possessive about them; she would have done the same if she and Chrissa had any. "I wish we had more of my mom."

"I'm sorry," Cord said quietly.

"It's fine." She shrugged, though of course it wasn't fine. It wouldn't be fine ever again.

The tension was broken by a sudden rumble sounding in the room. It took Rylin a moment to realize that it had come from her own stomach. Cord looked at her curiously. "You hungry?" he asked, though the answer was obvious. "We could break out the leftovers, if you want."

"*Yes,*" Rylin said, more enthusiastically than she'd meant to. She hadn't eaten since lunch.

"Next time you should eat the catering," Cord said as they started out of the holoden and down the sweeping glass staircase. "Guess I should have told you that." Rylin wondered what made him think there would be a next time.

When they reached the kitchen, the fridge cheerfully informed Cord that he'd consumed four thousand calories so far today, 40 percent of which were from alcohol, and per his "Muscle Regime 2118" he was allowed nothing else. A glass of water materialized in the fridge's export slot.

"Muscle regime. I should get one of those," Rylin deadpanned.

"I'm trying to be healthy." Cord turned back to the machine. "Guest override, please," he mumbled, then looked at Rylin, redder than she'd ever seen him. "Um, could you just put your hand on the fridge to prove you're here?"

Rylin placed her palm on the refrigerator, which dutifully swung open. Cord began pulling out containers at random, pumpkin seed milk bars and hundred-layer lasagna and fresh appleberries. Rylin grabbed a box of pizza cones out of his hand and tore into one. It was cheesy and fried and perfect, maybe even better cold. When Cord handed her a napkin, she realized that sauce had dripped onto her chin, but somehow she didn't care.

As he leaned back against the counter, Rylin caught sight of something over his shoulder, and let out a squeal. "Oh my god. Are those Gummy Buddies? Do they actually move when you bite off their heads, like they do in the adverts?"

"You've never had a Gummy Buddy?"

"No." A bag of Gummy Buddies cost more than what she and Chrissa spent on food in a week. They were the first edible electronics, with microscopic radio frequency ID tags inside each candy.

"Come on." Cord tossed her the bag. "Try one."

Rylin pulled out a bright green gummy and popped it whole into her mouth. She chewed expectantly, then glowered at him when nothing happened.

"You didn't do it right." Cord seemed to be struggling to keep his face straight. "You have to bite off the head, or the legs. You can't just eat it all at once."

She grabbed another gummy and bit off the bottom half. The RFID chip in the remaining top part of the gummy abruptly let out a high-pitched scream.

"Crap!" Rylin yelled, dropping the gummy head on the floor. It kept twitching near her feet, and she took a step back.

Cord laughed and grabbed the rest of the gummy, tossing it into the trash, which suctioned it off to the sorting center. "Here, try again," he said, holding out the bag. "If you bite off the head, they don't scream, just move around."

"I'm good, thanks." Rylin tucked a strand of hair behind one ear and glanced back up at Cord. Something about the way he was looking at her made her fall silent.

Then he was closing the distance between them, and lowering his mouth to hers.

At first Rylin was too startled to react. Cord kissed her slowly, almost languidly, pressing her back against the counter. The edge of it dug sharply into Rylin's hip, jarring her back to reality. She put both hands on his chest and pushed, hard.

She crossed her arms as Cord stumbled backward, his breath ragged, his eyes dancing with amusement. A smile curled at the corners of his lips.

Something about that look made Rylin shake with anger. She was furious with Cord for laughing at the situation, with herself for letting it unfold—and deep down, for *enjoying* it, for a single bewildered instant.

Without stopping to think, she raised her arm and slapped him. The noise cracked through the air like a whip.

"I'm sorry," Cord finally said, into the painful stillness. "I obviously misread the situation."

Rylin watched the red mark of her hand blossoming on his face. She'd gone too far. He wouldn't pay her for tonight, and all that hard work would have been for nothing. "I—um, I should get going."

She was halfway out the front door when she heard footsteps in the entryway. "Hey, Myers," Cord called out from behind her. "Catch."

She turned and caught the bag of Gummy Buddies in midair.

"Thanks," she said, confused, but the door was already closing behind him.

Rylin leaned against the door of Cord's apartment and closed her eyes, trying to gather the frayed and tangled strands of her thoughts. Her mouth felt bruised, almost seared. She could still feel where Cord had held her tight around the waist.

With an angry sigh, she hurried down the three brick stairs that led to his entrance and started down the carbon-paved streets.

The entire two and a half miles home, Rylin pulled the heads off the Gummy Buddies one by one, letting their small screams fill the empty elevator car.

WATT

"WATT!" A TINY pink form barreled down the hallway as he walked inside the next day.

"Hey, Zahra." Watt laughed, scooping his five-year-old sister into his arms. Her dark curls had something sticky in them, and a costume tiara was perched precariously atop her head. Watt noticed that her pajama pants, which used to drag along the ground, now barely hit mid-calf. He made a mental note to buy her a new set the next time he was paid. Zahra giggled, then wriggled impatiently out of his arms to run back into the living room, where her twin brother, Amir, was building something out of plastifoam blocks.

"Watzahn, is that you?" Watt's mom called from the kitchen.

"Yeah, Mom?" It was never a good sign when she used his full name.

You might want to change first, Nadia suggested, but Watt was already at the doorway. Shirin hovered over the cook surface, pouring water into an instant noodle dinner. Watt remembered back before the twins were born, when she used to cook elaborate Persian meals from scratch: rich lamb stews and golden flatbreads and rice sprinkled with sumac. Then she'd unexpectedly gotten pregnant and stopped cooking altogether, claiming the smell of spices made her nauseous. But even after the twins were born, the home-cooked Persian meals never came back. There wasn't enough time anymore.

Shirin pushed the cook-dial to high heat and turned to Watt. "You were at Derrick's all day?" she asked, with a glance at his rumpled clothes from last night. Watt reddened. Nadia said nothing, but he could practically feel her thinking *I told you so*.

"Yeah. I stayed at Derrick's last night," Watt said to his mom, but she just stared at him blankly. "Today was our last day of summer, and we wanted to try finishing this game. . . ." He trailed off.

It was true, though. He'd barely spent any time at Squid Ink Martini Girl's last night—Nadia was right, she didn't have much to say, and he felt somehow foolish for having left the bar with her. He'd ducked out almost immediately to head for Derrick's. He'd spent the night there, and this morning they'd eaten enormous sandwiches from the bagel shop and watched soccer on the tiny screen in Derrick's living room. It wasn't that Watt had been *avoiding* home, exactly. But Derrick didn't have two younger siblings who needed constant attention. His parents basically let him do what he wanted, as long as he kept up his grades.

"I could have used your help today," Shirin went on, sounding more defeated than angry. "The twins had a checkup this afternoon. I had to get Tasha to fill in for me at the center so that I could take them, since I couldn't find you. I'll have to work double shifts the rest of the week just to make up the time."

Watt felt like utter crap. "You could have pinged me," he said lamely, pretty sure he'd ignored a call at some point last night.

"You were too busy playing that *holo* game," his mom snapped, then let out a sigh. "It's fine. Just get your brother and sister." She set bowls and spoons on the table as the door opened again, eliciting more excited squeals from Zahra. Moments later Watt's dad was in the kitchen, a twin on each hip. He usually had to work much later than this—having him home for dinner was practically a special occasion.

"Dinner's ready, Rashid." Watt's mom greeted him with a tired kiss on the cheek.

They all crammed around the small table. Watt shoved the instant noodles and canned vegetables into his mouth without tasting them, not that they had much taste to begin with. He was angry with his mom for making him feel guilty. What was wrong with him occasionally blowing off steam at a midTower bar? Or spending the last day of summer hanging out with his friend?

The moment Zahra yawned, her hands making small fists over her head, Watt stood up as if on cue. "The bedtime monorail is about to leave! All aboard!" he announced, in a too-deep voice.

"Choo choo!" Zahra and Amir attempted a train noise and trotted alongside Watt. The actual monorail was silent, of course, but the twins watched tons of animated train holos and loved making that sound. Watt's dad smiled, watching them. Shirin pursed her lips and said nothing.

Watt led the twins down a winding imaginary train track to the end of the hall. Their room was tiny, but still bigger than his: this used to be Watt's room, actually, before they were born and he moved into the office nook. The dim light barely illuminated the bunk beds built into the wall. Watt had repeatedly tried to route more electricity to the twins, but it never seemed to be enough. He had a sinking suspicion that it was his fault, because of all the power-hungry hardware he'd set up in his room.

He helped the twins laser-clean their teeth and tucked them

into bed. They didn't have a room comp down here, of course, but Nadia did the best vitals check she could, watching the twins' breathing and eye movement. When she'd confirmed they were asleep, Watt shut the door quietly and moved down the hallway to his makeshift bedroom.

He sank gratefully into his ergonomic swivel chair—which he'd lifted from an office space that was about to be foreclosed— and clicked on the high-def screen at his desk, which took up most of the room. His bed was shoved far to the corner, his clothes tucked on hoverbeams up near the ceiling. Nadia didn't need the screen, of course, since she could project anything directly onto his contacts. But Watt still liked surfing the i-Net this way whenever possible. Even he thought it was weird sometimes, replacing your entire field of vision with the digital overlay.

He flipped through all the messages from the girls he'd met at Pulse last night, then closed out without answering any of them. Instead he logged into H@cker Haus, his favorite dark-web site for postings of "data services" jobs.

Watt's family always needed money. His parents had moved from Isfahad to New York the year before he was born, when the Tower was new and the whole world was excited about it: before Shanghai and Hong Kong and São Paulo all got their own thousand-story megatowers. Watt knew his parents had immigrated for his sake, hoping he would have a chance at a better future.

It hadn't turned out the way they'd hoped. Back in Iran, Watt's dad had attended the top mechanical engineering school, and his mom had been studying as a doctor. But Rashid now worked repairing industrial coolant and sewage systems. Shirin had been forced to get a job as a caregiver at a nursing home, just so they could keep their apartment. They never complained, but Watt knew it wasn't easy on them, working long days hammering machinery and dealing with crotchety old people, then coming downstairs to take care of the family. And no matter how hard they tried, money always seemed to be tight. Especially now that the twins were getting older.

Which was why Watt had started saving for college. Well, for MIT. Their microsystems engineering program was the best in the world—and Watt's best shot at someday working on one of the few legal quants left, the ones owned by the UN and NASA. He wasn't applying to any safety schools. His parents worried that his insistence was stubborn and overconfident, but Watt didn't care; he knew he would get in. The real question was how he would pay for it. He'd been applying to scholarships, and had won a few small grants here and there, but nowhere near enough to pay for four years at an expensive private university.

So Watt had started making money a different way: by venturing to the darker part of the i-Net, and answering ads for what were euphemistically called "information services." In other words, hacking. Together he and Nadia falsified employment records, changed students' grades at various school systems, even broke into flicker accounts for people who thought their significant others were cheating. Only once did they try hacking a bank's security system, and that ended almost immediately, when Nadia detected a virus hurtling toward them and shut herself off.

After that, Watt tried to steer clear of anything *too* illegal, except of course for the fact of Nadia's existence. But he took on jobs whenever he could, depositing most of the proceeds in a savings account and giving the rest to his parents. They knew he was good with technology; when he told them the money came from tech support jobs online, they didn't question it.

He scrolled idly through the H@cker Haus requests, stifling a yawn. As usual, most were too absurd or too illegal for him to take on, but he flagged a few for later review. One in particular caught his eye, asking for information on a missing person. Those were usually easy jobs if the person was still in the country; Nadia had long ago hacked the national security-cam link, and could use facial recognition to find people in a matter of minutes. Curious, Watt read further, an eyebrow raised. It certainly was an unusual request.

The author of the post wanted information on someone who *had* been missing this past year, but who had since returned. *I need to know where he's been this whole time, and why he came home*, the person requested. Sounded easy enough.

Watt immediately composed a reply, introducing himself as Nadia—the name he used for all his hacking jobs, because, well, why not?—and saying that he'd love to help. He leaned back, drumming his fingers on the armrests.

I might be interested, the person who'd written the post replied. *But I need proof you can actually do what you say you can do.*

Well, well. A newbie. Everyone who repeatedly posted on these forums knew enough about Watt to know he was a professional. He wondered who this person was. "Nadia, can you—"

"Yes," Nadia answered, knowing his question before he even finished speaking, and hacking into the sender's security to find the hardware address. "Got her. Here she is."

On the screen appeared the girl's feed profile. She was Watt's age, and lived right here in the Tower, up on the 962nd floor.

What did you have in mind? he answered, a little intrigued.

His name is Atlas Fuller. Tell me something I don't know about him, and the job is yours.

Nadia found Atlas instantly. He was at home—on the thousandth floor. Watt was stunned. This guy actually *lived* on the thousandth floor? Not that Watt had given the Tower's penthouse much thought, but if pressed, he wouldn't have guessed a teenager lived there. *What an idiot*, Watt thought, *running away when* that *was your life.*

"Can we hack their home comp?" Watt asked Nadia, thinking maybe he could get a snap of Atlas in his bedroom.

But Nadia wasn't having any luck. "It's an incredibly sophisticated system," she told Watt, which he knew meant that it could take weeks. Better to get something now. This job was too good to lose.

His messages, then. That would be easier to hack. Sure enough, Nadia immediately pulled up Atlas's most recent messages. A few had been sent to guys named Ty and Maxton, and the rest to someone named Avery. None were that exciting. Watt sent them all over anyway.

Moments later the girl's reply came in.

Congratulations, you're hired. Now I need you to find as much as you can about what Atlas has been doing the past year.

As you wish, Watt couldn't help replying.

In addition, the girl went on, ignoring the sarcastic turn of phrase, *I'm offering a weekly payment in exchange for constant updates on him—what he's doing, where he's going, any information you can provide. This is all for his own safety,* she concluded, in an incredibly unconvincing afterthought.

His safety, sure, Watt thought with a laugh. He knew a spurned-lover post when he saw one. This had to be either Atlas's ex-girlfriend trying to win him back, or a current girlfriend worried about him cheating on her. Either way, the job was a freaking gold mine. Watt had never even *seen* a request for a hacker on retainer before; most H@cker Haus posts were one-time gigs, because most hacks were, by nature, one-and-dones. This girl wanted to send him weekly payments, just to track her crush's movements? It was easy money, and he had no intention of messing it up.

"Leda Cole," Watt said aloud as he pushed SEND, "it's going to be a real pleasure doing business with you."

LEDA

"GOOD AFTERNOON, MISS Cole," said Jeffrey, the doorman at Altitude Club, as Leda walked up to the elevator bank the next day. Altitude had biosecurity too, of course: Leda knew her retina had been scanned the moment she stepped into the entrance hall. But Jeffrey was the kind of personalized and old-fashioned touch that made Altitude membership so expensive. He was a constant fixture of the club, practically an institution himself by now—always at the elevator wearing white gloves and a green jacket and a warm, crinkly smile.

Jeffrey moved aside, and Leda walked into the enormous brass members-only elevator. The doors closed behind her with a satisfying click as she was whisked up from the 930th floor entrance hall, past the tennis courts and spa treatment rooms to the club's main floor.

The Altitude lobby was lined with imposing dark mahogany and portraits of dead members. Afternoon sunlight streamed through the floor-to-ceiling windows that lined the north and west walls. Leda glanced at the various groups gathered near empty fireplaces and clusters of couches, trying to seem nonchalant as she searched for Atlas. If this so-called "Nadia" person was right, his squash game should be ending right about now.

She still couldn't believe she'd posted on that sketchy website. It had been nerve-racking—and yet a little thrilling too, doing something so clearly illegal, and dangerous.

She'd tried to upgrade her security first, but Leda still couldn't help wondering if Nadia knew more than he or she was letting on: about who Leda was, and why she was curious about Atlas. *Oh well*, she thought, none of it really mattered. "Nadia" probably didn't live in the Tower—probably wasn't even a girl. And Leda had no intentions of dealing with her, or him, ever again once she'd gotten what she wanted.

A moment later she saw Atlas walking out of the locker room. He had on a soft blue polo that brought out the caramel-colored strands of his hair, still wet from the shower. *Nice work, Nadia.* "Atlas," she said, with what she hoped was the right amount of surprise. "What are you up to?"

"Just finished a squash match with David York." He flashed her a smile.

"Sounds like it's all back to normal, then," Leda replied, a little more sarcastically than she'd meant to. She wondered what the Fullers thought about his reappearance, the way he'd just materialized inexplicably at Cord's party and jumped right back into their lives as if nothing had happened. Then again, they were the ones obsessed with maintaining appearances; this whole illusion of normalcy was probably their idea.

"About that." He sighed. "I wish I could explain everything, but it's complicated."

Isn't it always, with you? "I'm just glad you're back okay."

"Me too," Atlas said softly, then glanced around the club as if noticing the flow of activity for the first time: kids heading to afternoon tennis lessons and friends meeting up for drinks on the enclosed terrace. "Sorry, were you waiting for someone?"

"I was on my way to the juice bar," Leda lied. "Want to come?"

"You and Avery still drink that liquid spinach?" Atlas laughed, shaking his head. "I'll pass, thanks. Wanna do the Grill instead?"

"I guess I have time," Leda said casually, though this was exactly the kind of thing she'd been hoping for.

They headed across the lobby to Altitude's casual grill and grabbed a table near the back, next to the window. Even though she loved the view here, Leda took the seat that faced away from the flexiglass so she could look out over the restaurant. She liked keeping track of everyone coming and going.

"I haven't been here in ages," Leda admitted as they settled in. She thought suddenly of middle school, before her family had gotten into the club, when she always spent the night at Avery's and then came to Saturday brunch here with the Fullers. She and Avery would pile their plates with egg whites and lemon cakes and try to sneak sips from the mimosa fountain, while Atlas rolled his eyes at their antics and messaged his friends.

"Yeah, me neither," Atlas said, then laughed. "Obviously."

Drew, who'd been the waiter at the Grill since Leda could remember, walked up to their table. "Miss Cole. And Mr. Fuller! We're all so glad you're back."

"Glad to be back." Atlas smiled.

"Can I get you two something to drink?"

"I'd love a beer, actually," Atlas said, and Drew winked; Atlas had recently turned eighteen, so he was legal, but Drew had been sneaking them drinks for years now.

"Iced tea would be great, thanks," Leda murmured.

"What, no whiskeycream?" Atlas quipped as Drew walked away.

"You know that's an Andes-only drink." Leda tried to play it cool, but her heart was racing. What was he doing, referencing that?

"Thanks, by the way, for the other night," Atlas went on. Leda hesitated. "About Avery," he clarified. "You were right, she *was* really drunk. I ended up taking her home after that game of Spinners."

"Oh. Sure," Leda agreed, hiding her confusion. She'd just made that up in order to keep from playing Spinners. She was surprised, actually, to learn that it had been true; Avery wasn't usually the girl who needed to be taken home. She hoped everything was okay.

"Anyway." He grinned, and Leda felt that rush again, of being the focus of Atlas's attention. It was a frighteningly addictive sensation. "I'm so out of the loop. Tell me everything I've missed this year."

She saw what he was doing, deflecting attention away from himself, from questions about where he'd been. Well, she could play along.

"I'm sure you've heard about Eris and Cord," Leda began, taking a quick breath to steady herself. She tried to mentally recite a meditation chant, but none came to mind. "Did you hear about Anandra, though?"

The conversation meandered. Leda told him about Anandra Khemka's stealing spree, about Grayson Baxter's parents getting back together, about Avery and Zay, everything that had happened in the year he was away. Thankfully Atlas didn't seem to notice that her stories were light on details about the past summer. He just listened, and nodded, and even suggested that they share an order of nachos. "Sure," Leda agreed, trying not to read into it; but there was something intimate about eating off the same plate, the way their hands kept brushing as they reached for the same avocado-smothered quinoa chips. Was it her imagination, or was this feeling more and more like a date?

Drew finally came back over. The table's view screen projected the bill in front of them, the numbers a dark blue holo on a white background. "Do you want me to charge to your separate—" he started, but Atlas was already waving his hand to put the whole charge on the Fullers' account.

"No way. It's my treat," Atlas said.

Maybe he was just being chivalrous . . . or maybe she was right, and this *was* turning into a date. "What are your plans this week? Want to do something?" she ventured.

Time seemed to freeze, the way it used to right before an exam when she'd popped a xenperheidren. Atlas's hand lay there on the table between them. Leda couldn't think of anything but the way that hand had been tangled up in her hair, tipping her head back, that night ten months ago. She wondered if Atlas thought back on that night the way she did. If he wondered what could've happened between them, if he hadn't left.

She looked up and met his gaze. Her heart was pounding so hard she almost couldn't hear. He was about to say something. She leaned in—

"Hey!" Avery pulled up a seat next to Leda and pulled a perfectly toned, tanned arm forward in a stretch. "Man, antigrav yoga today was killer. How are you guys?"

"Hey, Avery." Leda smiled, hiding her disappointment at her best friend's timing. She couldn't believe she hadn't noticed her arrival; she'd been so focused on Atlas that she'd forgotten to watch the Grill's entrance the way she usually did.

"I missed you in class, Leda." It wasn't a reproof, just a question. Avery's eyes flicked to Leda and Atlas, his empty beer mug and the remains of the nachos on the table between them.

Leda shifted uncomfortably. She'd gotten so excited about Nadia's intel on Atlas that she'd forgotten to answer Avery's flicker from last night, about hanging out today. "Oh, yeah," she said guiltily. "I just came by for a juice. I've been totally lazy all day."

"And then I talked Leda into nachos instead. Sorry we didn't leave you any." Atlas gestured wryly at the empty plate.

"No worries." Avery's eyes were back to Leda. "Are you guys heading home? Want to share a hover?"

"Works for me. You ready to go?" Atlas said, turning to her.

"Sure," Leda said, telling herself that she'd get more time with Atlas soon enough. What Nadia had done once, she could easily do again.

As they started back toward the club's entrance, Avery reached to pull Leda back. "Can we talk about last night?"

"Right. Sorry I left without telling you," Leda said, deliberately misunderstanding. "I just got really tired all of a sudden, and I couldn't find you to say bye. You know how it is."

"No, I meant about earlier. I didn't mean to push you, about—"

"I told you, it's *fine*," Leda said, more curtly than she meant to. But seriously, couldn't Avery just take a hint?

"Okay. If you want to talk about it, I'm here."

"Thanks." Leda glanced warily at Avery and decided to turn the tables. "What about you? Atlas said you were really drunk at the end of the night? That he had to take you home?"

"First party back, guess I got a little carried away." There was something funny in Avery's tone, though Leda couldn't say exactly what.

"I get it. That was a great party," she concurred, not sure why she was overcompensating.

"Definitely." Avery wasn't even looking at Leda. "It was great."

They didn't say anything else until they caught up with Atlas near the entrance. Leda couldn't remember the last time she and Avery had been at a loss for words.

Then again, I've never kept a secret from her before, Leda thought, just as Atlas turned back to smile at them both, and she realized of course that wasn't true at all; her biggest secret was standing right there before her.

She just hoped he wasn't also her biggest mistake.

AVERY

"SO THERE I was, standing alone on a rainy cobblestone street—and I couldn't get any kind of signal because, you know, Florence is a tech-dark mess—and this group of midTower kids comes up!" Avery was telling the story on autopilot, talking without fully registering what she was saying, a skill she'd picked up from her mom. She couldn't shake the strange feeling that had settled over her when she saw Leda and Atlas together. *It doesn't mean anything*, she kept telling herself, but part of her knew that wasn't true. It meant something to Leda.

When she'd first seen them across the grill, Avery had smiled and waved, only to lower her hand self-consciously. They were too absorbed in their conversation to notice her. For a brief instant, she wondered what they were talking about—and then she saw the look on Leda's face, and the realization hit her like a punch to the stomach.

Leda liked Atlas.

Why hadn't Leda ever *told* her? *Because he's your brother*, the rational part of her mind supplied, but Avery was too shocked and hurt to think rationally. *There aren't supposed to be any secrets between me and Leda*, she thought bitterly, momentarily forgetting that she was keeping the same secret.

Not to mention Leda's defensive, overwrought reaction when Avery caught her in a lie about the summer. *Why can't you just let it go?* Leda had exclaimed—and Avery wanted to let it go, except Leda's reaction had worried her. She felt a sudden flash of anger. She'd been so concerned about her friend that she'd been planning to stop by Leda's on the way home from yoga. And the whole time Leda had been eating nachos and flirting with Atlas.

When had she and Leda started hiding so much from each other?

"Then what happened?" Atlas prompted.

Avery turned in her seat to answer; she'd selfishly, and strategically, taken the hover's middle spot. "They offered to help me find my dorm! Because I was wearing your old hockey sweatshirt and they apparently played us last year. Can you believe it? Mile-high kids, all the way in Italy! What are the chances?"

"That's crazy," Leda said flatly, and Avery felt a burst of shame for the way she'd told the story. "Mile-high" was the term upTower kids used for the suburban wasteland of the middle floors, since it was literally a mile above ground level. Leda had been a mile-higher, once upon a time.

"I just can't believe you were wearing that old sweatshirt abroad," Atlas teased.

"Yeah, it looked ridiculous." Avery shrugged and fell silent, suddenly embarrassed that she'd snuck into Atlas's room and grabbed the sweatshirt. Even though he'd been gone for months by then, it had still smelled like him.

The hover turned out of the vertical corridor onto floor 962, toward Treadwell, the gated luxury community where the Coles lived. "Hey, Avery," Leda began. The hover pulled up to the gate and she leaned out, letting the scanner review her retina and confirm that she was a resident. "Are you doing antigrav yoga again tomorrow? Want to go together?"

"Maybe." Avery shrugged noncommittally. "I'm kind of sore from today."

The hover turned onto Treadwell's wide, tree-lined boulevard, which felt even bigger thanks to the elevated ceiling that stretched five stories overhead. Treadwell was modeled after the old Upper East Side brownstones. Some of its homes had actually been salvaged from the old neighborhood, then reconstructed stone by stone inside the Tower.

Avery liked it down here, the way the buildings all felt unique, with their own scrolling ironwork and their own facades. Each structure caught the afternoon light in a different way. It reminded her of Istanbul, or Florence, anywhere that people still injected personality into their homes—a far cry from most neighborhoods upTower, where the streets were lined with bright white doors like fat, frosted slices of wedding cake.

Finally they pulled up to the Coles'. Leda pressed a button overhead, releasing the safety magnetron that held her in her seat. "Well, see you soon." Her gaze turned to Atlas and her smile softened by an imperceptible degree. "Thanks for the ride, guys."

The hover started up the remaining thirty-eight levels to the Fullers' place. "Did you and Leda have fun?" Avery asked, hating herself for prying but unable to stop.

"We had a great time. Actually," Atlas said, "Leda sort of asked me out."

Avery stared out the window. She knew she would lose control if she so much as looked at Atlas.

"Is that weird?" he asked. She was being completely awkward,

Avery realized; she needed to say something or she'd give herself away.

"No, of course not! I mean, you should definitely go out with her," she managed.

"Right." Atlas looked at her curiously. Funny how without Leda here, there was more space in the hover, yet now it felt small.

"It's a great idea," Avery added. *It's a terrible idea. Please don't do it.*

"Okay, then."

Avery pinched her forearm to keep from tearing up. Her best friend and the boy she could never admit to loving. It was like the universe was playing a cruel joke on her.

Silence fell over the hover. Avery tried to say something, anything, but she was at a loss. Every time Atlas had pinged her during the past year, she'd felt like she had *too* much to tell him, stories tumbling out breathlessly, disorganized, until Atlas invariably had to go.

Now he was here in person, and Avery had nothing to say.

"Hey." Atlas turned to her as if getting an idea. "Are you still dating that Zay guy? Would you two want to come?"

"We were never dating," Avery said automatically. Zay hadn't spoken to her since the party at the Aquarium, and besides, she'd seen him with Daniela last night. Whatever. She had no desire to double-date with Atlas and Leda.

Then again, maybe it wasn't a bad idea.

"I could invite other people, though," she said quickly.

"Who were you thinking?"

"Eris, of course. Risha and Ming and Jess. Ty, Maxton, Andrew, even Cord."

"I'm not sure a big group thing is the best idea," Atlas protested, but Avery had nodded as she said all the names, already composing a flicker.

"Leda won't care, trust me. Come on," Avery said. "It'll be fun! We can all go out to dinner, or a movie—whatever you want!"

"That does sound fun," Atlas admitted. "You know Leda better than anyone, I guess. If you say it's fine, then you're right."

Avery ignored the guilt that reared its head at that comment. Really she was just doing her best friend a favor, helping Leda see that she and Atlas didn't belong together before Leda got too invested and ended up hurt. She wished she could just *talk* to Leda about all of this. But Leda had shifted things between them, with all her secrets—about this summer, about liking Atlas. Avery wasn't sure how she would even begin the conversation.

"Of course I'm right," she said lightly. "Aren't I always?"

ERIS

ERIS LAY ON her stomach, head tilted to one side, eyes firmly shut as a children's cartoon played across the back of her eyelids. This was the absolute laziest way to watch something, but right now she didn't particularly care. She wasn't even sure what time of day it was. She'd been lying there for hours, ever since her mom had knocked on her door that morning asking if she was okay. Eris had ignored her.

"Eris?" It was her mom again. Eris burrowed deeper into the covers like an animal hiding in its nest, pumping up the volume on her eartennas. She refused to see her mom right now. Much better to stay here, in bed, where last night seemed like nothing but a bad dream.

"Please, Eris. I need to talk to you." The pounding persisted. Something in her mom's tone made Eris lean over and, gritting her teeth, type into the touch screen by her bed to unlock her bedroom door.

"What do you want?" she snapped, still lying down. Eris was perversely pleased to see that Caroline looked terrible, her eyes lined with hollow circles.

"How are you feeling?" Her mom started to sit on the curved edge of Eris's bed, but Eris glared at her, and she retreated a step.

"How do you *think* I'm feeling?" Eris knew she was being spiteful, but she couldn't bring herself to care.

Caroline let the question go. "There's something I need to talk to you about," she said, watching her daughter's reaction. She wrung her hands and took a careful breath. "I know this is the last thing you want to deal with right now, but we can't stay here."

"What?" It was enough to make Eris sit straight up, hugging one of her hand-stitched pillows to her chest.

"It's best that we leave. Your father should be able to come back here, without having to face . . . everything that's going on." Eris felt a rush of anger at the phrasing. It seemed cowardly to her somehow, as if Caroline were pretending she wasn't the one responsible. "Your father needs some space right now, from us," her mom finished.

"You mean from *you*! You said it yesterday, this isn't my fault!"

"Yes, but—"

"You go ahead," Eris said, turning away. Her entire body felt strangely numb. She found that she didn't care what her mom did, one way or the other. "I'll wait here for Dad."

"I don't know what your dad wants right now," Caroline said softly. "I know he loves you, but it's up to him to figure out how all this is going to work. And just in case, we should be prepared for the worst."

The worst? Wasn't this already the worst?

"It's you and me now, Eris," Caroline finished, with the ghost of a smile.

Eris wanted to argue but lacked the heart for it. "Where are we going?"

"I found us a new apartment downTower."

"DownTower? We aren't just going to the Nuage?"

"We can't afford the Nuage," Eris's mom said quietly.

Suddenly Eris understood. Her mom, the former model, and her much older dad. The revelation that Eris's mom had been with someone else. "You aren't taking anything from Dad, are you? You want to prove that you didn't marry him for the money."

Her mom nodded. "It's the right thing to do. I owe your father that much, at least. Don't worry," she said quickly, "I'm trying to keep this as normal as possible for you. I have some money saved, and your tuition is covered through the year, so you won't have to change schools. I promise, it'll all be okay."

Eris felt a little sick at that statement. The idea that she might have to go to a downTower school wouldn't even have occurred to her.

Her mom stood there a moment, as if she wanted to give Eris a hug, but Eris made no move toward her. After a moment, Caroline faltered and started for the door.

"Just one suitcase for now," she said. "We'll figure out the rest later."

As the door shut behind her mom, Eris collapsed onto her pillows and turned the cartoons back on, wishing she could escape into them indefinitely.

———

An hour later Eris sat in a hover across from her mom, bags and boxes stacked around them in the tiny space. Her skin crawled with dread as the numbers etched into the vertical corridor's titanium walls grew ever smaller. She kept expecting their hover to slow down and turn onto one of these floors, but it showed no signs of stopping.

"Mom," she said sharply, "just how low, exactly, are we going?"

"It was the best I could do, given the short notice."

"That's not an answer," Eris persisted.

The numbers dipped below three hundred. Her mom sighed. "I was poor once, too, you know."

The dim light from the walls caught on Caroline's bracelet, the one piece of jewelry she'd brought with her, as far as Eris could tell. It looked fake, probably because it predated Eris's dad. *There are millions of dollars worth of jewels in that safe*, she thought in mounting frustration. Yet her mom had apparently picked today to abide by a strict moral code.

Eris looked out the window, crossing and uncrossing her legs, feeling suddenly itchy in her Denna jeans, as if her skin no longer fit. She got on her tablet and looked over her messages again—she didn't want to do it on her contacts, in case her mom heard the verbal command and got upset with her for checking them constantly.

Still nothing. Like every other time she'd looked at them today.

Finally Eris felt the familiar weight of the hover decelerating, rotating just slightly as its electromagnetic propulsion slowed. She glanced up at the numbers marking the floor they had turned onto, and thought she might throw up. They were going to live on the *103rd floor*?

The streets down here were so narrow that the hover was barely able to turn the corners. They weren't even streets at all, really, certainly not the expansive streets of the upper floors that were designed to convince you that you might be outside, with real live trees and air that pumped through the floor in soft, breezy patterns. This was more of a hallway, with flickering fluorescent lights overhead and depressing, institutional white walls. Several heads turned and watched as they skimmed past. Eris got the sense that no one down here took hovers all that often.

They pulled to a stop in front of a dingy door marked 2704. Eris gulped. They were so far down, the floor here so big, that the numbers of each apartment didn't even begin with the floor number. God, the 103rd floor must be almost as big as the Tower's base. Up on 985, there had only been ten apartments total. Eris had known all her neighbors individually.

Bags on each shoulder swinging wildly, Caroline opened the door to the hover and began fishing in her purse for some kind of ID chip. No bioscanners down here, that was for sure.

Eris waited until the last possible instant, when the hover started beeping and informing her angrily that it would charge for the delay, before she peeled herself from the seat and walked slowly inside.

It was worse than she'd imagined. The ceilings were low, the lighting was bad, and there was nothing even resembling a window. Feeling dizzy, Eris held her wrist up to her nose and inhaled her jasmine perfume, but it wasn't enough to cover the lingering odors of rot and trash that permeated this place. There were several boxes stacked in the middle of what was apparently her mom's bedroom, containing the few things Caroline had managed to send ahead. A tiny bathroom was tucked off the main bedroom, as well as a narrow kitchen, not that Eris or her mom knew the first thing about cooking.

Caroline began sorting through the boxes. "This is just temporary, Eris," she said, without looking up. "I'm going to get a job, figure something out." *A job doing what?* Eris thought, kicking open the only door left, the one that must lead to her bedroom.

It was dusty and cramped, about half the size of Eris's closet in her old life. There would barely be room for anything else once they got a bed moved in there.

Something crawled across the toe of her sandal. Eris looked down and saw a giant cockroach, its feet twitching madly. She jumped back with a wild shriek, and it skittered away.

"Eris?" her mom called from the other room. "Are you okay?"

"Of course not! None of this is okay!"

Her mom started toward her, but Eris was on a roll and there was no stopping her. "I hope it was worth it!" she screamed. "Cheating on Dad with some random guy. I really hope it was worth *ruining* our lives!"

"It wasn't some random guy," Caroline began, but Eris cut her off, putting her hands dramatically over her ears.

"Oh my god, I don't want to hear about it!"

"Eris—"

"How can I believe anything you say anymore?" She stumbled blindly out the door and slammed it behind her, not caring where she went as long as she got away.

Just then, her eartennas began to ring, and her contacts lit up with an incoming ping. *Avery.* Eris declined it. Avery had no idea what was going on, of course: Eris hadn't told anyone. But whatever Avery wanted to talk about, Eris couldn't handle it right now. The problems of the upper floors felt a lifetime away.

She slumped against the wall in the hallway, biting back a scream.

"I know you."

Eris turned, furious at whoever dared talk to her. A Hispanic girl about her own age stood several doors down. She was wearing fake-leather pants, a gold bandeau top, and jangly earrings. One hand was holding a plain black halluci-lighter, which she held up now to take a long, slow drag, puckering her lips into an *O* as she exhaled the bright green smoke. Potshots, then.

"I don't think so," Eris said shortly.

"You're a member at the club where I work. Altitude."

Eris glanced at the girl—her heart-shaped face framed by black bangs, her legs casually crossed, ending in bright blue cowboy boots. She didn't recognize her. "You were sort of rude to me, in fact," the girl went on, dark eyes narrowed.

Eris said nothing. If this girl was looking for an apology, she wasn't going to get it.

"So." The girl's eyes traveled up and down Eris's outfit, her designer jeans and the pearl studs in her ears. "What the hell are you doing down here?"

"It's a long story."

"Suit yourself." The girl shrugged.

Eris eyed the girl's halluci-lighter. No way that it was the good stuff she usually smoked, but suddenly she felt an overwhelming and desperate urge for a hit. *Screw it.* Her life was already in shambles; why not smoke up with an Altitude waitress who apparently hated her?

"I just found out that my dad's not my dad," Eris said bluntly, and walked over. The girl held out the halluci-lighter, revealing a small inktat at the base of her wrist. "What's that supposed to be?" Eris asked, distracted. She didn't recognize the angular shape.

"It's part of a set."

"Where are the others?"

The girl laughed, giving her crisp dark curls a shake. She smelled like smoke and cheap perfume, and underneath, something spicy, like the scent of amber candles. "Like you'll ever see them."

Eris couldn't be bothered to rise to the bait. She took a long, deep drag of the lighter, exhaling the smoke in a perfect ring. The girl raised an eyebrow, impressed. "Anyway," Eris went on, "my dad had all the money, so now . . . it's just the two of us."

"Wow. Wasn't expecting that."

"Yeah, me neither, obviously."

They stood in a strange silence for a while, passing the halluci-lighter back and forth. Eris kept waiting for someone to come tell them off—up on 985, she'd always had to smoke right by the vents, to keep the regulators from showing up—but the girl seemed surprisingly nonchalant. Maybe no one cared what went on down here.

Eventually the lighter was almost out of weed. The girl dropped it carelessly to the ground and crunched it to a fine black powder under her feet, then smeared the powder around with her heel. It was one of those cheap disposable lighters, Eris realized. "See you around. My name is Mariel, by the way."

"Eris."

"Well, Eris," Mariel repeated, with a hint of laughter, still seeming amused at finding Eris down here. "Welcome to Baneberry Lane."

"Is that really what this street is called?" Eris couldn't believe anyone would give this dismal place such a happy-sounding name. It was delusional.

"Look up baneberries," Mariel called out, disappearing into her apartment. So Eris did.

They were highly poisonous plants, often used in medieval suicides.

"Now it makes sense," Eris muttered, wiping at a sudden angry tear.

She started to turn back toward 2704, but hesitated upon hearing voices in Mariel's apartment—a low, adult voice in particular. Probably Mariel's dad. For some reason the sound of it sparked Eris into motion. She couldn't just wait around smoking any longer, wondering what her dad was thinking. She had to talk to him.

She turned in the opposite direction and headed for the nearest express lift upTower.

It was Sunday, so the plastisurge department of the Vensonn-Seyun Hospital on floor 890 wasn't all that crowded.

"Hey, Eris. He's in his office," Slaite, the department's receptionist, offered as she walked up. Eris barely nodded, already hurrying onward.

She passed the experimental center, where various DNA forms were being recombined in tiny petri dishes, and the nerve farm, where spinal cords were grown in enormous translucent tanks, heading toward her dad's office at the end of the hall.

EVERETT RADSON, MD, DIRECTOR OF COSMETIC PROCEDURES AND MODIFICATIONS, read the printed nameplate above the door. Eris took a breath and stepped inside.

He was slumped at his desk, wearing a half-zip golf sweater and blue scrubs pants, one hand wrapped around a mostly empty handle of Scotch. The unflattering hospital light caught the strands of gray in his hair, and there were new worry lines at the corners of his eyes and mouth. He looked, for the first time in her life, like an old man.

"Eris." He sighed, his hand gripped tight around the Scotch. There was something funny about the way he pronounced her name, like his mouth was having trouble forming the sounds.

She opened her mouth, uncertain what she should say now that she was actually here. "I kept waiting for you to ping me," she began, knowing it sounded accusatory.

"I'm sorry," her father said. "I just needed to get away, for a little while."

Neither of them spoke.

Eris glanced around the office, from the 3-D screens in the corner to the closet with the real human skeleton, which she used to come look at sometimes in elementary school, fascinated, until Avery had told her it was morbid and weird. But Eris hadn't been afraid of the skeleton. She'd never feared much of anything, she realized, until now.

Her eyes drifted back to her dad. He was holding something in his hand, staring at it in bewilderment, as if uncertain what it was. It was his gold wedding ring.

All the words she'd planned on saying were wiped from her mind. "What's going to happen with you and Mom?"

"I don't know." Her dad sighed and placed the ring on his desk, then finally glanced up at Eris. "You look so much like her," he added, and his voice was laced with sadness.

Eris had never before hated how much she resembled her mom. It was probably all her father saw now, when he looked at her—she was the living proof of her mom's betrayal. Nothing connected her to him anymore, she realized with a jolt, except that they'd both spent the past eighteen years being lied to by the same person.

"I'm sorry," Eris whispered.

"Me too." He started to pick up the Scotch, then stopped, as if remembering she was there.

"Dad—or Everett—"

"I'm sorry, Eris, but I need some time," he interrupted. His voice was shaking. "I'm just . . . struggling here."

Eris bit her lip. She'd come to the hospital hoping her dad would fix everything the way he always did, and yet he seemed even more broken than she was. "I miss you," she said helplessly.

"I miss the way things were," he said in answer, and Eris's heart sank. Part of her wanted to shake him, scream at him— *Look at me*, she wanted to say, *I'm hurting too. I don't want to lose you!* Tears welled in her specially surged amber eyes. But the old familiar pride held them back, stuck the words in her throat.

"I'm sorry. I just need time," Everett said again. "Please."

Eris nodded, feeling as though she were falling a great distance. She didn't know what would happen to her parents; she didn't know when—or even *if*—her father would be ready to see her again.

She started back out toward the crowded elevator. But even pressed into the crushing sea of people, Eris had never felt more acutely alone.

RYLIN

HERE GOES NOTHING, Rylin thought, and stepped up to Cord Anderton's door for the second time in three days. Hard to believe that after everything that happened, she was back again—and by her own design no less.

The previous morning, when her communals hangover had finally dissipated and her anger cooled a bit, Rylin had opened her tablet to find herself 250 nanodollars richer. She wondered if the extra fifty was a standard Cord Anderton tip, or an attempt to make up for his late-night behavior.

She'd wavered between paying rent and the bank—the bank, she decided, seeing how impossibly high that debt had grown. Besides, she could always fend off their landlord when it came down to it. He tended to cut Rylin and Chrissa a little slack, because he'd known their mom.

Hey, Fenton, Rylin had written, sending him a quick message. *Just wanted to let you know that this month's rent will be coming to you a few weeks from now.* They were behind on last month's too, Rylin had remembered with a sudden twinge of discomfort, but it was too late; she'd already sent in the bank deposit. *I'm really sorry. It won't happen again*, she went on, hoping he was in a good mood today.

Then, swallowing her pride, she had called Cord.

He'd answered on the fifth ring. She jumped in, trying to sound normal. "Hey, it's Rylin. Myers," she added clumsily, after a moment of silence.

"Rylin. How . . . unexpected to hear from you." Cord had sounded amused. Rylin tried not to, but all she could picture was the bright red mark on his face after she'd slapped it.

"About last night." She was sitting at the kitchen table, tracing a crinkled advert for Later Gators cereal, the instapaper so old and cheap that the cartoon alligators no longer danced. Only their eyes flicked creepily back and forth, their tails barely twitching. Rylin took a deep breath and tried again. "I want to apologize. I was tired, and I overreacted. I'm sorry."

"Words are cheap," Cord answered. "If you really are sorry, why don't you show me?"

Rylin slammed her hands on the table. "You seriously think, after—"

"Get your mind out of the gutter, Myers," Cord said, drawling out her name in that way of his. "I was going to ask if you would *clean* again. I don't know if you've met my brother, Brice, but he's here this week, and he's kind of a mess."

"I could do that. Same rate?" Rylin said carefully. It was what she'd been about to suggest; after seeing that cash in her account this morning, she'd realized she should squeeze as much money out of Cord as she could. Yet somehow it seemed like the upper hand had shifted back to him.

"Sure. I'll have the uniform sent over. Wearing it is optional, of course." Cord chuckled. Rylin had rolled her eyes and started to reply, but he'd already hung up.

So now it was Monday morning, and here she stood, waiting for Cord Anderton to comm her in. She tugged self-consciously at the shapeless black dress and white apron the drone had delivered last night. She'd already called in sick to Buza, her boss at the monorail stop: she even had official "proof," since she and Chrissa had long ago rigged their mediwand to log a false positive for nasopharyngitis. She wasn't sure how long she could hold down her real job without showing up, but she couldn't afford not to try.

As the door clicked open, Rylin stepped inside—and paused for a moment, speechless. On Saturday these rooms had been overheated and crowded, full of people and noise and light. Now they felt vast, and empty. Rylin's eyes traveled to the greenhouse with its cobblestone flooring and insect-like heat lamps, to the cavernous high-tech kitchen, to the two-story living room with its curving glass staircase.

"Care to tell me why you're here?"

Rylin jumped, whirling around, and almost collided with a dark-haired stranger wearing a navy suit and a smirk. "Where's Cord?" she said without thinking, and instantly regretted it.

"Who knows?" The guy flashed a grin. "Maybe I can help you instead. I'm Cord's brother, Brice." Of course, Rylin thought; they looked alike, though Brice was almost ten years older.

"Rylin Myers. Sorry to bother you," she said quickly. "I'll get to work."

"Work?"

"Cord asked me to come clean for you guys." She shifted her weight, feeling uncomfortable.

"Ah," Brice said quietly, his eyes traveling up and down her body. "Well, I'm glad Cord's taste is improving. You're certainly better than the last one."

Rylin didn't say anything, just went to the closet of cleaning supplies and gathered the bucket of spray cleaners and disposable scrub-balls. But when she went back out into the living room, Brice was still there. He'd leaned back on the couch, his tie loosened and his arms crossed behind his head. "Please, don't let me stop you," he said lazily. "It won't bother me if you clean around me."

Rylin gritted her teeth and started up the stairs, ignoring him.

Later that afternoon, she stood outside the door to Cord's bedroom, steeling herself to go in.

It's not that weird, she told herself. *He's just a guy.* But even though she'd been in Hiral's room plenty of times, walking into the bedroom of a stranger felt somehow weird. It was far too intimate.

She started with the bed, changing the sheets and fluffing the pillows, then sprayed the windows and UV-cleaned the carpets. Finally, as she was running a duster over the top of Cord's heavy wooden dresser, she hesitated, overwhelmed by a powerful curiosity. Who *was* Cord Anderton, anyway?

Impulsively she opened the top drawer and glanced through its contents, an assortment of very masculine things. Some of them she didn't even recognize. But it had been so long since her dad left, all Rylin could really remember was living in a house full of women. She pushed aside cuff links, a small bottle of cologne, a leather billfold embossed with WEA—Cord's father's initials, she guessed. Rylin was a little impressed to find it full of illegal old paper greenbacks, which still circulated wildly through the black markets since, unlike nanodollars, they were untraceable. Maybe they were just heirlooms. But if Cord actually paid people in this, he was ballsier than she had realized.

In the bottom drawer she found something that gave her

pause—an antique metal box filled entirely with custom-made BeSpoke drugs. Spokes, everyone called them. Rylin had never seen so many in one place. But she lifted up the lid of the box and there they all were, her own personal treasure trove of tiny black envelopes, each of them marked with the signature yellow prescription label and containing a single pill.

Spokes were exorbitantly expensive, worth more than Rylin made in weeks at her monorail job, precisely because they were *legal* drugs: prescribed by a doctor after countless brain scans and psych evaluations. They were tailor-made for wealthy clients to "relieve stress and calm anxieties." Rylin glanced at the date on the original prescription. Just as she'd guessed—right after his parents passed.

She leaned back on her heels, thinking about how strange the world was, that both she and Cord had lost their parents. Yet while she was working for an hourly wage just to keep her family together, with barely any time to properly grieve her mom; Cord had been given custom-made drugs to help with his grief.

It wasn't fair, Rylin thought bitterly, then felt a little ashamed of herself for the thought. Cord had lost his parents. She of all people shouldn't judge what he did to handle it.

Shutting the drawer with a sigh, Rylin gave one last glance around the room before heading downstairs. She pushed open the front door only to bump into Cord on the steps.

"Oh. Um, hi," she said clumsily. She didn't know what to say to him. She'd never before had to face someone she'd recently slapped.

"Heading home?" Cord was wearing workout clothes, as if he'd come straight from the gym. Or maybe he'd been running; there was dirt caked around his shoes, leaving prints on the white limestone step.

"It's four o'clock." Rylin crossed her arms over her chest,

feeling suddenly self-conscious of the uniform, which was tight across the boobs.

"No, of course, I didn't mean . . ."

"Thanks for the Gummy Buddies, by the way. My sister loves them." Rylin wasn't sure why she'd said that. She wasn't getting paid to stand here and make conversation. She moved down a step, so she was on the same level as Cord, and started to walk past him.

"Chrissa, right?" Cord asked, shocking Rylin into stillness. She couldn't believe Cord remembered Chrissa's name.

"Yeah. She's three years younger," Rylin said quietly.

Cord nodded. "That's great, that you two have each other." Rylin thought of Cord and Brice. She wondered how close they were.

"Sorry," Cord went on after a moment, "I didn't mean to keep you. You're obviously headed somewhere."

"To meet—to meet Chrissa, actually," Rylin said, stumbling over her words a little. She'd been about to say "my boyfriend" and then some instinct had stopped her, though she didn't know why.

"Tell her there're more Gummy Buddies where those came from—if she promises not to torture them the way you did."

Rylin couldn't help smiling at that. "See you tomorrow," she started to say, but he'd shut the door quietly behind him.

Whatever, Rylin told herself as she started down the F lift; Cord Anderton was impossible to understand and there was no use trying.

When she reached Park and Central, the intersection at the exact center of the Tower, Rylin stepped through the metal double door marked LIFT MAINTENANCE ONLY.

She had to wait only a few minutes before Hiral appeared from the lifties' locker room in jeans and the thin black shirt he wore under his swing suit. His hair was still damp with sweat from the ecramold helmet. "Hey, babe. Didn't know you were coming by today."

Rylin leaned into the hug. He smelled comfortingly familiar, like metal and sweat. "I wanted to see you."

"What's with the costume?" Hiral laughed.

"Oh, right." Rylin glanced down at the maid's uniform she'd half forgotten she was wearing. "I worked for Cord Anderton today. You know, my mom's old job. And—"

"Seriously?" His tone sharpened, all his good humor gone. Hiral hated the highliers, with a fury that sometimes shocked even Rylin. "Why the hell would you work for that asshole?"

"It pays more than the monorail stop. And I called in sick there. It's just temporary," she said impatiently.

"Oh. I get it. Well, as long as you didn't quit your real job." Hiral put an arm around her waist. "New gig, this calls for a celebration. Wanna go to Habanas?" It was their favorite divey Cuban place, with spicy street corn and deep-fried queso.

"Absolutely." Rylin followed him out into the thoroughfare, where the lights had dimmed to evening setting.

Just then, a message came through on her tablet: Fenton's response to her earlier message.

Rylin: I've tried so hard to be generous with you and your sister, but I can't keep making exceptions for you, it read. *You're two months behind on rent. If you don't pay by the end of the week, you're evicted.*

Rylin felt nauseated. She immediately tried to call, but he didn't pick up.

"Everything okay?" Hiral was watching her.

Rylin didn't answer. She felt like the world was spinning. This was her fault—why had she paid the bank earlier instead of the rent? She'd been so sure of herself, of her ability to squeeze another month's grace period out of Fenton; she'd done it plenty of times before. But now everything was crashing down, and she didn't know how to fix it.

You'll get your money by Friday, she typed back, her hands shaking, though she had no idea on earth how she would manage it. Maybe she could borrow some from Hiral, except his family needed every penny too. Or maybe Cord could give her an advance.

Cord. Her mind flashed to what she'd found in his bottom drawer, earlier that afternoon. There was her answer.

"It'll be okay," she told Hiral, hating what she was considering.

But more than that, Rylin hated that she didn't really have a choice.

AVERY

AVERY'S STOMACH TWISTED nervously as she and Atlas pulled up to the Coles' apartment. Through sheer force of will, she'd managed to turn Atlas and Leda's date into a big Augmented Reality group game. She told herself it was fine, that she hadn't done anything all that bad, but deep down Avery knew she was being selfish.

She glanced up at Leda's doorstep, suddenly remembering the first time she and Leda had gotten drunk. Well, *tried* to get drunk; they'd just been giddy and ridiculous, only slightly buzzed off the spritzers Cord had given them. But they had decided they shouldn't go inside until they were totally sober again, in case Leda's parents heard them. They'd ended up spending half the night sitting together on the Coles' front step, telling stories and giggling at nothing in particular.

"Want to tell Leda we're here?" Atlas asked.

"Oh. Sure." *We're outside*, Avery flickered, realizing as she sent it how sparse their message thread had become. Normally she and Leda were in constant communication, sending each other selfie-snaps, complaints about school, messages from boys to analyze. But over the past couple of days, they'd barely messaged each other at all.

"Thanks for picking me up," Leda said as the hover door slid open. She had on a navy silk top and white jeans, with red-soled espadrilles. Avery moved aside to make room for her, glancing down at her own outfit, all-black artech and her comfy turquoise sneaks.

"No worries." Atlas smiled.

"Are you really wearing those to AR?" Avery blurted out, looking at Leda's shoes.

"You've seen me run in heels." Leda gave a brusque laugh.

"Right." She felt a sudden urge to diffuse the tension, to pretend this had all been everyone's idea to begin with. "I'm so glad we decided to do this," she gushed, lamely. "I haven't been to AR in forever!"

"Get ready, because we're gonna kick your ass, Aves." The light danced in Atlas's warm brown eyes.

"Avery," Leda interrupted, "how was shopping with Eris? Did you get anything?"

Avery felt a stab of guilt. When Leda had flickered her yesterday morning she'd said she was shopping with Eris, knowing it would put Leda off. But Eris hadn't answered any of her flickers, and Avery had stopped by her apartment only to find that no one was there.

"Oh, um, I got some jeans," Avery fumbled, naming the first thing she could think of. "At Denna."

"Don't you have those in pretty much every color?" Leda asked. Avery faltered, caught off guard.

"Like that's ever stopped either of you," Atlas joked, oblivious.

They pulled up to the ARena, which sprawled over a corner of the 623rd floor, just as its massive walls shifted from army-green camouflage to a depiction of a dark stone dungeon. Risha, Jess, and Ming all stood outside, dressed like Leda in cute jeans and impractical shoes. Avery refrained from rolling her eyes. She wished Eris were here; she could use a dose of her irreverent sarcasm right about now. Though come to think of it, the last time they'd all done AR Eris had shown up in a black leather catsuit, just for fun.

"The guys are inside," Risha offered as they gathered in front of the doors, which now showed a dragon swooping over an icy mountain peak.

"Probably arguing about whether to play cowboys or aliens," Atlas said, holding open the doors. Avery fought the urge to stay back, walk with him, reach for his hand.

"I heard that," Ty Rodrick called out from the ticket counter. A group of middle school boys all clutching the special-edition lightsaber accessory stood in line behind him. "The cowboy arena is old news, Fuller. We're playing Alien Invasion. Who's on my team?" Ty typed into the 3-D printer, which spit out electronic-coded game tickets for each of them, four black and four white. Each was shaped like a tiny miniature alien head, unique to the game and impossible to counterfeit. Apparently there were people so obsessed with AR that they collected these tickets, even though they were useless once the game was over.

"Aren't we doing boys against girls?" Avery said quickly. They'd played a lot of boys-versus-girls games here, back in the day. And the last thing she wanted right now was to imagine Leda and Atlas on the same team, together in the adrenaline-fueled darkness.

"That's uneven, though," Maxton Feld pointed out. "Five versus three."

Avery silently cursed Cord for not showing up. "Maybe we randomizer it?" she suggested, pulling up the dice-shaped icon on her tablet.

Leda jumped in. "Atlas and I already said we'd be on a team."

Avery stayed quiet as the teams were sorted out: her, Ty, Ming, and Jess against Maxton, Risha, Atlas, and Leda. She kept on saying nothing as they went to their respective team locker rooms to gear up. Ty was babbling about strategy, explaining his plan to "swarm and surround," but Avery wasn't listening. She just nodded, gripped by a strange and sudden apathy.

Finally the four of them stood assembled in the staging area, haptic vests fastened around their torsos, their plastic radar pistols holstered to their belts. Avery pulled on the thin mesh gloves that would track her hand movements for the master computer. Her virtual reality headset gave a loud beep, clamoring for her attention: it wanted her to select her avatar, the image that all her competitors and teammates would see once they entered the arena itself. Everyone else was waving and pointing, adding hair and armor and facial features. But Avery just selected the base avatar, with no defining characteristics at all. People paid too much attention to her real-life appearance for her to bother customizing a virtual one.

3 . . . 2 . . . The countdown board lit up. Next to her Ming was leaning back on her heels in anticipation. Ty turned and grinned at Avery. "Ready, Fuller?" he asked with a wink. Avery ignored it. She'd made out with Ty once at Jess's parents' holiday party, and he kept acting as though it would happen again.

1. The doors opened to reveal a spaceship on red alert, emergency lights blinking the length of the abandoned hallways. If she took off her headset Avery would see just an empty, industrial-looking space, filled with steam vents and shifting

carbon-foam walls. Somewhere, the other team was walking out of another exit pod into a different part of the spaceship arena.

Avery pressed a button on her wristband to comm the others. "Ming and I will take the left," she whispered, pushing a silver door that led to a side hall. Ming, dressed as a pink fairy princess—there really were no avatar restrictions, though she looked ridiculous in the middle of a space game—nodded and followed.

Something exploded to their left. Avery crouched next to a heavy pipe, then jumped up and launched into a sprint, no longer worrying about Ming. She fired her radar pistol into the opaque mist at the corners of the room. A ladder was suspended before her in midair, reminding Avery of nothing so much as her own ladder up to the hidden roof-deck. *Why not?* she thought, jumping up and starting to climb. It felt good, moving like this through the dark anonymity of the arena, her blood pumping hot and fast through her veins. If she moved quickly enough she could forget about Atlas and Leda, about everything except the game itself.

At the end of the ladder she swung herself onto the higher level and began shooting at two figures up ahead, illuminated with glowing arrows that marked them as members of the opposite team. They ducked behind a stack of boxes marked with radiation signs, one of them tripping forward over her feet. That had to be Leda, in her stupid espadrilles.

Avery moved slowly, creeping around from the opposite side so they wouldn't see her—and froze.

Crouched next to Leda was Atlas. She knew from the tattoos on the inside of his wrist; it was his tell, the matching yin and yang tattoos that he'd never get in real life, but always put on his avatar in ARena games. Avery watched as Leda put her hand lightly on his shoulder. Atlas didn't pull away.

Avery held her breath, willing herself to stop watching, but she couldn't look away. Leda's gesture seemed saturated with meaning: possessive, somehow. It was the kind of touch you gave someone you'd already touched in other ways, or who you really wanted to. The kind of touch Avery could never, ever give Atlas.

"Disengage," she whispered, pulling the red tab on her wristband. Immediately Avery's weapons were rendered inactive and she became invisible to everyone in the game, able to do nothing except walk back to the staging room until she reactivated. It was like she wasn't even there, like she'd suddenly erased herself. Which was exactly how she felt.

WATT

SO MUCH FOR *easy money*, Watt thought as he walked into the 623rd floor ARena. It had only been a few days, and already Leda Cole was proving a complete pain in the ass.

When he'd taken this job, he hadn't realized just how difficult she would be. She was constantly flickering him for updates on Atlas—on his movements, his messages, what holo shows he was watching and whether he thought they were funny. Watt had answered all the queries he could, but he still hadn't managed to hack the Fullers' home network, so he didn't know anything that happened within their walls unless Atlas flickered someone about it.

Now he was dealing with her latest demand, for help on this Augmented Reality group date. Watt had stupidly agreed to break into the ARena's system and manipulate the game, to force Leda and Atlas together—but he'd said that before he and Nadia had actually looked at the system's architecture. Turned out the ARena handled such a high volume of data that even Nadia couldn't get through their heavy firewall. Watt had finally realized that the only way to do what Leda wanted, what he'd so foolishly promised, was to infiltrate the system from within.

How did we get ourselves involved in such a dumb hack, Nadia?

As I seem to recall, I'm not the one who signed on for this job, she replied.

He stepped up to the 3-D ticket printer and studied the options, getting excited in spite of himself. There were fantasy games and an Aztec jungle adventure and even something called Dragon Riders. Watt wondered how on earth they simulated *that*. Well, if he had to buy a ticket to get in, he might as well play, right? If only Derrick were here. He would lose it over this place.

Just as he selected a wizarding game and started to print his ticket, Watt looked up at the staging area—and caught his breath. Walking across the room was unquestionably the most beautiful girl he had ever seen.

Nadia, who is *that?* he asked. Nadia pulled up the girl's feed, and Watt almost laughed aloud.

She was Avery Fuller—the sister of the guy he was supposed to be spying on, and Leda's best friend.

Watt stared, transfixed, as Avery reached up to pull out her ponytail, letting her blond hair fall loose down her back and giving it an impatient toss. He thought he saw tears in her sky-blue eyes.

What do I say to her?

Buy a pack of grapefruit M&M's from the vending machine, take the seat next to her, and start eating them, Nadia prompted.

Really? It was weird advice, even for Nadia, who often suggested the strangest and most oblique solutions to problems.

Have I ever led you wrong before?

That was true. Watt did as she said, buying the candy and

walking over to settle on the bench next to Avery, deliberately ignoring her. He pulled the grapefruit M&M's from his pocket and began popping them in his mouth one by one.

He felt Avery's attention shift to him, heard her clear her throat, sensed the weight of her gaze on the M&M's. He pretended he wasn't aware of it. Sure enough, after a moment—

"I'm sorry," she murmured, tapping him on the shoulder. "I was just wondering . . . could I have one?"

Watt blinked, a little stunned when she spoke to him, even though he'd been expecting it. She really was the most breathtakingly beautiful girl he'd ever seen. Finally he recovered enough to say something. "Sorry?" He made a confused gesture to his ears, as if he'd been listening to something on his eartennas, though of course he hadn't. But at least that explained why he'd just blinked silently at her like a complete moron.

Avery repeated her request, and Watt passed her the bag, hiding a smile. *Thanks, Nadia.*

Ye of little faith.

"What are you listening to?" Avery asked politely, passing back the bag, but he could tell her mind was elsewhere.

"This guy named Jake Saunders. I doubt you know him."

"No way! You like country?" Avery exclaimed.

Watt nodded, though he'd never heard a country song before in his life.

"What do you think of Jake's new album?" Avery went on, eagerly.

"I like it," Watt said carefully, reading almost word-for-word the commentary Avery had sent to Atlas a few weeks ago. "But it's not as good as his early stuff. My favorite song of his has always been 'Crash and Burn.'"

"Me too," Avery gushed, then surprised him by singing the chorus under her breath. *"I'm not comin' over, you and I are long done, you can crash and burn . . ."* Her singing voice was low, with a seductive huskiness that Watt hadn't expected.

"With another one," he managed, singing the last few words along with her, and she laughed.

"So what brings you here?" she asked after a moment.

She was mesmerizing: her eyes, her laugh, that unexpected song. "I'm meeting some friends to play Wizards," he said.

"Oh, that used to be my favorite. You know the part where you get to the sword in the stone, and you have to pull it out?"

Watt opened his mouth to lie—Nadia had pulled up the ARena's map for him, along with a description of that scene, from a game enthusiast's website—but for some reason he didn't want to. "Actually I've never been here before," he admitted.

"Really?" Avery sounded surprised by that. "Well, I won't ruin it for you. But piece of advice: When the alchemist offers you the potions, take the smallest goblet."

"Will that one help you win?"

"Oh no, they all get you to the next level. That one just tastes better than the others," Avery said seriously, and Watt smiled.

"I'm Avery, by the way," she added, belatedly.

"Avery," he repeated, as if he hadn't been on her feeds this whole time. "I'm Watt."

She looked back at the door, and he realized he might be about to lose her. "What game were you playing in there?" he asked, with a nod at the pistols holstered to her waist.

"Aliens." Avery shrugged. "I needed some air, I guess."

Watt nodded, following Nadia's advice even though he felt like he should speak. But Nadia was watching Avery's breathing and pulse, and seemed to think there was something else she wanted to say, if given the chance.

"It's all just so . . . *exhausting* sometimes, you know?" Avery looked away, fiddling with her haptic glove.

Watt hesitated. *Nadia?* he asked. He wasn't accustomed to being confused by girls, especially ones this gorgeous. In his experience, beauty and complexity were often inversely correlated.

"What do you mean?"

"Do you ever feel like people think they know you, but they can't, because they don't know the most important thing about you?"

"Actually yeah." No one knew about Nadia, yet she was so deeply, inextricably intertwined in everything Watt thought and knew and did. He wondered what big secret Avery felt like she was hiding. Whatever it was, it couldn't be as bad as having a quant in your brain.

"I'm sorry. I don't know why I said that." Avery had reverted to her formal, more distant tone, the one she'd used when she first asked Watt for an M&M. He looked up sharply and saw that she was reaching up to pull her hair back, letting him briefly catch the scent of her lavender shampoo.

She was shutting herself away, hiding away the vulnerable side she'd given him a brief glimpse of. Watt thought frantically of ways to stop her. She couldn't leave, not yet.

"Avery," Watt said, just as her wristband beeped, indicating that she'd been out for too much time already. If she stayed in the staging room much longer, the arena wouldn't let her back in.

"Looks like I should get back in there." She gave him a smile, but it lacked the warmth he'd seen just a minute ago.

"Before you leave, can we exchange flick-links?" He stood up as he said it, feeling awkward. He hadn't been this nervous around a girl since before Nadia.

"Oh. Sure." Avery waited as their contacts connected, enabling them to flicker and ping each other. "See you around," she added, and pulled her headset on. The doors slid open, giving

Watt a glimpse of the arena as it truly was, a series of gray walls covered in misters and motion sensors.

"Good luck in there," he called out, but Avery was already a world away.

ERIS

"YOU'RE HERE!" AVERY exclaimed, moving down the hallway toward Eris. The crowds instinctively parted to let her pass. "I thought maybe you were skipping. I haven't seen you in ages." Avery's voice pitched upward at the end, turning that last sentence into a question.

"Even I wouldn't skip the first day," Eris said lightly, though it had been the absolute worst first day of school ever. She'd actually come upTower early, wearing a plain black windbreaker over her uniform to hide from the lower-floor stares, and showered in the school locker room. Anything to avoid getting ready in that cramped bathroom she shared with her mom.

Normally on the first day of school, Eris's parents made her take an awkwardly posed picture by the front door, to add to the collection they'd started way back when she was in preschool. "Good luck!" they would both exclaim, hugging her until she finally escaped to the lift, laughing at their silly picture tradition but secretly loving it.

There hadn't been any pics this morning, of course. Eris wondered if her dad even knew it was the first day of school. At that thought, she felt a sudden, sharp pain gathering behind her eyes. She closed them for a moment, trying to calm the storm of hurt and bewilderment that tore through her. She couldn't let Avery see.

"Okay, but, Eris—is something going on?" Avery asked as the two started toward the exit. The afternoon bell had just rung. Students clustered in the hallways like flocks of monochromatic birds, all of them wearing pleated skirts or pressed khakis and button-down shirts. For the first time in her life, Eris was grateful for their stupid school uniform. She wasn't sure how many outfit combinations she could make with the clothes she'd brought down to 103, but she knew they wouldn't be enough.

"What do you mean?" she asked, pleased at how normal her voice sounded.

"I haven't seen you at all since Cord's, you missed the AR game yesterday, and when I went by your apartment to check on you, no one was there." Avery shot her a look. "Is everything okay?"

Eris didn't want to talk about any of this. It was too raw and tender; and besides, as soon as anyone knew the truth, it would all be irrevocably real. But she'd already thought of the perfect excuse. "My parents decided to renovate our apartment. *Again.* You know how they are." She gave an exaggerated eye roll. "We're at the Nuage for a while. I'm sorry about yesterday," she added.

"I'm just glad everything is okay. I mean, not that I was *too* worried; I figured you were off doing something fabulous. Like that time you came back a week late from summer break, because you and your mom took 'the long way home' from Myanmar," Avery teased. Eris felt a pang at the memory. She and her mom had so much fun on that vacation, traipsing around Asia wearing brightly printed dresses without a care in the world.

"Anyway, I'm jealous you're at the Nuage," Avery was saying. "We should start sleeping over at your place so we can wear those fluffy robes and order ricotta-blackberry pancakes in the morning!"

"Absolutely," Eris agreed, with false brightness.

They stepped out of the doors and onto the lawn in front of school, where manicured green grass sloped down toward Madison Avenue. A chorus of voices instantly surrounded them, Ming and Risha and Leda all debating how to spend the afternoon, exchanging gossip and stories from the day. Eris just stood there and let it wash over her. When the group decided on yoga and smoothies at Altitude Club, she let herself be swept along, nodding and smiling with the rest of them. She needed this time with Avery and her friends, doing what they always did. She needed to pretend that everything was normal, that her life wasn't crashing down around her. That she was still Eris Dodd-Radson.

As they walked past the tech-net—the boundary surrounding campus that caused all contacts, tablets, and other nonacademic hardware to go dark—Eris immediately pulled up her inbox. It was delusional, she knew, but she kept hoping for something from her dad. She got that he needed space, but still . . . was this really how it would be from now on? What if they never spoke again?

The top message in her inbox made her cringe. It was from the Altitude Club's member services desk: a courtesy notification that her membership had been discontinued.

Eris was overwhelmed by a sudden flush of anger. Her mom had done this—she'd been the one to insist they join Altitude in the first place, the one who managed all their memberships and social appointments and everything else that was fun or luxurious in their lives. Of course, Eris knew her mom didn't want to spend any of Everett's money anymore; that was the whole point of moving. But what harm would it really do if Eris stayed on his Altitude membership?

Then she thought of what her mom had said, about letting her dad set the tone of their relationship moving forward, and she realized that might be the reason Caroline didn't want Eris at Altitude. So that she wouldn't risk running into Everett there.

This is really happening, she thought, a little stunned, though of course she had known it was coming. Her life was falling apart before her eyes, piece by gilded piece.

She opened her mouth to say something but no sound came out. And what could she tell her friends anyway? "Sorry, guys, I can't come to Altitude because I'm too poor"? Everyone piled on the elevator to 930, shuffling a helpless Eris along with them. She kept nodding, not registering what anyone was saying. Her mind whirred with excuses to extricate herself, each wilder and more frantic than the last. That she had to go intern at her dad's office again. That Cord had booty-called her. That her parents had grounded her after Saturday's party and put a location-monitor on her contacts so they would know her every movement.

They started down the oak-shaded cobblestone lane that led to the Altitude entrance. Eris felt dizzy, her breath coming in abbreviated gasps. She couldn't walk in—couldn't face the pity on Jeffrey's face as he politely but firmly told her she wasn't allowed inside, the knowing glances and hushed whispers her friends would exchange once they realized the truth. She felt sick at the prospect. But it was as if her feet were moving of their own accord, drawing her ever closer to her own destruction, a weak mechanical smile pasted on her face. She watched as Risha and Leda headed into the elevator and up to the yoga level. Ming hung back, waiting for Avery, who was looking at Eris, a questioning expression on her face—

"I don't feel well," Eris blurted out. "I think I'm gonna head home."

"Are you sure?" Avery frowned.

Ming let out a single, bitter laugh. "Don't worry, Aves. She's totally just going for an afternoon workout session of her own. At Cord's."

Eris flinched at that. Normally she didn't let Ming's little barbs get to her, but with everything else that was happening, it was hard to maintain her calm. And why was Ming calling Avery "Aves" anyway? Everyone knew that was Atlas's nickname for her.

"That was kind of rude of you," Eris said, trying not to sound defensive. "I really don't feel great."

"Chill out, Eris, it was just a joke." Ming narrowed her eyes. "You do look pretty terrible, though, come to think of it."

"Oh my god, leave me *alone*!" Eris snapped, all niceties gone.

Ming looked to Avery as if expecting her to argue, but Avery just sighed. "I'll meet you upstairs," she said, not looking at Ming, digging through her bright red hobo bag. Ming tossed her head angrily and marched into the elevator. "Here we go!" Avery triumphantly produced a silver mediwand.

Eris recoiled. "It's fine, really," she insisted. But Avery was already waving the wand over Eris's head and torso, her wrist flicking as if it were a toy. After a moment the wand beeped, having quickly detected and summarized all Eris's vital signs, and the bulb at the end of it lit up a bright telltale green. The sign of perfect health.

"Look, you're clearly just tired." Avery sounded infuriatingly calm. "Why don't you come sit by the pool instead? Maybe get a facial while we're at yoga? Then you can still meet us for smoothies afterward."

"No, thanks," Eris repeated, her voice strained.

"You didn't need to snap at Ming," Avery admonished gently. "I know her joke was lame, but I don't think she meant any harm by it."

Eris shook her head, overwhelmed by a sudden bitter anger. Avery didn't *get* it. She was the same as she'd always been, still sailing effortlessly above everyone else's sordid little problems up there in her thousandth-floor palace, while Eris had lost everything. In their whole lifetime of friendship, Eris had never truly resented Avery until this moment. "You know, I really don't feel well," she repeated, overemphasizing each word. "I'm going home." She saw Jeffrey meet her eyes knowingly, and felt like she might scream.

"Okay. Call me later?" Avery asked, worried, but she didn't press any further. Eris turned back out of the entryway, contemplating the long, dismal trip to 103.

She hadn't made it halfway down the block before everything was blurry. She wiped angrily at the tears, but they were coming faster now, in ugly jagged sobs, and the only thing she could do was turn blindly into a side alley and try to pull herself together.

Who was she anymore, anyway? She couldn't be Eris Dodd. The name didn't fit her any better than the stuffy, cramped apartment down on 103. Eris crossed her arms over her chest, hugging herself tight, and took a few deep breaths to regain control. At least this alley was hidden enough from the main street that no other Altitude members had seen her breakdown.

"I wouldn't have guessed you're the type to sit around crying."

Eris looked up to see Mariel in front of her, hand on hip, wearing jeans and a tight-fitting tank top. "What, are you stalking me or something?"

"Shocking, I know, but the world doesn't revolve around you." Mariel gestured at the door behind Eris. "You're blocking the service entrance."

Eris stepped aside, racking her brain for a witty comeback, but none came.

"Thanks." Mariel walked past. "If you're looking for a better place to cry about your club membership, there's a nice closet in here."

"You have no idea what I'm going through, okay?" Eris shot back. "You don't know what it's like to have your family—your entire *world*—just fall apart."

Mariel stood in the doorway, her eyes locked on Eris, who shifted uncomfortably under the weight of her gaze. After a moment Mariel shook her head. "You'd be surprised," she said. The door shut automatically behind her.

Four hours later, Eris had stayed upTower as long as she could. She'd roamed through her favorite boutiques, pretending to consider dresses and bags she could no longer pay for. It felt fantastic at first, the rush of salesgirls locating designs they had pulled for her, the reassuring clack of their heels on the floor, the cold glasses of orange water they handed to her while she reviewed the scans of each design on her 3-D body projection. Yeah, it all felt fantastic—until they started to get serious about placing orders, and Eris had to mutter an excuse and flee the store.

She'd gone to Hyacinthe, her favorite organic grocery shop, to try the free samples they put out at dinnertime. She'd even gone to the download storefront and ordered a hot foam latte just so she could sit in the comfy chair for a while and flip through magazines on their tablets. It felt weird, really, spending the afternoon alone with nothing but her thoughts. But by now it was late, and Eris was running out of places to go.

She'd flickered Cord a couple of times, but he hadn't answered. He was probably napping or playing a holo-game, or smoking up with friends. She hadn't slept over since before his party, she realized; less than a week, but after everything that had happened, it felt like a lifetime ago.

Eris stood up with a sigh, about to head home. But the thought of the smell and the roaches and, most of all, of having to talk to her mom froze her feet in place. Before she'd consciously changed her mind she was already turning around and on her way to Cord's.

The front door swung open as Eris stepped onto his doorstep; she'd been on the approved entry list for months. "Cord?" she called out, venturing inside. He wasn't in the living room, though she saw a bunch of stuff that didn't look like his strewn out on the couches. Brice was in town, then.

She found Cord in his bedroom, leaning back on his expensive down pillows as he read something on a tablet. Strange, she hadn't seen him read all that often before. Maybe ever.

"Eris," he said, seeing her there. "What are you . . ."

"I wanted to pay you a visit." She pulled the door shut behind her.

"This isn't a good time, actually." Cord's gaze was distant, not with the distracted look of being on contacts, but truly lost in thought. Eris felt a little flutter of anxiety. She wondered if her eyes were still red-rimmed from crying earlier. *Screw it,* she thought, and reached for the top button of her oxford shirt. Then she walked slowly toward the bed, as she carefully, sensually, undid the buttons of her shirt one by one. But Cord's eyes didn't light up in appreciation the way they usually did.

When the shirt was undone, revealing her pink lace bra beneath, Eris climbed onto the bed next to him. He wasn't *doing* anything, she thought, a little panicked, not turning out the lights or reaching up to touch her or *anything.* "Eris—" he said, but she leaned forward to cover his mouth with hers, reaching for the hem of his shirt and starting to pull it up.

He allowed the kiss for a moment before resting his hands on her shoulders and pushing her gently to the side. "I'm serious," he said, and there was a new edge to his voice. "Not now."

Eris knew that was her cue to leave, to laugh and put her shirt back on as if nothing was wrong—but she couldn't do it. Cord's rejection had shaken loose whatever tendrils of control she had left. Tears burned at the corners of her eyes. She tried furiously to will them away. The last thing she wanted was to let Cord see her cry.

"Can I just stay here a little?" she asked, her voice small. She didn't even care about hooking up with Cord, she just wanted to snuggle under the thousand-thread-count sheets on his ultrafoam mattress, and wake up to the morning sun streaming in through his windows.

"Is everything okay? Do you want me to call Avery?" he answered. Eris felt like she'd been slapped. She understood the subtext: *Whatever you're going through, I'm not dealing with it.* Cord only wanted fun, flirty, happy Eris, not any of the other Erises that came along with her. She knew they weren't officially dating, that he wasn't her boyfriend or anything, but she'd thought that by now Cord cared about her a little—at the very least the way a friend would.

"Do you have any feelings for me at *all*?" she blurted out, and winced as soon as she said the words; she'd sounded shrill and clingy. "Never mind. Forget it," she stammered, but it was too late.

Cord was sitting up straight, looking her in the eye. "Eris, I'm so sorry," he said, as sincere as she'd ever heard him. "I thought we were on the same page."

"We are!" she cried out, but he was shaking his head.

"I thought we were just having fun. I can't do anything serious right now. I'm sorry," he said again, sounding regretful. "I think it's best if we end things, before we do any more damage."

Eris started to reply, to tell him that she was fine keeping things casual, but something stopped her. She couldn't bear to lose what little pride she still had left. With quick, concise movements she buttoned her top and tossed her hair. "Sure. See you around," she added, in as normal a voice as she could manage.

"See you." There was a note of grudging respect in Cord's tone, as if he hadn't expected her to take everything so easily.

On her way out the front door, Eris realized that she would almost certainly be off the retinal scanner's admit list starting tomorrow. *Oh well*, she thought, with a surprising lack of emotion. She was far less upset about the breakup—if it even counted as a breakup when you weren't really dating—than she'd thought she'd be.

Maybe because it seemed so unimportant, in light of everything she'd already lost.

LEDA

THE NEXT AFTERNOON, Leda stood at the East Asian rock garden on the edge of campus. It was quiet here, and cold. Hardly anyone ever came this way. The only sounds were those of the tiny garden-bot, raking the stones into a rippled pattern, and a fountain burbling cheerfully in the corner.

She was waiting for Avery. They both had chemistry lab this period; they'd made sure of it when they picked classes last spring. They always scheduled their science classes together, and they always met here at the Zen garden before the first lab session, to walk over together and make sure they were partners. It had been their tradition since eighth grade.

Leda paced tight circles around the garden, watching the time on her school-issued tablet, waiting as long as she dared. Her contacts didn't work within school grounds, so she couldn't reach Avery. The garden-bot started to undo the swirls it had raked, replacing them with tiny squares. Real natural sunlight, filtered from outside the Tower using a system of mirrors, spilled through the skylight overhead. Leda bit her lip, frustrated. What a pointless garden. How could anyone feel Zen with this stupid thing constantly *raking* the stones?

Avery wasn't coming. Leda needed to go—but first she stepped forward and gave the bot a sudden, violent kick. It sailed in an arc through the air, landing on its back with a satisfying crunch. Its wheels spun helplessly. If Avery had been there, she would have laughed. The thought only made Leda feel more upset. She left the bot there and hurried toward the science wing.

She made it to chemistry just as the three-tone chime sounded the beginning of class, only to find that Avery was already in the second row, her long legs crossed negligently in front of her. "Hey," Leda hissed as she slid into the empty seat next to her friend. "I looked for you at the garden. Did you forget?"

"Oh, right. I'm sorry." Avery turned back toward the front of the room, her stylus poised on the tablet to take notes.

Leda bit back a reply and tried to focus on Professor Pitkin's opening remarks. He had a PhD in materials science and had authored the national chemistry textbook. That was the reason parents paid for Berkeley, because the teachers were leaders in their fields: the people who composed the lecture vids everyone else watched rather than public school preceptors. But when Leda looked at the professor, all she could think was that with his bald pate and blood-shot complexion, he resembled nothing so much as a purple, overripe fruit. Professor Plum, they would call him. She started writing the joke to Avery, then put down her stylus with a sigh.

Things between her and Avery were weird. Leda wasn't sure whether it was because of Cord's party—if Avery was still upset that Leda hadn't told her the truth about this summer—or whether it was about Atlas. She'd acted a little strange during the whole AR thing, after all. Hadn't she left the game at one point?

Leda wondered if Avery was upset that Leda hadn't checked with her first, before asking Atlas out. It *would* be kind of weird for Avery, if her best friend started dating her brother. But this still seemed like an overreaction.

An overreaction if your friend dated your brother, sure, but not if she'd slept *with him*, Leda thought suddenly. The realization made her nauseated. Did Avery know about the Andes? That would certainly explain her behavior: she was pissed that Leda had lost her virginity to Atlas and didn't even tell his sister, her *best friend*, about it.

But how exactly was Leda supposed to talk about that when Avery was always so weirdly protective of Atlas?

She glanced over at Avery's profile, desperately trying to figure out what her friend was thinking. Should she apologize? She didn't want to unless Avery actually knew. And Leda had no desire to march up to Atlas and ask whether he'd told his sister about their hookup.

The old familiar xenperheidren urge nipped at her, whispering that it had the answers, that it would smooth away all her insecurities. *I am enough in myself*, Leda repeated silently, but the mantra didn't soothe her the way it had back at Silver Cove.

Maybe Nadia could figure out what was up with Avery. The hacker had been tracking Atlas's movements over the last few days, providing transcripts of his flickers and receipts from his bitbanc, although none of it was particularly helpful. It wasn't Nadia's fault. The problem was Atlas; he was too private for any of that to be much use.

Avery looked up and met her gaze head-on, and Leda glanced away, annoyed that she'd been caught staring. She was uncomfortably reminded of the beginning of seventh grade, when she'd been so anxious about what everyone thought of her.

Compared to midTower, the upper floors had felt sleek and

high-tech and oppressively expensive. And her classmates had done everything so *fast*, punch lines snapping back and forth between them in some kind of code. Leda wished she knew what they were saying, who their jokes were referencing. She had watched one group of girls in particular, blazing with confidence, led by a tall blonde almost too perfect to be real. She had wanted, desperately, to be one of them.

It wasn't long before she learned some of these kids took xenperheidren—the anxiety pills, the same ones her mom took—as a study aid.

Getting her mom's pills had been far too easy. Leda's parents were so trusting that they'd never activated the biosecurity on their new apartment's touch surfaces. That night, Leda had slipped into their bathroom while they were watching holos and grabbed her mom's xenperheidren from the medicine cabinet. She shook two of the pills into her palm and was back in the hall in a matter of seconds. The next day, before school, she took one of them.

Instantly the world had become brighter, more focused. Her brain was moving at warp speed, mining her long-term memory for facts she'd forgotten, watchful and alert for every detail of the world. She felt more confident than she'd ever been. When she walked up to Avery at lunch and asked to sit at her table, Avery had just smiled and said sure. Fueled by the xenperheidren, Leda laughed at all the right jokes, said exactly the right thing. She knew in that moment that she was in.

She took more and more of the pills over the next few years, eventually buying from a dealer named Ross so she wouldn't get caught stealing her mom's. She had tried to space them out, to take them only before exams or big parties—she didn't need them socially anymore, now that she was friends with Avery. But she loved the Leda the pills brought out. That Leda was sharper and cleverer and more insightful, able to read the nuances of a situation and manipulate it to her advantage. *That* Leda figured out how to get everything she wanted.

Except, of course, Atlas.

Leda startled to sudden attention, aware that everyone around her was standing up, chairs scraping the floor as they paired off into lab partners. She turned to Avery, but Avery had her back to Leda and was talking to Sid Pinkelstein.

"Avery?" Leda said, reaching around to tap her friend on the shoulder. "We're partners, right?"

"I just promised Sid," Avery apologized. Sid stood there looking a little bewildered by his good fortune. "Junior year, college applications and all. I need to really ace this," she added quickly. "I'm sorry."

Wow. Avery was so desperate to avoid her that she'd rather hang out with the kid they'd always called Sid Pimpleface? "Sure," Leda said. "Risha?" She grabbed the other girl's arm and dragged her, seething, to the lab table.

"Here it is." Risha pulled up the lab instructions on her tablet. Her eyes darted back and forth between Leda and Avery, who was working with Sid two tables away. But Leda had already started to mix things, throwing powders and chemicals into the bowl at random and grinding them with a pestle.

"So according to the instructions we don't actually need magnesium . . ." Risha said warily, lowering her goggles over her eyes.

"Too late," Leda replied. *What the hell*, she thought a little wildly. With any luck maybe she would create an explosion.

RYLIN

SATURDAY AFTERNOON, RYLIN stepped into Cord's bed-room and pulled the door quickly shut behind her. She'd been waiting for this chance all day. Cord had been gone since she arrived this morning—come to think of it, he hadn't been home much at all this week, though she had no idea where he went every afternoon. Maybe he was avoiding her after that weird moment on his step, she considered, then felt foolish for even thinking it. Cord Anderton had probably never made a decision based on a girl in his entire life, let alone a girl who worked for him.

But even with Cord gone, Rylin didn't feel comfortable enacting her plan until Brice left the apartment. He'd skulked around for hours, watching her clean, until ten minutes ago when he finally left to "hit the cardio," whatever that meant. She shuddered at the memory of how he'd looked at her on the way out, the way his eyes had traveled over her form and he'd wet his lips, like a lizard. Small wonder Cord was so messed up, when the only real family he had left was a debauched twenty-six-year-old who did nothing but jet from one expensive playground to another.

Rylin had dealt with worse than Brice, though; she could put up with him for a while longer. Truthfully she owed him, for being the reason she'd kept this job all week. She was starting to dread her inevitable return to the monorail snack station, with its screeching train cars and endless flow of angry customers. But her options as a seventeen-year-old high school dropout were kind of limited.

Working at Cord's was a nice change. His apartment was cool and quiet, and she could get things done at her own pace, alone with her thoughts for once in her life. Cord paid better too.

And if her plan worked, he would be the reason she and Chrissa didn't get evicted.

Heart racing, Rylin knelt down to pull open the bottom drawer of Cord's dresser and grabbed three of the individually wrapped Spokes, their paper thick and waxy in her hands. *Cord doesn't need these the way I do*, she reminded herself. He had so many already; he'd never notice a few missing. Besides, if he ran out, he would just go see his long list of doctors and get a refill prescription.

Suddenly all she could think of was the look on Cord's face when he'd been watching those old family vids. There'd been something so earnest, almost young, in his expression, his face clear of its normal skepticism and sarcasm. And here she was, stealing the drugs that he'd been prescribed right after his parents' funeral. How would her mom react, if she knew what Rylin was up to right now?

The door swung open.

Rylin jumped, holding the Spokes guiltily behind her back. Cord stood in the doorway.

"Hey," he said, sounding puzzled. Rylin opened her mouth, but no words came out. She knew she was only making herself look *more* suspicious, standing in the middle of his room without cleaning supplies, but she wasn't sure what to say. She stared stupidly at Cord, trying to read the emotions dancing like lightning across his face. If he caught her stealing from him, she wouldn't just be fired—she could be arrested.

Rylin did the only thing she could think of. She leaned in, her hand still closed tight around the drugs, and kissed him.

She felt desperate and panicked, as utterly terrified as she'd felt when she followed Hiral to an elevator shaft and looked down the impossible distance to the bottom. After an endless moment, Cord returned the kiss. But it was guarded, cautious, nothing at all like the way he'd kissed her last weekend.

By the time they pulled away Rylin had managed to stuff the Spokes into her pocket. Cord was watching her, curious. His broad-shouldered presence seemed to draw the air from the room. Had he noticed? She steeled herself, ready to deny everything, to run away—

"You're kind of confusing, you know, slapping me one weekend and then kissing me the next."

"What can I say?" Rylin's tone was flippant, but her heart was still racing in panic. "I'm complicated."

"Apparently." Cord stared at her a moment longer, then reached into his pocket for something. "I was going to give you this, by the way."

Rylin inhaled sharply. It was an instaphoto of her mom, taken in what looked like the Andertons' greenhouse. She watched, transfixed, as the moving image of her mom leaned in to smell a blooming pink amaryllis, her smile glowing. "How did you . . . ?" she whispered, fighting to hold back sudden tears.

"My mom took it. She was constantly taking snaps," Cord

replied. "I remembered you saying you didn't have many of your mom, from before. I stumbled across this and . . . anyway, you should have it."

"I love it."

"She had a ton of old files. You're welcome to look through them. Who knows—there might be more of your mom." His voice was rough with some emotion she couldn't place.

"Thank you." Rylin fell silent, touched.

They both stood there, neither of them quite sure what to say next. Rylin realized she was staring at the quick rise and fall of Cord's breath, the neat row of stitches along his collar and the tanned smoothness of his chest underneath. She caught herself with a start. "I should get going, I guess," she mumbled, and side-stepped past him.

Cord nodded, saying nothing. He just watched as she clattered down the stairs and out the door, clutching the photo with both hands.

———

"You're never going to believe what I got today," Rylin announced as she walked into the apartment.

"Arrested. A promotion. A new boyfriend!" Chrissa stood at the all-purpose cooktop in their kitchen nook, fiddling with the knob to change the setting from grill to steamer. She reached into the produce drawer and pulled out several oversized broccoli, then tossed them onto the cook surface and sprayed them with honey-sriracha glaze from a can. The steam curled her hair in little ringlets around her face.

"What? No," Rylin said, too excited to respond to the dig at Hiral. Chrissa had liked him fine before, but ever since he started dealing last year, she'd made her disapproval abundantly clear. "Look at this!" Rylin exclaimed, holding out the instaphoto. She hadn't been able to tear her eyes from it the whole commute home.

Chrissa turned, impatient, and nearly dropped the box of feta pops she was holding. "Oh, Ry." She rushed over for a closer look.

"I know." The two of them stared at the photo for a moment, transfixed.

"She's so . . . *happy*. I'd almost forgotten how beautiful she was, before—" Chrissa sniffed. "Where did you get this?"

"Cord gave it to me." Rylin wondered, suddenly, how Cord had stumbled across it. She and Chrissa had been looking for photos of their mom for a year, but most of the ones they had were pics that Rose had taken of the two of them. In the few they did have, she always looked tired or worn down. *This* was how Rylin remembered her: laughing and healthy, her green eyes sparkling, her face illuminated from within.

Chrissa had started crying. Not the quiet tears that they'd wept in the last days of their mom's illness, when she was suffering in the next room and they didn't want her to hear, but huge sobs that shook her skinny shoulders. "Shhh," Rylin murmured, pulling her sister into a hug. She felt Chrissa's pain as if it were her own, which of course it was, it always had been, ever since their dad left when Chrissa was a toddler, and Rylin's mom had started working all the time. Even then, it had been the two of them against the world.

"I just miss her so much," Chrissa whispered.

"I know. Me too."

The front door pushed open. Startled, both girls turned to look, but it was only Hiral. "Hey hey, what's cooking?" he asked, and paused when he saw that they were crying. "Sorry. What happened? Did someone die?"

Rylin tried to forgive his bluntness. "It's okay," she said, feeling Chrissa bristle next to her. "I just got this today. Cord gave it to me." She gestured to the instaphoto on the table, the moving image of her mom laughing and smelling the flower in joyful eternity.

"Oh. That's nice."

"We need to hang it." Chrissa pointed to a spot on the wall. "Right here, in the middle of the room."

"Yes." Rylin nodded enthusiastically. She went over to the cabinet and rummaged through drawers until she unearthed a package of adhesive dots. "Hiral, can you reach?"

He shrugged and stuck the dots onto the back of the photo, then mounted it where Chrissa directed, sticking it to the wall with a slap.

"I have to get some air," Chrissa said suddenly, and stepped outside. Rylin wondered if she'd started crying again.

"I have something for you, by the way," Rylin said to Hiral, pulling the Spokes out of her pocket.

His eyes widened. "You stole those from Anderton? Nice."

"He had so many, he'll never miss them," Rylin said, feeling suddenly uneasy. She hoped she was right. "How soon can you clear them for me?"

"I'll move them as fast as I can." Hiral held one of the Spokes up to the light and studied it from various angles, emitting a low whistle. "We should hit one of these, though, before we unload the others."

"No!" Rylin almost shouted. She took a breath to calm herself. "I need that cash. I'm behind on rent."

"You're always behind on rent," Hiral said easily. "Come on, they're Cord Anderton's Spokes, they have to be powerful stuff! I mean, isn't he totally messed up?"

"What, because his parents are *dead*?"

Hiral flushed a sudden bright red. "You know that's not what I meant. I'm just saying, it would be one hell of a ride. And then . . ." His hand dropped lower on her waist.

"I'm serious," Rylin snapped, shoving him away.

"Fine, fine." Hiral threw up his hands, trying to laugh it off. "You snagged 'em, you decide what to do with 'em. I'll take them to V when I make my next drop."

"Thank you," Rylin said quietly.

"Maybe we can take one of the next round." Hiral tucked the Spokes quickly into his pocket.

Rylin frowned. "There's not going to be a next round. I won't steal from him again."

"Why not? You said it yourself, that douche bag won't even notice."

"He's not a douche bag. He gave me that photo," Rylin replied, though she wasn't sure why she was defending Cord Anderton. For some reason her mind jumped to the kiss, and she flushed a little, hoping her thoughts weren't written there on her face.

"Whatever." Hiral made a dismissive gesture.

"What's going on with you?" Rylin asked sharply, just as Chrissa walked back in the door, her eyes red. Rylin made eye contact with her sister, then looked back at Hiral, wondering what had set him off. Unless . . . her gaze drifted to the insta-photo. Could he be *jealous*?

"Nothing. I'm sorry." Hiral passed a hand over his face, and his features settled back into their usual indifference. "I'll give these to V tonight. Speaking of which, do you want to change? We should probably get going."

Oh, right. They were all supposed to go to some party for one of Indigo's friends. But for the first Saturday in a year, Rylin wasn't desperate to get out and get high. She felt exhausted, and she missed her sister.

"It's okay," she said. "I'm kind of tired. Why don't you go without me this time?"

"Whatever you want, babe." Hiral gave her a quick kiss. "We'll miss you, though. See you tomorrow?"

The moment the door shut behind him, Rylin turned to Chrissa. "So," she said, as if it were totally normal for her to be staying in, "I'm gonna put on sweatpants and set the table. Are there any good vids you've been wanting to watch?"

Her sister looked at her in disbelief, then up at the insta-photo, and it seemed to Rylin that they were both doing the same thing—trying to rewind to before Hiral walked in. After a moment, Chrissa broke out into a smile.

"Mais oui," she said, in the terrible French accent that Rylin had missed more than she realized. "Café Paris is open for business."

ERIS

ERIS STEPPED UP to 2704 Baneberry Lane and opened the front door as quietly as she could. The last thing she wanted right now was for her mom to hear her coming in and try to start a conversation. Eris had barely spoken to her all week. Her feelings were still too raw and tender, like a bruise that she kept pressing on.

As the door swung inward, Eris threw a hand up to cover her mouth, trying not to gag. Their apartment had that smell again, the gross sewage-y one that occasionally wafted from the upstairs neighbors'. She pushed the front door all the way open, which usually helped ventilate a little, and wedged one of her shiny black stilettos to hold it in place. Then she sailed through the entire apartment spraying her jasmine perfume, dousing the vents in it until her eyes watered. But at least now she could breathe again.

Eris heard a noise coming from her mom's room and stepped a little closer, only to realize that what she heard were muffled sobs. She felt a sudden flush of guilt, and shame. Her mom had been acting so optimistic all week, telling Eris about jobs she'd applied for, and trying to spruce up this awful apartment in whatever little ways she could. Caroline hadn't once cried around Eris. Now here she was, clearly letting out her grief only because she didn't realize that Eris was home.

Eris moved quickly past. She hated seeing her mom like this. But she wasn't ready to go in there and hug her either. She hadn't yet forgiven her for everything that had happened. It was like her dad—Everett, she reminded herself—had said. *I just need more time, okay?*

Eris sighed and opened the refrigerator. She wasn't even hungry; it was a hollow and aimless gesture, because she wasn't sure what else to do. For the first time in years Eris had no plans on a Saturday night. Instead she would be here, alone, in a smelly apartment while all her friends did something fabulous that she could no longer afford.

At least she'd managed to go upTower earlier today. She'd spent the afternoon shopping with Avery and the girls—not that she bought anything, but she'd been desperate to escape the lower-floor claustrophobia. They'd all gone out for icefruit afterward, and Eris had ended up spending some of her rapidly dwindling bitbanc balance on a lemon freeze, just so she wouldn't be the only girl without one. She'd practically had to restrain herself from licking the bright pink compostable cup when she was done. She couldn't believe she used to buy stuff like that, eat two bites, and throw the rest away without another thought.

Now the rest of the girls were all headed out, to dinner at Amuse-Bouche and then the new tiki bar Painkiller. Eris had heard that the bar looked out on a simulated ocean, where the sun set repeatedly all night long, over and over every forty minutes. In her old life Eris would be getting dressed right now. She let herself briefly fantasize about it, planning her outfit—her white crocheted halter top and the flowy skirt with the slit up the side. And a big, expensive hibiscus flower in her hair, which she would have to special order from the florist, but which would be totally worth it when all the other girls saw it and wished they'd had the same idea.

They'd all been shocked when she said she couldn't come tonight. "Are you sure?" Avery had begged, and Eris almost blurted out the truth right then and there. But she knew the moment she did, everything would change, and she couldn't handle that yet. None of the girls would be *mean* about it, of course; but they would feel awkward and uncomfortable around her, and the invitations would slowly stop coming. No one would want to make Eris feel bad by asking her to expensive dinners or yoga classes she couldn't afford. And she needed that pretense of normalcy. It was the only thing keeping her stable right now.

Instead she'd told everyone that her parents were forcing her to come home for family dinner. *Family dinner, ha.* In an attempt to be nice, the girls had insisted on walking her "home" to the Nuage. Eris ended up waving good-bye and getting in the elevator, then wandered the halls upstairs for fifteen minutes before she dared come back down. It was getting exhausting, keeping up with her lies.

She started toward her bedroom but paused at the sound of commotion out in the hall, the voices traveling clearly through the doorway, which was still propped wide-open. "I know, I know, I'll tell her!" It sounded like Mariel.

Eris glanced out and sure enough, there was Mariel, rolling her eyes as she shut the apartment door behind her. "Going out?" Eris said without thinking. Mariel was wearing a tight dress with an uneven hem, red heels, and a compact chrome bag.

"Staying in?" Mariel answered.

"Guess so. Not much to do around here, is there?"

Mariel raised an eyebrow. "Yeah, our parties aren't all champagne flutes and lame music."

"You're going to a party?" Eris wasn't sure why she was doing this, except that she didn't want to go inside and be alone again.

Mariel stared at her for a moment in evident disbelief. "You want to come?"

"Yes," Eris breathed, sounding pathetically eager.

Mariel walked over to Eris, her lips pursed. Then, in a single dramatic gesture, she ripped all the buttons from Eris's silk button-down, revealing the white camisole beneath.

"What the hell?" Eris stepped back, but Mariel was laughing. For someone so brusque, her laugh was surprisingly soft, floating lazily upward like rings of halluci-lighter smoke. Eris found herself wanting to hear it again.

"Sorry," Mariel said cheerfully, "but it's not a costume party, so you can't go as an uptight highlier bitch. Here." She pulled one of the long chain necklaces from around her neck and handed it to Eris. "That'll help."

"Thanks." Eris glanced down at her outfit, jeans and sand-colored wedges and the white undershirt, which was way too low-cut to be worn as an actual top. The necklace drew attention to her cleavage in a slutty way. Whatever, it didn't matter how she looked down here. And her spirits had lifted a bit, in spite of everything, at the mention of a party.

"Where are we going?" Eris trotted to catch up with Mariel, who was already moving down the hall.

"Have you ever taken the monorail?"

Only once, on a field trip in elementary school, but Mariel didn't need to know that. Eris wondered with some trepidation where they were headed. The monorails were commuter trains, leading only to dismal places like New Jersey or Queens. Everyone upTower just took copters instead.

"Of course I have," she said, more confidently than she felt.

———

"Welcome to Brooklyn," Mariel announced when they finally disembarked. They started down a street lined with shops, a few stubbornly open despite the lack of foot traffic, the halogen lights out front flickering halfheartedly. Mariel pulled out her tablet and began texting, her brow furrowed. Eris said nothing.

She'd never been to Brooklyn before. It used to be a fairly popular neighborhood, she knew, back before the Tower was built—and cast part of the borough in perpetual shadow. The township of Brooklyn was still locked in a lawsuit with the engineering firm that had designed the Tower, but no one thought they would actually win. In the meantime, people had been trickling out of the area for the past two decades. Eris wasn't sure who even lived here anymore.

"Here we are," Mariel said, walking up a staircase that led to an old, once stately brick town house. FORECLOSURE: PROPERTY OF FULLER WEALTH MANAGEMENT, read a bright red sign taped across the front door, which had been sealed off and then crudely broken into. Eris heard music thumping behind it. She gave a dark chuckle at the irony that she was going to a party in a house owned by Avery's dad. Avery would find it hilarious. Too bad Eris could never tell her.

Mariel gave a series of knocks at the door, which swung inward, revealing a burly guy with inktats and a beard. His frown melted into a smile when he saw Mariel. "Where've you been?" he asked, pulling her into a hug. "My mom keeps asking about you!"

"Tell your mom we'll come by soon," Mariel promised, and

stepped past him. Eris tried to follow, but the guy put an arm up, blocking her way.

"Thirty nanos," he said firmly.

"Oh—um—" She might have thirty nanos left in her bitbanc, but only just.

"She's with *me*, José," Mariel called over her shoulder.

"Sorry." José lowered his arm. "I didn't realize. Have fun."

Mariel looped an arm in Eris's and pulled her forward, toward what looked like the living room, empty of furniture but crowded with teenagers wearing cheap-looking clothes and broad smiles. Bars had been set up at both ends of the room, and there were speakers in all four corners, including floating speakers that followed the highest concentration of people. It wasn't a bad party, for being in Brooklyn.

"My cousin José," Mariel explained.

"It's his party?" Eris still didn't understand why they were in a foreclosed house.

"You could say that. This is his side business—throwing parties in abandoned and foreclosed houses, then charging for entry. He actually makes decent money off it."

"Oh. Well, thank you for getting me in without paying," Eris said awkwardly. She hated being in anyone's debt, especially this girl's.

"Don't thank me too much," Mariel said. "Now you can't flirt with anyone here, since I told José we're together."

"What?" Eris stared at her, even more confused.

"Sorry," Mariel said, "but he stopped letting me bring my friends for free, because I abused it too much. Now he only comps whoever I'm hooking up with. I figured you're strapped for cash right now, so . . ." she trailed off awkwardly.

"Thanks." Eris had no idea what to make of that. She looked around. "Who are all these people?"

"Friends from school, from the neighborhood. You might know some of them, actually—a few of my Altitude coworkers are here." Mariel grinned wickedly.

Eris looked around the room and realized that she did, in fact, recognize several people. Wasn't that tall brunette girl the barre instructor she'd flirted with all last summer? "I need a drink," Eris announced, heading for the bar as Mariel laughed behind her.

The night wore on. Eris introduced herself to almost everyone; they were all perfectly friendly, and all seemed to know Mariel, as if Mariel were the social glue holding this group together. But something ineffable kept Eris separated from them, with their easy laughter and high energy. Maybe it was the hot coal of resentment still burning in her chest, or maybe it was just that she came from upTower. But whatever it was, Eris felt somehow *apart* from them all. She kept drinking, hoping the alcohol would close the distance between them: kept drinking until she too could laugh easily, dance carelessly. It felt good, floating around this abandoned house without caring what any of them thought of her. She had needed a night like this.

At some point she discovered the stairs to the roof. This house was so low to the ground, only four floors up; no one in the Tower would consider this a view at all. Eris leaned against the low protective wall, looking at the dark forms of the surrounding buildings. Light fell in golden rings on the street below. She could see straight into another house's living room, where a couple was seated at a tiny table, holding hands over their food. Eris looked quickly away, feeling somehow invasive.

Across the water loomed the massive hulk of the Tower. She let her eyes skim up, up, up, wondering which of the tiny twinkling lights—which little slice of sky—was her old apartment up on 985. *Forget them*, she told herself, the resentment still warming her from within. They had all treated her terribly, her mom,

159

her dad, even her birth dad, whoever he was. She didn't need any of them. She didn't need anyone at all. She was doing just fine without them.

Eris tipped her head all the way back, even higher than the Tower, to look up at the dark expanse of night sky. She remembered all the nights she'd snuck into Greenwich Park hand in hand with whomever she was dating at the time, to look up at the vast holoscreen of stars. No matter how good holo technology got, it would never come close to this.

"There you are." Mariel appeared at the top of the stairs. Snippets of the music drifted through the doorway with her. "I'm heading out, if you want to come."

"I don't want to leave yet." Eris was still looking up at the stars.

"Really? You're gonna take the monorail alone later tonight?" Mariel teased.

"Fine." She heaved a dramatic sigh and turned around, stumbling a little.

"Hey there." Mariel reached forward to steady Eris, who was swaying in her wedges. "Drinking yourself stupid won't make it better. Trust me, I've tried," she said, surprisingly earnest.

"Whatever." Eris wasn't really listening. She was studying the sooty thickness of Mariel's lashes, the bright cherry red of her lips, the soft curve of her neck. She wanted to trace it, so she reached out and did just that. Mariel stood there, utterly motionless.

Eris leaned in to kiss her.

She tasted exactly like Eris had thought she would, like smoke and rum and waxy paintstick. Eris kept a hand lightly on Mariel's neck, enjoying the feeling of her pulse skipping erratically, and reached the other around her head.

Mariel broke away and took a step back. "Eris! What are

you—never mind. You're drunk," she said, stating the obvious. "You need to get home."

"That's right. Let's go home." Eris started to pull Mariel down the stairs, but Mariel dug her heels in.

"Eris—"

"Come *on*. I want to see all your inktats," she teased mercilessly, though she wouldn't have really cared if Mariel pushed her away; she was past caring about anything. Still, this was fun, the teasing and the flush on Mariel's cheeks and the stolen kiss. Eris loved these games. She was good at them. *Play to your strengths*, her dad used to say. She'd always assumed he was talking about her beauty. Everyone knew that was her greatest strength.

No. She shouldn't be thinking about her dad anymore.

"Well . . . okay," Mariel said, and laughed. "Let's go. You are my date, after all."

Eris nodded, feeling reckless, not caring about anything but this moment.

———

Eris's head was pounding. She started to reach for the sheets she'd kicked down near her feet—and froze, blinking into the unfamiliar darkness. The bright pink contacts-clock at the corner of her vision told her it was 4:09 a.m. Next to her was the sound of quiet, steady breathing.

Slowly, carefully, Eris turned. Mariel lay sprawled alongside her, her dark hair spilling out over the flat white pillow.

Shit, shit, shit.

Eris stayed utterly still, practically holding her breath, as she pieced together the events of the night before. She remembered taking all those shots of cheap liquor at the party . . . kissing Mariel on the roof . . . then heading out together into the warm summer night, to come back here, to Mariel's room. . . .

Mariel shifted in her sleep, and Eris's heart lurched in sudden panic. She needed to leave. Moving as hurriedly as she dared, she slid out of the bed and hunted for her clothes, which were strewn all over the floor. Buttoning her jeans with one hand and holding her wedges in the other, she walked barefoot out of Mariel's room.

Eris hesitated a moment in the hallway of their apartment, disoriented—she hadn't been paying attention when they stumbled inside a few hours ago. But then she heard muffled footsteps and a low voice, and she jumped to action. She could *not* be confronted by Mariel's parents right now. In a sheer panic, she grabbed what looked like the front door, and escaped into the cheap fluorescent lighting of Baneberry Lane.

Seconds later Eris had slunk the three doors back to her apartment and was safe in her room. She didn't even bother changing into pajamas, just curled up in her bed and squeezed her eyes shut. God, she missed their old apartment. She missed her old bed, with its soft rounded edges and aromatherapy pillows and her expensive Dreamweaver.

Tonight had been a mistake. Eris blamed all the shots she'd taken, and her bizarre mood. Thank god she'd at least woken up when she did, and saved herself the awkward morning-after conversation. And thank god none of her friends knew what she'd done tonight.

So she'd hooked up with Mariel—oh god, what was her last name? Eris winced. Well, it didn't count and didn't matter, she thought as she drifted restlessly back to sleep. It would be like the whole thing had never happened at all.

AVERY

LATER THAT WEEK Avery stood in the middle of her closet, skirts and dresses and tops from last season strewn around her on the floor like piles of brightly colored leaves. "To Leda," she muttered, composing a flicker on her contacts. "Designer Day cleanout! Come over?" She started to turn her head all the way to the right, the motion she'd programmed to send messages, only to change her mind, whipping her head back around to save it as a draft. She wasn't actually sure she wanted one-on-one time with Leda right now.

Leda still hadn't said anything about the growing distance between them. Avery knew she should try harder, but everything between them lately felt stiff and forced. She couldn't stop thinking about what was going on with Leda and Atlas. Had they hung out again since the date she'd managed to sabotage? Had they *kissed*? Avery couldn't ask either of them about it, so she kept torturing herself by imagining them together. It was a constant source of anguish.

Besides, she thought unfairly, Leda was the one who'd started it all, by acting weird when she came back from summer break— lying to Avery about where she'd been, hiding her crush on Atlas. And Leda wasn't exactly making a huge effort with her right now either.

Avery sighed and turned back to the clothes scattered over her pale blue carpet. She was cleaning out her closet before next week's Designer Day, when all the best international designers would set up in boutiques throughout the Tower and reveal their next season's collections. By now the designers all recognized Avery. A lot of them invited her into their portable privacy-coned dressing rooms, so she could actually try on the sample items they'd brought, which was way more fun than just projecting clothes onto her 3-D body scan. But it could also be embarrassing; every year at least one designer would proclaim that Avery was his or her muse, that she'd inspired the whole collection, and then she'd feel uncomfortably obligated to buy one of everything until Leda led her firmly away. That was the nice thing about shopping with Leda. She was the only person, aside from Atlas, whom Avery could trust to tell her no.

At some point Avery and Leda had started this tradition, of cleaning out their closets the week before Designer Day to make room for new purchases. It was always a fun game, trying on their old things and making fun of each other's fashion faux pas, reminiscing about past adventures. Avery felt a pang of loss. She missed the way she and Leda had been before, back when everything was easy. They would have it again, though, she promised herself; once things between Leda and Atlas fizzled out, as surely they would.

She stepped into a flowy white-and-yellow dress she'd worn to her cousin's wedding two years ago and tapped the smart mirror, changing her reflection so that it showed a braided updo instead of her current style, long and wavy. But not even fixing the hairstyle could save this one. "Too dated," she said aloud, and hung the dress on her closet's input rod, where it was swept into the donation bin.

Next she pulled on a vibrant tangerine Oscar de la Renta gown, with a long train and a bow on one hip—from last summer's Whitney young members' gala, if Avery remembered right. She was struggling with the zipper when a knock sounded at her door.

"Come on in, Mom," she called out, thinking she'd heard her mom's voice. "I need you to zip me up—"

Atlas walked through the door. "I thought you were out," Avery stammered, holding her dress awkwardly in place.

"I was," Atlas said simply. Avery wondered if he'd been with Leda but didn't dare ask. "*I* can zip you, if you want," he offered.

Avery turned around, shivering at the intimacy of the gesture. His hands were warm where they brushed her back.

"You look amazing," Atlas told her as she swished back to face him, the heavy skirt dragging over the carpet. "But it still needs something."

"What do you mean?"

"I've been wanting to give you this." Atlas pulled a drawstring pouch from his pocket. Avery reached for it, her breath catching a little.

Inside was a necklace that glittered with unfamiliar stones. They looked almost like black diamonds, but each had a swirling orange streak through the middle, reminding Avery of the smoldering embers of a real wood fire.

"Volcanic glass from Kilimanjaro. The moment I saw it, I thought of you." Atlas looped the necklace around her neck, reaching to pull the blond curtain of her hair from underneath. His hands were certain, no fumbling with the clasp, and Avery couldn't help wondering how often he'd done this before, with other girls. Her heart sank a little.

She turned and looked at her reflection. Atlas was still standing behind her, his tall, broad silhouette outlining hers. Their eyes met in the mirror just as his hands released the clasp and fell to his sides. Avery wished he would grab her bare shoulders, whisper in her ear, kiss her at the base of her neck where his hands had just been.

She stepped quickly away, as if to get a closer look at the necklace.

It really was beautiful. Usually Avery looked all bright and sunshiny, but the dark stones captured something else in her, the shadows flitting across her face and along the curve of her collarbone. "Thank you," she said, and turned back around. "When were you at Kilimanjaro?"

"For a few days in April. I worked my way from South Africa up to Tanzania. You would have loved it, Aves. The view's even better than this." He gestured toward the windows that lined two of her walls, where a bright orange sunset burned its way into the atmosphere.

"Why did you do it, though? Leave like that?" Avery whispered. She'd promised herself she wouldn't press him on this, but she couldn't help it anymore; she was sick of not talking about it, of pretending that nothing in their perfect family had ever gone wrong.

He looked away. "A lot of reasons," he said. "I don't really want to talk about it."

"Atlas—" She reached out and grabbed his arm, feeling suddenly desperate, as if he might float off unless she anchored him here. "Promise me you won't do that again. You can't just run off like that, okay? I was worried."

Atlas looked at her. For a moment Avery thought there was

something alert and watchful in his gaze, but it disappeared before she could be sure of it. "I promise," he told her. "Sorry I made you worry. That was why I kept calling you—so that at least *you* would know everything was fine," he added.

"I know." *But everything* isn't *fine*, she thought. Now Leda liked Atlas, and meanwhile, she, Avery, was caught in some impossible place, loving him more than ever. She never imagined she'd say this, but she almost missed the days when he was half-way across the world. At least then he'd been all hers.

"Well, I'll let you get back to your closet. Looks like you have a lot to clean out," he said, sensing the subtle change in her mood, as he always did.

"Wait," Avery called out. Atlas paused in the doorway. "Um, thanks. For the necklace," she said, not totally sure why she'd stopped him, just wanting to delay his leaving her. "It means a lot, that you were thinking of me."

"I'm always thinking of you, Aves." Atlas shut the door behind him.

Avery reached up to feel the cold glass of her necklace. The silence of her room felt suddenly deafening. She needed to get out.

"Ping to Eris," she said aloud, but Eris didn't pick up. Avery flickered her too, stepping out of the tangerine gown—which of course she had to keep now—and into white jeans and a navy top. She started to take off the necklace, but hesitated, and let it fall back onto her throat.

Why wasn't Eris answering? Avery knew her family was renovating, but that didn't explain how absent she'd been lately.

Maybe she should just go to the Nuage and surprise Eris. Actually, Avery realized on second thought, that was a fantastic idea. They could get dinner at the sashimi bar there, or go to the steam room; anything to keep her from being alone in this closet, thinking of Atlas.

Fifteen minutes later she was getting off on the 940th floor and walking into the massive lobby of the Nuage, the most expensive—and highest—luxury hotel in the Tower. Tourists and businesspeople sat on the plush couches, which were incredibly soft despite the carbon polymers woven into each thread, which changed the color of the couches to match the color of the sky. Through the Nuage's full-length windows, Avery saw that the sun was just sinking below the horizon. The couches matched: the same deep cobalt blue, shot through with glowing tendrils of red.

She and Leda used to come here to take sunset vids, back in eighth grade when they went through their hopeful-models phase. They would wear white dresses and pose on the couches for the half hour that they changed color, then edit the vid to a thirty-second speed frame and post it to the feeds. It had been silly and embarrassing and a ton of fun.

Avery sighed and made her way to the front desk, a slab of white Tuscan granite suspended in midair by powerful micro-hovers. "Can I help you?" the guy behind the desk asked. He wore a crisp white shirt and trousers, and his name tag read *Pierre*, which meant that he was probably a lower-floor kid named Peter.

"I'm looking for Eris Dodd-Radson," Avery said. "She and her family have been staying here for a week or so."

"I'm sorry, but we can't give out guests' room numbers, for privacy reasons."

"Of course." Avery flashed him her most dazzling smile, the one she held in reserve for occasions like this, and saw him waver. "I understand. I was just wondering if you could call up to their room for me, pass along a message? She's my best friend, and I haven't heard from her in a while. I'm getting worried."

Pierre bit his lip, then began waving in the air in front of him, studying a holoscreen visible only to him. "I don't see an Eris Dodd-Radson in our system," he said. "Are you sure she's staying here?"

"She's with her parents, Caroline Dodd and Everett Radson."

"I see an Everett Radson—"

"That's it!" Avery interrupted. "Can you call up?"

Pierre scowled, looking down his nose at her. "Mr. Radson is registered alone. You must be mistaken about your friend. Perhaps she's at a different hotel?"

Avery paused. "Okay. Thanks," she said, hiding her confusion, and stepped away.

She sank onto one of the couches, whose few remaining red-orange threads were rapidly turning a dusky blue, and ordered a lemonade from the touch screen in front of her. She didn't want to go home just yet. She needed a minute to think. The drink arrived almost instantly, and Avery took a long sip, wondering why Eris would have lied about renovating their apartment, and why her dad would be staying here at the Nuage alone.

Mr. Radson had been divorced twice before. Was he doing it again, leaving Eris's mom? And if so, where was Eris?

"Drinking alone?" Cord settled onto the couch opposite her and leaned back into the cushions.

"It's lemonade," Avery said wearily.

"How disappointing." He smiled, showing his perfect white teeth. "You used to be more fun, you know, Fuller."

"And you used to actually be tolerable," Avery answered, though they both knew she didn't mean it. She'd known Cord too long not to forgive him almost anything. "Are you looking for Eris too?" she went on, wondering if he had any answers for her.

"You didn't know? Eris and I aren't . . . anymore."

"Oh, I—she didn't tell me." Avery's worry flared up stronger than before; why hadn't Eris called her? She always came to

Avery after her breakups, and then they commiserated and ate ice cream and plotted Eris's next conquest. Something was really wrong.

"What happened?" she asked Cord. She wasn't really surprised they'd broken up—neither of them had seemed particularly invested in it—but she was still curious what he would say. Cord just shrugged, not answering. "Is there someone else?" Avery prodded, watching him. She knew all his tells.

"No, we just got bored," he said. He was a good liar; Avery had to give him that, at least. She wondered who the new girl was.

"I'm looking for Brice," Cord went on. "Have you seen him?"

"Brice is in town?" Avery didn't particularly like Cord's older brother. She blamed him for the asshole attitude Cord tried to put on these days.

"Who knows?" Cord shrugged it off, but Avery could tell he was bothered. "He got here last weekend, and his stuff's still at home, but he hasn't been by the apartment since yesterday. I thought I'd check a few places before I start going through his bank charges."

"I hope you find him," Avery said earnestly, though she was far more worried about Eris. "Hey," she added, realizing she was hungry, "wanna get some truffle fries? I've been craving them lately." She and Cord used to come here for truffle fries with Atlas sometimes, late at night after a party. It was the best comfort food in the entire Tower.

Cord shook his head. A few threads of the couch behind him were still lit up a fiery crimson, producing the strange effect of a halo. "I'm okay. You should get some, though." His eyes softened a little. "You look tired, Avery."

"Gee, thanks," she said sarcastically, though in a way she was grateful, to have at least one person in her life who didn't always tell her how great she looked.

"Anytime." He laughed, and headed off.

Avery sat there a few minutes longer, pinging Eris again—though by now she'd given up on an answer—and finishing the last of her lemonade. The hotel bar was getting more crowded as she watched, filled with businesspeople talking in low tones, a group of women clinking champagne glasses. Avery's eyes were drawn to a couple who seemed to be on their first date, their body language still a little stiff but their interest in each other apparent. The girl leaned forward, as if she wanted to put a hand on the guy's arm but didn't dare. For some reason it all saddened Avery, and she headed home.

Waiting in the delivery chute in their kitchen was a brown paper delivery bag. Avery looked at the reference tag, wondering if Atlas had ordered something, but the package was addressed to her. Puzzled, she opened it—and was greeted by the smell of warm, truffled grease. *Cord.* Sure enough, the receipt inside had been billed to him.

She took a bite of one of the fries, hot and crispy with truffle oil, and gave a reluctant smile. What a messed-up start to junior year, she thought, that the only friend she could count on right now was Cord Anderton.

ERIS

ERIS WALKED DOWN the hallway at school, automatically nodding at or ignoring people based on whether she liked the way they looked, keeping her expression as icily calm and unflappable as ever. But inside, she was seriously losing it.

She still couldn't believe she'd gone home with Mariel on Saturday. She'd been trying to act like the whole thing never happened, but Mariel didn't seem to get it. She'd messaged Eris *twice*, asking if she'd gotten home okay, then referencing some song they'd listened to that night. Eris had deleted the messages without responding. She was writing the whole thing off and moving on, and the sooner Mariel figured that out, the better.

She headed into the cafeteria and went through the line on autopilot. At the blender bar she had the robot make a raspberry smoothie with almond butter, then grabbed a protein snack for later. Lately she'd been trying to squeeze everything she could out of her meal plan, since home was mostly cheap sandwiches and ramen bowls. Eris had no idea what they would do when they ran out of money.

"Eris." Avery fell into step next to her as they started toward their usual table. "We need to talk."

"Uh-oh," Eris teased, "are you breaking up with me?" But her heart was hammering; she could hear the solemnity in Avery's voice and she had a feeling, somehow, that Avery knew.

"Let's go over here, just the two of us," Avery suggested, and led Eris toward the school's shaded interior courtyard. It felt so much like outdoors it was practically real, with live oak trees growing in the soil, even a hammock strung between two of them, though no one ever used it. They settled down in the projected sunshine, sitting mermaid-style with their pleated uniform skirts belling around their waists.

Avery took a tiny pink speaker from her bag and put it on silencer, which used similar technology to the privacy cone, blocking all sound waves in a seven-foot radius. The world was abruptly hushed, as if they'd stuck their heads underwater. "Great," Avery said, opening her kale-and-mango salad and setting it on her lap, "now we can talk in private. Eris, what's going on?"

"What do you mean?" Eris asked unsteadily.

"I went to the Nuage yesterday, to look for you." Eris's heart sank. She should have thought of a better lie. "When I got there, they said you aren't staying there—but that your dad is. Alone."

"Right. Well, the thing is . . . um . . ."

Avery looked at her expectantly. And Eris found that she couldn't do it anymore. She burst into tears.

Avery wrapped her arms around Eris's shoulders, letting her cry. "Hey, it's okay," she murmured. "Whatever it is, it'll all be okay."

Eris pulled back and shook her head, tears running down her face. "It won't, though," she whispered.

"Are your parents splitting up?" Avery prompted.

"It's worse than that." Eris caught a shaky breath, then said it, the thing she couldn't bear to say aloud. "Turns out my dad isn't my dad." There. Now the truth was out in the open.

Slowly, as they ate their lunches and regained a sense of normalcy, Eris told Avery everything—how she'd learned the truth because of the DNA test she'd had to do as part of her trust fund paperwork. How her father was brokenhearted, barely able to even look at her, he felt so betrayed. How she and her mom had moved down to 103, and had practically no money. How Eris's old life was gone forever.

Avery listened quietly, horror flitting across her face at the mention of the 103rd floor, though she quickly masked it. "I'm so sorry," she said when Eris had finished.

Eris didn't answer. She had no words left.

Avery twirled a piece of grass between her thumb and forefinger, seeming to think carefully about something. "What about your birth father?"

"What *about* him? I have zero interest in him," Eris said tersely.

"I'm sorry," Avery apologized, immediately backing down. "I didn't mean to—never mind."

They were silent for a while. Eventually Eris's curiosity overcame her defensiveness. "You think I should try to meet him or something?"

"Oh, Eris." Avery sighed. "That's up to you. I just know that if it was me, I would want to know. Besides, he might be more interested in seeing you than your dad—than Everett is."

"That's not exactly a high bar," Eris replied, and for some reason she laughed. It was a bizarre laugh, half ironic and bitter, but Avery joined in. Afterward Eris felt slightly better, the hard knot in her chest loosening just a little.

"So," Avery asked finally, "what can I do to help?"

"Just don't tell anyone. I don't want them . . . you know."
Pitying me.

"Of course. But, Eris, you should sleep at my place anytime, borrow clothes, whatever you want. I still can't believe all this," she said, a little wonderingly. Eris just nodded. "Wait," Avery added, "what about your birthday?"

"You mean the reason I'm in this mess to begin with? My mom and I haven't exactly talked about it. I think we're ignoring it this year."

"Absolutely not." The bell rang signaling the end of lunch, and Avery stood up, holding out a hand to pull Eris to her feet. An elegant diamond tennis bracelet was stacked next to an Hermès bangle on her wrist, a fresh manicolor on her nails. Eris's nails were chipped and dry in comparison. She curled her hands into fists at her side. "Please, let me throw you a party," Avery was saying. "Bubble Lounge, Saturday night?"

"I can't let you do that," Eris protested weakly. But her heart had leapt at the mention of a party, and Avery could see it in her eyes.

"Come on. Let me take care of everything," Avery insisted. "Besides, I could use something to distract myself with right now."

Eris wasn't sure what she meant by that. "Okay," she conceded. "If you're sure. Thank you."

"You'd do the same for me."

They turned out of the courtyard and into the hallway. "Dress shopping later?" Avery went on, pausing outside the door to her next class. "My treat, obviously."

"Avery, you're doing too much already, I can't—" Eris argued, but Avery talked over her.

"Eris. That's what friends are for," she said firmly, and ducked into her class as the bell rang.

Eris walked slowly down the now empty halls, late to calculus and not caring at all. Her heart felt lighter than it had in weeks.

———————

That afternoon when Eris came home, she found her mom in the living room. She was sitting cross-legged in a sea of document scans, wearing cropped artech pants and a drapey sweater, and her riot of red-gold hair was pinned up with an enormous white clip. Old-fashioned eyeglasses were perched on her nose. She looked thin, and tired, barely older than her daughter. Eris fought the urge to go hug her.

"Why are you wearing those?" Eris couldn't help asking, as she stepped over a stack of papers on her way to the kitchen. The glasses looked silly and outdated. Hadn't her mom gotten her eyes lasered a long time ago?

"I used to wear these in college. Thought they might help me focus on all these job applications," Caroline said with a rueful shrug.

Oh, right; Eris always forgot her mom had attended a year of undergrad before she dropped out to move to New York. "So what do you want for dinner?" Caroline went on, as cheerfully as she could manage, the way she used to say it back when they were deciding between expensive sushi and black truffle pizza. "I was thinking maybe—"

"Who's my birth father?" Eris interrupted. She was half surprised to hear herself ask the question, yet the moment she asked it, she was glad she did; it had been there in the back of her mind, slowly gaining significance, ever since Avery had brought it up at lunch.

"Oh," Caroline breathed, stunned. "I thought you didn't want to meet him?"

"Maybe. I don't know."

Eris's mom studied her daughter, as if uncertain what she

really meant. "I'll reach out to him, then, tell him everything. I'll do my best," she promised.

It took a second for the meaning of those words to sink in. "You're saying he doesn't *know* about me yet?"

"It's all very . . . complicated, you know."

"No, I *don't* know!"

"Eris—"

"You've been lying to everyone! This is why I need to meet my birth father! Because I need at least *one* functioning parental relationship in my life, and I clearly can't get it from you!"

Her mom winced. "I'm sorry." She sounded small and broken, but Eris had already moved toward her bedroom door.

She wasn't sure why it saddened her so much, this realization that her birth father didn't even know she existed. But on top of everything else—losing her dad, losing Cord, losing her entire life—it felt like more than she could handle.

Eris felt like those wadded-up pieces of trash that she'd seen the kids on this floor kicking idly around. Unwanted and useless, and belonging to no one.

WATT

WATT'S FEET POUNDED on the thick black polyresin as he followed the running trail through the forest. Electronic music blasted in his eartennas. He hadn't been to Redwood Park in ages. He hadn't gone *running* in ages, come to think of it, unless you counted the pickup soccer games he occasionally joined. Boxing was more his thing these days. But he'd been running almost every day since he met Avery at the ARena last week. To get in shape, he told himself, though it wasn't a coincidence that he was following the same loop Avery always posted about.

It wasn't like Watt to go to such lengths for a girl. Yet he had no idea what else to do. He couldn't stop thinking about Avery; he'd flickered her a couple of times, and while she always responded, the conversation was never more than friendly. Not even Nadia was quite sure what to say to her, which only made Watt more intrigued. He'd been reading through Avery's feeds all week—a task he usually left to Nadia, but in this case he wanted to do it himself. Avery was brilliant. He loved hearing all her thoughts, teasing through the way her mind worked.

And on top of all that, of course, was her near-terrifying beauty. By now Watt had figured out Avery's history, that her parents had custom designed her from the pool of their combined DNA. He was crazy to think he might ever have a shot. What could a guy from downTower ever hope for, with the most beautiful girl on earth—a girl who literally lived on top of the world? Avery probably had dozens of guys constantly asking her out, all of them taller or richer than Watt.

Still, none of them had Nadia.

He sped up as the trees thinned ahead, and the dark ribbon of the path turned along the edge of a wide illusion lake. The water wasn't real, but the redwood trees around him were, their roots sinking deep into the agri levels below and their tops stretching far overhead. Watt took a deep breath, relishing the burn in his calves. The air was heavy with the scent of clean, dry needles. No wonder Avery liked it here. Redwood Park was technically open to the public, but its location—tucked away on the 811th floor, on a local elevator line—meant that most people who came here were highliers.

Do you know where Atlas is? came an incoming message on his contacts.

What an obsessive weirdo, Watt remarked to Nadia as she pulled up Atlas's location and sent it to Leda. Not that he particularly cared. It was Leda's craziness that had put several hundred NDs in his college savings account, and let him buy Zarah and Amir some new clothes.

I fail to see how Leda's behavior differs from what you're doing.

At least I'm not constantly tracking Avery the way she is Atlas, Watt thought angrily.

I can do the hack for you, if you want, Nadia replied.

Watt suddenly felt ashamed. Nadia was right; he should give up and head home.

And then he saw her.

She was running the opposite direction down the path, wearing a lime-green shirt and camo-printed running pants. Even running she was somehow elegant, her hair spilling carelessly over one shoulder.

It wasn't until she was a couple of meters away that Avery blinked in recognition. "Hey," she breathed, and slowed to a walk. "Watt, right?"

He felt a momentary dismay that she hadn't been thinking about their meeting in the ARena the way he had. Clearly his flickers hadn't made that much of an impression either. Maybe he was right, and she was talking to a ton of guys at once. Well, he thought, shoving aside the doubt that threatened to creep in, he would just have to be that much more memorable.

"Avery." He turned around, falling into step alongside her. "I didn't know you ran up here. Are you training for something?" A reasonable question; this was a pretty long loop. Watt remembered from the feeds that she'd run a half marathon the last couple of years.

"Not right now. I just love running here." She made a gesture that encompassed the bright green trees, the cool air that smelled rich and woodsy, the light dancing on the artificial water. This far into the park, the walls weren't even visible. "It's nice how you can go miles without seeing anyone, you know?" she asked, then seemed to realize what she'd just said. "Present company excluded, of course."

"No, I know what you mean," Watt agreed. "Hard to believe we're inside right now, isn't it?"

Avery smiled. "What about you, are you training for something?"

"Oh, just my next Wizards game," Watt said lightly. "And—"

"Want to race?"

"What?"

But Avery was already tearing headlong down the path. After a split second of hesitation Watt took off after her, suddenly grateful for all the soccer games. Avery was *fast*. He wondered if they'd somehow found an extra high-twitch muscle gene in her parents' DNA.

Finally she slowed to a stop at the path that led to the elevator, where a small water fountain was disguised as a tree stump. "Thanks for that." She smiled broadly, splashing water on her face. A few droplets trickled down the curve of her neck and onto the front of her shirt. "I haven't done that in a while."

"Me neither," Watt said truthfully.

Her eyes dilated; she was looking something up on her contacts, probably an incoming flicker. *Now or never*, Nadia urged him.

"Hey, Avery?" he began, and immediately cursed himself for making the sentence pitch up like a question. "Want to do something this weekend?"

"Oh, god. This weekend I'm throwing a huge party for my friend Eris's birthday," Avery replied, pulling her leg behind her into a stretch. For a moment Watt thought he was being completely blown off. But then—

"Want to come?"

Watt tried to hide his excitement. "Yeah, sure. I mean, I'd love to."

"Great. It's at Bubble Lounge, Saturday night." Avery leaned back down to take one last sip from the water fountain, then turned back to head the other direction. "See you then."

"You will," Watt said, watching her disappear into the trees.

RYLIN

RYLIN STOOD AT the counter of her monorail snack station, unaware that several miles above her, all the highlier kids were in a flurry of activity over Eris Dodd-Radson's eighteenth birthday party, which Avery Fuller was hosting tonight. But even if Rylin had known, those names would have meant nothing to her. All she knew was that it was too early on a Saturday morning to be awake.

Yet here she was, working a job that somehow seemed worse than it used to. If that was even possible.

Rylin had worked at Cord's all week. She hadn't taken any more of his Spokes after that close call and the subsequent kiss, which she really needed to stop thinking about. Still, every morning she'd called in sick to the monorail cart and headed upTower to the Andertons'. She told Chrissa and Hiral it was for the pay—which she'd levered to pay off their last few months' rent and kept them from getting evicted. Hiral still hadn't managed to sell the Spokes, he told her. She didn't really care. She sort of wished she'd never taken them.

If she were being honest with herself, though, the money wasn't the only reason she stayed. Cord was part of it too. Something had changed between them, something unspoken and confusing, and Rylin was curious about it. He came home earlier in the afternoons and always chatted with her for a few minutes on her way out, asking questions about her family, her monorail job, why she'd dropped out of school. He bought more Gummy Buddies and left them out on the counter. Once she caught him napping on the couch in the living room, a wistful smile on his face, the same smile she'd seen when she caught him watching the family holovids. Only when Brice was around did Cord seem different, as though he acted tougher for his brother's sake. *I can't wait till he leaves again*, Rylin had caught herself thinking; but of course it didn't matter, because once Brice left, she would be gone too.

Then yesterday, Buza—her boss at the monorail cart—had called Rylin, refusing to let her take any more sick leave no matter what the mediwand said. "Either get to a hospital or get back to work," he'd snarled, and hung up. Rylin had messaged Cord that she was done, feeling surprisingly disappointed.

Now here she was, back to smelly, depressing reality. It was for the best, though, she assured herself. Better that she leave now, while she still had her actual job, than be fired whenever Brice left town and have nowhere to go.

"Myers! Look alive!" Buza said as he walked past. Rylin clenched her jaw, saying nothing. A monorail was just pulling up to the station. She allowed herself a brief glance out the window, way over on the far wall, then squared her shoulders and settled in for the typical Saturday-morning rush.

She hated weekends, when the crowd was mostly tourists. At

least the weekday commuters always knew what they wanted, ordered quickly and moved down the line and occasionally even tipped her, since they knew her and would see her again. Tourists dithered over their orders, asked a million questions, and never tipped. Sure enough, the first group to reach her from the overfull train was a family wearing matching I ♥ NYC sweatshirts outlined with the Tower's silhouette. The two children fought over the single banana-nut muffin their mom agreed to buy, while she pestered Rylin, micromanaging exactly how much foam she wanted in her coffeeccino.

The next customers were all just as bad. Sometimes Rylin wondered if people forgot she was a human and not a bot. Cord had once asked why her job even existed, why they didn't just have bots at each monorail stop like they did at upper-floor lift stations. "Because I'm cheaper than a bot," she'd told him, which was true.

Handing a package of baked apple bites to an older man, she turned to her next customer, about to ask what the person wanted. But when she saw who stood there, she was speechless.

"I admit, I haven't been here before," said Cord, who was lounging at the counter as if it were the most normal thing in the world. "What do you recommend?"

"You know this is all crap," Rylin blurted out, hardly aware what she was saying. She couldn't believe Cord even knew how to *get* to a monorail stop, let alone that he remembered which one she worked at.

"Yes, so I've heard." Cord's eyes glittered, amused. "But I'm trying to talk to the girl who works here, and if that means I have to buy some crap, so be it."

"Myers!" Buza called out from the back room, where he was working his way steadily through a bag of bacon-flavored chips. "Stop flirting!"

Rylin bit her lip to keep from answering. She turned back to Cord, her voice tight. "Apparently we need to keep moving. So, what can I get you?" she asked, still uncertain why he was here.

"Whatever takes longest," Cord replied, looking at Buza, who frowned.

Rylin set about making a whipped hazelnut frappé, tossing ingredients in the blender and putting it on the loudest setting. "So, this is where the magic happens," Cord spoke under the noise of the blender, leaning back on his heels.

"Cord, why are you here?" she asked bluntly.

"Would you believe it if I told you I miss your cleaning?"

"What happened to your old maid service?"

"They aren't as fun as you."

"Cord—"

"Wanna play hooky?" he asked.

"I thought Brice was leaving town." She took the blender out of its socket and poured the creamy drink into a white elastifoam cup, marked with an obnoxious yellow smiley face.

"I wasn't talking about cleaning," he clarified. "I'm going on an adventure, and I want you to come."

"I don't know." The line waiting behind Cord was starting to get loud, insistent. "Fifteen NDs," Rylin said, and slid him the hazelnut frappé.

"If you come, I promise to drink this nasty concoction you're forcing me to buy," Cord said, looking up at the retinal scanner and nodding to confirm payment.

"Myers!" Buza bellowed. "Hurry it up out there!"

That was the final straw. Her blood boiling, Rylin whirled around and stood in the doorway, hand on hip. "You know what?" she said. "I don't feel well. I think I came back to work too soon. Probably because my boss bullied me, and told me that if I didn't come back, I'd get fired," she replied angrily.

He looked up, bacon-chili powder smeared on his upper lip. "You leave now, you *are* fired," he threatened.

Rylin took off her name tag in a dramatic gesture. "Good-bye, then," she said, and threw it on the floor.

"Let's get out of here," she told Cord as she hurried out the employee entrance, laughing at the thought of Buza trying to handle that angry crowd of customers alone. *God, that felt good.* She'd been fantasizing about quitting since her first day working there. She knew she'd freak out about this tomorrow, once she had to start looking for a new job, but right now it was deeply satisfying.

"Bottoms up," Cord said, and took a swig of the frozen, syrupy mess. He choked but managed to swallow the sip. Rylin couldn't help laughing, a little hysterically.

"Where are we headed?" she asked, stepping with Cord onto the monorail back toward the Tower.

"I was thinking dinner," he said. "Are you hungry?"

Rylin looked at him, her brow furrowed, but for once he didn't sound teasing. "It's only ten a.m.," she pointed out.

He grinned. "Not where we're going."

Rylin didn't quite figure it out until they disembarked at Grand Central, the transport hub that sprawled over six floors in a massive chunk of the Tower's east side. She let Cord lead her down the iconic marble steps that had been excavated from the original Grand Central, past the monorail lines and elevator banks, toward the farthest part of the station. "Wait," she said slowly, as understanding dawned, "you didn't—I'm not—"

"Too late, our train is already boarding," Cord argued, pulling her along the Hyperloop platform and onto a curved, bullet-shaped car, the sign above it flashing PARIS GARE D'OUEST. Rylin followed, in too much shock to protest. The inside of the car consisted of four pairs of seats, the oversized lay-flat chairs a deep purple, each with its own silencing privacy walls.

"Seats 1A and 1B, that's us," Cord said, finding their row.

Rylin planted her feet in the aisle. "Cord, I can't accept this. It's too much." She wasn't sure how much a first-class Hyperloop ticket cost, but she had the feeling she didn't want to know.

"Suit yourself." Cord sank into the window seat. "If you don't want to come, don't come. I'm going to Paris either way. But decide soon," he added as a countdown sounded over the speakers, "because in ninety seconds this train will be deep under the Atlantic, heading to Europe at twelve hundred kilometers per hour."

Rylin spun back toward the vestibule, ready to jump onto the platform and write off this whole crazy day, maybe even go to Buza and beg him for her job back. But something stopped her. She watched, her eyes glued to the screen as the countdown fell to under a minute. Then she returned to the first row, her mind made up.

"Switch with me."

"You know there's no view out the window, except the sides of the tunnel," Cord told her, but he was already unbuckling his magnetic safety belt and moving to the aisle seat.

"I don't care about the tunnel. I just want to see Paris the absolute first moment that I can," Rylin said, and settled in as the train began to accelerate.

The three-hour train ride passed faster than Rylin would've guessed. Cord ordered them croissants and café au lait, and she watched an old 2-D vid in French that she didn't really understand, something about a Frenchman with a big nose who was in love with a dark-haired woman. "You know you can put that on in English," Cord whispered, but she just swatted him away. She liked the way the French fell on her ears, mellifluous and soft. It sounded the way honey tasted.

When they emerged back aboveground and began speeding

through the French countryside, Rylin pressed her face to the glass, drinking in every detail. None of it felt real yet. *I wish Mom could have seen this,* she kept thinking. *She wouldn't believe it either.*

"Where to?" Cord asked when they finally stepped off the train and passed through the visitors' bioscanner line, which cross-referenced their retinas with their digital passport profiles before letting them through. The late afternoon sunshine spilled in glorious golden pools onto the ancient-looking streets.

"The Eiffel Tower," Rylin said automatically, reaching for her necklace.

"From one Tower to another. I see how it is," Cord teased, but her gesture hadn't been lost on him.

The Parisian streets had never been excavated and lined with the magnetic pieces needed to keep hovers afloat, so they got into an auto-taxi and started down the funny old cobblestone roads toward the Eiffel Tower.

They arrived just in time to climb the steps. By the end Rylin was racing like a child, gasping as she reached the upper platform. Dusk had settled over the streets of Paris below, making everything feel enchanted.

"Is it like you expected?" Cord asked, stepping up behind her.

Rylin thought of the virtual-reality headsets at the school library, of all the afternoons she'd spent waiting in line for one, just so she could do the Eiffel Tower simulation again. She'd played it so many times that by now she knew the whole thing by heart. Rylin curled her fingers around the railing, worn down by centuries of hands, and inhaled deeply, breathing through her mouth so she could taste the cool Parisian air. "It's way better. It's just . . . beautiful," she whispered, watching the final rays of sun gilding the white dome of Sacré-Coeur. The streets below were a constant flicker of men and women and beeping electric autocars, everything cheerfully humming and disorganized, nothing like the ruthless efficiency of streets in the Tower.

"It is," Cord said, but he was looking at her.

They wandered the wrought-iron structure until its six p.m. closing time, then started along the river toward the Quartier Saint-Germain-des-Prés. They passed dozens of small bakeries that smelled like icing and spun sugar, and Rylin kept trying to stop, insisting that they get éclairs for Chrissa. "I have a better bakery," Cord kept saying, leading her on through the winding cobblestone streets.

Eventually they walked up to a nondescript blue door on a corner. Rylin gasped when they stepped inside. It was a tiny space, richly decorated in exquisite antique mirrors and gold-leafed wallpaper. *"Bonsoir, monsieur, mademoiselle."* The white-gloved maître d' nodded. "Welcome to Café Paris."

Rylin looked curiously at Cord. "How did you know?"

"You told me, remember?"

They followed the maître d' into the dining room, illuminated by hundreds of candles that floated in brass candlesticks lifted by invisible microhovers. The dim light gleamed on gold plates, crystal champagne flutes, the jewelry sparkling at the wrists and necks of the other guests. In the corner, a violin covered in lavish scrollwork was playing itself. Rylin knew the movement was just for effect, the music streaming from tiny high-frequency speakers scattered around the room, but it was still magical to watch.

Maybe a little too *magical,* she thought, her rational brain kicking in. She realized, feeling suddenly foolish, that it was late and she was halfway around the world with a boy she really didn't know that well. She started mentally adding up everything he'd spent today, and felt a little queasy. What did he expect from her, in exchange?

"Cord. Why are you doing all this?"

"Because I want to. Because I can." He waved over a bottle of champagne and started to pour her a glass, but Rylin refused to be distracted. She was thinking back to when she'd met Brice, how he'd said Cord's taste was improving, that she was "better than the last one."

"If you think I'm going to sleep with you because of all this, you're dead wrong." She reached for her napkin, whose smart-threads had shifted to match the exact lavender of her jeans, and started to stand up.

"God, Rylin, I hope you don't think that," Cord said, and she settled back down, a little mollified. He broke out into a grin. "I promise, if you ever sleep with me, it won't be because of 'all this'"—he repeated her words, holding out both hands to indicate the restaurant, Paris, everything—"but because you can't help yourself. Because of my devastating good looks and crushing wit."

"Right," Rylin said, straight-faced. "That right there, that wit gets me every time."

"If I get too forward, by all means, slap me."

Rylin burst out laughing.

"If I ask a question, will you answer it honestly?" Cord's voice sounded as irreverent as always, but she sensed a real purpose there.

"Only if you answer mine too."

"Fair enough." Cord leaned forward on his elbows. He'd rolled his shirtsleeves up, as if in challenge to the solemnity of their surroundings, revealing the dark hair on his forearms. "What do you want most?"

"To be happy," Rylin said without thinking.

"That's a cop-out answer. Of course you want to be happy. Everyone wants to be happy." Cord made a dismissive gesture. "Maybe a better question is, what makes you happy?"

Rylin swirled the champagne, buying time. Suddenly she

wasn't sure what made her happy anymore. "What do you dream about?" Cord tried again, seeing her hesitation.

"That's easy. My mom."

"That she's alive again?"

"Yeah."

Cord nodded. "I have that dream too," he said quietly, as serious as she'd ever seen him.

"My turn." Rylin wanted to edge away from this kind of talk. They were in Paris, after all. "Where do you go when you cut school?" she asked, genuinely interested.

"Wha— How do you know I cut school?" Cord asked sharply.

"I pay attention. Come on, it's my turn to ask questions, remember?"

Cord shook his head, laughing a little under his breath. "I'm sorry, I can't answer that one. Ask something else."

Rylin was still curious, but she let it go. "What would you have done if I hadn't come today?"

"Of course you were going to come. Why deal in hypotheticals?"

"But what if I hadn't?" she persisted.

"I'd have tried to return the tickets, probably. Or I might have come alone, you never know. Someone's got to get those éclairs for Chrissa."

"You aren't as much of an asshole as you pretend to be," Rylin remarked.

"And you aren't as tough as *you* pretend to be. Besides," Cord said, with a bit of a smirk, "my pretend assholedom got you here, didn't it?"

"*Paris* got me here," Rylin corrected, and Cord laughed.

"Well, then, to Paris." He lifted his glass.

"To Paris," Rylin repeated softly. She clinked her champagne to his in the flickering candlelight, wondering what exactly she thought she was doing. But she couldn't summon even a shred of regret.

Two hours later, stuffed with whipped pepper potatoes and an unbelievable animal-sourced steak—not the lab-grown stuff, but a real steak from a real cow that had lived and eaten grass and died—Rylin and Cord were walking back to the train station. At some point they had started holding hands, their fingers interlaced, Cord running his thumb lightly over the back of her wrist. It sent shivers up and down her body. Rylin knew she should pull away, and yet she didn't.

"Oh! It's the bridge of locks!" she exclaimed, catching sight of the Pont des Arts, which had been restored years ago with the same ultra-strong carbon composites used in the Tower. The moonlight silvered the padlocks fastened all over the bridge, where so many countless lovers had locked their hearts and thrown the key into the river. The sky stretched endlessly overhead, unobstructed by any tall buildings. The river lapped beneath their feet.

Rylin stopped in the middle of the bridge and turned in a slow circle, arms outstretched. She hoped, belatedly, that she wasn't being overly romantic by bringing Cord here. But of course she was. This was the lovers' bridge.

Sure enough, Cord stepped up to reach for her shoulders. Rylin's arms fell to her sides as she turned slowly to face him. *You can stop this*, she reminded herself, but she didn't, she couldn't, or maybe she just didn't want to. It seemed to Rylin that she was in a sort of trance, that time had halted and the whole world was holding its breath.

Cord's lips on hers felt like fire. Without another thought she was rising on tiptoe to kiss him back, clinging tight to his shoulders as the only solid thing in a dizzying world. She knew this was wrong, but Hiral felt so far away, like someone she'd imagined in another life.

Rylin wasn't sure how long they stood there, intertwined on

the lovers' bridge in Paris. Eventually Cord pulled away. His hair was disheveled and he was grinning, and he still hadn't let go of her hand. "Now," he said, "let's go get those éclairs for Chrissa, before we miss the last train back."

A splash sounded in the water behind them, as another pair of lovers tossed a key off the bridge and into the night.

WATT

IT WAS DARK inside Bubble Lounge.

Watt walked in slowly, trying to look around without making it obvious that he'd never been here before. The space was huge, with sable walls and a black-lacquered bar manned by pale, thin bartenders. The ultraviolet light overhead picked out spots of neon color: the napkins, the glitter on most girls' arms and faces, even their neon-painted fingernails. But most striking were the dozens of glowing neon bubbles, each about the size of a dinner plate, that floated around the room at eye level. Hence the name Bubble Lounge, Watt realized. He'd thought this would be a champagne bar, but that only showed how little he knew about the upper floors.

"Straw?" murmured a cocktail waitress, holding a platter of white straws, each about half a meter in length. Watt looked around and saw that each guest had one. People were using the straws to drink from the various bubbles, which apparently functioned like shared punch bowls.

"Um, thanks," he murmured, grabbing a straw and holding it at his side. *You didn't research this place, Nadia?*

I didn't realize you needed help figuring out how to drink alcohol, given how many times you've done it before.

Watt ignored her. He stepped deeper into the crowds, keeping an eye out for Avery's tall blond form. But before he saw her, he found another familiar face.

"Atlas," he said with a smile, sidling over to Avery's brother, who stood under an amber-colored bubble. "It's been a while." *If only you knew how much of my mindshare you've taken up recently, thanks to your crazy ex, or whatever she is.*

Atlas frowned, clearly struggling to place Watt, who held out his hand. "Watt Bakradi. We met on Carter Hafner's boat party last year," he lied.

"Watt, of course. I'm sorry." Atlas gave his hand a friendly shake. "That day was kind of a blur, to be honest," he added ruefully.

"Tell me about it," Watt commiserated. "What was that rum bar we ended up at? Where Carter fell into the pool of fish?"

"Ed's Chowder Shack!" Atlas exclaimed, laughing. "I'd forgotten about that! What a day." He held up his straw and took a sip from the amber bubble. "This one's whiskey and ginger ale, by the way," he offered. "Probably the only thing you'll want here. I begged Avery to order it; the blue bubbles are atomic and soda, and the pinks are champagne."

"My dad always said not to drink alcohol from a straw, because there's no way to look manly while doing it." That was true, actually. He chuckled at the thought of what Rashid Bakradi would say if he could see Watt here now, standing next to a billionaire and drinking whiskey from a floating bubble. "But what the hell. When in Rome, right?" He took a long sip.

"I'm in your dad's camp. We look ridiculous," Atlas agreed

with a laugh. "But the girls love this place, so we're stuck with it."

Watt nodded. "So," he said once Atlas had taken another sip. "I heard you were gone this year. Traveling, right?"

He felt Atlas stiffen a little, the ease between them gone. "I needed some time off," was all he said. "I'd already finished my high school credits fall semester, so I was eligible to graduate."

"Where'd you go? Anywhere worth recommending?" Watt tried.

"Tons of places. Europe, Asia—all over, really." Atlas didn't offer anything else. *Sorry, Leda. I tried*, Watt thought, murmuring a good-bye and moving deeper into the party. Atlas was as boring and introspective as all of Watt's hacking had led him to believe.

He saw Avery and Leda's other friend Eris first, standing at the center of a group of people, wearing a black leather dress that hugged her curves. He recognized her from all the pics he'd seen of her and Avery together. Her long hair spilled sumptuously over her bare shoulders, and her eyes, heavily lined with makeup, glowed golden in the light like a cat's. She was gorgeous, sure, in a bold, in-your-face kind of way. On any other night he might be trying to talk to her. But then Avery turned around and saw him, and the rest of the room dimmed by comparison.

"Watt." Her face broke out into that blindingly perfect smile. "I'm so glad you could make it."

"You throw a great party."

"This is Eris's favorite place," Avery offered by way of explanation.

"You wouldn't want to have your own birthday here?"

"I always try to do something a little less . . ." Avery trailed off, looking away.

"Less glow-in-the-dark floating drinks? Less tortured pets?" Watt nodded at Monica Salih's shoes, which had live neon jellyfish swimming in each heel. Avery snorted at that, and shook her head.

"Just . . . *less*," she said. "I like birthdays with nothing but a few friends, delicious food, maybe getting out of the city. Not checking our contacts a single time the whole day."

"Really?" Though Watt shouldn't have been surprised, given what she had said at Redwood Park the other day. "Where would you go?"

"Somewhere green."

"Don't you have a garden in your apartment?" He winced the moment he said it; he wasn't supposed to know that. "I just assume you would," he tried to recover, but Avery hadn't noticed the slip.

"Yeah, but it's hard to grow some things high up. A lot of plants need to put down deeper roots." She sighed, a little wistful. "I was in Florence on my birthday this summer," she went on, though of course Watt already knew her birthday was July 7. "Some friends and I rented boats and went out on the lake, and did absolutely nothing all day. I love that—just doing nothing. Here it feels like we're always trying to do too much."

"That sounds like a great birthday," Watt said, looking at her curiously. The more he talked to Avery, the more complicated she seemed. They were both seventeen, and yet sometimes it felt like she was far older, as though she'd already been everywhere and seen everything, and was exhausted by it all. Then she waved over a rose-colored bubble, laughing in delight, and suddenly she seemed young and girlish again.

"Have you ever—" Avery began, and Watt knew even before Nadia told him that she was going to ask if he'd been to Florence.

"Tell me more about your program," he said, neatly dodging the question. Avery took a sip of champagne and launched into an explanation, telling him about her classes, the funny boardinghouse she stayed in, the long road she took to class every day, past a cheesy New York–themed bagel shop that always made her laugh. Watt loved listening to Avery talk. God, he would probably listen even if she was just reading the dictionary aloud.

The conversation flowed easily between them. Watt was careful with what he said, not technically telling any lies about himself, but referencing enough names and real-life incidents that Avery didn't question his presence in her world. He tried his best to keep the conversation focused on her. And thanks to Nadia he was asking all the right questions, specific enough to seem insightful without being *too* specific. Every time Avery smiled, he felt a small rush of victory. He was at the top of his game.

And then, suddenly, she went pale at something she saw in the crowd. Watt turned to look behind him, wondering what had happened to upset her, but of course all he saw was a packed mass of people. "By the way, have you met Ming?" Avery said, and a girl with shoulder-length dark hair and a deep red smile stepped forward. "Ming loves that show too," she went on, and Watt remembered they'd been talking about something on the holos that he'd never even seen; he'd only referenced it because Avery followed it.

"Ming, this is Watt." Avery sidelined them both with a gracious smile. "Sorry, I have to go check on something. I'll be back," she promised, though of course she wouldn't be back and all three of them knew it.

"Hi, Watt. So where are you—" Ming began.

"Excuse me," Watt interrupted, and headed toward the entrance. He needed a moment to think, to clear his head and figure out what had happened to mess things up with Avery.

She wasn't *un*interested. He knew that much for sure. If she didn't like him at all she would have detached herself from the conversation much earlier. She'd talked to him for twenty minutes at least, practically an eternity at a party like this. She'd laughed at his jokes, been genuinely engaged, until something—or someone—had upset her. Maybe a friend, he guessed, or something to do with the party planning. *Or another guy*, a more cynical part of him thought.

Watt leaned against the wall, watching the glowing bubbles move slowly around the room like alcoholic blimps. Normally he would have given up by now, called it a sunk cost and moved on. The problem was, he didn't want to move on. He didn't want to talk to any other girls, not anymore.

You really like her, Nadia remarked when he didn't speak for a while.

Yeah, maybe. Watt's eyes were still glued to Avery as she moved through the crowded room, a bright golden beacon.

LEDA

LEDA PROWLED AROUND the edges of Bubble Lounge, clutching her ridiculous white straw so tight that it left an indentation in her palm. It was a great party—she expected nothing less from Avery—and she knew she looked amazing in her new one-shouldered dress. But Leda still felt unsettled. It was making her want to drink, even though she'd vowed not to have anything tonight, a vow she'd managed to keep. So far.

She saw Avery and Eris together toward the center of the room, and was momentarily struck by the old familiar envy. Avery, of course, was utterly perfect. But Leda was jealous of Eris too, of the way she somehow managed to stand there in a too-short leather dress looking like the queen of everything. It was in the way she moved, the easy confidence with which she carried herself, the scornful entitlement that echoed behind her commands. Leda would rather die than admit it, but back in seventh grade she'd tried to emulate Eris's movements before the mirror. She never could get it right.

She considered walking over to join them, but decided against it. Avery's weird hostility was really getting to her.

And why hadn't she seen Atlas yet tonight? Leda still wasn't quite sure what was going on between them. When their plans to hang out turned into the group AR game, she'd worried that he wasn't interested. But they'd been flickering back and forth ever since—about stupid stuff, just school and their favorite holoseries *Mike Drop* and whether it was worth going to the hockey team's away games this season. Leda felt certain that some of the flickers were flirty. Yet it had been almost two weeks since their almost date at the Altitude Grill, and Atlas still hadn't made any kind of move. What was he waiting for?

She eyed an amber bubble floating lazily nearby. One taste wouldn't do any harm, right? She allowed herself one long sip, relishing the feeling as the whiskey sent a pleasant warmth down her body, all the way to her toes curling in her tall silver heels.

The crowds in front of her shifted, and she caught sight of Atlas across the room.

Without another thought Leda was walking over. "Hey," she said, excited by the smile that flitted over his face when he saw her. "How's your night so far?"

"Oh, you know." He gestured at the room, the crowded guests, the effervescent bubbles. "It's all very . . ."

"Very Eris?" Leda supplied, and Atlas laughed.

"Exactly."

"And I heard about your new job," she added, wishing it didn't sound so much like small talk.

"Yeah. It's been great so far." Atlas had started working at one of his dad's portfolio companies, and deferred his Columbia acceptance till next fall. He shrugged. "I'm actually thinking of applying some other places for college, too, since I have time."

"You want to leave New York? Again?" No matter how long

she knew Atlas, Leda thought, she would never truly understand him.

"There are other places in the world aside from New York," Atlas said.

"Right, and because you backpacked around the world and spent a week in each of them, now you're an expert," Leda replied, a little provoked.

To her surprise, Atlas laughed. "You're right, I'm no expert. It's like they say, the more you see, the less you know."

Leda had never heard that expression. She was sick of trying to guess what Atlas meant, what he wanted. "You're confusing," she said frankly.

"So are you."

Leda watched Atlas take a sip from her amber bubble. The music seemed suddenly faster, in time with the frantic beat of her heart.

She couldn't take it anymore. Impulsively, just like she'd done in the Andes, she leaned in and kissed him.

He kissed her back. Leda moved closer, twining an arm up in his hair, all her nerves suddenly afire. Pure oxytocin was snapping through her veins. *Finally.*

But after a moment they pulled apart. Leda looked up to gauge his reaction—only to see *Avery* instead. Her friend was standing barely a meter away. She looked pale, her brows drawn upward in disgust and horror.

Leda blinked and took a step forward, but before she could say anything, Avery had turned and slipped into the crowd.

ERIS

FOR THE FIRST time in weeks, Eris's life was as it should be.

It was an incredible party. Avery had outdone herself on every detail, from the picstream projected in the side room to the customized straws that said HAPPY BIRTHDAY, ERIS! in tiny glowing letters. Bubble Lounge was more crowded than Eris had ever seen it. Everyone who was anyone was here: talking, drinking, celebrating *her*.

The only no-show that bothered her a little was Cord. She didn't expect them to hook up tonight or anything, but she'd thought he might still come, as a friend. Parties were always more fun when Cord was there. She briefly considered flickering him, but after the way they'd ended things she wasn't sure she wanted to.

Another part of her—a small, stupid part of her—wondered if she should have invited Mariel. Not that she wanted to hook up with *her* again either. But Mariel had been nice to her when no one else was, and Eris couldn't help thinking, a little uncomfortably, that she'd wronged her.

Stop it, Eris told herself, determinedly pushing those memories aside. This was her party and nothing could ruin it.

"Eris?"

She turned around, a little surprised to see Leda approaching her alone, without Avery. It wasn't that she didn't like Leda, exactly. They just never had much to talk about. Eris always felt that Leda said one thing and meant another, as if she were secretly amusing herself at everyone else's expense. Even her compliments seemed double-edged.

But standing there now, Leda looked earnest, almost hopeful. "Happy birthday! What an amazing party," she exclaimed.

"Thanks. It was all Avery, though," Eris said, venturing a confused smile.

"I was wondering . . ." Leda took a breath, hesitant. "I mean, I wanted to ask you, has Avery said anything about—"

"Eris!" Ming was cutting a line through the crowds toward her, a strange smile playing around her mouth, which was paint-sticked a shocking deep red. "Avery's looking for you in the side room."

Eris started to turn, but Leda was standing there. "Do you want to—" she started to ask, but Leda shook her head, something unreadable in her eyes.

"It's okay," Leda said. "Go be the birthday girl."

Eris nodded, excitement thrumming through her as she fell into step alongside Ming. She could feel the glances of everyone in the room following their movement, the murmurs as they commented on the party, admired her dress. She stole another glance at Ming, who was walking stiffly alongside her. She'd always found the other girl irritating, the way she simpered around after her and Avery, copying everything they did. But her conversation with Leda had put her in a strangely generous mood. "That dress looks great on you," she said, nodding at Ming's gold-sequined shift.

"Mmm." Ming acknowledged the compliment noncommittally.

"Are you having fun?" Eris tried again, a little irritated.

"Of course. Are you?" When Eris nodded, Ming smiled again. "Well, it'll be a night full of surprises," she said mysteriously.

"I *knew* Avery had something else planned!" Eris exclaimed as they turned the corner. She gasped at what she saw. Floating in the center of the room was a stage, decorated with pink glitter and holding a multilayer cake as tall as Eris. Avery, Risha, and Jess were already on the middle of the platform. As it sailed slowly past Eris and Ming, Avery leaned over the side, and the two girls climbed up to stand next to her.

"I can't believe this!" Eris laughed, delighted at her best friend's secrecy.

Avery just smiled and pulled her into a hug. "You deserve it," she said, and pushed Eris toward the center as the stage floated higher, lifting over everyone's heads to float back into the main room.

The music playing through the speakers came to a sudden halt. The room fell to a hush, everyone looking expectantly at Eris. She thought her face would break from smiling so wide.

"Thank you all for coming," she said into the microphone, and they all broke out in a raucous cheer. She waited for the commotion to die down, basking in it. "And thanks to Avery, for planning everything."

Avery stepped forward, her own voice amplified throughout the room. "Happy birthday, Eris!" she exclaimed.

"After-party later!" Ming jumped in, pushing forward. She looked pointedly at Eris. "Not at your place, I'm guessing, right?"

Avery recovered first. "Eris isn't hosting an after-party, but maybe I can—"

"Yeah, that makes sense. I assumed Eris couldn't host, given her dad's thinking of selling the apartment. My mom is the broker assigned to appraise it," Ming persisted. She turned to Eris, her eyes all innocence. "I guess you aren't renovating, like you told everyone?"

Eris knew with a sudden sinking feeling what was going on. This was about Cord, and the snide comment she'd made before yoga last week, and all the other infinite micro-aggressions she'd inflicted on Ming. She'd brought this on herself, in a way.

"Um, well, we thought about it, but then—"

"I wanted to throw you an after-party at the Nuage," Ming went on, relentless, "but I went to their special events desk, and they said you weren't staying there." A few murmurs rose up in the crowd. Eris felt her face redden. "Where *are* you living, Eris?"

"Well, we're moving, and—"

"Happy birthday to you," Avery interrupted, throwing her hands into the air to illuminate the candles, which lit up with custom pink flames. The song continued, but in a halfhearted way. Eris could see that everyone was murmuring to one another, looking things up on their contacts. Ming had started something, and now the insatiable gossip machine wanted answers.

Tears pricked at the corners of Eris's eyes. She looked out over the party she'd been so excited about all evening, the beautifully dressed crowd and expensive booze bubbles, and felt suddenly like an imposter. Her old life didn't belong to her anymore. She was a nobody who would go home to a cramped, cockroach-filled apartment two miles below them. She couldn't even return to her old apartment if she wanted to, because her dad apparently might sell it. She'd known he was staying at the Nuage, but she hadn't quite realized how painful the apartment must be to him, with all the memories flitting around it like ghosts. She felt an aching sense of loss, at the realization that she'd likely lost her childhood home forever.

It was the last fragment of her old life, falling away for good. She wasn't Eris Dodd-Radson. Not anymore.

The song died down. "Make a wish, Eris!" Avery said brightly, but Eris just shook her head, not trusting herself to speak.

"Eris—" Avery reached for her, but it was too late. Eris had turned and was running blindly out of Bubble Lounge, tears streaming down her face for all the world to see.

LEDA

"THERE YOU ARE."

Leda strode violently over to where Avery was standing alone, drinking from one of the bubbles. Its blue light flickered over her face, picking up the glo-makeup dusted on her lips and eyelids, making her seem almost otherworldly. Most of the girls here were wearing that glow stuff, except for Leda. It always came out clownish on her darker complexion.

"Hey, Leda," Avery said wearily. She started to turn away.

"Are you *serious*?" Leda reached to grab Avery's wrist. She was done acting like nothing was wrong. She'd tried to talk to Avery earlier, right after she and Atlas had kissed and Avery had looked so horrified about it, but she'd lost her friend in the crowd. She'd been forced to wait until Avery came down from a *floating birthday cake*—which she hadn't invited Leda to join them on. God, Leda had even gotten so desperate that she'd attempted to ask *Eris* for advice. She didn't know what else to do anymore.

Avery's eyes narrowed. "I was trying to ping Eris again, if you would just *let me go*."

Leda dropped her friend's arm as if scalded. "Why have you been avoiding me?"

"I'm not avoiding you," Avery said, her voice eerily calm.

"It's about Atlas, isn't it? You don't think I'm good enough for him," Leda said, and it wasn't a question. "You looked really upset when you saw us together."

Avery flinched. She seemed to be struggling with what to say. "I guess it's a little weird for me. My best friend and my brother."

"I get that it's weird. But don't you think you're overreacting, just a little?" *Weirdness* didn't explain why Avery had been cutting Leda out of her life since the start of the school year. Something else was going on.

"You could have at least *told* me that you liked him."

"Clearly I was right not to, since this is how you're reacting," Leda snapped, frustrated.

Avery crossed her arms over her chest. "I just don't want to see you get hurt."

"Can't you see I'm already hurt?"

Avery's mouth opened, but no sound come out. "I'm sorry," she managed, and Leda could hear the strain in her words.

"I just want things to go back to normal." Leda watched her best friend's face. She hated that it sounded like she was begging. But she didn't care about her pride anymore. She missed Avery, and she'd apologize for anything she had to just to make things right between them.

Avery sighed. "Leda," she said, "you're the one who started acting strange, and keeping secrets from me."

"Oh my god," Leda breathed, because now it all made sense. Avery *definitely* knew. "Atlas told you, didn't he? About the Andes?"

Avery pursed her lips and didn't reply. Leda pressed onward, the words coming out so fast they were tripping over one another. "I'm sorry I didn't tell you sooner. But you were already in New York for surgery, and it only happened that one time. And then Atlas *disappeared*, and I didn't want to bring it up." It felt so good to say this at last, to clear the air between them once and for all.

"Yeah," Avery said cautiously.

Leda looked down. "I know it's stupid and clichéd, losing it to your best friend's brother. That's part of why I didn't want to tell you. I felt so embarrassed, you know? I thought it actually might *mean* something. But then he just ran off."

Avery had gone pale, and wasn't saying anything. Leda floundered a little. "It's just . . . I really like him," she persisted. "Even if you think it's a bad idea. I want to at least try."

"Right. I mean, of course," Avery said woodenly.

"I'm sorry," Leda said again. "I know I should have told you. I promise, no more secrets between us." *Except for rehab,* her mind whispered, but she shoved that aside. It wasn't important right now.

Avery nodded slowly. "I get why you didn't tell me," she said. "And even though I'm . . . a little weirded out"—she laughed, but there was no humor to it—"I'm happy for you guys. Now, um, I really need to go ping Eris. Is that okay?" She turned toward the entrance.

"Okay," Leda said softly. But she knew with a sinking feeling that her apology, or confession, or whatever it was, hadn't worked. Things between her and Avery were still strained.

It isn't fair, Leda thought with a new wave of bitterness. What more did Avery want from her? Was she supposed to just accept the role of Avery's sidekick, accept that Avery would never let Leda date her beloved brother? And why did Avery get to call all the shots, anyway?

Leda stood there alone, anger emanating from her in mounting waves. She pulled the engraved white straw out of her bag and began searching for an amber bubble.

AVERY

AVERY STUMBLED DOWN the hallway, cursing as she tripped over a vacuum bot, her breath coming in deep, ragged gasps. She knew she shouldn't have left early from a party she had thrown, but there was no way she could stay.

It had been awful enough seeing Leda and Atlas kiss. She'd run away from Watt mid-conversation and fled to the side room, where she sent a bartender for a tray of atomic shots—she needed something stronger than what was in the bubbles—and knocked back several of them by herself. Then she'd shakily gathered the others for Eris's surprise. Which had turned out to be yet another disaster.

She'd still had a handle on things, though, until Leda capped off the night by telling her how she'd *slept* with Atlas. At that news, Avery's last shreds of self-control had snapped.

Now she was home, running into the pantry, flinging open the door and yanking down the ladder, her elaborate updo shaking loose. She pushed on the trapdoor, feeling dangerously on edge as she stepped out onto the roof.

There was a downpour coming; Avery could feel it. The wind was already gaining strength, tearing out the last of her hairpins, whipping her dress close to her body. The air was heavy with the scent of rain. Avery leaned on the railing. Her thoughts circled frantically in her mind, pressing so hard she thought she would burst.

A falcon that had been perched farther along the railing turned a beady eye on her, curious. Avery watched it unfurl its wings and take off. She felt a sudden kinship with the bird, the way it flew screaming into the sky like a wild thing. She wished she could follow it straight into the gathering storm.

"Avery?" Atlas's voice sounded behind her.

She realized in a panic that she'd left the trapdoor open. But Avery's fear was immediately followed by a perverse wave of relief that Atlas hadn't gone home with Leda.

"What is this?" he asked, walking unsteadily toward her.

"The roof."

Atlas nodded. It was a sign of how drunk he was that he skipped right over her sarcasm. "We should go back down."

"You go. I like it up here."

Atlas shot her a look. "Wait," he said slowly, "have you been up here before?"

Avery didn't answer, just stared out at the dark line of the horizon in the distance.

"How did you find this, Avery?"

She shrugged. "I just did, okay?" She was still angry with him for sleeping with Leda, which she knew wasn't fair.

"We should call maintenance and have them close it off."

Avery whirled around to face him, panic rising in her chest. "You can't! Then I'll have nowhere to go!"

"What do you mean, you'll have nowhere to go?" He came to stand next to her at the railing, nervousness flitting across his expression as he saw how very high they were. "You have plenty of places to go."

"Yeah, well, *this* place helps me clear my head." She stared determinedly down into the shadows below, trying to keep from crying. The roof was all she had left. She was losing Leda, she'd already lost Atlas, and now she was about to lose the only place she could escape.

"Are you okay, Aves?"

"I'm *fine*," she protested.

"Avery." He reached out to touch her arm. "What's going on?"

"Leda told me," she said flatly, still looking fixedly away from him. She knew she shouldn't bring it up, but some stupid part of her wanted to. "About January, in the Andes."

Atlas was quiet for a moment. "I'm sorry I didn't tell you before," he said, using almost the same words Leda had used earlier. Avery wanted to laugh at the absurdity of it all.

"I know she's your best friend," he went on, watching her. He was speaking very slowly, as if he were choosing his words as carefully as he could. He was even drunker than she'd realized.

"You didn't go home with her tonight, though."

"No, I didn't."

"Do you love her?" Avery blurted out. She dreaded the answer but she needed, desperately, to hear it.

There was another silence. Avery couldn't really see Atlas's face in the darkness. "I don't . . ." He trailed off. Avery wondered whether he was about to say he didn't love Leda—or didn't know.

"How could you?" she whispered.

He turned to look at her. His face was an unreadable shadow against the darkness of the sky.

Then he leaned in and kissed her.

Avery froze, hardly daring to breathe. The touch of Atlas's lips on hers was featherlight, tentative, uncertain. She closed her eyes as the kiss sent a thrill through her body, until it felt like her hair was standing on end, like her whole body was a live wire, humming with electricity. She wanted to wrap her arms around Atlas, to pull him close and never let go. But she didn't dare move, terrified to break the spell.

Finally Atlas pulled away. "Night, Aves," he said before clattering down the ladder and out of sight.

Avery stood there in a daze. Had that really just happened? She braced her palms on the railing for balance, feeling dizzy.

The skies began to open overhead. Sudden rain poured down, the droplets so cold and fast that they stung Avery's face. But she couldn't move. She just stood there like a lightning rod as the storm gathered around her, her feet rooted in place, a hand raised to touch her lips in wonder.

RYLIN

RYLIN STOOD AT the back of the Ifty car, clutching an overhead metal railing as the train slowed to a stop at Bedton. The Tower narrowed as it got higher, so unlike Cord's floor, which was only several blocks square, the 32nd floor was enormous. It stretched the whole breadth of the Tower's base, from 42nd Street all the way up to 145th, and from East Avenue to Jersey Highway in the west. Hiral lived on the same floor as Rylin, but almost thirty blocks away, at least fifteen minutes on the Ifty.

A giggling posse of twelve-year-old girls piled onto the railcar, and Rylin turned her music up louder, trying to drown them out. She needed to think. Her mind was jumbled, everything from yesterday morning onward all blurred together and confused. But from the tangled knot of her feelings she'd extracted a single crucial thread.

She didn't love Hiral anymore.

She hadn't loved him for a while now. Maybe she never had.

She'd certainly thought she did, back when they were so young that words like *love* and *grief* described burgers and exams. Back when their biggest problems were things like the air regulator in Rylin's apartment breaking—Hiral had climbed up into the vents to fix it for them—or when Hiral forgot his brother's birthday and Rylin helped him bake a cake last minute. Before Rylin's mom died, and they both became harder, flintier versions of themselves.

She'd arrived home from Paris last night and stumbled straight into bed. For once Chrissa's snoring didn't even keep her awake. This morning she'd woken to find Chrissa already at volleyball practice, a bacon bagel in the toaster and a pod of coffee in the brewer. Rylin sat for a while at the kitchen table, picking the bacon chunks from the bagel like she always did, thinking over everything that had happened. Finally she stood up with a sigh and got dressed.

After all this time, she was going to break up with Hiral. Yet she didn't feel guilty, or even very sad—only relieved, and vaguely nostalgic for the way they used to be. She knew Hiral wouldn't take it well. He didn't like change; he would've been fine staying with her indefinitely, if only out of sheer inertia. He would agree with her eventually, though, wouldn't he?

The Ifty slowed to a stop again, and Rylin swayed forward, toying with her Eiffel Tower necklace. She didn't quite understand what was going on between her and Cord, but whatever it was, she wanted to see where it headed. She'd been surprised at how much fun she had had with him yesterday—of course she'd loved Paris, but it wasn't just that. It was being in Paris with *Cord*.

She got out her chunky gray MacBash tablet and tried pinging Hiral again, but he didn't pick up. *Are you awake? I'm coming over*, she wrote, biting her lip in impatience. She'd thought about waiting till this afternoon, tomorrow even. But she hated delaying any action once she'd decided on it. As her mom used to say, better now than later.

She stepped off the Ifty at Niale, the closest stop to Hiral's family's apartment. Most of the shops that littered the main thoroughfare were still asleep, their neon signs flashing booze logos or one-stop clothing stores, or the tech pawnshops that everyone knew carried stolen holo hardware in their basements. A stray cat peed into a doorway. Pets were supposed to exist in the Tower by permit only, and permits were expensive; but no matter how hard Animal Control tried to clear them out, the cats always reappeared. Rylin remembered the time Chrissa had brought home a bright orange kitten, its ribs sticking out starkly beneath its scruffy fur. Their mom had let Chrissa feed it, but later that night Rylin had caught her nudging the kitten out the front door. "We can't afford it," Rose had said defensively to ten-year-old Rylin, who had nodded. The next morning, they both told Chrissa it had run away.

Rylin kept her head down as she turned right, toward the residential area, and onto Hiral's street. The occasional worker walked past on the way to an upper-floor service job, their starched uniforms and glazed exhaustion giving them away.

"Rylin!" Davi, Hiral's mom, answered the door while Rylin was still knocking. Her broad face broke into a smile. "Come in, come in."

Rylin shifted her weight, staying in the doorway. "I was wondering if—"

"*Hiral!*" Davi bellowed, not that she needed to; the apartment was barely bigger than Rylin's, and for twice as many people. Hiral's older brother, Sandeep, had just moved out last year; but Hiral still shared a room with his brother Dhruv, who'd been in Rylin's class at school before she dropped out.

"I think the boys are still asleep." Davi turned to her. "Can I make you some breakfast while you wait?"

"I'm okay," Rylin said quickly.

"Some tea, at least." Davi's tone brooked no argument. She put her hands on Rylin's shoulders and steered her forcibly toward the kitchen. Instaphotos of the family were tacked all over the fridge. Rylin's attention was caught by a pic of her and Hiral at an eighth-grade formal, back before they both became too cool for stuff like that. Rylin had on a bright green dress that brought out her eyes, and her arms were wrapped tight around Hiral, whose face looked rounder and more boyish than it did now. She'd forgotten about this party, this photo. How long had it been since she came to the Karadjans' apartment? Whenever she and Hiral spent time together anymore, it was always out somewhere.

"I haven't seen you in a while," Davi said gently, clearly thinking the same thing. "How are you? How is your sister?"

"We're okay." Rylin wished Hiral would hurry. Here she was, about to break up with him, and his mom was being so damned nice.

"You know you can always come to me, whatever you need." Davi curled Rylin's fingers around a mug of hot tea.

"I—"

"Ry?" Hiral stepped into the kitchen, wearing nothing but the black fleece sweatpants she'd gotten him last year. "What's up?"

"How many times have I told you to wear a shirt around guests!" Davi exclaimed.

"Rylin's not a guest," Hiral protested.

"I was wondering if you wanted to go on a walk," Rylin jumped in, before Hiral's mom could reply. She didn't want to do this here.

"Sure." Hiral shrugged. "I'll just get a shirt, I guess."

But as they turned back toward the narrow hallway, a sudden banging sounded on the front door. *"Police!"* a low voice yelled, pounding relentlessly.

"Get back," Hiral's mom hissed, pushing them both aside and

setting her shoulders in determination. Rylin glanced at Hiral. His face was ashen.

Davi opened the front door. "Can I help you, officers?" she asked, standing squarely in the doorway to block Rylin and Hiral from view.

"We're looking for Hiral Karadjan. Is he home?" The two officers were trying to push through, craning their necks to see inside.

"I'm sorry, what—"

"We have a warrant for his arrest."

Rylin made a strangled noise deep in her throat. Hiral shot her a look, panicked, but it was too late; the police were already barging past Davi to surround him. "Hiral Karadjan, you are under arrest for the distribution and sale of illegal substances. You have the right to remain silent. Anything you say can and will be used against you. . . ." The officer's voice was gruff. His partner flashed a search warrant and stormed into Hiral and Dhruv's room, where Dhruv mumbled an outraged but sleepy protest. The officer ignored it and began overturning furniture, lifting up mattresses, sifting through drawers. Rylin knew he wouldn't find anything. She wasn't sure where Hiral kept his drug stash, but he was too smart to keep it at home.

Davi stood aside, wringing her hands. Rylin felt Dhruv come to stand beside her. Rylin reached for his hand and gave it a supportive squeeze. She couldn't look away from Hiral. His upper lip was curled into a sneer, his bare shoulders flexed as his wrists were yanked behind his back and fastened with magnetic cuffs. Something in his eyes seemed almost frightening.

Rylin stood there as the police took Hiral away, her whole body trembling with shock. "What are we going to do?" Dhruv turned to her.

"I don't know," Rylin whispered. She wasn't really sure of anything anymore.

LEDA

LEDA STOOD AT the Fullers' entryway, debating whether to ring the doorbell or just let herself in. If she were here to see Avery, she would already be inside by now; Avery had added her retinal scan to the instant access list years ago. But Leda wanted to see Atlas.

She decided to push the button, shifting Atlas's coat onto one elbow. He'd put it over her shoulders last night, when she shivered in the hover home from Bubble Lounge. It had seemed like a good sign. Until the hover pulled up to her place, and he wished her good night before she had a chance to invite him inside. He hadn't even tried to kiss her at all.

Maybe he didn't like her, a doubtful voice in her mind whispered. Maybe he liked someone else. After all, *she* had been the one to initiate their kiss at Eris's party. Yet he'd kissed her back easily enough.

Still, she was glad he'd forgotten to ask for his jacket back at the end of the night. It was the perfect excuse to drop by and see him.

No one was answering her entrance comm. Leda looked up into the retinal scanner with a sigh, and the door obediently swung open for her. "Atlas?" she called out, walking into the enormous entryway. She gave an involuntary glance at the mirrored walls, where her reflection—looking almost slinky in a casual wrap dress and gladiator sandals, her hair carefully styled, her makeup flawless—danced alongside her.

"Leda?" Avery walked in from the kitchen, wearing a monogrammed knit robe and alpaca slippers, her hair a wild blond cloud around her perfect face. Leda felt a flash of irritation that she'd worked so hard to get dressed up this morning, yet Avery looked better without even trying.

"Hey," she said cautiously. She wasn't sure what the protocol was anymore, between her and Avery.

"You're up early." Avery gave a self-conscious shrug, looking down at her robe and slippers. "Or maybe I'm just moving a little slow."

"It was a great party," Leda said lamely.

Avery shuffled one fluffy slipper against the floor. "Thanks. I meant to tell you, by the way, I loved your dress. Was it new?"

"Yeah." *Oh my god*, Leda thought, *we sound like complete strangers.* Is this what it was going to be like now, this weird stilted politeness? It was worse than not talking at all.

They stood looking at each other in some weird kind of détente. Leda realized that she hadn't even set foot in this apartment since school started. Normally she was here all the time, treating the space like her own home, eating from the fridge without asking. Now she wouldn't have even taken a seat on the couch without being invited first.

"Do you want to sit down?" Avery asked, as if reading her mind. Her eyes darted to Atlas's jacket.

"It's okay," Leda hurried to say. "I was just looking for Atlas."

"I can give that to him for you." Avery reached for the jacket, but Leda took a step back, clutching it tight.

"Actually I was—"

"Leda?" Atlas appeared in the hallway, looking even more hungover than Avery. His eyes were bloodshot, his face pale under a shadow of stubble, and he was still wearing his crumpled white dress shirt from the night before, though he'd managed to put on red mesh athletic shorts. Leda felt a strange sense of relief. Surely this was the reason he hadn't tried anything with her at the end of the night: he'd gotten so drunk he needed to send himself home.

"Hey," she said, ignoring Avery. "Crazy night last night, huh?"

"Tell me about it." As Atlas stepped forward, Leda saw something on his collar—the unmistakable glint of glo-makeup, just barely visible in the morning light.

The entire world began spinning. *Atlas kissed someone last night.* Someone who had been at the party. How else could that horrible makeup have ended up there?

"Anyway. I just wanted to give you this." She tossed Atlas the jacket, pleased at how cool her voice sounded.

"Thanks." He snatched it from the air, seeming caught off guard. "So, um—"

"I have to go," Leda said quickly. "See you guys later."

They both called out good-bye, but Leda was already in the hall. She kept her eyes forward, avoiding the incriminating glances of all the mirror Ledas moving alongside her, reminding her of her pathetic attempt to look cute for a boy who didn't even care, who had another girl's makeup smeared all over his shirt.

"To Nadia," she muttered as she got in the elevator, composing a new message. "I think Atlas was with someone last night. I need to know who."

As you wish, the hacker replied. A moment later there was an additional line of text. *But if I need to hack someone else aside from Atlas, it'll cost extra.*

"Tell you what. You find this out for me, I'll *quadruple* your usual fee," she snapped in reply.

The elevator doors opened and Leda walked briskly out, already feeling a bit better. There had never been a problem she couldn't solve, once she set her mind to it.

Except Atlas.

Well, she wasn't giving up yet. Not without a fight.

AVERY

AVERY WATCHED HER best friend walk away. She knew she should say something, shouldn't let things end on this note, but she was too focused on Atlas to think clearly. She'd been waiting all morning for him to wake up, her whole body tingling with a heady, delirious sense of anticipation. She'd barely kept herself from running into his room and jumping on his bed the way she used to every Christmas.

Their kiss on the roof last night was replaying nonstop in her mind. And Avery was brimming with questions. How would they handle things, after what had happened last night? What would they tell Leda? What would they do about their parents? "Atlas?" she said, not sure exactly how to phrase this—only to realize that he wasn't looking at her. His eyes were focused on where the front door had just shut behind Leda.

"Yeah?" he asked slowly, turning to her.

Avery's resolve faltered. Why wasn't he smiling at her, now that they were alone?

"I was wondering . . . um . . ."

A beep sounded from the kitchen, indicating the arrival of a food delivery. The next thing Avery knew, Atlas was walking in to pick it up, not even looking at her. She followed him, deflating a little, as he reached for the delivery box that had just been whisked up from their favorite bakery.

"Wait. You ordered from Bakehouse?"

"Yeah. Want one?" he asked, and she shook her head.

She couldn't believe it. She'd been pacing her room all morning, her heart about to burst—while Atlas had been lying in bed ordering *waffles*?

"Sorry. What was it you wanted to ask me?"

"Oh—I . . ." A sick worry settled over her. She couldn't do it. "Never mind," she said, trying to play it off.

This was all wrong. Avery wanted to scream. She stirred a rehydration tablet into a glass of orange juice, just to have something to do.

"Can I have one of those?" Atlas said awkwardly, after a moment. Avery wordlessly tossed him the bottle. "Thanks," he went on, and popped a couple of the tablets. "God, I'm really hungover."

"It was a crazy night, wasn't it?" She hoped it would provoke him. She couldn't believe he was doing this, pretending the kiss had never happened.

"You throw great parties, Aves." The microcooker beeped and Atlas pulled out the waffle, dousing it in syrup. He was still doing that thing where his eyes didn't quite meet hers. "I can't remember the last time I got after it that hard. Those whiskey-soda bubbles . . ." He shook his head and took a huge bite. "Man, I'm hungover," he said again.

"Me too," Avery agreed, at a loss. What was going on? Atlas was just sitting at the counter, eating breakfast as if it was any old morning—as if they hadn't *kissed* last night. As if the entire world hadn't just shifted on its axis, as if the very fabric of Avery's existence hadn't been forever changed.

Could Atlas really have been so drunk that he didn't remember what had happened? Or worse, was he pretending it hadn't happened because it didn't mean anything to him—because he regretted it?

"Avery? This just arrived for you." Their maid, Sarah, stood in the doorway, hugging a flower arrangement in a hammered metal tin. Avery immediately glanced at Atlas, wondering if he'd sent it. Maybe he'd just been acting cautious earlier, and the flowers were his way of showing how he felt while keeping everything a secret.

Avery strode over, keeping her robe tied close around her, and pulled the heavy cream notecard from the side of the flowers. *Avery,* was written in antique loopy handwriting on the front. Of course, she thought with a little thrill of pleasure, Atlas remembered her favorite calligraphy style. She opened the note, hiding her smile.

But it wasn't from Atlas. *Some long roots, for your greenhouse,* it read. *Watt.*

Watt? Avery registered, bewildered. She thought back to their conversation last night. Who was this guy, exactly, and why didn't she know more about him? She buried her face in the bouquet to hide her confusion and inhaled deeply. It was an intoxicating scent, light and airy. Avery realized that the flowers had been very carefully selected, baby's breath and peonies and a single white rose at the center. All flowers with long roots. And there was soil in the tin, which was wide and deep. These plants weren't cuttings: they were all still alive, so if she wanted to, she could try to transplant them to deeper soil.

Watt had clearly put a lot of thought into this gift. She was touched, in spite of everything.

"Should I take them to your room?" Sarah asked.

"What about right here instead, on the kitchen table?" Avery's eyes were on Atlas as she said it. She hoped the flowers would elicit some kind of reaction from him: jealousy, or at least curiosity. But he was just chewing his waffle, not even looking their way. "Atlas, what do you think of these?" she pressed, irritated.

"They look great."

He hadn't even asked who sent them. Her heart aching, Avery leaned her elbows on the table and looked down at her new flowers. They seemed so beautiful now, but they were all doomed, she thought darkly, their tiny roots racing toward the inflexible confines of the pot.

She broke off a sprig of baby's breath and tucked it into the pocket of her robe, then retreated to her room and shut the door quietly behind her.

ERIS

ERIS STOOD IN line at the grocery on the corner, a tiny shopping basket slung over one arm, clutching a stack of coupons that flashed with the cheap instapaper of lower-floor flyers. Her mom had transferred her a few nanodollars so that Eris could buy dinner for tonight. Caroline was out meeting with "someone very important," she'd said, putting on a white pressed blouse and pearls for the first time in weeks. Eris had wondered, briefly, if that someone was Everett. Not that she really cared what he did anymore. Besides, it was much more likely that it was some kind of job interview, she'd concluded, losing interest.

On the bright side, she'd have the apartment to herself tonight, instead of sitting across from her mom at the high-top table where their knees bumped each other, eating noodles and veggie broth in silence.

Eris had been alone a lot recently. Ever since her disastrous birthday party, when everyone learned the truth about how poor she was, she'd felt isolated and left out. Of course, all her friends kept *saying* that everything was fine; they'd all texted her supportive messages the next day, still hung out with her at school, repeatedly asked if she needed anything. Not that Eris really believed them. Being friends with Avery was staving off the worst of it, but she still walked through the hallways at the center of a storm of whispers, eyes following her every movement. She could hear people murmuring in pitying tones about how terrible it must be, even though many of them, Eris knew, were probably glad to witness her fall from grace.

She'd come straight home from school every day for the past week, actually doing her homework for once—she had nothing else to do—and going to bed early, where she lay blinking up into the darkness. Even after she finally fell asleep, her dreams were filled with locked rooms and frantic chases down endless dark hallways, a far cry from the flying dreams and Technicolor fantasies she used to upload to the Dreamweaver.

Overall, it had been a pretty awful week. Eris wished she had someone else to bother aside from Avery. If only she and Cord were still hooking up, she could at least escape to his place. She kept pausing at Mariel's apartment each time she walked home, only to sigh and keep going. Given the way she'd ignored Mariel after that night two weekends ago, she couldn't exactly knock on the door and just ask her to hang out.

She shifted her weight impatiently. Everything was so much faster on the upper floors, where robots scanned groceries and charged for them via contact-link in a matter of seconds, then whisked them away to be delivered by drone. But she was learning that nothing down here was automated or efficient.

Finally Eris stepped up to the register, and the grizzled old cashier began clicking at her items with an ancient-looking hand-held scanner. Eris zoned out, her gaze traveling over the dusty displays of cheese product; the nut-butter dispenser grinding its loud gears; the girl working the next cash register over, with a long sand-colored braid and wide, sad eyes. She looked about thirteen.

"That'll be sixty-two dollars and twenty-six cents," the cashier intoned. Eris dug her tablet out of her bag to wave it over the scanner, and the machine gave an angry beep. "It looks like the transaction was denied," the cashier said, irritation creeping into his voice. "Do you have another account you can use?"

"Oh, um—" Eris looked down, her fingers flying over the screen as she pulled up her account balance, and felt suddenly nauseous. She had less than fifty NDs in her account. When the hell had *that* happened? "Sorry," she mumbled, her face turning bright red, "let me just take out a few things, then you can ring me up again." She heard muffled complaints from the customers in line behind her, and wished she could just sink into the floor and disappear.

She kept the meganoodles and pasta sauce, hesitating between losing the chicken or the chocolate–key lime ice cream cup. Finally, with a little sigh of defeat, she put aside the ice cream. "This should go through," she said as a hand reached from behind her to pluck out the ice cream.

"You know you can add up the price of everything while you're shopping." Mariel rolled her eyes. "And if you can't do the math, there's a program for it on your tablet."

"Hey," Eris said quietly, unsurprised. "How's it going?" She took her bag of groceries, the transaction approved now, and stood aside as Mariel's few items were scanned.

"Like you care." Mariel swiped her tablet and tossed Eris the ice cream cup. "Here you go."

"It's okay, you don't have to do that." Eris followed Mariel down the hallway, feeling discomfited. She hadn't quite realized Mariel was buying the ice cream cup for *her*.

"I did have to. You looked so pathetic about it." Mariel shrugged. "Consider it a late birthday present. I saw on the feeds that you celebrated last weekend."

Eris felt a stab of guilt. "Look, I didn't—"

"Forget it. You don't owe me anything."

"I'm *sorry*!"

A few heads turned to look at them, curious, and Eris lowered her voice. "I'm sorry," she said again, fumbling the words; she wasn't used to apologizing. "What I did was shitty. It's been a rough month for me. I didn't mean to . . ." She trailed off helplessly. "Anyway, I really am sorry. Thank you for the ice cream."

"Whatever. It's fine." They had reached Mariel's door. She pushed on it with her hip; it was unlocked, and she started to step inside.

"Wait!" Eris hated begging, but she was already here and what the hell. "Do you want to maybe do something tonight?"

Mariel laughed once, darkly. "Sorry, Eris, I can't just clear my schedule every time you need a hookup."

"I meant as friends." Eris tried not to sound defensive. "I just . . . I don't know anyone else down here. It's been lonely."

"I have plans tonight. And I don't mean a party," Mariel said, but her voice had softened a little. Eris wondered if she'd struck a chord.

"Can I come?"

Mariel raised an eyebrow, studying her. "You're not eating your ice cream."

"Please?"

Mariel snatched the ice cream cup from Eris's hand and ripped off the lid, then stuck a red-painted nail in and took a bite with her finger. "Mmm. Chocolate–key lime. Excellent choice.

And yes," she said as Eris opened her mouth again, "you can come. But if you do, there's no ducking out early. Also, no drinking the wine."

"So it *is* a party," Eris said triumphantly.

Mariel just laughed again, saying nothing.

"You brought me to *church*?" Eris hissed, standing outside the hulking carved wooden doors of the Cathedral of St. Paul. "You do know it's Friday, right?"

"My mom works weekends, so we always go Friday night instead of Sunday morning." Mariel turned to Eris. "You can head home, if you want."

Eris hesitated. They weren't far. She'd never even noticed this church, but it was barely ten blocks from their street. "No," she decided.

"No leaving early," Mariel reminded her, and pushed on the heavy door, which swung inward. She dipped her hand in the holy water next to the entrance. When Eris passed the marble font without taking any, Mariel sighed, and turned to rub a few droplets from her thumb onto Eris's forehead. Eris stood absolutely still.

She followed Mariel down a side aisle and into a pew, where a middle-aged couple with dark hair and a boy who looked about twelve were already seated. Mariel's parents and brother, Eris guessed. Mariel whispered something that Eris couldn't hear, gesturing at her. They all smiled and nodded at her, then faced forward as the choir began to sing.

Eris looked around, curious. It was cool and dim inside, most of the light blazing in from the stained-glass windows that lined the walls. Eris knew they weren't anywhere near a side of the Tower, so these must be false windows, lit up from behind with solar lamps. The ceiling arced high overhead, taking up all of the next floor and maybe even some of the 105th. Stone statues of people in robes and halos lined the walls.

Belatedly Eris realized everyone was kneeling. She hurried to follow, sliding down onto the cushioned kneeler. They all began chanting something she didn't know the words to. She looked over at Mariel. "Just pray," Mariel whispered. So Eris closed her eyes and let the unfamiliar words wash over her.

For the rest of the service she followed the movements of the congregation: sitting, kneeling, standing, sitting again; humming along with the songs and sitting quietly during the prayers. The choir was enchanting, their voices mingling with the piano recordings to weave a kind of temporary magic over her. Eris felt soothed, almost peaceful. Her mind wandered. She thought about her parents—what they'd been like when they met, when her mom was just a young model who left her career for an older man, and her dad fresh off his second divorce. She let herself imagine her birth father; where he was now, what traits they shared.

She looked over at Mariel's family, the four of them holding hands, and found herself hoping that everything would turn out all right for them. And for her own twisted, broken family too. Maybe that's all that praying was, she thought, just wishing good outcomes on other people.

The priest said something and everyone was suddenly on their feet, shaking hands, murmuring good wishes to one another. It was utterly foreign to Eris, this idea of touching people you didn't even know. But it was nice too—being someplace where no one judged her, or cared about her history, or even knew her name. After she'd shaken hands with Mariel's family and the entire pew in front of them, Eris finally turned to Mariel. "Peace be with you," she whispered, her voice a little scratchy.

"And with your spirit," Mariel said in return, clasping Eris's hand.

As they sat back down, Mariel didn't quite let go. Instead she ran her hand along Eris's arm to intertwine their fingers. Eris said nothing, just looked straight ahead, but her hand was tightly interlaced with Mariel's. She gave Mariel a little squeeze, and after a moment, Mariel squeezed her back.

They sat quietly holding hands for the rest of the service.

————

When mass ended, Eris followed Mariel's family as they joined the other churchgoers streaming out. After the calm peacefulness within the church, the world outside suddenly felt loud and over-crowded. Eris jumped a little as a medical hover, its siren wailing, swerved angrily past.

"Thanks for letting me come to church with you," Eris said. Mariel just nodded.

"Eris," Mariel's mom said, breaking the silence. "Tell me about yourself. What brought you and your family to Baneberry Lane?"

Eris shot Mariel a glance, surprised that the other girl hadn't shared any of this. "My family is going through some stuff," she admitted. "It's actually just me and my mom down here. My parents are splitting up." It was easier each time she said that, she realized. Maybe eventually she would be able to say it without wanting to cry.

"I'm sorry to hear that," Mariel's mom said, and surprised Eris by giving her a hug. Eris had never been hugged by anyone else's parents before, not even Avery's. "Do you and your mom want to come over for dinner?" she asked as they stepped up to her apartment.

Eris hesitated, surprised at how much she wanted to stay. "My mom is out, but I'd love to," she admitted.

Mariel's mom grinned and stepped inside. Mariel stood there looking at Eris, a funny expression on her face.

"What is it? Do you not want me to stay?" Eris asked.

Mariel shook her head. "No, it's just . . . Every time I think I've figured you out, you do something unexpected."

Eris laughed. "Good luck with that," she said. "Even I haven't figured me out, and I've been trying for eighteen years."

Mariel rolled her eyes and led Eris inside.

Eris sat contentedly at the Valconsuelos' kitchen table—turned out that was Mariel's last name—while Mariel's parents clattered pots and pans around in their warm, cozily cluttered kitchen. Moments later Eris heard the sizzle of tomatoes and sausages cooking. Her mouth watered; she hadn't had anything lately but canned food and takeout, except what she got at the school cafeteria.

Dinner was delicious, and cheerfully chaotic. Eris loved the way the Valconsuelos kept teasing and challenging one another, arguing about some basketball match, naming players Eris had never even heard of. Finally Mariel's dad went to take a ping in the bedroom, and her mom led a yawning Marcos out of the room. "Eris and I have got the dishes," Mariel volunteered, watching Eris's face.

"Oh, Eris is a guest," Mariel's mom called out from the hall-way.

"I'm happy to help," Eris insisted, and stood up to clear the table, gratified by the astonishment in Mariel's expression. *Please*, she thought, amused, *I can handle washing a few plates.*

They cleaned the kitchen in silence. "Why did you let me come with you tonight?" Eris asked after a while.

Mariel shrugged. "You said you were lonely. Mass always helps me, when I'm feeling that way."

Finally, when everything was cleared, Mariel reached up to

turn out the overhead lights and clicked on an artificial candle. "Sorry," she said, setting the candle in the middle of the table. "We're just trying to lower the electric bill."

"Is that my cue to leave?" Eris asked, feeling a little reckless.

The candle made strange shadows dance across Mariel's face, strong-boned and willful, her eyes pools of darkness that Eris couldn't read. She'd never felt this way about anyone before—that they were achingly familiar and yet at the same time a stranger. She started to reach across the table for Mariel's hand, but Mariel yanked it away, shaking her head.

"It *is* your cue to leave, actually," Mariel said, and sighed. "I can't go down that road with you again, Eris, knowing how it will end."

Eris knew she should go, but Mariel was leaning forward imperceptibly, her eyes locked on Eris's. She hadn't quite made up her mind yet. "It won't end the same way this time," Eris heard herself say.

"Why should I believe that?"

"What if we take things slow?" Eris offered, standing up. She wasn't sure why she wanted this, exactly, but she knew that she did.

Mariel tilted her head in consideration. The candlelight caught the cheap red stones of her earrings, a spark of red fire against the dark curtain of her hair. "Maybe," she said at last.

Eris nodded. "You know where to find me," she called out, and shut the door behind her.

Eris Dodd-Radson, she thought, *self-professed queen of the casual hookup, offering to take things slow. Who would have guessed?*

RYLIN

RYLIN STOOD IN her kitchen, her tablet pressed to her ear, trying to get through to the police station yet again. It had been a week since Hiral's arrest, and they still hadn't put him on the approved list for visitors. What was taking them so long?

"Hi," she said, the moment the front desk officer picked up. "I'm calling to ask about Hiral—"

"Miss Myers, like I told you yesterday, your boyfriend isn't cleared yet," the guard snapped, recognizing her voice. "We'll let you know, okay?" With that, he hung up.

Rylin leaned her elbows on the counter, her head in her hands. Even if she didn't love Hiral anymore, she hated the thought of him in jail, suffering. She'd gone to see his parents every night over the past week, just to check on them, to assure them that Hiral was innocent and everything would turn out fine. Dhruv would look at her, an eyebrow raised, and Rylin would blush at being caught in the lie. But what was she *supposed* to tell the Karadjans—that there wasn't any hope?

She sighed and kept packing Cord's sleek silver cooler with electrolyte drinks and energy bars. In spite of everything else going on, Rylin was determined to make it to Chrissa's volleyball tournament this morning. She hadn't seen Chrissa play in months. She was even bringing team snacks like some of the other girls' moms always did. It had been Cord's idea, actually; he'd insisted on lending her the cooler, because of course Rylin didn't own one.

A smile played around her lips at the thought of Cord. It was weird, how easily he'd transitioned from being her employer to . . . well, to whatever he was. It was weird—and yet it also felt natural, almost inevitable.

Cord had insisted on continuing to pay her all week, claiming it was his fault that she'd gotten fired from the monorail job. Rylin took the money—she couldn't exactly afford not to—but she determinedly kept cleaning despite Cord's assurance that she didn't need to. The only times she left were to go on interviews for other jobs, none of which had worked out. She'd been rejected from five positions in the past week. "I don't see why you won't just stay here," Cord kept telling her. "You should be going back to school instead of getting another dead-end job. You're too smart for that stuff, Rylin." It was tempting, the idea of just taking Cord's help, but Rylin was already uncomfortable with the imbalance in their relationship. Maybe he *was* right about graduating, but she'd have to figure out the money some other way first.

Still, she and Cord had spent more time together since Paris; in the afternoons when he got home from school, or wherever it was that he mysteriously disappeared to. They stayed mainly at his place, just hanging out, watching holovids, laughing—and kissing. There was a lot more kissing. They hadn't gone further yet, though, mainly because Rylin felt guilty. She needed to break up with Hiral before anything else happened. Which she was desperate to do: she felt twisted up inside, living a lie.

A knock sounded on the door. Rylin looked up, startled, and went to answer it.

"Lux!" she exclaimed, giving her friend a hug. Lux was wearing silky gray drawstring pants and a tank top, the same candy-apple green as her ponytail. "Your hair this week would look fantastic with my eyes," Rylin added, with a nod to the new color.

Lux gave a halfhearted smile at the observation. She was still in school, but worked afternoons at a hair salon up on the 90th floor, cleaning the dye-cones and sweeping cut locks of hair off the floor. The stylists didn't care when Lux used the dye on herself, and as a result her hair was now a constantly shifting kaleidoscope of color. "You've barely answered my texts this week. I was getting worried," Lux said.

"I'm sorry. It's just been kind of crazy." Rylin felt a stab of guilt. She hadn't meant to ignore her friend; she just hadn't known how to respond. Lux had been texting her constantly since Hiral was arrested, probably assuming that Rylin needed cheering up. If only she knew the truth, Rylin thought, that she was trying to break up with Hiral but hadn't been able to yet. And oh, by the way, she was starting to have feelings for the upper-floor guy she worked for.

"That's why I've been trying to reach out, Ry," Lux said softly. She lifted her hand in an exasperated gesture, and Rylin saw that she was holding a brown recyclable grocery bag. "I brought over stuff to make chocolate-nambo pancakes. Thought you could use a little breakfast comfort food. But it looks like you're busy." She glanced from the cooler to Rylin's brushed-out hair and cute blue dress.

Rylin smiled, remembering all the times her mom had made those pancakes when they were kids. They were nothing special, just banana mix pancakes with chocolate flakes thrown in. Chrissa loved them and always tried to ask for them, but she couldn't pronounce *banana* yet, so she'd run around the kitchen exclaiming "Nambo! Nambo!" until Rylin and Lux produced the pancake mix box, and her toddler face would break out in a grin of recognition.

"Chocolate-nambo pancakes sound amazing," Rylin said truthfully. "But I was just heading to Chrissa's tournament. Want to come with me? And then we could all do breakfast for dinner later?"

Lux hesitated, then nodded. "Sure," she said, still watching Rylin, clearly confused by something in her expression.

"How is everyone?" Rylin asked as they left the apartment, realizing how little she'd seen of her friends since she'd started working for Cord. "Have you seen Andrés or V lately?" V in particular she wondered about—she still didn't understand how Hiral had gotten caught, while V, who handled a much higher volume, was still dealing like normal.

"We went to the steel forest last night. The DJ was kind of lame, so we ducked out and just did halluci-lighters in that back corner by the Seventieth Street exit." Rylin knew that corner. It was where they'd all smoked up for the first time, several years ago, and she'd felt so hungry suddenly that she thought she might puke. *It'll pass*, Lux had assured her, giggling, *and when it does it'll suddenly feel amazing*. She'd been right.

"It's not the same without you and Hiral, though," Lux added.

"Yeah. I'm worried about him. I just want to *talk* to him, but they won't let me." Rylin sighed as they stepped out of the Ifty stop near school, the cooler rolling gently along after her. Lux eyed it, but didn't say anything.

They reached the wide double doors of the Irving Middle School gymnasium. Rylin felt a strange twitch of apprehension, being back here. It had been a while since she had set foot in a school.

They filed into the gym as the tournament was starting. It was just the way Rylin remembered, musty and faintly smelling of sweat, with a scratched-up polyresin floor. Rylin didn't understand how the gym, which like everything in the Tower was only twenty years old, already looked like something out of the last century. Probably because no one maintained or cleaned it, ever.

The gym was crowded; Rylin knew this was a district tournament, but she hadn't quite realized what a big deal it was. There was Chrissa and the rest of the Irving team, huddled on their side of the net, their heads bent together. Their school's holographic mascot, an enormous gray wolf, prowled around the stands, eliciting squeals from a few of the younger spectators. Rylin even saw a few of those mini hovercams that flew around behind the star players, projecting their perspective onto the giant screens overhead.

She and Lux slid onto one of the rows of benches. Chrissa was about to serve, weighing the ball in her hand and rocking back onto her heels. Her dark ponytail swayed back and forth. Rylin watched, a little awed, as she tossed the ball into the air and slammed it across the net.

"She's really good," Lux whispered.

Rylin nodded. "Yeah." She loved watching Chrissa, the way her body would be crouched utterly still, then slam into sudden action with all the ruthlessness of a machine. She moved gracefully, like a dancer, like she was in one of those fancy low-grav chambers and her feet barely touched the ground. Rylin's heart clenched in pride. At times like this, everything she had given up seemed worth it.

Her tablet buzzed with a message from Cord. *Dinner tonight?*

I can't, Rylin replied, with a glance at Lux, whose eyes were fixed on the game. She needed this time with her friend. *We're doing breakfast for dinner. You know how it is.*

Breakfast for dinner is only worth having if it's breakfast in bed, Cord replied. Rylin bit back an exasperated smile, and slid the tablet back into her pocket—but not before Lux caught the expression on her face.

"Good news?" Lux asked.

Rylin wished desperately that she could tell Lux everything. But she wasn't sure Lux would understand. How could she, when Rylin didn't even really understand it all herself? "Not really," she said, hoping Lux would drop it.

When the game was over and the buzzer sounded, Rylin dragged the cooler down to where Chrissa's team was all gathered, Lux following behind. Their faces were flush with victory, and they were all high-fiving one another. "Rylin! I didn't know you were coming! And Lux!" Chrissa exclaimed, pulling Rylin into a sweaty hug. There was a small red patch stuck on her lower arm—a VitalsMonitor, Rylin realized, to track Chrissa's heart rate and metabolism, and the contents of her sweat.

"When did you get that?" she asked.

Chrissa shrugged. "They're making everyone who's early recruiting wear them," she said, and Rylin had a sudden flashback to the night in the steel forest, the last time she'd worn a patch of her own. It felt like ages ago.

"You brought snacks?" Chrissa went on, catching sight of the cooler and grinning in delight.

"I know, I'm totally the coolest older sister here." Rylin wheeled it forward and opened the top, and the girls began eagerly reaching for drinks.

Chrissa grabbed an electrolyte drink and took a long, slow

sip. Then she lowered the bottle and stared at Rylin. "You look different," she said. "Is it your hair?"

"You're confusing me with Lux," Rylin said lightly, and Chrissa laughed.

"You're right. It's probably just that you're wearing a dress," Chrissa replied. But Rylin knew what Chrissa was seeing, even if Chrissa hadn't figured it out yet.

Somehow, despite everything that was going on, Rylin was happy.

LEDA

"**MOM? ARE YOU** here?" Leda called out as she walked inside. She shivered a little, damp with sweat, still wearing the white nausea-blocking wristbands from antigrav yoga. It had only been Leda and Ming in class today. Avery hadn't come to yoga with them for over a week now. She claimed she was trying to run more often, but Leda knew Avery was avoiding her—and Ming, whom Avery still hadn't forgiven for what she'd done at Eris's party.

Leda and Avery had barely spoken since that weird interaction the next morning, when Leda had shown up with Atlas's jacket. They didn't even sit next to each other at lunch anymore. One day Avery had just walked up and taken the seat on the end, next to Eris, leaving Leda to slide in between Risha and Jess. No one said anything about the shift, yet Leda felt they were all watching her, waiting for a reaction that she refused to give.

And then there was Atlas. Nadia insisted that he hadn't seen anyone else that night: she'd even hacked the centralized hover records, found the one that picked him up, and proved that he went straight home after dropping off Leda. She saw it herself, right there in the hover's tracked itinerary. He didn't go back to the party, or to any other girl's house. And yet . . . Leda still couldn't shake the feeling that something was going on, if she could only figure it out.

Leda wished she could stop obsessing about the Fullers. But they were everywhere—hell, just now when she'd headed to the Altitude juice bar after yoga, she'd almost run into Avery and her family leaving brunch. She'd ducked instinctively into a corner as they passed, just to avoid talking with them. She knew she was acting insane, but she couldn't face Avery *or* Atlas. At least not until she felt a little more in control of everything.

"Leda?" Her mom's voice came from her office. "What do you need, hon?"

Leda went into the kitchen and began punching buttons on the liquifuser, making herself the cashew smoothie that she'd wanted before she had to flee the juice bar. What did she need? To fix things between her and Avery. To have sex with Atlas again. Anything except what she was doing right now, because her current strategy clearly sucked.

"Nothing, I guess," she replied, not really sure why she'd yelled for her mom. The smoothie poured itself into a chilled glass. Leda sprinkled it with cinnamon before taking a sip. She couldn't shake the image of Avery and Atlas and their parents walking through Altitude all together, something proud and fierce and tawny about all of them.

"How was the workout class?" Ilara Cole appeared in the doorway.

"It was fine," Leda said impatiently.

"Your father and I have the Hollenbrands' party tonight," her mom reminded her. "I'm not sure what Jamie's doing. Do you and Avery have plans?"

"I think I'm staying in tonight. I'm kind of tired, actually," Leda hurried to say.

She was annoyed by the flash of relief in her mom's eyes. Ilara hadn't been too pleased that Leda had gone to Eris's birthday last weekend, but Leda had promised she would be fine, that she wouldn't drink. She hadn't *really* broken the promise all that much, she told herself. Though it was hard to keep track of, drinking from those absurd bubbles.

"Why don't you have Avery over? I can have Haley stay and make homemade pizza for you girls," her mom offered. She reached up to tuck a loose curl behind Leda's ear, but Leda jerked her head away.

"I told you, I'm fine!"

"Leda." Her mom's voice lowered in concern. "Is everything okay? Do you want me to schedule an appointment with Dr. Vanderstein?"

Leda was spared from answering by the front door's beep. Her dad must be home. Thank god, because the last thing she wanted was an appointment with her mom's shrink. "Hey, you two," he said, walking into the kitchen. He sounded exhausted. "How's it going?"

"Where've you been?" Leda asked. Her dad was usually home on Saturdays, falling asleep on the living room sofa. Or if he had to work, taking calls in his office.

"I golfed with Pierson and a new client, at Links." He spoke into the fridge as he grabbed a lemon spritzer.

"Mr. Fuller?" Leda repeated. An internal alarm sounded.

"Yes, Mr. Fuller," her dad said shortly, as if she were being ridiculous to even ask. She held her breath to keep from saying anything. She'd seen the Fullers at brunch just twenty minutes ago; Mr. Fuller couldn't have been golfing all morning. Why had her dad lied?

"How was the game?" Ilara walked around the counter to give Leda's dad a quick kiss.

"Well, we let the client win, which is the most important thing." Her dad laughed at his own joke, but it rang a little false, as if his mind were elsewhere. Was he hiding something? But her mom just smiled and nodded, oblivious.

"I'm going to shower," Leda said shortly, grabbing the remains of her smoothie.

She stormed down the hall and slammed her bedroom door shut behind her. Quickly she began to peel off her damp exercise clothes, tossing them into the hamper in the corner, which fed directly to the laundry room. Hugging herself, she stepped into the shower and turned her rain ceiling on, setting the steam at full blast. But for some reason she couldn't stop shivering.

Leda lowered herself to sit on the shower floor, made of red tiles that had been reclaimed from a villa on Capri. Leda had picked them out herself, on vacation two summers ago. Her hair curled into wiry tendrils in the aromatherapy steam. She pulled her knees to her chest and tried to think. Her mind felt scattered, spinning wildly from one subject to another. Kissing Atlas at the party. Who else he was seeing. Why her dad was lying about where he'd been. The expression on Avery's face lately, when she saw Leda in the hallways at school. The way Leda pretended it didn't bother her at all.

Everything was wearing on her. Weighing on her. The water stung like a million tiny needles pricking at her raw skin.

She needed a hit.

She still had the flick-link for her old dealer, Ross. It had been Cord who connected them; she'd had a few too-close calls, stealing her mom's xenperheidren, and one night at a party she decided to ask him for help. She didn't know who else to turn to. Leda knew it was risky, putting her secret in Cord's hands like that, yet she sensed that under all his bluster, he had his own sort of loyalty.

"Sure," he'd said when she asked, and sent her a flick-link labeled simply *Ross*.

Ross gave her xenperheidren, all right, as much as she wanted. But he gave her other stuff too, stuff she didn't even pay for. "I have all these extra relaxants," he'd said once, when she bought several xenperheidrens before the PSATs. "Why don't you take a couple? You'll probably need them, after your test." And so she did.

It wasn't long afterward that Leda started smoking up occasionally with Cord and his friends, sometimes Brice. A couple of times she tried harder stuff, for no real reason except that she was curious about it; but she refused to let herself do it too often. It was just kind of nice every now and then, loosening her grip on herself, which was normally twisted so very tight.

And she was totally fine until last winter—until Catyan, and Atlas's disappearance. That was when Leda had *really* started to lose it.

Hey. How's it going?

Leda's head shot up at Atlas's message. *Hey*, she replied cautiously, trying to ignore the excitement shooting through her veins. *I'm good. What's up?*

I was wondering, do you want to go to the University Club thing with me?

Leda closed her eyes, flooded with a giddy relief. *Yes*, she replied. *I'd love to.*

She relaxed for what felt like the first time in weeks, taking deep, rose-scented breaths, letting the skin of her hands wither into prunes. It didn't matter how much water she used; it was all being collected and filtered for some other use anyway. So she stayed, letting the tension seep out of her tired body.

Eventually Leda stood and began to thread soap beads into her hair, feeling almost settled again. The way she used to feel, back in the safety of the Silver Cove meditation tent.

AVERY

SUNDAY EVENING, AVERY sat at her family's massive hand-carved dining table, trying to focus on her asparagus and not the infuriating boy across from her.

"Atlas, I spoke with James today and he said you're doing very well. That you've stayed late every night this week?" Pierson Fuller nodded at Atlas across the table, scraping his fork as he took a bite of almond-baked salmon.

"Yeah. I'm trying to learn everything as fast as I can, prove that I can do the work even if I didn't—you know. Graduate high school."

"You *did* graduate high school, you just didn't walk with your class!" Avery's dad exclaimed, at the same time her mom cried out, "Everyone knows you took a gap year! It's very common to travel at your age! I did!"

Atlas ignored them and looked at Avery. "Hey, Aves, can you pass the pepper?" he asked.

Don't think you can "Aves" me and everything will be back to normal, Avery thought, pursing her lips and sliding the auto-spicer across the table to him. Typical Atlas, trying to stir drama from their parents in an attempt to cheer her up. But it wouldn't work this time.

She looked out the window to avoid making eye contact with him. It was a foggy night, moisture clinging in droplets to the floor-to-ceiling windows that lined three of their dining room walls, obstructing the views that normally looked out toward the East River.

Ever since Atlas came home, the Fullers had been eating meals as a family more often. They had dinner almost every night now; they'd even had brunch yesterday, on a Saturday, when her dad was usually out golfing and her mom neck-deep in spa treatments. Avery had loved it at first . . . until last weekend's kiss. Now she just felt confused. Atlas had been the one person she could confide in, and she didn't even know how to talk to him anymore. It seemed impossible that they could just go back to normal, yet Atlas was apparently doing it easily enough.

Avery almost wished the kiss had never happened. Almost, but not quite. Because at least now she had the memory of it, could replay it in her head as often as she wanted. It was torture sometimes, remembering the brush of his lips, the warmth of his breath on her cheek, the way his hands had rested on her waist. But Avery couldn't bring herself to regret it. If she never kissed anyone again, she knew she could live on the memory of that kiss for the rest of her life.

"By the way, Atlas, I placed your new tux order today." Elizabeth Fuller drew her perfectly lasered brows together into a frown. She clearly wanted to know what had happened to the last one but refused to broach the subject. Normally Avery would have been curious too, but right now she couldn't make herself care. Probably Atlas had forgotten it at some stupid yacht party in Croatia. Avery made eye contact with her mom, and they exchanged a look.

It was often baffling to Avery that half her genes actually came from her mom. Of course, it was all the unexpressed recessive genes, the ones that her mom carried but didn't demonstrate, that Dr. Shore had mined out and given to Avery. Because the two of them truly looked nothing alike.

Avery's mom was far from beautiful. Her frame was too stout and her arms were too short, and her hair, no matter how much time and money she spent treating it, tended toward frizzy. But she attacked her appearance with the gritty determination of a full-time job, undergoing annual plastisurgeries and a grueling Pilates regimen. Still, Avery knew her mother was achingly self-conscious about the way she looked. It was the whole reason she'd insisted they pay so much, to ensure that Avery would never have to worry about it.

"Well, the tux will be ready for the University Club fall gala," Elizabeth went on. "By the way, are you two taking anyone?"

"I'm going with Leda, but her family are members anyway, so you don't need to get her a ticket," Atlas answered.

That was news to Avery. She reached for her glass of merlot—thankfully her parents were laissez-faire enough to serve wine to their teenage children—and took a long sip, the light glinting on the ruby liquid in its unbreakable flexiglass. She was floored that Atlas was still talking about Leda, after kissing *her*.

"Oh, that's wonderful," Elizabeth said, clearly a little surprised. "Pierson, should we have the Coles at our table, then? I'd asked the Reeds and the Delmonds, but I think we can bump up the table size to ten. . . ."

"Whatever you want," Avery's dad murmured, probably trying to read messages on his contacts.

Great, Avery thought, *now the parents are involved*. It felt more real that way, as if Leda had now officially become Atlas's girlfriend.

"Are you going with anyone, Avery?" her father asked. Concern crept in at the edges of his tone. He was always asking Avery why she wasn't dating anyone, as if Avery's single status was the most confusing puzzle the world had ever presented him.

Avery hesitated. She hadn't given much thought to the fall gala, but now that Atlas was going with Leda, she wanted to be there, and with a date, to prove that she was as unaffected by the kiss as he was. But Zay had gotten sick of waiting around for her and was officially with Daniela now, so she couldn't ask him. She briefly considered Cord—he was always fun at these things—but Atlas knew she and Cord were just friends, so it wouldn't make him jealous.

Avery's eyes darted to the flowers that Watt had given her, still in their hammered metal pot on the kitchen counter. A few of the baby's breath had died, but the white rose at the center was in full bloom, its velvet-soft petals beautifully unfurled. *Why not?* she thought. Watt had seemed to know a few people at Eris's birthday—which she hadn't really expected him to come to, though now she was glad he had. Actually, hadn't she seen him talking to Atlas at one point?

"I'm bringing Watt Bakradi. The guy who sent me those." Avery gestured to the flowers. She looked at Atlas's face as she said it, watching for some kind of reaction, but he seemed as nonchalant as ever.

"I wondered who those were from!" Avery's mom exclaimed. "I'll add another ticket to our order. How do you know him, Avery?"

"I don't, really. Atlas knows him, though," she said pointedly. Atlas looked up, clearly confused. "Didn't I see you talking to him at Eris's?" Avery went on, still on the offensive. Let Atlas think she'd had eyes for Watt all night.

"Right. Watt! He's a nice guy," Atlas said, and turned back to his risotto.

"Well, I look forward to meeting him. It's going to be a lovely evening." Elizabeth smiled.

It'll be something, Avery thought, wondering what exactly she'd gotten herself into.

WATT

WATT LEANED LAZILY on one elbow, bubbling in the answers to his honors American history midterm. Everyone around him had spent days cramming for this exam—he could practically hear the gears in their minds whirring as they scoured their brains for facts they didn't know, their styluses faltering as they decided what guess to make. Poor suckers. They had to rely on their own flawed, human memory to pass this test. Unlike Watt.

Not even the tech-net surrounding the school—which rendered everyone else's contacts and tablets useless—could affect Nadia; she was far too sophisticated. Currently she was flashing the answers to each question onto Watt's eyes, even suggesting which ones he should miss on purpose. After all, he knew better than to get 100 percent on every exam he took.

Watt put his stylus down and looked out the window at the vertical garden that surrounded the school, ferns and succulents crawling over walls in an explosion of viridescence. "Two minutes remaining," said the preceptor, Mrs. Keeley, with a shake of her overly hair-glued helmet of hair. There was a small shuffle of anxiety from the other twenty kids in the class, not that Watt could see them, thanks to the invisibility screens that separated everyone on test days. He just kept looking out the window.

If only Watt could find a way to prove that Atlas wasn't hooking up with anyone. Ever since Leda's message last week—that she would quadruple his pay if he could figure out who Atlas was seeing behind her back—he'd been working nonstop, tracking Atlas's movements and cross-referencing them with every girl who could have possibly been there. So far, nothing. Watt had a feeling there *was* nothing to turn up, because Leda was being paranoid and crazy.

Especially because he now knew Leda was a recovering xenperheidren addict. He hadn't done a deep dive into her past before, just pulled up her feeds that first day she hired him. Until the other day, when in a fit of frustration he'd asked Nadia to track everywhere Leda had been, ever. Nadia had been the one to discover Leda's stint in rehab. Now Watt was even more convinced that Leda was wrong about Atlas—she was seeing things that weren't even there.

He wondered what was going on with Avery lately too. He'd hoped that the flower arrangement he'd sent to her house would win her over, or at least spark a conversation, but all she'd done was send a polite thank-you flicker when she received it. It had been over a week since then, and he'd barely heard from her at all.

The bell rang signaling the end of class, eliciting a frantic tapping from the other students as they filled in the last bubbles before their school-issued tablets closed out of the exam. Watt just stretched his arms overhead in a lazy stretch. Depending on the grading of the essay, which Nadia had composed and he'd tweaked to sound more authentic, he should have scored somewhere between a 95 and a 98 on that midterm.

He slung his backpack over one shoulder and started out into the hallway. Girls stood at their lockers, conjuring up temporary mirrors with their beauty-wands and checking their hairstyles. The football team passed by in athletic gear, heading to the hoverbus that would take them to the practice field three floors down, in the Park Zone. Banners strung in the hallways changed from yellow to purple, alternately reading CONGRATS, JEFFERSON: HIGH SAT SCORES 3 YEARS RUNNING! and HOMECOMING DANCE: BUY YOUR TICKETS! A paper airplane, lifted on tiny microhovers, whizzed overhead as if by magic.

"Killer exam, huh?" Cynthia, an Asian girl with wide-set eyes and black bangs who'd been friends with Watt and Derrick since middle school, fell into step alongside him.

"Yeah, definitely." They walked out the main double doors to stand in the broad paved area in front of school. Directly across the street was an Ifty stop, and an ice cream parlor that they'd cut class to go to countless times. Derrick was standing in the crowd of kids along the edge of the tech-net, all of them eagerly looking through their messages and feeds. He started over when he saw them.

"Hey, Cynthia," Watt said suddenly, "can I ask your advice on something?"

"Absolutely not. I've told you before, don't come to me with your girl stuff. Just because we're friends doesn't mean I approve of what you do when I'm not around." She raised an eyebrow, challenging.

"How did you know . . ." Watt fell silent as a flicker appeared on his contacts.

"I hear things," Cynthia said.

Watt couldn't believe it. The message was from none other than Avery. *Hey, I hope you had a good weekend*, it read. *I was wondering, if you're not busy Saturday, do you want to come to the University Club fall gala with me?*

Watt couldn't hide a smile of excitement. The flowers had worked after all. *I'd love to*, he replied, sending the message transcranially through Nadia.

Great! I'll send you the details. Just a heads-up, my parents and brother will be there too. It's kind of a family thing, Avery added, and Watt could almost hear the caution in her tone. Well, he didn't care if he had to charm Avery's grandparents and cousins and the guy who cut her hair. He was going to be Avery Fuller's date.

"What things do you hear?" Derrick asked, having fought his way through the crowds to join them.

"Watt asked me for girl advice, but I refuse to get involved. Honestly, I feel sorry for whoever his next victim is," Cynthia explained, with mock solemnity.

"He came to *you* for advice?" Derrick scoffed. "Is this about Avery? Wow," he said, turning to Watt, "you must be more desperate than I realized."

"Actually," Watt interrupted, "she just invited me to an event. The University Club fall gala." He tried not to sound smug, but he couldn't help it. He'd done the impossible, and gotten Avery Fuller to ask him out. He felt like doing a victory dance.

"The University Club? Who is this girl?" Cynthia sounded skeptical.

"She's a highlier," Derrick volunteered, as if that explained everything.

Watt nodded, but he wasn't really listening. He pulled up Avery's message and instructed Nadia to help with a witty but confident reply. *Sounds great*, he began. *And*—

"You know the University Club is formal," Cynthia went on. "You probably need a tux."

Watt looked up sharply at that. "I need a tux? Are you sure?" Now he really needed that bonus payment from Leda. He'd never bought a tux, but he knew enough to know they weren't cheap.

He looked back at his contacts, about to finish the message— and realized in a panic that the words he'd spoken had just been sent to Avery: *sounds great, and I need a tux, are you sure?*

What the hell, Nadia? You knew *I didn't mean for that to go to Avery*, he thought at her, furious.

You were in message-composing mode, Nadia replied. *Perhaps if you upgrade me, I will be better able to intuit unspoken intentions.* He thought she sounded sarcastic. Stupid recursive algorithms. He should have just programmed her with linear logic the way most quants had been, before the ban.

Watt squirmed, wondering how he could damage control this, but Avery had already replied. *Yeah, it's black tie. I can help you shop for a tux. I know exactly where to go!*

"You definitely need a tux at University Club," Cynthia was saying.

Derrick laughed. "Where the hell are you going to get the money for a tux?"

"He can rent one, you moron. There's a rental place on this floor. On the east side, I think," Cynthia added, trying to be helpful.

But Watt was focused on his reply to Avery. *It's okay. Mine just got red wine spilled on it at my last event.*

Well, if you end up needing a new one, I'm happy to go with you this week.

Watt was about to protest again, trying to hide his embarrassment, his complete inexperience with formal events and really her whole world in general. But Nadia chimed in before he could think of a reply. *I hacked the store records where Avery usually shops*, Nadia volunteered, sounding almost apologetic. *It doesn't seem that she's gone with anyone but her brother in the past. I calculate this as a good sign, that she's offering to take you there?*

I'm still annoyed with you, Watt replied. But Nadia was right. What was he thinking, turning down a chance to spend time with Avery, no matter where it was? *Okay . . . I may take you up on that after all*, he flickered to Avery.

"I'm not renting," he said, in answer to Derrick's question. He'd finally gotten his chance with Avery, and he wanted to do it right. "I've got some money saved. It'll be fine."

"I just hope this girl is worth it." Cynthia looked curiously at Watt.

"And you said you didn't want to get involved," Watt teased, purposefully dodging the question. Of course Avery was worth it.

Derrick laughed. "Are we still studying calculus at your place tonight?" he asked Cynthia, who nodded. They normally had a rotating study schedule during midterms week, though they rarely came to Watt's place anymore, because the twins were too loud and disruptive.

"Can't," Watt said. He loved hanging out with his friends, but he didn't actually need the study time. He wanted to focus on the Atlas thing instead so he could hopefully collect payment from Leda before tux shopping.

"But my mom already made your favorite cookies!" Cynthia protested as Watt waved good-bye.

Back at home, Watt grabbed a bag of cheesy popcorn from the pantry, then settled at his desk and pulled up his view screen. "Nadia," he said aloud, "we need to hack the Fullers' home system. Now."

"You want to joint-hack?" Nadia asked, sounding almost

excited, if that were possible. The longer he spent with Nadia in his head, the more he attributed human emotions to her, Watt thought.

"Yeah. Let's do it." It had been a while since he and Nadia had needed to hack something together. Most of the time Nadia was faster on her own, without his interference. But every now and then, when a system was especially complicated—usually the idiosyncratic ones, the ones that had been coded by insanely creative human designers—they were better off together.

Watt settled in, finding his rhythm, his fingers flying across the touch screen as he manipulated pieces of invisible information, like pulling on the strings of a massive, intricate net. He and Nadia worked well together. Even as he made his way slowly and methodically through the hack, Watt could feel her there, a ghostly presence, like the light of a candle flickering just at the edge of his vision. He lost all sense of time and place, his entire being reduced to the string of numerics on the screen before him, waiting for the flash of intuition that would enable him to see a pattern, a blind spot, anything at all.

Eleven hours later, they got it.

"Yes!" Watt exclaimed with a stab of elation, realizing belatedly that he'd missed dinner, that it was practically morning by now. But it didn't matter. Nadia had been trying to break into the Fullers' security for weeks, and now they'd finally accomplished it. "You've got access to Atlas's room comp now?" he asked Nadia.

"Yes. Do you want to look at the live feed?"

"Not really," Watt admitted. He had no desire to watch whatever Atlas did, alone in his room. "But you can monitor it for me, right?"

"I will," Nadia said simply.

Watt leaned back in his chair, lacing his hands behind his head and closing his eyes with a contented sigh. "How much do you think Leda would pay, to see what you're seeing?" he mused aloud.

"Well, right now Atlas is teeing up his Dreamweaver for the night, so it's not that exciting," Nadia told him.

"What's on his Dreamweaver?" Watt asked, a little curious in spite of himself.

"Amazon rain forest visuals and sounds."

"That's kind of weird," Watt said, thinking aloud. Unless . . .

"Do you still have a way into the State Department?" he asked. Nadia had slipped into their system dozens of times, for missing persons and police reports and even the aviation board once.

"Of course."

"Let's start running facial reg on all the South American satellite cams." Maybe Atlas just happened to like rain-forest dreams, Watt thought, and this was all a waste of time.

Or maybe he would crack this Atlas thing once and for all.

He headed to the kitchen to make himself a sandwich, feeling almost hollow, his body aching a little from the hack. But it was a good tired. He'd almost forgotten how satisfying it felt to finish a complicated hack, like he'd scaled some intangible mountain, or conquered an impossible puzzle. He should do it more often.

"We're a good team, you know, Nadia," Watt said, spreading nut butter on a slice of bread. He was too tired and excited to even care that he was talking to himself in the kitchen.

"I know," Nadia agreed, and it sounded like she was smiling.

RYLIN

"I'M HERE TO see Hiral Karadjan," Rylin said clearly. She stepped up to the visitors' counter at the Greycroft Correctional Facility up in Queens, where Hiral was being held until his trial, unless by some miracle his family could find the money for bail.

"That boy sure is popular," the middle-aged guard said drily, and gestured for her to hold out her bag for inspection.

"Hiral? Really?" Rylin lifted up the satchel, packed with as many gifts as she was legally allowed to bring.

"You tell me. You're the third one who's come by today, and he only just got cleared for visitors." The guard pursed his lips as he sorted through Rylin's presents: shampoos, a package of Mrs. Karadjan's shortbread cookies, even an old tablet with the i-Net disabled, preloaded with dozens of books and vids. "Okay. Walk over there for security check," he added, and pointed her to the bioscanner, where her retina images were instantly recorded and her body mili-scanned for evidence of weapons. Finally, when the machine flashed green, a door ahead of her opened. "He'll be in soon," the guard told her, and turned back wearily to his tablet.

Rylin stepped into a bare, whitewashed room, empty except for four tables and chairs bolted to the ground. There was something funny about the walls; they almost glimmered, and Rylin wondered how solid they really were. Probably they were made of that polarizing glass that looked opaque on one side but clear on the other, so police could observe the inmates' conversations. She took the chair at the middle table, farthest from the walls, and put her bag on its dinged metal surface.

Rylin shifted uncomfortably, trying to plan what she would say when Hiral walked in. It seemed unbearably cruel to break up with him when he was already at his lowest. But she couldn't take any more of this, spending time with Cord when she hadn't truly ended things with Hiral. She imagined this was how Hiral felt during his elevator repair jobs: hanging in a breathless state of suspension, where one wrong move could ruin everything.

The wall across from her slid open. Rylin looked up to see Hiral stumbling forward, his hands cuffed in front of him, two cylindrical security bots sliding alongside him on ghostly wheels. He was wearing a nauseating orange jumpsuit and regulation white sneakers, and his hair had been shaved in a buzz cut close to his scalp. Freed of his boyish curls, the planes of his face became more starkly visible. He looked harder, grimmer—he looked *guilty*, Rylin realized. Which he was.

"Hiral," she said softly as he plopped into the seat opposite her. Magnetic cuffs retracted from the chair legs to circle his calves. "How are you holding up?"

"How do you *think* I'm holding up?" he snapped. Rylin's eyes widened. "I'm sorry," he said swiftly, turning back into the Hiral she knew, the boy she'd fallen in love with once upon a time. "It's just been really hard."

"Of course it has," she commiserated, and remembered what the guard had said. "At least your family came by to visit?" She wished she could just cut right to the chase, but she couldn't just breeze in and break up with him, not here.

"My family?" Hiral reached for the bag and began sorting carelessly through the gifts.

"The guard said you'd already had two visitors today?"

"Those weren't my family." Hiral took a bite of one of the cookies, not looking at her.

"Oh." Rylin's stomach fluttered. She wondered if it had been V, or someone else involved in that whole twisted mess. She didn't want to know. Maybe it would be better if she did just dive right in. "Listen, Hiral—"

"Ry," he cut her off. "I need you to do something for me."

Once upon a time she would have agreed on the spot, but now she knew better. "What is it?" she asked carefully.

"I need you to help me post bail."

She started to laugh at the absurdity of it, but Hiral scowled, and she fell silent. God. He was serious.

He leaned his elbows on the table, his forehead in his hands. "My stash is at the liftie entrance to the C line, on seventeen." His eyes were still closed, his shoulders hunched in apparent defeat.

"Hiral!" she hissed, panicked—what if the table was bugged?—but he just went on, speaking in low, rapid tones.

"It's fine. Put your hand on my shoulder. They don't actually listen in. I just don't want them to see my mouth, use LipRead or anything."

Rylin did as he said, her heart hammering. Anyone looking in would think he was overwhelmed, hanging his head in his hands, and she was comforting him. His fists were almost at his chin, blocking his mouth from view.

"The C line, on seventeen," he went on. "Behind the left-side mech panel. I need you to clear it out. All of it. Don't leave anything there, especially not the Anderton Spokes. V will reach out to you soon, to set up a time and place for the handoff. Give everything to him. It should be enough to cover my bail. Mainly thanks to you, stealing those Spokes," he added.

Rylin was speechless. Had Hiral really amassed fifteen thousand nanodollars of drugs? When had *that* happened? "Hiral, you know I can't," she said slowly. "Not with Chrissa. If I get caught, she ends up in foster care."

His eyes hardened, and he looked up sharply. "So the rest of us can risk jail all the time, but you're too good for it?"

"I'm sorry." Rylin tried to keep her voice even. "What about V? He could handle it."

"You know he can't get into the locker room. Besides, I only trust you with this."

"Hiral, please—"

"Do you *want* me to stay in here? Is that it?" he snarled, his face reddening.

"Of course not, but—"

"Damn it, Ry!" Hiral slammed his fist on the table. She jolted back, but he grabbed her wrist with an iron grip. "You're going to do this for me, okay? This is what people in relationships do for each other. They help each other, *protect* each other. You're going to help me get out of here, because you're my girlfriend." He said it as if it were a curse word. "And, because you're my *girlfriend*, I'll protect your secrets."

"My secrets?" Rylin whispered.

"What you took from Cord. I *love* you, Rylin. I would never tell on you, no matter how many times they ask me about it."

Rylin felt as though she'd been kicked in the chest. He was *threatening* her about the stolen Spokes. Her eyes flicked up to the walls, feeling dazed. Could the cops be listening to this?

"I told you, I'm not important enough for them to eavesdrop on," Hiral said, reading her mind. He leaned back and released her hand. Rylin pulled it into her lap. He'd been holding it so tight her fingers had gone numb.

"Okay. I'll help," she said, the words torn forcibly out of her. She didn't have a choice.

"Of course you will."

Rylin braced her hands on the table. It felt suddenly like there was no air in the room. The walls closed in on her as if she were the one imprisoned.

She couldn't break up with Hiral. At least, not yet. She had to stay with him until she got through this, and got him out of jail.

"Now come give me a kiss," Hiral said, with a nod to his shackled ankles. Obediently Rylin stood and walked around the table. She started to brush her lips lightly on his, but Hiral reached up and grabbed her forcibly, his lips hard and unyielding, almost bruising.

After a moment she pulled back. She felt cold all over. "I should get home," she said, and turned to walk back through the guard's room and out the front door.

"See you soon!" Hiral called out behind her.

For a few minutes Rylin walked without even realizing where she was going. Hiral's ugly threat kept replaying in her head. Finally she stopped in her tracks and wrapped her arms around herself, still trembling uncontrollably.

She was standing at the entrance to the A line, the one that went straight up to Cord's place. *Why not?* she decided; he wouldn't be home till much later anyway. It would be nice to escape for a while into Cord's safe, blackmail-free, upper-floor world.

Several hours later Rylin was curled up on an armchair in Cord's library, with the fireplace holo turned on and an old instaphoto book of his mom's in her lap, when she heard a noise in the door-way. "Cord, I'm sorry," she said, only to look up and see Brice. She hadn't even realized he was back in town.

"Looks like you're working hard," he drawled.

"Cord lets me take breaks," she said defensively. But she knew what it looked like, her making herself at home like this, and he knew it too.

Brice threw up his hands in surrender. "Far be it from me to criticize. I like jobs with benefits too, you know."

"I don't know what you mean," Rylin said. He took a step forward, and she shrunk back, holding the book in front of her like a shield. "Listen, why don't you—"

"What's going on?" Cord stood in the doorway. Rylin's heart gave a grateful lurch.

"I was just having a scintillating conversation with our maid here, about work ethics." Brice winked and slunk out the door.

"I'm sorry," Rylin said uncertainly, though why she was apol-ogizing, she wasn't sure.

"Oh, that's just Brice. He acts all scary, but his heart's in the right place."

Is it, though? Rylin thought. She knew that Cord's assholeness was just an act—and she knew where he'd learned it from—but she wasn't so sure with Brice.

"What are you looking at?" Cord nodded at the book as he took the seat next to her.

"Nothing, really." Rylin had been flipping idly through the photos, looking for more images of her mom, though she hadn't found any so far. "I didn't mean to lose track of time," she added, but Cord waved her protest away.

"I love this room too." He glanced around at the shelves of antique books, the floral-printed carpet under their feet, the simulated fire, crackling and emanating heat so convincingly that it seemed real.

Rylin looked from the antique clock on the wall to Cord. He was wearing a plain gray T-shirt, and there was dirt caked around the hems of his jeans. "You skipped school again today?" she asked, though she already knew the answer.

"Special occasion," was all he said. Then, "Hey, I haven't seen those pics in forever! Are those of my fourth-birthday party? The Aladdin-themed one with the holo genie?"

Rylin wordlessly held out the photo album, and Cord began flipping through the pages; stopping here and there to point out childhood versions of his current friends, an enormous cake with far more than four candles, a holographic magic show that apparently scared Brice so much he wet his pants. Rylin nodded from time to time, not really paying attention. In her mind she was still in that prison visiting room, seeing Hiral in a new light.

Cord had stopped talking and was looking at her expectantly, clearly waiting for an answer to something. "Oh!" Rylin exclaimed, startled. "That's so . . . um . . ."

Cord put his hand over hers. "Rylin. What's going on?"

Rylin flipped her hand over and laced her fingers in his. She hated that she couldn't be fully honest with Cord. She was trapped by all the lies she'd told, building and building on top of one another like that old party game where you stacked tiles until they fell over. "A friend of mine was arrested. I visited him in jail today," she admitted, telling as much of the truth as she could. "It's got me a little shaken up, to be honest."

"I'm sorry," Cord said. Rylin gave a helpless shrug. "What was he arrested for?" he added after a moment.

"Dealing."

"Did he do it?"

Something about the question put Rylin on the defensive. "Yeah, he did," she said shortly.

"Well—"

"You don't get it, okay? You don't understand what it's like downTower, that sometimes you have to do things you don't want to! Because you don't have a *choice*!"

"You always have a choice," Cord said quietly.

Rylin stood up abruptly, closing the instaphoto album and putting it back on the shelf. A rational part of her knew that Cord was right. But for some reason she was still upset.

"Hey. I'm sorry." Cord came up and wrapped his arms around her from behind. "You've had a rough day. I didn't mean to . . . I'm sorry," he said again.

"I'm fine," Rylin protested, though she didn't move.

They stood for a while like that, saying nothing. There was something strangely calming about his stillness. Finally Cord stepped back.

"I, for one, am starving," he said, in a clear effort to break the tension. "What should we order?"

"Do you always get delivery?"

"Well, I'd offer to cook for you, but my skills in the kitchen are limited to frozen noodles and, apparently, making an ass of myself."

"You deserved that slap," Rylin said, smiling in spite of herself at the memory. It seemed like a long time ago.

———

Later that night, after they'd eaten—Rylin had insisted on cooking, even wrapping the roast chicken in bacon, which she never could afford to do at home—she curled up on the couch in the living room. She should go back. Chrissa would be getting home soon; she'd had late practice all week, with the state tournament coming up. But Rylin felt drained by the spectrum of emotions she'd whirled through today. She needed to rest, just for a minute.

"Do you want to stay?" Cord asked, his usual confidence faltering a little. Rylin knew what he was asking. She couldn't go there, not yet.

"I need to get home," she said, and gave a huge yawn. "Can I just . . . for five minutes . . ." She leaned her head back on the pillow. Cord started to walk away, but Rylin found that she didn't want him to. "Wait," she protested sleepily.

He settled next to her, and Rylin shifted so that her back was against his chest. Slowly her breathing became more regular.

Eventually Cord wriggled off the couch. Rylin was asleep by then, so she didn't see him search for a blanket in the cupboard and tuck it carefully around her. She didn't see him look at her for a moment, studying the way her lashes fluttered in her sleep. She didn't see him lean down and brush back her hair, then kiss her lightly on the brow before heading to his room and shutting the door behind him.

But when she woke up in the middle of the night and felt the blanket around her, Rylin snuggled deeper into it, and smiled into the darkness.

ERIS

ERIS WAS LYING on the floor of her art history classroom, looking up at the ceiling along with her classmates as they watched a holographic Michelangelo paint the Sistine Chapel. She could hear Avery next to her, sighing each time the painter made another brushstroke. She never understood why Avery loved this stuff so much—it was Avery's fault Eris had enrolled in this class in the first place. Their teacher began lecturing about something, popes maybe, but Eris wasn't listening. She moved her purse under her head to get more comfortable. Her eyes drifted to a figure in the corner of the ceiling, holding a scroll and looking anxiously over her shoulder at a painted angel. The girl's hair was the same color as her own.

She wondered what Mariel would say about this immersive learning. Probably she would just laugh and roll her eyes, and make some comment about how rich people didn't spend their money very well. Eris looked around the room. Gone were the desks and display board and windows. Thanks to an elaborate, incredibly expensive system of holograms and mirrors, every surface was utterly transformed into the sixteenth-century church. Eris wondered, suddenly, how many lower-floor families they could feed for the cost of the tech equipment in this room alone.

She couldn't wait till this class ended, when she could sneak to the edge of the tech-net and see if Mariel had messaged her. They'd spent most of the last week together, ever since Mariel came by Eris's apartment the morning after church. "Okay," Mariel had said simply, and Eris had nodded, and that was that.

They'd fallen into an unspoken pattern of meeting up in the evenings, when Mariel got off work. Sometimes they would just do homework together, or sit on the couch and watch mindless comedies on the vid-screen, or run errands for Mariel's mom, who was a salesperson at a department store. Most of the time Mariel's mom would insist that Eris stay for dinner. Eris had eaten at their place the past three nights. It was nice, being part of a family again. The more time Eris spent with Mariel, the more she wanted to keep spending time with her.

A high beeping noise cut through the sounds of holographic Michelangelo's humming. A message from the front office, Eris thought, her interest piqued. And then she heard her own name.

"Eris Dodd-Radson?"

The old Eris would have loved this moment, stood up slowly and tossed her hair, letting everyone think she was off somewhere fabulous. But now she just lurched to her feet and grabbed her things. She ignored Avery's whisper and walked quickly out the door to the headmaster's office.

The last person she expected to see waiting there was her mom.

"Eris!" Caroline exclaimed, striding forward and hugging

her. Eris stood there numbly, shocked that her mom was here, at school, picking her up. "Let's get going." Her mom put a hand firmly behind her back and steered her out the school's side door. The headmaster's secretary gave them a fake smile, already turning back to her tablet screen.

A hover waited for them on the side of the school. "We can't afford to take a hover." Eris turned, reminding her mom, but Caroline was already shooing her inside and keying in the destination. "Here," she said, handing Eris a self-steaming garment bag. "Change now. We're running late as it is."

"Are you serious?" Eris asked.

"Please. Like this is the first time you've changed in a hover," her mom replied. She had a point.

Eris shimmied out of her school uniform and into the sundress inside the bag—her nicest one, a purple Lanvin with big splashes of blue and white. Eris hadn't managed to pack this one before the move. She shot her mom a glance, but Caroline just shrugged. "I got it from storage for you," she said, and Eris felt a pang of gratefulness.

Finally they pulled up to the paved courtyard of the Lemark Hotel on 910. Eris still had no idea what was going on. "Mom," she snapped, losing her patience, "you can't just pull me out of school and expect me to—"

"We're here to meet your birth father."

The world seemed to go silent, everything spinning dizzyingly around her. Eris couldn't think. "Oh," she said at last, in a tiny breath. She followed her mom out of the hover, into the courtyard. A nearby fountain sprayed water in the shape of a giant cursive L.

"After you asked me about him a few weeks ago, I reached out, told him everything. He wants to meet you."

Eris's eyes darted up to the hotel, tears blurring her vision. "He's here?" she whispered.

Her mom nodded. "He's inside right now."

Eris stood there for a moment, uncertain. "Okay," she heard herself say, and knew it was the right thing. If she didn't meet her birth father now—when he was here, waiting for her—the what-if of it would haunt her forever.

Caroline stepped forward. Eris started to pull away but thought better of it. *I've punished her enough*, she decided, and accepted her mom's hug.

"I love you, Eris," Caroline whispered. Eris felt dampness on her neck, and realized that her mom was crying.

"I love you too, Mom," Eris said, as the wall she'd built between them began to crack, just a little.

———

Eris said nothing as they stepped inside the cool, hushed lobby of the Lemark, where a white-gloved concierge was speaking with an overweight lady in golf clothes. A little out of the way at 17th and Riverside, the Lemark was a favorite spot for businesspeople holding secret meetings—and, Eris had heard, couples having affairs. Supposedly the president himself used to sneak away to meet his current wife here, before he divorced the former First Lady. Eris wondered what it meant, that her birth father had suggested this place. For some reason it made her feel uncomfortable, as if she and her mom were a sordid little secret. *It's fine*, she told herself, *he probably just wants privacy.*

They walked into the dining room, filled with dark leather banquettes that were so widely separated, it was impossible for someone at one table to see the guests at any other. Eris realized she couldn't hear a single shred of conversation, only the music pumping in over the speakers. Maybe all the tables were equipped with silencers.

The hostess, a dark-eyed brunette in a tight uniform skirt, looked them over. "We're the Dodd-Radsons," Caroline said, stubbornly using their old name, or maybe she'd just forgotten the same way Eris kept doing. But the hostess seemed to already know who they were.

"This way," she said, weaving through the secluded tables to the back corner. "He's been waiting for you."

Eris felt a shudder of apprehension and reached instinctively for her mom's hand. They arrived at the table just as a gentleman stood up from the shadows, and Eris gave a sharp, helpless laugh.

She turned to the hostess. "We're at the wrong table. I'm meeting someone else," she said, marveling at the coincidence, because she actually knew this person. It was Matt Cole, Leda's dad.

But the hostess had turned away, and Mr. Cole was clearing his throat. "Caroline," he said, his voice low and hoarse. "It's good to see you, as always." He held out his hand awkwardly. "Eris, thank you for coming." And she realized, stunned, that there hadn't been a mistake at all.

Leda's dad was her dad too.

She and her mom sat down, sliding awkwardly along the banquette so that Eris was between her parents. The silence felt strained and heavy. Mr. Cole was looking at her as if he'd never seen her before, his eyes tracing over her features, probably searching for himself in them. They had similar mouths, Eris realized, and his skin was as fair as hers. But she looked so much like her mom it was hard to tell.

A bot rolled over with a tray of drinks on its surface and began to dole them out. "I'm sorry, I went ahead and ordered," Mr. Cole said self-consciously. "Caroline, the spritz is for you, and Eris, I got you a lemonade. I remember it's your favorite, right?" She just nodded dumbly. *Yeah, it was my favorite, back in eighth grade, the one and only time Leda had me over.*

They sat there idly swirling their drinks, everyone waiting

for someone else to speak. Eris refused to be the first to talk. She was still making sense of all this. A thousand moments were replaying in her mind—the way her mom always asked which other parents would be there, before she came to any school function; her seemingly casual questions about Leda, which evidently weren't so casual at all. Now it all made sense. But—

"When?" she blurted out, shaking her head in bewilderment. "I mean, when did you . . ." *hook up?* She didn't know how to phrase the question, but her mom understood.

"Matt and I met in our early twenties," Caroline said, watching Eris. "Before I met your father. We were part of the same group of friends, all new to the city. The Tower was just under construction. Everyone was scattered in the boroughs waiting for it to be done. We were all so poor," she added, turning to Mr. Cole. "We were living paycheck to paycheck. Remember how my first apartment in Jersey City had beach towels for curtains?"

"You couldn't even afford furniture," Mr. Cole said, amusement creeping into his tone. "You stacked wooden boxes as your coffee table."

"In the summers when it was hot, we'd sneak into the indoor farmers' market and wander the aisles until they kicked us out, because we couldn't afford air-conditioning."

Eris looked back and forth between them, totally unnerved by this reminiscing. Her mom smiled softly at the memory, then turned back to Eris, the moment over.

"Anyway," Caroline said, "that's when my modeling career took off. I met Everett, and Matt went back home to Illinois for a while. By the time we saw each other again, it was several years later, and I was married. . . ."

And so was Mr. Cole, Eris thought. She remembered that he'd picked things back up with Leda's mom—his high school sweetheart—when he moved home to take care of his ailing dad, then convinced her to move with him back to New York, to the brand-new Tower. God, Mrs. Cole had probably been pregnant with *Jamie* when they saw each other again. But neither of them mentioned that particular detail.

"Well, we reconnected, and then . . ." Caroline looked at Eris. "And then there was you." She looked away, wringing the napkin in her lap until her knuckles were white.

"Eris," Leda's dad—*her* dad—interrupted, "I had no idea until your mother called me. I never even guessed that you were mine. As you know, Caroline and I haven't been . . . involved, for years now." He cleared his throat in a businesslike way. Of course, Eris thought, he was still shocked himself. "I want to tell you how sorry I am for everything you're going through," he went on. "I imagine this is all incredibly hard on you."

"Yeah. It sucks," Eris said drily. Caroline squeezed her hand.

"Please," Mr. Cole said, "whatever I can do to help, let me know."

Eris looked at her mom. Did he know they were on the 103rd floor? What was he going to tell his family? But as she opened her mouth to ask, Mr. Cole tapped on the center of the table, pulling up the holographic menu. "Should we all get some lunch?" he offered, hesitantly. "The shishito spring rolls here are amazing. If you have time, that is."

"We'd love to," Caroline said firmly.

Eris took a long sip of the lemonade she didn't want, her mind still trying to adjust to this strange new reality. Mr. Cole met her eyes across the table and gave a tentative smile. Eris felt herself soften a little. She thought suddenly of when she'd gone to church with Mariel, the way strangers forged a connection with her through nothing but a touch and a look. And this was her birth father, not a stranger at all, trying in his own way to connect with her.

Whereas the man who'd been her father for the last eighteen years had stopped speaking to her altogether.

Leda's dad was her dad. It was pretty much the last thing in the world she'd expected. But he was here, and he was trying.

Eris looked up at him and smiled. "Sure," she said, as cheerfully as she could manage. "Lunch sounds great."

LEDA

LEDA SAT BOLT upright, gasping, her silk pajama set drenched in sweat. Her hands wound tightly in her sheets, clutching at them with clawlike fingers.

She was having the dreams again.

The lights came slowly to life as the room comp detected her alertness. Leda sat huddled in the center of her enormous bed, her arms wrapped around herself. She was shaking. Her limbs felt too heavy to move, like she had shrunk to some miniature creature standing at the controls of an enormous, unwieldy body.

She wanted a hit. Desperately. God, she hadn't wanted one this badly since the early days of rehab. Back then she'd had these dreams every night: of drowning in ink-black water; of fingers reaching for her, still and cold as death. *I am my own greatest ally*, Leda repeated, trying to center herself, but she couldn't, it was freezing in here and her brain felt muted and all she wanted was a burst of xenperheidren to bring her back to life.

When she finally felt like she could move, she threw back the covers and twisted her hair up, heading toward the kitchen. She wanted a glass of water. She could've asked the room comp for it, of course, but she thought walking around might calm her a little. It felt like someone had scraped out her head from within.

The apartment was eerily silent. Leda moved a little faster, her bare feet skirting around the squares of moonlight on the floor just like she used to do when she and Jamie were little, and pretended that touching the light was bad luck. In the kitchen, she opened the refrigerator door and stood there awhile, letting the cool air kiss her face.

Her eyelids were shut, but behind them, almost without realizing it, Leda had drafted a flicker to her old dealer, Ross. It was costing every ounce of her self-control not to send it. Everything was fine, she kept telling herself—not just fine, it was great. She was going to the benefit with Atlas, no matter that it was costing her friendship with Avery. Well, that was Avery's fault for acting so weird. She deserved Atlas, Leda reminded herself. She deserved to be *happy*.

Her jaw tensed, she turned and started back toward her room—only to stumble over something in the entry hall. She cursed under her breath. It was her dad's briefcase, plopped right where he'd left it when he came home. Leda paused at the sight of a flat orange box peeking from the bag's side pocket. Apparently her dad had been shopping at Calvadour. Her parents' anniversary was in a few days; this must be his present for Leda's mom.

Leda didn't feel any scruples about lifting up a corner of the box to see what her dad had gotten. It was exquisite, a cream-colored silk scarf with what looked like hand-stitched embroidery on the edge. She gave a quick verbal command to her contacts and they looked it up with ShopMatch. When she saw how much it cost, Leda gasped. Her dad must be feeling really in love these days.

Or really guilty about something.

Leda tucked the box away and moved back down the hall. But even after she crawled into bed, she couldn't fall asleep. She felt anxious. She wished she could flicker Atlas, but it was the middle of the night and she didn't want to seem crazy.

What's the latest on Atlas? she wrote to Nadia instead, not really expecting to hear back right away.

Moments later, though, she got a reply. *I have something now, actually.*

Leda started reading, and felt immediately stunned. It seemed that Atlas had been in the Amazon for the last few months, working at some kind of wilderness lodge. Nadia had even attached a few aerial photos as proof, taken by what must have been passing satellites.

You hacked the State Department? Leda couldn't help asking. These images could only have come from the government comm network.

I told you, I'm the best.

Leda lay there in bed, her eyes closed, muttering to her contacts as they projected one image after another for her. The guy in the photos was more deeply tanned, and he had the beginnings of a beard, but it was definitely Atlas.

She tossed back and forth, wishing she could fall asleep. Dark, twisted images from the nightmare flitted through her mind. The flicker to Ross was still projected on the inside of her eyelids. God, she wanted to send it.

Did anyone else ever feel this way, alone and frantic, haunted by a fear she couldn't quite place? Did Avery? Leda doubted it. But part of her wondered if Atlas might understand. Maybe he had disappeared last year because he'd been running away from something too. Something big, if he had to go all the way to the rain forest to escape it.

Whatever it was, she wondered if Atlas had ever figured it out—or if his demons still chased him at night the way hers did.

WATT

WATT STOOD OUTSIDE Norton Harcrow Men's Attire on the 951st floor, waiting impatiently for Avery.

Many social scientists find that nervousness can be reduced by rituals such as counting, especially while picturing an innocuous animal. For instance, sheep, Nadia projected onto his eyes.

I'm not nervous, Watt thought at her, irritated.

You happen to be exhibiting many physiological signs of nervousness: elevated heart rate, sweaty palms. A cartoon sheep overlaid his vision. Watt gave his head a shake to dissolve it.

Can you just be quiet unless I ask you a question? He self-consciously wiped his hands on the inside of his pockets as a hover pulled up, and Avery stepped out.

"Watt!" She tossed her waves of sunflower hair over one shoulder. She had on a simple white dress that showed off her lean, tanned body. A necklace of dark stones glittered distractingly at her neckline. "I'm so glad we're doing this," she said, leading him forward into the store.

"Thanks for coming with me," he replied. "And for inviting me to the gala, of course."

"We are talking about the same event, aren't we?" she teased. "I mean, I feel kind of guilty for dragging you along. You know how these things can be."

No, I don't know. But I don't care. You'll be there. Watt was saved from replying as they passed straight through the solid wooden doors of the store, which, it turned out, weren't solid wood at all but a location-based holo that shimmered and re-formed after they passed. He looked back over his shoulder and saw that the entrance had now shifted to resemble marble Greek columns. "How weirdly Ionic of them," he remarked dryly, just as Avery sighed and said, "I love those doors."

Watt felt a flash of guilt—he'd never insulted something that a girl cared about, Nadia always saved him from this kind of thing—but to his delight, Avery had started laughing at the pun. "I think those are Doric, but nice work," she said with mock seriousness. "Eris and I are in art history this year, you know."

"That must be torture for you and Eris, looking at lots of pretty things you're not allowed to buy," Watt ventured, and immediately worried he'd gone too far. He wasn't accustomed to handling this kind of banter alone.

But Avery just laughed again. "You know, no one's ever put it to me quite like that, but you might be onto something."

"How's Eris doing, by the way?" Watt asked, thinking of the party.

"I'm not sure, honestly," Avery said. "She left school in the middle of the day today, which can't be good, right?"

Watt wished he could offer to help, to look up where Eris had gone if that would calm Avery's fears, but of course that was impossible.

As they walked through the store toward the formal section,

salespeople at various counters nodded and murmured hellos to Avery, greeting her by name. "Everyone here seems to know you," Watt said, a bit intimidated.

"I shop a lot." Avery shrugged.

"It's a men's store," Watt couldn't help pointing out.

Avery smiled. "I know."

He followed her past racks of brightly colored ties, belts and boxers and sleek briefcases, to a spacious area marked FORMAL. The walls and floor of this section were a stark industrial white, the space littered with leather chairs and small couches. Watt looked around but didn't see any clothes.

"A little blinding in here, isn't it?" he pointed out. The white was so bright he almost put his contacts on light-blocking.

Avery gave him a funny look. "That's so they can build settings. Didn't they do that at your last tux fitting?"

"Avery, my dear." A pale, drawn salesgirl with dark circles around her eyes glided from a back room, the sleeves of her charcoal sweater dipping past her skinny wrists. She looked familiar, but Watt couldn't place her. *Nadia?* "Who have you brought for me today? Not Atlas?"

"Rebecca, this is Watt, a friend of mine. He needs a new tux."

Rebecca pursed her lips when she saw Watt, and her eyes narrowed in recognition. She looked a few years older than Watt and Avery, but not many. Hadn't he . . .

December 11 last year, Anchor Bar. She told you her name was Bex and that she was a freshman at Amherst. She saw you again the next night but you ignored her to talk to her friend, Nadia informed him.

Well, that explained why she seemed familiar.

"Let's get started," Rebecca said, in clipped tones. "Watt, can you—oh." She paused, wrinkling her nose in distaste at Watt, who'd started unbuttoning the top button of his shirt. "There's no need to disrobe here. We're not at Bloomingdale's." She shuddered.

"Don't you want to measure me?" Watt asked, and Rebecca barked out a laugh.

"Norton Harcrow took a 4-D scan of your body when you walked inside," Avery said gently. "It's accurate down to the millimeter, and the tux will be made to fit. You know their motto, 'No alterations needed.'"

"How is it 4-D?" Watt said without thinking, trying to hide his embarrassment.

"They track you each time you come in, keep your measurements updated, let you know how your body's changing over time," Avery explained. "I know guys who come in here just to track their workout progress." Rebecca began typing on a tablet, and a holographic scan of Watt's body, a big blue silhouette, was projected in the middle of the room.

"What kinds of details will you be wanting? Button size, lining, lapels . . . ?" Rebecca asked, a little edge to her voice, and looked at Watt expectantly.

Nadia? Where are you?

"Why don't you set the scene," Avery suggested to Rebecca, reading Watt's silence. "It's for the University Club gala, so I'd say cherry floors, dim lighting, and the dark walls lined with those terrible white curtains—you know which ones I'm talking about."

You told me not to volunteer information unless it was requested directly, Nadia answered.

Well, I take it back, Watt snapped.

Rebecca clicked away at the tablet some more, and instantly the room transformed into the empty dance floor of a distinguished wooden ballroom, with high, narrow windows looking out into the night. A few more taps, and holographic couples in tuxes and floor-length dresses appeared in several small clusters.

The silhouette of Watt's body was still hovering there, like a ghostly headless mannequin. Rebecca nodded and a black tux materialized on it, the exact size and shape that it would be when it was sewed to Watt's specifications. "Midnight blue, navy, or black?" she asked.

"Black?" Watt guessed. He watched as she approached and began moving her hands through the air, pinching her fingers to zoom out or widening them to focus on certain details. She chose the lapel first, scrolling between various widths and textures of silk, glancing from the projection to Watt and back.

"Formal attire is supposed to be minimalist, to detract attention from the body of the wearer," she was saying, almost under her breath, "but you have such a wide chest, I'm thinking you might want a broad notched lapel, to balance you out."

"Sure," he said helplessly. Was that supposed to be an insult?

"Is your bow tie butterfly or bat-winged?"

Nadia had projected a guide to bow-tie shapes onto his eyes, but Watt was still floundering. Avery and Rebecca were both looking at him, expectant. "I don't have a bow tie," he said. "I mean, it got ruined too, with my last tux. I need everything."

Understanding flashed in Avery's eyes, and she stepped forward. "I like butterfly, myself," she said quickly. "I prefer more classic styles. What do you think of jetted pocket, cummerbund, and optional suspenders?"

"That's perfect," Watt said, grateful, as Rebecca glared at him and made the necessary adjustments to the projection.

Watt swallowed when he saw the bill, but he could afford it thanks to all the payments he'd collected from Leda lately, especially the bonus she'd given him for the pics of Atlas in the Amazon. Really he owed this entire date to Leda, he thought, with a strange amusement. If it wasn't for her, he would never have realized that Avery existed.

As he and Avery walked out the front doors—which had now taken the form of old ironwork gates, with holographic vines creeping over them—Avery turned to him. "This is your first tux, isn't it?" she asked softly.

Nadia offered him an array of excuses, but Watt felt tired of hiding the truth. "It is," he told her.

Avery looked unsurprised. "You didn't have to lie to me, you know."

"I didn't lie. At least, not about anything important. I just didn't tell you everything," Watt hastened to say. He'd told Avery the truth whenever she asked—about how many siblings he had, for instance, or what he liked to do. Whenever she asked a question he didn't want to answer he had neatly dodged it, and let her fill in the blanks with the assumptions he knew she would make. He'd been so proud of himself, but suddenly it did seem a lot like lying.

"Actually I live on the two hundred fortieth floor," he confessed, then glanced away, unwilling to see her reaction.

"Watt." Something in Avery's voice made him look up. "That stuff doesn't matter to me. Please don't lie to me again. Too many people lie to me as is. I thought—" She pursed her lips, frustrated. "One of the reasons I like you was that I thought you were actually honest with me."

"I am," Watt assured her, thinking guiltily of Nadia, and all the information she'd given him on Avery, to help his chances. But wait—had Avery just said she liked him?

"Oh no. Watt!" Avery exclaimed, blushing. "We need to go cancel your tux order!"

"Why?"

She blushed adorably. "Because! Don't you want to go

somewhere less expensive? Or you can rent one! I'm sorry, I didn't realize, when I suggested Norton Harcrow, that you—"

"I'm getting the tux," Watt said firmly, and Avery fell silent. "I can buy it and I want to buy it, and mostly, I'm excited for the chance to wear it, with you. Besides," he went on, confident again, "I'm hoping this isn't the last gala I get to take you to."

Avery smiled at that. "Who knows? Maybe you're right," she said opaquely.

"I'll take a maybe for now." Watt paused on the sidewalk, not wanting this to end. "In the meantime, can I buy you a coffee to thank you for helping me with my first tux?"

"There's a place down the street that has awesome hemp milk chai. And hot coffee," she added, catching his expression, "if you don't like hemp milk."

"Who wouldn't like hemp milk?" Watt said in mock seriousness.

As he followed Avery to the coffee shop, Watt's mind was racing, thinking over everything she had said—and everything he hadn't.

Avery was right. She deserved more than the way he'd been treating her, pretending to be something he wasn't, trying to tell her exactly the right thing. He wasn't just trying to sleep with her—well, he amended, he wasn't *only* trying to sleep with her—so why was he acting like it? What he really wanted was to pursue Avery. For real.

And so Watt made a decision he'd never made before. He would stop using Nadia when he and Avery were together.

See you later, Nadia, he thought, then sent the command that would power her all the way down. *Quant off.*

He felt the sudden emptiness like a sound, or rather a lack of sound, like the silence that echoed after a summer storm. He hadn't turned her off since the day she was installed in his head.

"Here it is," Avery said, pushing open the door and looking back over her shoulder at Watt. Her eyes were so startlingly blue it almost took his breath away. "I hope you're ready for the best coffee you've ever tasted."

"Oh, I'm ready," Watt said, and followed her inside.

RYLIN

SATURDAY AFTERNOON, RYLIN stood outside the 50th floor entrance to Lift Maintenance, steeling herself. She could do this, she told herself. She had no other choice.

Pasting a smile on her face, she walked in the metal double doors and winked at the craggy old security guard behind the flexiglass sign-in counter. He grunted, barely looking up as she sailed past, recognizing her from all the times she'd been here with Hiral. Technically only lifties were allowed past this point, but Rylin had seen plenty of their significant others in the locker room before, delivering forgotten items or cleaning out dirty laundry.

The locker room was musty, and smelled like stale sweat and grease. Rylin walked confidently to the far side, past two guys in the corner who were stripped to the waist, playing some game on their tablets to kill time. They were the skeleton weekend crew, on call in case of emergencies. Moving quickly, she punched in the passcode to Hiral's locker and swung the door open.

Hiral was a climber, one of the guys who actually hung from a wire in midair while the rest of the crew manned the operation from the tunnel above—a job that took courage, or maybe just blind hubris. Because of that, he had a full-length locker, in a prime location near the exit door. She pushed aside his dark gray swing suit, made of a thin but nearly impenetrable carbon-composite fiber, and his heavy-duty ecramold helmet, which supposedly could prevent brain damage from a fall of up to two hundred stories. Not often useful, given that most repairs were needed in the upper floors, where altitude and cable strain led to lift closures.

Under Hiral's climbing boots and magnetic grip gloves, Rylin found what she was looking for: the tiny ID chip that snapped into place on his helmet.

"You shouldn't be in here."

She whirled around, shoving the ID chip the only place she could think of—in the crevice of her bra. "I'm sorry," she said to the young man who stood before her, his burly arms crossed. "I'm getting some things for Hiral Karadjan."

"The kid who got picked up for drugs?" he growled.

Kid? This guy couldn't be more than a few years older than Hiral. But she just nodded as she said, "Yeah. I'm his girlfriend."

"I've seen her here before," the other guy called out from the corner. "Leave her alone, Nuru."

But Nuru stood there watching as Rylin grabbed the first thing she could think of—Hiral's high-pitched silent whistle, as if that mattered at all to him in prison—and slammed the locker shut. "Sorry. I'll be going," she mumbled.

As she hurried out, she could hear them talking in low tones behind her. Most of the words were too quiet for her to make out, but she heard "damn shame," and "shouldn't do that to her," and she thought she heard V's name mentioned. She wondered, suddenly, if they hadn't been fooled at all by her excuse.

She made her way hastily to the C local train and got off on 17, wrinkling her nose at the smell of oily machinery. It had been a while since Rylin went lower than 32. She'd almost forgotten how depressing it was down here. The bottom twenty floors housed most of the Tower's cooling facilities, with dim warrens of rooms crowded in the spaces between. The walls were thicker down here, and the ceilings lower, lined with the triple-enforced steel that supported the unthinkable weight of the Tower over their heads.

The lift was mostly empty. Still, Rylin waited for everyone else to filter off, turning toward the machine rooms or their dismal apartments. When the coast was clear, she fished Hiral's ID chip from where it was nestled in her cleavage and used it to open the tiny, almost invisible door on the corridor marked MAINTENANCE ONLY.

It was utterly black inside, the darkness pressing down on her like a weight. Rylin fumbled for a light button. She found it, then hesitated. She couldn't risk drawing any kind of attention to herself. Maybe someone, somewhere, could see what lights were on throughout the maintenance areas, and would notice that the liftie tunnel on 17 was occupied when it shouldn't be.

Cursing under her breath, she unearthed her tablet and put it in flashlight mode. A thin beam of light blinked into being. Rylin waved it before her, stepping carefully over the boxes on the floor, until she found the mech panel on the left-hand side. Biting the tablet with her teeth to keep the light steady, she pried the panel open.

There they were: dozens of plastic baggies filled with multicolored powders, pill bottles whose contents she didn't even recognize, and, at the back, the dark envelopes of Cord's Spokes. Rylin stood a moment in sick shock. She was trembling, causing the tablet's light to dance wildly over the panel, as if she were some messed-up version of an explorer standing over a pile of buried treasure. She'd taken drugs so many times with Hiral, and yet the sight of all this stuff was sobering. He'd become a complete stranger to her. How long had he been squirreling things away here?

She swung her empty backpack off her shoulder and began filling it, tossing handfuls inside as fast as she could. But she froze at the sight of Cord's name on the Spokes packets, in small capitals at the top of each individual prescription label. DR. VERONICA FISS, COLUMBIA HILL PHARMACOGENOMICS; PATIENT: CORD HAYES ANDERTON JR.; DOSAGE: AS NEEDED (MAX ONE TABLET DAILY).

Quickly she peeled Cord's name from each label and shoved the sticky paper into her pocket, where she wadded it into a tiny ball. Then she zipped the bag back up and closed the mech panel—carefully, using the hem of her shirt so she didn't leave fingerprints—before retreating into the hallway. On the lift upTower, she pulled out her tablet and replied to the message she'd received earlier this week. *It's done.*

Excellent. Meet here. There was a location drop attached to the message.

Rylin reached to put her hair up in a ponytail, trying her best to look like a normal high schooler, just walking around on Saturday with a backpack full of homework. Following the message's instructions, she got out on the 233rd floor. An old woman bumped into her as she stepped off the lift, and Rylin reflexively pulled the straps of her backpack closer over her shoulders. The lights overhead were dimming as the day grew later; it must be at least six o'clock by now. Rylin passed a few Laundromats and takeout noodle shops, turning onto High Street ahead.

The location drop led to Fisher Elementary School. Really?

She slowed as she walked past, a little creeped out by the dark, empty windows of the school leering at her.

"Glad you could make it," she heard V say, from the play-ground.

Rylin looked both ways before climbing the low-tech metal fence. Her hands were white by the time she jumped to the other side. "I'm here," she said, glancing around the monkey bars, where during recess holographic monkeys would clamber along-side the kids. A treetop canopy soared overhead, dotted with tree houses that resembled whimsical shapes like a tortoise shell or a giant cloud. This was way nicer than her own elementary school had been, just seventy floors down.

Rylin's shoes sank into the recycled rubber covering the ground. V stepped forward from the shadows, an impish smile dancing across his face.

"Why couldn't we have just met at the steel forest?" she asked, but V shook his head.

"Too many people. Now let's see it. What do you have for me?"

Rylin shrugged off her backpack but held it tight. She didn't like the feel of this at all. Her deep-rooted survival instincts were stirring, warning her that something wasn't right. "I need to get paid first."

"Let's just see what you've got." V laughed and snatched the backpack from her grasp.

Rylin ground her jaw angrily as he dumped the contents of the backpack onto the playground and sorted through it. "You've taken the name off these Spokes," he said, an eyebrow raised.

She struggled to keep her face impassive. "You know it doesn't matter. No one gives a shit who their Spokes were originally pre-scribed to."

"Trying to protect him?"

Rylin's breath caught. She opened her mouth to say something, to deny any feelings for Cord—

"Whatever. You're right, it won't, really. You don't know where Hiral got these, though, do you?" V asked, with a sidelong glance. "He never did tell me."

Rylin shook her head, feeling stunned. Hiral had told V that *he* was the one stealing the Spokes? He must have done it to protect her.

V swept all the drugs into his bag and gave a dramatic sigh. "I'm sorry, but this isn't enough."

"What do you mean, it's not enough?"

V shook his head. "I can't give you fifteen thousand for this. It's barely worth ten."

"You lying little—" Rylin lunged forward, but V put his hands out and grabbed her shoulders, squeezing them so hard that Rylin felt she was running into a wall. He gave her a little shove and she stumbled back, her breath still coming fast.

"Come on, Rylin," V muttered, shaking his head. The inktats around his neck looked almost darker with his anger. "Play nice."

She stayed mutinously silent.

"Now, about the extra five thousand." His eyes traveled over her in a way she didn't like. "You and I could always just strike up a little trade of our own."

"Go to hell, V."

"Thought you'd say that. But for some reason I like you, so I'm giving you one last chance. Tell Hiral he needs more Spokes," V demanded, his words unyielding. "At least five more. You'll have to grab them, since he's locked up."

"No!" Rylin shouted, clenching her hands, feeling sick. "I won't do it, okay?"

V shrugged. "I don't care one way or another. But it's my final offer, take it or leave it, Myers. Now get the hell out of here." He muttered something under his breath and the school's security alarm went off.

Rylin stood there in stunned bewilderment. But V had already taken off, ducking through a gate she hadn't seen on the far side of the playground. An instant later Rylin's reflexes kicked in and she was running through the gate, sprinting headlong down the empty length of Maple Street. V was nowhere to be seen. Rylin kept running, so fast that she tripped over her own feet and fell forward, skidding angrily along the unforgiving pavement. But she picked herself back up and hurried on, adrenaline dulling the pain in her hands and knees, not daring to stop until she turned onto the main avenue.

Finally Rylin bent down and examined her knees. They were badly skinned, and blood was smeared on her palms where she'd fallen. Taking a deep, ragged breath, she started the long trip home.

AVERY

"I'VE GOT IT!" Avery called out, when the entrance comm buzzed later that night. Not that her parents were the type of people who answered their own door. But she wanted to give Watt a moment to collect himself before he met them, since they'd all be sharing a hover to the University Club. Atlas had already left to pick up Leda, which Avery was trying not to think about.

"Watt!" she said, flinging open the front door, and paused at the sight of him in his new tux. The elegant satin clung to his frame, making him seem taller than he really was; highlighting the strong, clean lines of his nose and jaw and the burnished brown of his skin. "It looks great on you," she said, her heart beating unexpectedly faster. "The tux, I mean."

"It was fun shopping for it." *It was fun, wasn't it?* Avery thought. "I got you something, by the way." Watt cleared his throat and held out a small velvet box.

"Oh, you didn't have to . . ." Avery trailed off as she opened the box. Inside was a miniature incandescent, one of the genetically engineered flowers that attracted light the way magnets attract metal. Already it was drawing some of the light from the room toward it, taking on a sort of ghostly glow, though it generated none of the light itself. Incandescents were funny; they'd become much cheaper since they were first bred decades ago, because they only lasted a few hours before dying. But they were truly beautiful if you caught them in the one night they bloomed.

"I know you hate cuttings," Watt was saying, "but I couldn't help it, I've been wanting to get you one of these ever since that night at Bubble Lounge."

"It's beautiful. Thank you," Avery breathed. The actual bud was tiny, smaller than her fingernail, and was now positively glowing with a soft golden light. She tucked it into her updo, behind her ear. It went perfectly with her gown, which was long and slinky and covered in tiny pieces of mirror. She'd loved the delicious irony of it, that when people tried to look at her, they'd be forced to look at themselves instead.

"Is this the famous Watt?" Avery's mom called out from the entryway. "Come in! We've heard so much about you!"

I mentioned him once. Avery flushed with embarrassment as she led Watt inside.

"Watt, it's wonderful to finally meet you." Elizabeth held out a hand, enormous diamond rings glittering on every finger.

Watt shook it, undeterred. "Thank you. You look lovely tonight, Mrs. Fuller." To Avery's surprise, he *winked*—quickly, but with just the right amount of flirtation to make Avery's mom melt a little. How had he known to use that little trick?

"Now tell me," Avery's mom asked, a new warmth in her voice, "because Avery refuses to. How did you two meet?"

"We ran into each other at an Augmented Reality game. Of course, after I saw Avery I couldn't really focus on the game,"

Watt said. "So I pestered her and sent her flowers until she agreed to go out with me."

"Yes, well, Avery's always been stubborn." Pierson Fuller strode briskly into the room. "You must be Watt," he said, and gave his hand a firm shake. "Have a seat. Can I get you something? Wine? Scotch?"

"Dad, we're already late." Avery glanced over at Watt, but he seemed to be thoroughly enjoying himself.

"Oh, I think we have time for one drink, don't you?" he asked mischievously.

"Exactly." Her dad stepped behind the bar and began sorting through the monogrammed crystal decanters. "Besides, they might have age scanners at the club, you never know. This could be the only drink you get tonight."

"Not at the University Club." Elizabeth stepped forward, the skirts of her dress giving a little swish as she walked. "Wine for me, Pierson."

"They're cracking down everywhere these days." Pierson poured drinks into prechilled glasses and passed them around, then settled on the sofa. "So, Watt, tell me about yourself. Where do you go to school?"

"I go to Jefferson High, actually, on the 240th floor." Watt said it confidently, unashamed. Avery found herself feeling oddly proud of him. To her relief, her parents just nodded, as if it were normal for boys to come two miles upstairs to go on dates with Avery.

"That's a charter school, isn't it?" Pierson asked.

"It is," Watt said, and Avery shot her dad a curious stare. How did he know that?

Her dad nodded. "I have a few properties in that neighborhood. One's at the corner of Seventeenth and Freedmore, the building with the bank inside. . . ."

Avery stifled a groan and met Watt's eyes, but he just grinned at her and took a sip of his Scotch. Up in her hair, the incandescent glowed like a living lightbulb.

Avery linked her arm in Watt's as they stood at the entrance to the University Club ballroom. The massive dark-wood room was decorated all in tones of blue and silver; even the columns seemed to be entirely covered by a blue-and-white profusion of flowers. Curving bars dotted the corners of the room, and along the far wall, a dance floor had been set up. The room was dim, but Avery could still see the vibrant colors of all the dresses, which seemed even richer alongside the stark black of the tuxedos. "You're terrible," she hissed at Watt, and led him forward into the crowd.

"It's not my fault your parents like me," he replied innocently, and Avery couldn't help smiling at that. He held out a hand. "Wanna dance?"

"Yes," she said eagerly, wondering how Watt could tell what she'd been thinking. It was still a little early to be on the dance floor. But Avery had always preferred dancing to socializing at these things. People tended to flock around her, bombard her with small talk, shoot glances at her from across the room. Even now she could see them studying her dress, whispering to one another about the new boy she'd brought. The dance floor was the only place she ever got any peace.

As they moved through the crowds, Avery saw that pretty much everyone was here. There was Risha, standing with Ming at the bar; and Jess with her boyfriend, Patrick; and her parents' friends the McClendons, who gave her a little wave. She knew why Eris was missing, but where was Cord? He and Brice were actually members in their own right, even though they were technically too young—the Club had bent the rules for them, since their parents were so beloved—but Avery didn't see either of the

Anderton boys around. She'd been sort of hoping Cord would show, just so she could find out what girl he'd broken up with Eris for.

They stepped onto the dance floor, and Watt reached for her arms to give her a perfect spin. He moved lightly and easily on his feet. "You're a great dancer," Avery said over the music, and felt immediately guilty for sounding so surprised.

"I had those shoes when we were younger. You know the ones that danced on their own, pulling you along for the ride?"

She snorted inelegantly at the image. "That sounds danger-ous. I would definitely fall."

"I did, hundreds of times. But eventually I started dancing like this." Watt spun her again, then dipped her low over one arm.

He pulled Avery back up and the band began to slow, the lead female singer crooning one of Avery's favorite old love ballads. She started to lead Watt deeper onto the dance floor just as he took a reflexive step back.

"Please? I love this song. Especially when it's sung live," she said, trying not to laugh at his dismay. It was so rare to hear live bands anymore, so few chances to listen to things like this.

Watt obediently stepped closer, seeming to hesitate before sliding a hand around her waist. He caught her other hand in his, swaying gently. "You really like old things, don't you?" he asked, his eyes on hers.

"What do you mean?" Avery looked at him.

"The way you talked about the song just now. Or what you said in Redwood Park, or how you talk about Florence. You're so . . . nostalgic. Why do you like ancient stuff so much?"

Avery was surprised at the insight. "You think it's useless, don't you?"

"Not at all. I'm just used to only thinking about the future."

"And what does the future look like, to you?" She was curious.

"Faster! More convenient and connected. And safer, hopefully."

Avery blinked. "Sorry," Watt said ruefully, looking almost embarrassed. "I do a lot of tech stuff, in my spare time. I'm trying to get into MIT's microsystems engineering program."

Avery didn't even know what microsystems engineering *was*. "Does that mean you can fix my tablet whenever it freezes?"

Watt seemed like he might laugh, and Avery found that she didn't mind, that she wanted to join in. "Yeah. I could definitely do that," he told her. A light danced in his eyes.

Avery let them drift closer to the band. People were forming a space around them, giving Avery a nearly imperceptible bubble, like always. "You're right," she said, thinking aloud. "I do love the romance that everything had, back when there were more obstacles in the world. Like, listen to this song." She sighed. "It's about being in love even when you never get to see the person, because you're a thousand miles apart. No one would write anything like this now, because our lives are so automated and easy. Which I guess is thanks to people like you," she added, teasing.

"Hey!" Watt said in mock protest. "Don't you like always getting everything you want?"

Avery looked down, suddenly sad. "I don't get everything," she murmured.

The song ended and the crowds began shifting, giving her a direct view of Leda and Atlas.

They were sitting together in a pair of chairs near the dance floor, their heads bent close. Avery watched, powerless to look away, as Leda whispered something in Atlas's ear. He looked incredible in his new tux, Avery thought, remembering the first time he'd gone for a fitting, when he insisted she come help. Leda looked beautiful tonight too, in a new strapless cobalt gown.

They looked happy together, Avery admitted grudgingly. They looked *right*.

Watt's eyes were on her. Avery couldn't bear it; she knew her emotions must be written there on her face, plain as day. She hooked her arm around his neck and pulled him closer, tilting her head to rest it on his shoulder. She felt him catch his breath, felt his heartbeat pulsing through the tux she'd made him buy.

She could never, ever be with Atlas the way Leda was: together, holding hands, in public. It was a helpless, hopeless dream. She knew she had to give up on it—on him. But it still hurt.

"I don't think I've told you enough how beautiful you look tonight," Watt murmured. His breath was warm on her ear. She shivered, and tilted her head back to meet his gaze.

"You don't look so bad yourself, you know."

"I clean up okay, with proper help," Watt said softly. "I'm really glad I got to come with you tonight, Avery."

The sincerity in his tone gave her pause. "Me too," she said, meaning it. She was glad she'd invited Watt. He was way better than the string of fake dates she'd previously brought to stuff like this.

In fact, this wasn't really feeling like a fake date at all.

She let go of Watt's hand and reached up to lace her fingers behind his neck. He was so close she could count each eyelash framing his deep brown eyes. Her eyes traveled to his lips, and she wondered, suddenly, what it would be like to kiss him.

She hadn't thought it was possible, but maybe, eventually, she could fall for someone who wasn't Atlas.

Avery closed her eyes and swayed to the music, next to Watt, letting that be enough for now.

LEDA

LEDA WALKED THROUGH the party with Atlas, flashing smiles at everyone she saw, in a gloriously expansive mood. Tonight was going even better than she'd hoped.

Technically this was only her and Atlas's first date. But it felt like more: a proclamation, almost. Everyone here, from their friends to the photographer, was treating them like an official couple. Already their parents were seated at the same table, smiling and shooting obvious glances at them. Leda had never felt so beautiful as when she stepped into the room on Atlas's arm, smiling ear to ear. All eyes had seemed to turn to her. *Avery must feel this way every single day*, she'd thought wonderingly.

It was perfect—everything she'd ever wanted since she'd moved up here four years ago.

Best of all, there was no sign of the mysterious glo-makeup girl—if she'd ever even existed, which Leda was starting to doubt. Nadia still hadn't found a shred of evidence that Atlas was with anyone but Leda, that night or any other. Maybe the makeup had smeared on his shirt some other way. Maybe he really hadn't kissed anyone else.

Besides, based on the way the night was going, Leda was starting to hope that she and Atlas would finally go home together.

It was all she'd been able to think of, in the hover on the way here. She'd registered Atlas making conversation, had somehow managed to answer his questions, but her mind kept tracing over his body on the cushions next to her. Every time he shifted his weight, Leda felt the movement reverberate through her. It was torture, having him so achingly close.

Now, on the dance floor, she was finding every excuse she could to touch him. She pulled him close, her hand tracing small circles on his back through his tux jacket. She couldn't wait to take it off him later.

"What's going on with you and Avery?"

"What?" Surely Leda had misheard. She'd been distracted by the direction of her thoughts.

"I asked what's going on with you and Avery," Atlas repeated. He'd moved to sit in a chair at the edge of the dance floor, and Leda wordlessly sank down next to him.

"It's fine," she said automatically, annoyed that even when Avery wasn't around, everything inevitably came back to her. "Why wouldn't it be?"

"Sorry. I didn't mean to bring up a sensitive subject. I just noticed that you two haven't spent much time together lately, and I wanted to make sure . . ." He sighed. "Normally I'd ask Avery about it, but we're not exactly on great terms right now."

That made Leda sit up a little straighter. Had Avery and Atlas fought about *her*? Maybe Avery had said something to Atlas, told him that Leda wasn't good enough for him, and Atlas had stood up for her. Leda didn't want to believe it of her best friend . . . but was Avery even her best friend anymore?

"Thank you for asking. I don't really want to talk about it, though."

"I'm sorry. Forget I said anything." Atlas sounded genuinely regretful. "Want to dance?"

Leda nodded gratefully, and he swept her back onto the dance floor. "Is it weird, being back?" she asked after a while.

"Kind of," Atlas admitted. "The Tower is just so different from everywhere else, you know?"

"Well, it certainly is different from the Amazon," Leda said without thinking.

Atlas's feet were suddenly rooted in place. "How did you know about the Amazon?" he asked, very slowly.

Shit. "You mentioned it, I think," she told him, wishing she could unspeak the words.

"I'm sure I didn't," he corrected her.

"Well, Avery, then, or your parents, I don't know. I heard it somewhere," she said offhandedly.

But Atlas wasn't so easily fooled. "Leda. What's going on with you?" His brown eyes narrowed.

"Nothing, I promise. I'm sorry."

Atlas nodded, seeming to let it go, and they kept dancing. But Leda could still see the tightness in his jaw, the tension in his body. She felt it strumming through the space between them.

After another song, he took a step back. "Want a drink?"

"Yes," Leda agreed, a little too emphatically. She started to follow him, but Atlas shook his head.

"The bar's so crowded—let me bring it to you. Champagne, right?"

"Thanks," Leda said helplessly, even though champagne wasn't her drink at all; it was Avery's.

She wandered toward the enormous side rooms off the ballroom, wondering where her friends were. But before she saw them her eyes were drawn to her dad, who was standing alone in a corner. He was folded in on himself, looking like he didn't want to be noticed, and muttering, clearly on a call.

Leda's mind went immediately to last weekend, when he'd lied about golf. Before she thought twice about it she'd logged into LipRead on her contacts and focused intently on her dad's mouth, dozens of meters away. LipRead was intended as a tool for the hearing-impaired, but Leda had discovered that it worked great for spying, when you used the new superzoom contacts.

"I can't tell my family yet," a robotic voice translated her dad's words into her ear, in a grating monotone. *What* couldn't he tell them, Leda wondered, the words giving her pause. A moment later: "Fine. I'll talk to her next weekend."

Leda, dazed at what she'd overheard, watched him end the ping and walk away, just as her mom appeared at her shoulder. "Leda! You look gorgeous!" Ilara exclaimed, as if she hadn't seen her daughter getting ready. "Where's Atlas?"

"Bringing us drinks," Leda said shortly.

"Leda . . ."

"I'll be good, I promise," she added, still thinking about her dad's behavior. She glanced over her mom's crimson gown and expensive jewelry, realizing that she didn't recognize the bracelet on her wrist. "Is that new?" she asked, momentarily distracted.

"Your father just gave it to me for our anniversary." Ilara held out the bracelet, an intricate wrought-gold net studded with tiny diamonds, for Leda to inspect.

"That *and* a Calvadour scarf? Wow." Leda had never seen her dad so generous.

"I didn't get a Calvadour," Ilara said, puzzled. "What do you mean, hon?"

"There are my two girls!" Leda's dad pushed through the crowd to hook his arm through her mom's. They made a striking pair, him so light and her so dark, the red pocket square in his tux mirroring the color of her dress. Leda wondered what his bizarre ping had been about, and what had happened to the scarf. Did he think better of it, and return it? It made sense, but still, she couldn't shake the feeling that something bigger was going on.

"I need to go find Atlas." Leda stepped back, feeling suddenly uneasy, almost panicked. She wanted a drink. Now.

"Leda—"

"See you at home," she called out over her shoulder.

When she got to the bar, she shoved shamelessly forward to the front of the line, looking for Atlas. "Excuse me. I'm sorry," she muttered, not really caring who she pushed past. Her need was like an itch crawling desperately over her skin. In some part of her mind, she registered this as a warning flag, but she'd deal with it later, when her chest wasn't so tight.

At the front of the line stood Avery's date. Watt, if she remembered right. Leda hadn't actually been introduced to him at Eris's party, though she'd seen him there, wandering around after Avery like a lost puppy. And now he was Avery's *date* to the University Club gala? It seemed impossible that he'd just appeared in their lives out of nowhere, with no backstory and no explanation.

"Watt, right?" she asked, sidling up to him. "You're here with Avery."

"You do realize you just cut an entire line of people to get to the front of the bar."

"It's fine, they're all friends," Leda said, with an airy gesture. Well, it was sort of true.

"Who am I to argue with that logic," Watt replied, his mouth twitching with a barely suppressed smile. Was he laughing at her? "Since you're clearly thirsty, let me buy you a drink."

"It's an open bar," Leda snapped in irritation, as the white-gloved bartender turned to Watt. She started to tell him that she wanted a—

"Whiskey soda for the lady. Beer for me. And a champagne," Watt said.

When the bartender handed him the drinks, Watt and Leda moved aside, to a high-topped table past the crush of people. "How did you know what I wanted?" Leda asked, a little discomfited. Whiskey soda wasn't exactly a ladylike drink, but it was the only thing that calmed her when she felt truly agitated.

"Lucky guess," Watt said easily. "But be careful. It only takes one."

She shot him a glance, startled. What the hell did he mean by that? *It only takes one* was what they used to say back at Silver Cove. But Watt was just sipping his beer innocently.

"I'm sorry," she said, in the nicest tone she could muster. "I haven't even introduced myself. I'm Leda Cole." She held out a hand, and Watt shook it, that maddening smirk still on his face.

"I know," he answered.

"Well, that doesn't seem fair," she went on, more flustered than she'd wanted to be. "I don't know anything about you! Tell me about yourself."

"Oh, I'm not very interesting," he said lightly.

"Where do you go to school?"

"Jefferson High."

She frowned, wishing she could look up things like this on her contacts without being obvious about it. "I don't know it. Are you—"

"It's on the two hundred fortieth floor," he interrupted, leaning on the table, watching her. He wasn't tall, but there was something imposing about his stance. She found herself wishing they were seated.

"I see." Leda had no idea how to respond. She hadn't talked to anyone from that far down even back when she was a mile-higher. "And how did you say you met Avery?"

"I didn't say." He winked. "You seem awfully curious about me. It's because Avery is your best friend, right?" He said it knowingly, and Leda flushed, angry. Had Avery told this guy about their falling out?

"She is," Leda said defensively.

Avery appeared as if on cue. Her hair was swept up in a twist, a few tendrils escaping to frame her face, an incandescent tucked behind one ear like everyone used to do in middle school. It was totally lame and yet, of course, Avery pulled it off effortlessly. God, by next week everyone would probably be wearing incandescents again. Avery moved forward and the light dazzled over her gown, which was high necked and covered in miniature shards of mirror. *Of course you picked that*, Leda thought, with a surprising bitterness. *It's a dress that literally reflects you to yourself ad infinitum.*

"Hi." Avery stepped close to Watt, only to stiffen once she noticed Leda. "Oh. Hey, Leda. How's your night?"

Oh, I just messed things up with the guy I like, and my dad's acting weird, and I really miss my best friend. Other than that, it's completely— "Fantastic," Leda said, a smile settling over her face like a mask.

Avery nodded. "I saw your mom earlier. She said you guys might go to Greece over Christmas? I had no idea," she added clumsily.

Of course you had no idea. We don't talk anymore. "Yeah," Leda said, suddenly sad. "Remember that time we had to be Greece for model UN?" she blurted out, not sure why she was bringing it up.

"And our homemade baklava made everyone sick?" Avery joined in.

"That's one way to win. Send everyone else running home," Leda said seriously, and then they both laughed. For a fleeting instant, the world seemed normal again.

Until their laughter died down, and they looked at each other across the table, and both seemed to realize that things weren't all right between them at all.

Avery was the first to escape. "Can we go dance?" she asked, turning to Watt and leaving her still full champagne on the table.

"As you wish." Watt took Avery's hand. "Nice meeting you, Leda."

"Bye, Leda," Avery called over her shoulder as she pulled Watt into the crowd.

"Yeah, see you," Leda mumbled, but they were already gone.

Leda stayed at the table for a while, downing the whiskey soda and then the champagne Avery had left behind. There was something weird about that Watt guy. She didn't trust him. She wanted to ask Avery about him . . . but then there was so much she needed to talk about with Avery, and she didn't know how anymore.

Leda thought she saw Atlas over by the dance floor, where he'd left her. She should go back and find him.

But she turned back toward the bar instead, her small shoulders drawn upward like a knife. First she would get another drink.

ERIS

ERIS LAY ON Mariel's bed, curled idly onto one side. Through half-closed lids she watched Mariel at her desk, furiously typing away at some assignment. The walls were painted a soft green, covered in instaphotos of Mariel and her friends, and various photography posters—the sun setting over a jagged mountain range, the moon lit up during an eclipse. Country music played on Mariel's speakers. Eris had never met anyone obsessed with country music except Avery, and she'd long ago written it off as one of those incomprehensible Avery quirks. It was kind of funny, that Eris's best friend and the girl she was dating had something so unusual in common.

"Are you almost finished?" Eris asked Mariel, though she didn't really mind. She liked it more than she would've expected, actually, spending time with Mariel in peaceful quiet while Mariel did her homework. She couldn't remember ever lying on someone else's bed and just hanging out, without any expectations at all.

"Almost," Mariel said, her brow furrowed in concentration.

Where are you? Caroline flickered. "I'm at Mariel's," Eris said aloud, composing a reply. Caroline had met Mariel, and knew that she and Eris were spending time together lately. "My mom," she added in explanation, since Mariel had heard the message.

Mariel nodded. "Seems like things are getting better between you two," she pointed out.

It was true. After their lunch with Leda's dad—after Eris learned that he was *her* dad too—she and her mom had fallen into a sort of truce. They'd started hanging out again, the way they used to: wandering through their favorite upper-floor haunts, even having dinner together most nights. It was nice, no longer feeling so resentful toward her mom. "Have you heard anything else from your birth dad?" Mariel asked. "When will you see him again?"

"I don't know," Eris told her. They hadn't made any plans to meet up again, hadn't discussed what kind of support, if any, Mr. Cole would give them. She'd mentioned it to her mom earlier, but Caroline had said not to worry, it was being taken care of. What did that mean? Eris wondered, crazily, if she and her mom would move upstairs and start being one big family with the Coles.

"Well, I'm sure he'll reach out," Mariel said, with more confidence than Eris felt. "It's probably just as weird and new for him as it is for you."

"Thanks," Eris said, glad she'd decided to tell Mariel the whole story.

She'd come and spilled everything to Mariel the afternoon that it happened. Partly because she needed to share the news with someone, and couldn't talk to anyone from the upper floors, since they all knew Leda. But mainly she told Mariel simply because she wanted the other girl to know, and was interested in her opinion. Eris didn't know anyone else who approached life the way Mariel did, who *thought* the way Mariel did.

"Let's not talk about me anymore," Eris said, suddenly eager for a distraction. "I want to talk about you."

"But I so enjoy always talking about you," Mariel quipped. Eris sat up and glared at her, and Mariel laughed. "Sorry," she said, though she didn't sound sorry at all. "What did you want to talk about?"

"I know I'm endlessly fascinating," Eris said drily. "But seriously. We met, what, a month ago? And there's still so much I don't know about you."

"Has it really been a month?"

Eris tossed a pillow at Mariel, who ducked. "Fine, fine, what do you want to know?"

"Favorite color," Eris said automatically.

"What a typical Eris question," Mariel replied, but before Eris could throw another pillow, she answered, "Green! Mint green, actually."

"Favorite class in school."

"That's easy. Debate."

"Really?" Eris couldn't help asking. All the debate kids she knew were so awful, with their obnoxious uniform vests and know-it-all attitudes. Mariel seemed way too cool to be one of them.

"If you're that surprised, clearly I haven't argued with you enough," Mariel teased.

"Feel free to try." Eris smiled. "What do you want to do, someday?"

"Be on the holos."

"Me too!"

Mariel laughed again. She'd spun her chair around to face Eris and pulled her feet up to cross them. One of her socks was pink with white polka dots, the other dotted with tiny orange pumpkins. "I don't think we'd have the same holos career," she said, her eyes dancing. "I want to be a political commentator."

"Those people who read the news?"

"The ones who lead presidential debates, and talk about the issues, and write articles for the newsfeeds." Mariel looked down, pulling at the sleeves of her sweater. "I just want to help people understand what's going on. Help them decide their opinions."

"Why don't you run for office, and then you won't just be helping people think, but actually *doing* stuff?" Eris suggested. She scooted toward the edge of the bed, close enough to touch Mariel's arm.

"Maybe," Mariel said, but she sounded as though she didn't really believe it. "One more question," she added, looking back at Eris.

Eris tilted her head, weighing her thoughts. She didn't know anything about Mariel's romantic history; she didn't even know whether she dated guys as well as girls. "Have you ever been in love?" she decided.

"No," Mariel said quickly—too quickly, Eris thought. She wondered who Mariel had loved, and was surprised to feel a pang of disappointment, or maybe jealousy. "Have you?" Mariel pressed.

"No, I mean, me neither."

The song switched to a fast, upbeat country track: a girl's voice crooning about how she was going to get revenge on someone who'd cheated on her. Mariel turned quietly back to her assignment, and Eris pulled out her tablet, flipping idly through the feeds, her heart pounding though she wasn't sure why.

The University Club fall gala was going on right now, miles above their heads. Avery had offered to bring her as a guest, but Eris had declined—she wasn't sure she wanted to face the stares, or the chance of seeing her dad—that is, the man she'd thought was her dad. *Either dad*, she mentally corrected, because Mr. Cole would of course be there too.

Still, as the minutes ticked by and Eris flipped through photo after photo of her friends all dressed up and having an amazing time, she began to regret telling Avery no. Her mind drifted to what she'd be wearing right now, if she were there. Maybe her blush-colored gown with the scalloped hem, or something silver—hadn't that been the theme of the party this year? She pulled up the invitation on her contacts. *The University Club invites you to an evening under the stars*, it read in elaborate cursive, with animated stars falling in bursts around the corners of her vision. There was a comet tonight, she remembered suddenly.

"Done," Mariel said, clicking to turn in her assignment. "What do you want to do tonight?"

"Get your coat." Eris grinned. "We're going on an adventure."

———————

"I'm confused," Mariel said as they walked along Jersey Highway at 35th Street. The solar-charged lamps cast interlocking rings of golden light on the sidewalk. Up ahead Eris could see the hulking form of the *Intrepid* naval museum, an enormous old ship anchored to the Hudson's floor. They'd gone on a field trip there in third grade. She still remembered how Cord had tried to dare her and Avery to jump off the side, to see whether the water would give them mermaid gills. Cord—she hadn't really thought about him in weeks, had she?

"All your questions are about to be answered, I promise." Eris stepped up to a gate marked PIER 30: EMPLOYEES ONLY. She entered the code she'd paid for online, and the door swung open.

They stepped out onto a wooden dock, with rows of corrugated iron doors on either side. Water lapped softly under their feet. Eris couldn't stop smiling. She loved this sensation: the delicious thrill of setting out on a wild quest for something you may or may not find, all the while knowing that whatever happened, the night itself would certainly be wonderful.

She punched the same code into one of the doors, which retracted up into the roof overhead, revealing a small space filled almost entirely by a four-person hoverboat. Its shape reminded Eris of the top of a mushroom, propeller jets peeking out from under the sleek white hull. The only decoration was a peeling American flag decal. "Put this on," she said, tossing Mariel a silver inflato-belt.

"Whose boat is this?" Mariel stepped onto the tiny enclosed dock, snapping the belt around her waist. Eris pushed a button and the hoverboat began to lower onto the water.

"We're borrowing it," she said simply. The after-hours rental she'd paid for was, she felt pretty certain, illegal. The lights around the boat turned the water in the slip a brackish green.

Eris kicked off her shoes before grabbing Mariel's hand and pulling her inside, onto the white vinyl seats that circled the interior of the boat.

"Do you know how to drive this thing?" Mariel asked, watching her. She seemed torn between skepticism and enthusiasm.

"It has autopilot. At least, that's what I was told." Eris grinned and pushed the start button, and the hoverboat took off into the night.

They skimmed across the surface of the water, which was as dark and impenetrable as the surface of a black mirror. Eris's hair whipped around in a reckless tangle. Spray flung up into her face. The sting of it felt shockingly good. Across the river in New Jersey, scattered lights twinkled warmly.

Mariel was looking out over the water, watching their progress. There was something almost regal in the shadowed line of her profile, her long nose and high brow. Then she turned and winked at Eris, and the illusion was broken.

"Where are you taking us, O intrepid captain?" Mariel raised her voice over the sound of the wind and the motor.

"Somewhere we can see around *that*." Eris pointed back at the Tower, which stretched impossibly high into the darkness.

They passed the shrouded form of the Statue of Liberty, heading south around the seaports, where Eris could hear the sounds of music and raucous laughter. Finally, when they were far enough away that the Tower no longer filled the whole sky, Eris killed the motor. She leaned over the side to trail her fingers in the water and pulled them quickly back. It was bitter cold.

"I love this. It's an amazing surprise, " Mariel said, in the sudden quiet.

"This isn't the surprise," Eris said, "at least, not all of it."

The cheers from South Street were getting louder. Eris could hear music playing, and saw the pink dancing lights of hallucilighters across the water. "Is there some kind of rave going on tonight?" Mariel asked.

Eris laughed. "They're all here for the same reason we are," she said, and drew her arm around Mariel. "Look." She pointed up, and they both tipped their faces to the stars.

A comet sliced through the velvet-dark sky, its tail streaming after it like a fan.

"It's beautiful," Mariel breathed.

Eris drank in the sight, trying not to think about the University Club, how Avery and Leda were probably pressed up against the windows this very moment, wearing expensive gowns and holding champagne flutes as the comet blazed past. *Stop it*, she told herself. This was so much better.

"It's almost named after me, you know," she said, recalling what she'd read earlier. "Eros instead of Eris. Supposedly it won't pass Earth again for a thousand years."

"The god of love." Mariel laughed. "Eris, on the other hand, is the goddess of—"

"Chaos," Eris said ruefully. She'd always teased her mom

about that. Caroline claimed she hadn't known, that she'd picked the name because she thought it was pretty.

"Sometimes love and chaos are the same thing," Mariel said softly.

Eris turned around and kissed her in reply, blocking the comet from her view.

Mariel responded eagerly, slipping her arms around Eris's shoulders. There was something new in the kiss, a tenderness Eris wasn't familiar with.

Eventually Mariel pulled back. "Eris. I'm afraid."

"What? Why?" The comet had faded from the sky. Downtown, they could hear the screams of revelers toasting its arrival. Eros, the love comet.

"I just . . ." Mariel seemed about to say something. Eris could feel nervousness crackling across the surface of her skin, like electricity. "I don't want to get hurt."

Eris felt for some reason that hadn't been what Mariel originally meant to say. But she just leaned in, resting her head lightly on Mariel's shoulder. "I'll never do anything to hurt you. I promise," she said softly.

The cynical, worldly part of Eris laughed at herself for saying that, for making a promise she could never hope to keep. Well, she would just have to keep it this time, she thought firmly.

She felt Mariel relax a little next to her. Their boat rocked back and forth, gently buffeted by the waves. "I promise," Eris said again, and the words drifted up like smoke into the darkness.

AVERY

"THANKS FOR THE ride home," Avery said when the hover pulled up to her apartment. Her parents had left the party hours ago, and she wasn't sure where any of her friends were by now, not even Leda or Atlas. She'd been too distracted by the dancing, the laughing, the swirl of coordinated excitement surrounding the comet. And by Watt.

She'd had fun with him tonight, far more fun than she'd expected to. He was somehow earnest without being serious, confident without being an asshole. As he walked her to the front door, Avery realized that Watt would have to go almost eight hundred floors downTower after dropping her off. She tried to picture his home life and drew a blank. Why hadn't she asked more questions about *him*? she thought, a little embarrassed at how self-centered he must think she was.

"Of course." Watt reached gingerly behind her ear for the

incandescent. It was dried and brown now, its fragrance cloyingly sweet. Just hours ago it had been a living star.

"I guess the night's really over, isn't it?" she remarked wistfully. Watt made a move to throw the flower away, but she stopped him. "No, don't—not yet. I want to keep it. Just for a little while."

He obediently held out the incandescent, his eyes on her, thoughtful. Avery reached for the dead blossom and held it tight in her palm. She felt like she could hear Watt's heartbeat echoing across the space between them.

Ever so lightly, Watt leaned down to place his lips on her forehead. He paused, giving Avery time to pull away. She didn't, but she didn't lean in either. She just stood still, and waited.

By the time he was brushing his lips to hers the kiss felt inevitable. Avery kissed him back without thinking, eager to see what Watt felt like, tasted like. The kiss was soft and slow and she loved how warm his hands were on her hips.

When they finally broke apart, neither of them spoke. Avery felt a strange, aching happiness. She'd finally done it: kissed someone who wasn't Atlas. For real this time, not someone she was halfheartedly avoiding, not a sloppy makeout at a holiday party, but someone she might actually like. It felt like sacrilege, and yet it hadn't been that hard at all.

Maybe this was what she needed, she thought, to help her get over Atlas once and for all. Maybe *Watt* was what she needed.

"Good night, Avery," he said, turning back toward the hover. The feelings swirling uncertainly around Avery's mind coalesced into a single word.

"Wait."

Watt stopped, the door halfway shut.

Avery's heart was beating too fast, her breathing uneven. She wondered if Atlas was home and would see them together. *Stop thinking of Atlas.* She didn't want Watt to leave, and yet she wasn't sure she was ready for this. But maybe she never would be.

"I was thinking . . ." She bit her lip. Watt stood there patiently, watching her watch him. And Avery realized her decision was made.

"Do you want to come in?"

WATT

AT FIRST WATT wasn't sure he'd heard correctly. "Yeah. I mean, I'd love to," he told Avery, trying not to sound too eager.

He let the hover drive off as she took his hand and led him inside, through the imposing mirrored entryway that opened onto their vast, two-storied living room. He half expected to go toward the couch, but instead Avery turned immediately to the right, down a carpeted hallway. Were they really going where he thought they were going? he wondered. He wasn't used to doing this stuff without Nadia's help.

"This is my room," Avery murmured, pushing open a door.

Watt was dimly aware of an ornate bedroom with a massive four-poster bed, everything decorated in soft blue and cream, antique prints and heavy-framed mirrors spaced evenly on the walls. But he couldn't focus on anything but Avery. He hesitated, his mind whirling, wondering if he should make the first move or if that would be too forward.

And then Avery leaned in and kissed him, and he was done thinking.

They fell backward onto the bed in a wild tangle. Watt wasn't being careful with his kisses anymore. Avery began impatiently unbuttoning his dress shirt, yanking the straps of his suspenders down over his shoulders, and then her hands were on the plane of his chest and she was pushing him back against her pillows, her kisses insistent, almost frantic. In whatever part of his mind was still functioning, Watt wanted to shout some primal victory cry.

He couldn't quite believe it. He was in Avery Fuller's bedroom, on Avery Fuller's bed, kissing Avery Fuller. The most beautiful, most incredible, most intriguing girl in the entire world. And of all the infinite guys she could have, she had somehow picked him.

He slipped his hands around to the zipper at the back of her dress. Avery made a sound deep in her throat. Mistaking her meaning, Watt tugged it down all the way, and Avery pulled back as if scalded.

He blinked, dazed. "I'm sorry. We can slow down," he said thickly.

"No. It's not— I just—" Avery took a deep, rattling breath. "I can't do this." She sounded close to tears.

Watt sat up and raked a hand through his hair. "I promise. Nothing you don't want to do." He searched for his shirt and threw it back on, feeling guilty.

"It's not that. . . ." She trailed off, biting her lip. "I think you should go," she said, and there was a finality in her voice that scared Watt more than anything she'd said.

"Okay. But . . . why?" he couldn't help asking.

Avery didn't say anything, didn't even look at him. He was reminded suddenly of Eris's birthday party, how they'd been talking, even flirting; then in a bewildering instant Avery had gone pale and dumped him on Ming. And what about that weird, wistful comment she made tonight, about not always getting everything she wanted? Even without Nadia, Watt's mind was capable of putting together the pieces.

"Is it someone else?" He knew it was an asshole thing to ask, but he wanted to know. Avery just looked at him in apparent distress. "Never mind. Forget it," Watt said, hating how bitter he sounded.

Without another word, he turned and walked out of Avery's room, out of her apartment, and maybe out of her life for good.

LEDA

LEDA SLID INTO the hover alongside Atlas. It was later than she'd realized, and she'd drunk more than she'd meant to. All the uncertainty in her life was throwing her off. But it didn't matter; she and Atlas were here, together, alone at last. She scooted closer to him, too drunk to worry anymore, and looked up at him through her lashes.

She was sick of waiting. She wanted him so acutely she couldn't think straight. The hover reached her house, and Leda started to kiss him.

"Leda." Atlas pulled back, circling her wrists with his hands and lowering them to her lap.

"You should come inside," she persisted.

Atlas shook his head. "We need to talk."

Those four words sent a cold finger of dread down her nerves, already buzzing and on edge with the alcohol. "So talk," she said bluntly.

"I had a lot of fun with you at the gala," Atlas began awkwardly. "You looked beautiful tonight, you know. But," he went on, and in that *but* she saw all her heartbreak, "I don't think we should go out again."

"You don't want to at least sleep with me before you run off this time?"

Atlas flinched. "I'm sorry. What happened in Catyan . . . I should have stopped it before it went so far."

"If it was such a mistake, then why did you ask me out again tonight?"

"Because you're incredible. Any guy would be lucky to go out with you." Atlas looked straight into her eyes. "You deserve better than me—you deserve the truth. And the truth is, I have feelings for someone else. It wouldn't be fair to you, letting things go on when I feel this way."

"All right, then."

Atlas started to come around to open the door for her, but she stepped out and slammed it shut before he had the chance. "I'm sorry, Leda. I hope we can stay friends," he said.

She just carefully climbed up her steps, letting him see how unaffected she was, stubbornness and wounded pride keeping her head aloft. She wondered what he would say, if he knew that the last time he'd pulled something like this, she'd gone on a wild tailspinning bender that ended in two months of rehab.

She should have known better. She should have known that Atlas would play boomerang with her emotions again, ask her out to big public events and then tell her stiffly that he wanted to be "fair." *I'll show you fair*, she thought, walking in her front door without turning her head even a fraction of a degree back in his direction.

But the moment she was safely in her room, Leda crumpled to the floor, cradling her head in her hands. A terrifying part of her hated Atlas for the way he'd treated her. She wanted to hurt him, him and whatever stupid girl he supposedly had *feelings* for.

Leda realized with a start that she still hadn't used the best weapon in her arsenal. She started mumbling, composing a message to Nadia. *You were wrong. Atlas just told me that he's in love with someone else. Figure out who it is, or you're fired.*

A moment later, a response she didn't expect flashed across her vision. *Too late. I quit.*

Her blood boiled. *No one quits on* me. *You can't quit, not now.*

And you wanted to fire me. It sure is hard to keep up with your mood swings.

You little—

Sorry, but I'm done with all of you, Nadia interrupted, and then the link was broken as Nadia blocked her permanently.

Leda didn't know what the hacker meant by "all of you," and she didn't particularly care. She felt blindsided. Everything was pressing in on her. Losing her best friend, then Atlas, and now Nadia on top of everything else . . . god, she just wanted to *talk* to someone . . . not to mention all the weirdness lately, about her dad . . . Leda felt cornered, panicked. She wanted to lash out. *Think,* she told herself, but her thoughts weren't coming. She closed her eyes and took a deep, shuddering breath.

She couldn't take it anymore.

She pulled up the unsent flicker to Ross, still waiting there in her drafts box, and sent it under her breath. *It's me. What have you got?*

AVERY

AVERY SIGHED AS she pulled her feet up onto the soft gray couch in the living room. She waved halfheartedly, the gesture scrolling through the thousands of channels on the holoscreen. But all she could think about was Watt, and the look on his face when she'd kicked him out of her room.

Avery felt terrible about how she'd ended the night. She really hadn't meant to lead Watt on. The moment he turned up on her doorstep, looking so magnificent in his tux, she'd felt a little thrill of excitement. And that feeling had only grown as the night wore on.

Maybe it was the way he tried to talk to her, *really* talk to her, and paid attention to things that mattered to her. Maybe it was the warm, clean scent of him, when she leaned her cheek on his shoulder on the dance floor. Or maybe it was just that something in Avery's life would have to change, drastically, if she had any hope of getting over Atlas, and this was the most drastic change she could think of. Whatever the reason, standing there at the end of the night, she'd decided to follow Jess's advice—to do it, and get it over with. She was going to have sex with Watt.

Yet when the moment came, Avery froze up completely. She liked Watt, she really did, and still she couldn't do it. She knew it was messed up, but she'd always imagined that moment with Atlas. No matter how hard she tried to convince herself, she couldn't bear the thought of being with anyone else.

She thought of what Watt had said earlier, about how she was always looking backward while he looked forward. She wondered, suddenly, if part of why she was so interested in the past was because it was easier than thinking of the future—of *her* future. Because a future with Atlas was impossible, and yet a future without him would be unbearable.

Avery glanced at her messages again. Still nothing from Watt. She'd sent him a brief flicker saying she was sorry for the way things ended, and she hoped he got home okay, but she hadn't heard back.

If only she could talk this out with Leda. But she had no idea if Leda and Atlas were still at the gala, or at Leda's place . . . Avery swiped at the holo channels again, trying desperately not to think about Leda and Atlas. Better to focus on the lesser hurt, of how royally she'd screwed things up with Watt.

She heard the telltale beep of the front door and sat up, startled, tucking her stray wisps of hair behind her ears. Her parents had come home hours ago and were asleep in their master at the far end of the hall. It had to be Atlas.

"Avery?" He stood in the doorway. "I didn't realize you were home."

"You're back," she pointed out, stupidly.

"Yeah." He settled on the couch next to her.

"I thought you were with Leda," Avery couldn't help saying.

"I was, but I dropped her off." He paused. "I told Leda we shouldn't go out again."

"Oh." Avery felt a surge of triumph at the news and hated herself for it, for rejoicing in her friend's suffering. Part of her knew that if it weren't Atlas, Leda would be calling her right now, to vent about the whole thing and scheme some Leda-esque revenge.

They sat there for a moment, both of them staring straight ahead at the holoscreen, where a commercial for a new dragon-fruit snack pack was playing. Animated dragons flew around the screen in circles, batting their long eyelashes.

Atlas turned to her. "So what's the deal with you and that Watt guy?"

"What do you mean?"

"What do you see in him, anyway?"

"You said last week that you thought he was nice!" Avery snapped. Atlas didn't answer. "Not that it's any of your business," she went on testily, "but we're over. Guess it's a night for breakups. Happy now?"

Atlas met her gaze, those deep brown eyes unblinking. "Aves. I only care if *you're* happy."

She felt her anger deflate. "The thing is," she said haltingly, "you were right. Watt *is* a nice guy. It's not his fault he's not—"

She couldn't afford to finish that thought.

"Not what?" Atlas prompted.

Avery was tired, so tired, of acting like the sight of Atlas with other girls didn't bother her, of hiding her hurt behind a smile. The pretense weighed on her so heavily, she felt she might snap in two.

Yet she hesitated. If she said it, if she told Atlas what she really wanted to, she risked losing him forever.

"Not you," she whispered at last.

The words hung there, quietly ending the world Avery had always lived in. In the silence a new world was unfolding. Avery held her breath.

And then suddenly Atlas's arms were around her, his lips on hers.

Avery responded eagerly, recklessly, her heart almost hurting with joy. Their kisses were frantic and feverish and she would never get enough of them.

At some point Atlas swung her up into his arms and started down the hall to his room. Avery's head was pressed against his chest and she could hear the erratic beat of his heart, its pulse matching her own. She felt it too—the exhilaration, and underneath it the thin electrifying undercurrent of fear, at the forbiddenness of what they were about to do. She shivered.

A crash sounded. She realized Atlas had knocked over the lamp by his bed. They both froze, hardly daring to breathe. Their parents were still home—asleep on the other end of the apartment, but still, they were here.

Nothing happened, and after a moment, Avery relaxed. "I'm sorry," Atlas began, but Avery just laughed and pulled him onto the bed with her.

"It doesn't matter. None of it matters but you." She reached up to kiss him again but Atlas beat her to it, his kisses burning her skin, obliterating all thought.

———

When Avery woke up, Atlas's sleeping form was curled around hers, his arm over her shoulder and his breath soft in her ear—living proof that it was real, that she hadn't imagined any of it. She lay still for a while, relishing the feel of Atlas so close to her. Then she turned on her side and kissed him.

Atlas stirred. "Hey there," he said drowsily, and smiled.

"What are you thinking?" Avery asked, because she wasn't sure how to say what she wanted to.

"Right now, I'm thinking how nice it is to lie here and hold you," he murmured, reaching an arm around to pull her closer.

She nestled contentedly into him, but a million questions still whirled through her mind. "Atlas," she tried again. "After Eris's party, when we kissed . . . you didn't even remember. . . ." She looked at him expectantly, but his brow was furrowed.

"*I* didn't remember?" he repeated. "Aves, you were the one who acted like it never happened!"

"No," she said automatically—that couldn't be true. Could it?

"You didn't even kiss me back, up on the roof!" Atlas went on. "It terrified me. Why do you think I ran away so fast?"

"But you were just standing there eating waffles the next morning like it never happened!"

"Only because I thought that was what you wanted me to do."

Avery shook her head. But as she played back through the events of that night, she remembered how fragile that kiss had seemed, how she hadn't dared move for fear of breaking the spell and sending Atlas running. Maybe she'd done that anyway. "I thought you didn't remember. Or didn't care," she whispered.

"Of course I remember. How could I forget kissing the girl I love?"

Avery caught her breath. "I love you too," she said, so glad to finally say it aloud.

It was close to dawn. She should get back to her room before her parents woke up. She stole another glance at Atlas, who lay propped on one elbow beneath the rumpled white sheets. He watched the play of emotions across her face, reading her as always. "You're leaving," he said.

Avery nodded and reluctantly sat up. But something else was

bothering her. "What about Leda?" she asked. Stubbornness, her one flaw, Atlas always said.

He looked away. "I feel terrible about how I've treated Leda in all this." *I should feel terrible too*, Avery thought, but even though Leda was her best friend, it was hard right now to think of her as anything but the obstacle that had kept her from Atlas. "I really didn't mean to lead her on," he added remorsefully, and Avery was reminded of her thoughts about Watt last night.

"Why did you sleep with her, in the Andes?"

"Because I couldn't have *you*, Aves." He shook his head. "I thought being with Leda might keep me from thinking about you all the time. That's why I went away—to escape the way I felt about you. I kept hoping that if I just ran far enough, eventually I'd figure out a way to stop loving you."

"I'm glad it didn't work."

"Of course it didn't work." Atlas smiled. "There's no way it ever could."

WATT

WATT HEADED HOME from the gym Sunday afternoon, taking a large sip of his painkiller protein shake, and winced at the soreness in his shoulders. It had been a particularly rough session with the boxing-bot, per his request. He'd hoped that if he punched the bot hard enough, he would forget the sting of Avery's rejection. So far it hadn't worked.

Watt had never answered the flicker Avery sent late last night. It sounded too much like a brush-off. Nadia, when he turned her back on, had suggested that he respond. But Watt was human and irrational, so he'd left it deliberately unanswered despite Nadia's advice, his silence some kind of stupid prideful statement.

He stepped up to the 236th floor observation deck, full of recycled-water fountains and gimmicky ice-pop stands and screaming kids. There were more crowds up here than usual. He caught a glimpse of the sky through the floor-to-ceiling windows, and saw a roiling mass of storm clouds gathering.

I didn't realize today was a rain day, Watt remarked to Nadia, moving closer. He'd loved rain days ever since he was a kid—the brightly colored dirigibles that rose into the air and released the hydrosulfates, the way moisture gathered around the exploding chemicals in perfectly symmetrical spirals, and then the satisfying hiss as the desired rain began to fall. Humans couldn't control the weather on a global scale, of course, but they'd figured out localized methods of rain induction and prevention almost fifty years ago. Watt wondered what it had been like back when people were at the mercy of the weather: if they, too, thought rain was beautiful, or if they hated it because they couldn't control it. *Avery would know*, he thought, then felt annoyed with himself for the thought.

"You're welcome," Nadia's voice sounded in his eartennas.

Wait—you're telling me this was you?

"You needed cheering up," she said simply.

Sometimes I worry that I'm wasting your talents. Watt shook his head, smiling a little. Leave it to Nadia to hack the Metropolitan Weather Bureau just because a seventeen-year-old kid had gotten rejected by the girl he liked. But he was grateful.

Do you *think Avery likes someone else?* he asked Nadia as the first fat raindrops began to clatter against the skylight overhead. The edges of the Tower were lined with them, everywhere the building narrowed as the floors went up.

"I know she does."

What do you mean, you know? Watt thought back, confused.

"Do you want me to tell you?"

Watt hesitated. Part of him was relieved that Avery's rejection hadn't actually been about *him*, that he hadn't done anything to make her change her mind. But another part was angry with her for even asking him out at all, feeling the way she clearly felt about this other person. Of course Watt wanted to know who it was.

If he asked, though, he would be just as bad as Leda. And knowing wouldn't change what had happened.

Thanks, Watt told Nadia, *but I don't want to know.*

He held firm the rest of the walk home, through when he walked in the front door and Zahra and Amir jumped up excitedly, begging him to play games. He held firm all through dinner, and helping his parents clean up, and putting the twins to bed.

Yet he couldn't stop thinking about it. Now that he knew that Nadia knew—that the message was literally *inside* his own brain—it was like an itch he felt desperate to scratch. Finally Watt's willpower snapped. He retreated into his room and shut the door firmly behind him.

"Changed my mind," he said aloud to Nadia. "I want to know." He didn't care that the knowledge wouldn't be helpful, that it would probably just upset him even more. He needed to know whom Avery had chosen over him.

"I'm going to play you the room comp audio, from Atlas's room," Nadia told him. "This is from last night, after you left their apartment."

"Okay." Watt didn't understand where this was going. Maybe Avery had told Atlas who she liked?

Watt frowned as he heard Atlas murmuring, and a moment later, a higher-pitched voice whispering. Okay, so he had a girl with him. Leda would want this, he realized. He could charge her a ton of money for it. He opened his mouth to tell Nadia to fast-forward to the part about Avery—

Watt's fingers tightened around the edges of his chair. *Oh god.* He recognized that girl's voice. And his anger dissolved into a sick nausea as he realized the truth.

RYLIN

LATER THAT WEEK, Rylin stood in the doorway of Cord's room, steeling herself for what she was about to do. She'd done it once before, she reminded herself. But it had felt different then, back when Cord was just the asshole who'd hit on her after his party, not the boy who'd taken her to Paris and made her laugh—made her happy—despite everything else going on in her life. The boy she was falling for despite all her better judgment.

She thought of V, and the looming threat of Hiral in jail, and shivered with foreboding. She needed to do it now; Cord had just left for school—she'd heard the front door close behind him—and she wanted to get these and off-load them before he was home. Moving quickly, decisively, she slipped into the room and grabbed five Spokes from Cord's hiding place, shoving them in her back jeans pocket. She walked out the door and halfway down the upstairs hallway—

And ran straight into Cord.

"Hey there," he said, grabbing her shoulders to steady her, "where are you headed in such a hurry?"

"I thought you left," she said, then winced; that was an odd thing to say. She couldn't stop thinking about the last time this had happened, when she'd kissed Cord to keep from being caught red-handed. But now he looked so trusting she didn't even need to distract him.

"I'm headed back out," he said, and she realized he was wearing jeans and a plain white shirt instead of his school uniform.

"You're cutting again," she realized aloud.

Cord looked at her closely, and for a single terrifying moment Rylin thought he had somehow figured out about the Spokes, but then he nodded as if coming to a decision. "Do you want to come?" he offered.

Rylin hesitated. The Spokes were burning a hole in her back pocket. "I don't know," she began—and stopped, seeing the imperceptible flash of hurt that crossed Cord's face. "All right," she amended. This was a terrible idea, going out with Cord when she was carrying so many packets. But this place clearly meant something to Cord.

"Trust me, you won't regret it," he said mysteriously, and grinned.

———

They deboarded the private copter and stepped out on the lawn of an abandoned-looking house in West Hampton. "What is this?" Rylin asked, her voice hushed, as Cord unlocked the front door. The copter's blades began to whirl, stirring up the grass in slow concentric circles before it took off again. Rylin inhaled deeply, relishing all the scents of the world outside the Tower, soil and smoke and ocean. It was nice to leave sometimes.

"My dad owned this place," Cord explained. "I didn't even know about it until after they died. He left it to me in the will."

He said it calmly, but Rylin's heart went out to him. "Just you? Not Brice?" she couldn't help asking.

"Yeah. I have no idea why. Maybe he thought I would appreciate it. Or that I needed it more, for some reason." He paused, the door open, and gave Rylin a searching look. "You're the first person I've ever brought here."

"Thank you for sharing it with me," she said quietly.

He led her into the house's entry hall, where automatic lights flickered on, revealing a small, cozy living room and stairs leading up to a second floor. For a moment Rylin wondered if they were here on some kind of romantic getaway, but Cord was already walking through the kitchen and opening another door.

"Here it is," he said in the most reverent tone she'd ever heard him use. High-beam lights flared overhead, illuminating a massive garage filled with at least a dozen cars.

Rylin walked inside, confused. Cars couldn't be driven within the Tower itself, only hovers, which were owned by Building Services and operated through a central algorithm. Almost no one in the Tower owned an actual auto, except a few upper-floor families who kept them suspended in hydraulic garages. Even in the suburbs, Rylin knew, people rarely owned individual cars anymore; it was so much easier to pool money and go in on a shared ownership, or just pay a subscription ride service.

One car, out here in the Hamptons, Rylin might understand. But why did Cord have so *many* cars?

Cord grinned, seeing her uncertainty. "Go look closer," he urged.

She ran her hands over the surface of the nearest one, sleek and red. Dust motes rose into the air. She realized that the car had a wheel, and a brake pedal—and was that an accelerator?

"Wait a minute," Rylin said, as understanding dawned on her. These weren't autocars. "Are they . . . ?"

"Yeah," Cord said proudly. "They're old, *really* old. Driver-run, pre-autocar models. My dad left them all to me." He looked fondly at the convertible Rylin was circling. "That one is almost eighty years old."

"But where did they all come from?" Wasn't this against the law?

"My dad collected them over the years. They're hard to find, mainly because they're illegal to drive, and insanely hard to get running again," Cord said easily. "Plus they drive on fossil fuels, not electricity, and petroleum is expensive."

"Why, though?" Rylin said bluntly.

Cord looked excited. "You've been in an autocar before, right?"

"Yeah, when we visited my grandparents in New Jersey, when I was little." Rylin remembered how her mom had called the car on the tablet and it appeared moments later, another family crammed inside since they could only afford the "share ride" option. They'd typed the address into the screen on the car's interior and off they went, driven by the highway system's automated central computer.

"Well, this is nothing like those cars, with their built-in speed limits. Come on, I'll show you."

Rylin stayed where she was. "You're telling me that you know how to operate that thing?" she asked, dubious. She wasn't sure she wanted to climb into a huge, dangerous piece of machinery with Cord at the controls.

"It has safety belts. And yes, I do."

But safety belts hadn't saved the millions of people who died in car accidents every year, before driver-run cars were made illegal. She remembered that much from health class. "How did you learn to drive?" she asked, stalling.

"I had help. And I practiced. Now come *on*," he teased, "where's your sense of adventure?" He held the passenger door gallantly open for her. Rylin sighed, mutinous, and took the proffered seat. The Spokes dug sharply into her rear, reminding her what she'd done earlier. She fought aside the fresh wave of guilt that rose up at the thought.

Cord reached for the handle of the garage door and manually lifted it up, letting the cool afternoon light stream in. Rylin brought her hand over her eyes to shade them. She watched as Cord reviewed the car, checking the tires, lifting the hood and studying the silver tangle of the engine beneath. His movements were clean and focused, his brows drawn together in concentration. Finally he slid into the driver's seat and turned the key in the ignition. The engine purred to life.

They started down the leaf-strewn residential road—lined with houses that peered out at them with empty eyes, abandoned in the off-season—toward the turnoff to the Long Island Expressway. Rylin marveled at the way Cord's hands moved on the wheel. "Want me to teach you to drive later?" he offered with a wink, following her gaze. She shook her head mutely.

The highway extended silent in both directions, on the left to Amagansett and the ferry to Montauk; and on the right, back to the city. Rylin could see the Tower far off, nothing but a dark haze in the distance. If she hadn't known better, she might have thought it was a storm cloud.

"Here goes," Cord said, and slammed his foot on the accelerator.

The car lurched forward like a living thing, the needle on the speedometer spiking up to fifty, then eighty, then ninety. The entire world seemed to shrink to a silent pinpoint. Rylin lost all sense of time or place. There was nothing but this, the car beneath them and the curve of the road before them and the rush of her blood pumping hot and fast through her veins. The landscape flashed past, a blur of sky and dark forest punctuated only by the yellow line glowing on the road.

The highway curved ahead. Rylin watched as Cord just barely moved the wheel, letting the car turn smoothly along with it. Her whole body thrummed with the energy of the vehicle beneath them. She understood why Cord loved this so much.

The wind pulled her hair in a loose tangle around her shoulders. She could feel Cord looking at her and she wanted to remind him to keep his eyes on the road but something told her she didn't need to. He let his right hand fall over the middle console, driving only with his left, and Rylin reached for it. Neither of them spoke.

Finally Cord turned onto a small country lane. Rylin was still trembling from the shock and exhilaration of the highway. She saw a sign that said NO PARKING and wanted to make a joke, something about how even though she'd only been in a car once, she knew what parking implied—until she saw the white ribbon of the beach, and everything else fell from her mind. "Oh!" she exclaimed, kicking off her shoes to run toward the water. The wind had carved the sand into small scallops, sloping down to the angry gray surf that mirrored the skies overhead.

"I love this," she said eagerly as Cord stepped up behind her. She and Lux had only ever been to a beach once, at Coney Island, and it was miserable and crowded. Here she could only see the sky and the sand and Cord, not even the houses that she knew were right there behind the dunes. It felt like they could be anywhere in the world.

Thunder broke, and a sudden downpour rained over them.

Cord muttered under his breath to his contacts. Almost instantly a hovercover emerged from where it had been folded in the trunk of the car, and floated through the rain toward them.

"Want to go back?" he asked over the increasing roar of the storm as they huddled for shelter on the beach, beneath the hovercover. It was the size of a very large blanket, printed with cheerful red-and-white stripes, like the old-fashioned umbrellas Rylin had seen in pics. But unlike umbrellas, which apparently had to be held aloft by anyone who wanted to use them, hover-covers were lifted by tiny aerial motors in each corner.

It could have been the storm, or that crazy car ride, or the fact that they were so far from everything resembling normal life. But Rylin was done waiting. None of the complications keeping her apart from Cord seemed important anymore, not even the stolen Spokes in her back pocket. It all faded to a distant blur, drowned out by the rainstorm and the beat of her heart.

She kissed him in answer, pulling him down deliberately onto the cold sand. The rain drummed even harder over their tiny hovercover-protected square of beach, but underneath, the sand was still warm.

Cord seemed to understand her sense of purpose. He didn't say anything, just kissed her back, slowly, as if they had all the time in the world.

ERIS

ERIS STOOD OUTSIDE Cascade, an out-of-the-way French restaurant on the 930th floor. She tried pinging her mom one last time, just in case; but Caroline didn't pick up, and she hadn't been at home earlier either. Eris shook her head in irritation and stepped inside. She would just have dinner with Mr. Cole on her own.

Ever since their lunch last week, Eris had been asking her mom constant questions. What did it mean that Mr. Cole was her father? When were they going to see him again? "I don't know, Eris. It's only been a few days," Caroline had said, then sighed. "I'll send him a message, and we'll see what he says."

So Mr. Cole had arranged this dinner. Eris had been looking forward to it all week, had discussed it at length with Mariel, who nodded and listened but didn't seem sure what advice to give.

The weirdest part was seeing Leda at school and being unable to say anything. Mr. Cole had asked Eris to let him be the one to tell her, in his own time. Of course, it *was* his secret to tell. Yet Eris hadn't been able to keep herself from stealing glances at Leda all week, marveling at the fact that they were half sisters, searching for some common features in their utterly different faces. Perhaps something around the mouths, she'd thought one day during lunch, watching Leda across the table. They both had that deep Cupid's bow, and a full, sensuous lower lip. Eris had always thought, uncharitably, that a mouth like that was wasted on Leda, who was clearly too uptight to put it to good use. But she'd never noticed how similar it was to her own.

"What? Do I have something in my teeth?" Leda had snapped, noticing her staring. Eris rolled her eyes and looked away, as if bored by the question.

Now she tossed her hair with the old entitled confidence and nodded at the hostess. "Mr. Cole's party," she murmured, and followed the girl to where her birth father was sitting, at a small round table by the windows.

"Eris," Mr. Cole said warmly as she took a seat. "You look lovely."

"Thank you." She was wearing a dress of Avery's that she'd borrowed, a navy shift with tiny darts that hugged her figure and flared around her knees. She'd thrown her mom's pearl necklace on over it, and felt almost normal again.

"I'm sorry my mom couldn't make it," she began, about to explain that she'd looked for Caroline everywhere, but Mr. Cole shook his head.

"I already spoke to her." For a moment his jaw tightened, but then the moment passed and he relaxed into a smile. "So, Eris," he said genially, "I hear I missed your birthday last month."

Had it really only been a month since her party at Bubble Lounge, since all the trappings of her former life were finally gone? It seemed like longer.

"It's okay," she said, but Mr. Cole was pulling something out of his briefcase—a signature orange Calvadour scarf box. Eris held her breath and untied the fat paper ribbon. Propelled by tiny compostable microsensors, it self-folded into an origami butterfly and flew off in search of the nearest recycle bin.

Eris gasped. Inside the box was a beautiful, hand-embroidered cashmere scarf, covered in a buckled equestrian print with a scarlet floral border. She'd seen this in the window at Calvadour; it was a one-of-a-kind piece, and inordinately expensive. Exactly the kind of thing Eris used to buy for herself, back when money was no object.

"This is too much. I can't accept it," she murmured, though of course she had no intention of giving it back. She buried her face in the cashmere and took a deep breath.

"Consider it seventeen years' worth of birthday presents from your father," Mr. Cole said gruffly.

Father. Wasn't that the first time he'd used that word in reference to her? Feeling impulsive, Eris stood up and leaned across the small table to kiss him lightly on the cheek, the way she always used to do with the man she'd thought was her dad.

Her father seemed a little surprised by the show of affection, but accepted it. Eris wondered if Leda didn't do stuff like that. Oh well, he'd just have to get used to Eris's impulsiveness. "Thank you," she said, and tied the scarf in a jaunty knot around her neck, letting the distinctive embroidery fall over her back. It was the perfect accessory for her navy dress.

The waiter approached and they ordered dinner. The lights overhead dimmed, candelabra on the walls flaming into life. Eris glanced out the old-fashioned mullioned windows that overlooked Haxley Park, a small, tucked-away public space with gardens and running fountains. She realized that someone might see them together, here by the windows. Her father, seeming to think the same thing, angled his chair a little closer toward the center of the restaurant.

"So, Eris. Tell me about your apartment."

"Our apartment?"

"Where you and your mother are living right now. It's not quite . . . spacious enough for the two of you, is it?"

"It's not huge," Eris admitted.

"What floor is it on?"

"The hundred and third."

He paled at the number. "Oh, god. I hadn't realized it was that bad." Eris didn't quite like the distaste in his voice, but let it go. "Poor Caroline," he said, almost to himself.

Their entrées arrived. Eris's father continued to pepper her with questions: about her mom, their life downstairs, her school-work, whether she'd heard anything from Everett Radson. Eris answered all his questions, wondering what exactly he was leading up to. Maybe the crazy thought she'd had wasn't so crazy after all. Maybe he really was going to suggest they start spending time together, all of them, as a family. Eris considered the possibility and found that she wasn't completely averse to it—though it would feel weird at first, being publicly and openly related to Leda. But if that was what he was hinting at, he didn't quite say it.

Finally they finished eating, and the waiter came to clear away their plates. "Thank you," Eris said as her father inclined his head to pick up the check. She shook the scarf out over her shoulders against the sudden chill. "I'll make sure my mom comes next time." Though it had been surprisingly nice, having her father to herself all evening.

"Eris," he said gently, "I'm not sure there should be a next time."

"What?"

He looked down at the tablecloth, and there was no mistaking the sudden clouding of his expression. "I've enjoyed getting to spend time with you recently, Eris; I really have. I'm proud of the beautiful young lady you've grown up to be. You're so like your mother was at your age, you know." His expression tightened. "But I'd be lying if I said this news hasn't been a shock to me. And I'm not sure it's wise for us to keep spending time together, in public settings."

Eris felt suddenly as if the air was too thick to breathe. "Why?" she managed.

"It's delicate, this relationship," Mr. Cole said. "It complicates things for me, for your mother, and for you as well."

"And for your family," Eris said, the cold realization washing over her. "Your wife, Jamie. And Leda."

He blinked a little at that. "Well, yes," Mr. Cole admitted. "I don't want them to find out, for obvious reasons. You understand, of course."

Eris did understand. She and her mom were the dirty little secret he wanted kept buried.

"Now, about your finances," Mr. Cole said, his tone utterly businesslike now. "I've already spoken about this with your mother, though she didn't accurately convey how dire your situation is." *It's not dire*, Eris wanted to say, her fierce stubborn pride kicking in. *We're doing okay, given everything.* "I'm transferring a lump sum to your account, as well as to your mom's, and I'll pay you both a monthly allowance as well. It's already been deposited, if you'd like to check."

A little shocked, Eris muttered the commands to open up her bank balance—and gasped at the number of zeroes that were now lined up there.

"Is that enough?" Mr. Cole asked, but of course the question was ridiculous. It was more than enough: to move out of the lower floors, buy a new apartment, replace all her clothes and then some. It was enough to buy her old life back. Eris knew what he was really asking: whether she understood the unspoken price. That she never tell anyone he was her birth father. Not even Leda, she thought—or rather, *especially* not Leda.

He was buying her silence.

Eris didn't answer right away. She was looking at her father's face, which she'd been studying all week in search of her own features, except this time she was trying to read his emotions. There was resignation there, and a little fear, and also something that might have been affection. She could see herself reflected in his eyes as he looked back at her, unspeaking.

Her birth father was disavowing all relation to her. It upset Eris more than she would have guessed. She felt lonely, and rejected, and angry. But emerging the strongest of all her warring emotions was a sense of relief that she wouldn't have to be poor anymore.

Never one to linger once her mind was made up, Eris stood abruptly. "It's more than enough," she said. "Thank you, for the scarf—and everything else."

Mr. Cole nodded, understanding her meaning. "Good-bye, Eris," he said softly.

Eris turned and walked out of the restaurant without another word, without even saying farewell to the only father she had left.

Abandoned by two dads, she thought sourly. What a great therapy candidate she was turning out to be.

LEDA

LEDA STOOD OUTSIDE the gates of Haxley Park on First Avenue, her eyes darting back and forth along the quiet, tree-lined street. She felt shaky and tense all over. It had been Ross's idea to meet here at Haxley, where they always used to do hand-offs before Leda's stint in rehab.

She took a deep breath and started into the park, the old-fashioned iron gates swinging smoothly inward on automatic sensors. A flood of memories washed over her. One of the first times she took xenperheidren, when she'd felt so laser focused she did all her homework for the rest of the year. The afternoon she'd smoked relaxants and lay here on the grass, looking up at the animated clouds on the ceiling in the hopes of finding a pattern. The time she and Cord took his Spokes together, and chased a mosquito around for hours until they stumbled back, laughing, to his apartment.

And now she was back again.

Everyone knew that Haxley was the best upper-floor park for getting high. There were tons of ventilators in its ceiling, since it was in a corner of the Tower, where the floor's overall airflow might otherwise slow down. It had no playgrounds, so there were no little kids or nannies around; in fact, it was conveniently empty most of the time, tucked away like this on the eastern side of a floor that was mostly office space. The only part that ever had any people was the section by the windows, where a couple of restaurants, a seafood place and a French bistro, looked out over the gardens.

Sure enough, the park's central pathway was completely empty, even on a Friday evening. "Where the hell *are* you?" Leda said quietly, sending a flicker to Ross.

The Tower's internal lights were dimming as the evening got later. A chill lifted the hairs on her arms. The centralized ventilation meant that it was always colder toward the edges of the Tower, especially in public places where no one wanted to foot the electric bill. Leda hugged herself, wishing she'd changed after school this afternoon. But she'd come straight from her SAT prep session, not even stopping back at home. She was too eager for a hit.

There was a garden up ahead with a fountain, blanketed in four-leaf clovers. Leda didn't see anyone in either direction. She'd wait for Ross there, she decided, her ballet flats crunching on the gravel underfoot.

Then she caught sight of a familiar face, and stopped in the middle of the path.

Her dad was seated at that French restaurant, the one with the heavy glass windows that looked out over the rose garden. Strange, Leda thought; hadn't she heard her mom say he was working late tonight? Maybe he'd gotten out early . . . but then, who was he with? Leda stood on tiptoe, craning her neck for a better look.

He was with a woman, and she most definitely wasn't Leda's mom. Not a woman, she realized, looking at the slight, pale form. A girl. Hell, she couldn't be much older than Leda.

And then the girl tossed her hair, a gorgeous red-gold river, and Leda realized she knew that hair, even if she couldn't see the face. It was unmistakable.

What the hell was her dad doing out with *Eris*?

"LipRead," she said, focusing as closely as she could on Eris's mouth, desperate to know what they were saying. A message flashed across her eyes: *read obstructed, shorter distance necessary.*

In spite of everything, Leda refused to believe the evidence in front of her. Surely there was some other explanation for what she was seeing—surely her dad wasn't having an *affair* with Eris. There had to be another reason they were having dinner alone, on a Friday night, in secret.

She watched, dumbstruck, as Eris reached across the table to take something from her dad. Eris smiled. And then she stood up and leaned forward, and *kissed* Leda's dad, the curtain of her hair blocking their mouths from Leda's view.

Leda watched it all as if it were happening in slow-motion. Her feet felt rooted to the ground. She watched as Eris, still smiling, settled a scarf around her shoulders. It was the one Leda had seen in her dad's briefcase, the ridiculously expensive one with scarlet flowers.

Leda stumbled forward blindly, wanting to scream. Or throw up. Now it all made sense: the weird way her father had been acting lately, the secrets he'd been keeping.

He was having an affair with Eris Dodd-Radson. Or Eris Dodd or whatever the hell her name was now.

"Leda?"

"About time!" she snapped, hurrying toward Ross. "What took you so long?"

"Somebody's a little antsy." He was young, with thick auburn hair and a face so beautiful and innocent it might have been surged onto him. His brown eyes were wide, thick lashed, with the slightly dilated pupils of someone wearing contacts—or someone constantly high. He blinked slowly, as if it were an unthinkable struggle to remain awake.

"So," he said, "I, um, have some bad news. I'm out of xenperheidren."

"What?" That was the whole reason Leda was meeting him, to get a pack of xenperheidren, and take them over and over until her world wasn't ripping apart at the seams. "Are you *serious*?"

He winced. "I'm sorry, I don't—"

"What the hell *do* you have?"

Ross opened his bag and began pulling things out one by one. "So I've got BFX, and some potshots, and relaxants, which honestly you need—"

"I'll take it all," Leda cut him off. She snatched the bag and began pawing through its contents.

"You know that's enough drugs for several—"

"I told you I don't care! I *need* it, okay?" she shrieked wildly. Ross didn't say anything. "All of it but these," she amended, grabbing the telltale black envelopes and shoving them back toward him. She knew from experience how terrible it was taking bad Spokes, and the fact that the prescription label had been tampered with was a sure sign that whoever's those were, Leda didn't want to get in their head.

Ross nodded and took the Spokes, his eyes still on her. "Why don't you keep one," he said after a beat. "Free of charge. If it's a bad trip, no skin off your back, right?"

"It's always the same with you, isn't it?" Leda said, rolling her eyes, remembering when it had just been relaxants that Ross comped her. *Guess I've graduated to the big leagues*, she thought with a dark humor. But she kept the Spokes packet. It was too expensive to turn down.

She nodded to pay Ross and made a little motion that could have meant thanks or could have meant leave me alone. Ross shrugged, accepting her payment, and shoved his hands in his pockets before heading out.

Leda clutched her red leather satchel tight to her chest, the paper sack of drugs crinkling reassuringly inside. She needed to get high, so high that even the sight of Eris kissing her father was erased brutally from her mind.

AVERY

"I'M SO HAPPY Mom and Dad are gone," Avery murmured. Her parents were at a wedding in Hawaii this weekend, not returning till Sunday.

"Me too." Atlas lay stretched out behind her on the couch, one arm curled beneath her. Avery still had on her school uniform, but Atlas wasn't wearing a shirt, and it was distracting her. "Mainly I'm just happy being with you, Aves," he said, and kissed her lightly at the base of her neck.

Avery shivered. She loved when he touched her like that. She loved when he touched her any way at all, really, even if it was just brushing her foot under the table, the way he'd done at dinner all week.

She knew what Atlas meant. She hadn't even known it was *possible* to be this happy. It was as if her entire life she'd lived in a world with limits, and then suddenly she'd discovered the way into a vaster, better, brighter world.

A message scrolled across her vision. *What are you up to?* Eris had written. Avery muttered under her breath, composing a reply, "Sorry, I'm just staying in and watching movies with Atlas."

"Eris," she said by way of explanation, because of course he'd heard her.

Atlas nodded. "You can invite her over, if you want," he said, but Avery shook her head.

"And make you put on a shirt? I don't think so."

She felt Atlas smile against her hair. "How's Eris doing, with all her family stuff?" he asked. He'd been there, of course, for the whole debacle at Eris's birthday.

"I think she's good, actually," Avery said, which was true. Eris had seemed better these days, her whole demeanor more buoyant. "She's even starting to see someone downTower. I've been dying to meet her."

"Cord can't be too happy about that," Atlas guessed, but Avery shook her head.

"Cord was the one who broke up with Eris, I think."

"Really? That must be a first." Eris was notorious for being the one to end relationships whenever things got complicated. She'd done it to at least two of Atlas's friends last year.

Avery flipped onto her other side, so that her face was just inches from Atlas's. "You know, Eris asked me something this week, about why I've been so happy lately."

"Oh yeah? What did you tell her?"

"That I have a new yoga instructor," Avery said, with mock seriousness.

"Yoga? Is that my code name?" Atlas leaned in to kiss her, and Avery pressed her body up against his, kissing him back.

They lay there contentedly, their breathing soft and even, neither of them eager to move. "Atlas," Avery ventured after a while, "when did you know that you loved me?"

"I've always loved you," he said earnestly.

"I mean, when did you truly realize it?"

Atlas shook his head. "I've known it forever. Why, did you have a moment in mind?"

Avery bit her lip; now she felt silly for bringing it up, but Atlas was looking at her expectantly. "It was one day after school. You probably won't even remember," she told him. "We walked across the street together to the lift line, but then you were going down-Tower to the hockey rink for practice and I was heading home. I stood there waiting, and I could see you across the empty elevator shaft. I don't think you looked over at me. . . ." She hesitated for a moment, remembering how Atlas had been illuminated from behind, the light streaming out to gild the edges of his form. "For some reason the thought that we were heading different directions made me sad. I know it sounds stupid," she said, rushing to get the words out. "But looking at you in that moment, I just thought, I never want to be apart from him."

"That wasn't what I expected you to say," Atlas admitted.

"Why?"

"I just thought you'd have some big, dramatic, epic moment. But I like this better."

She nodded, twining her hand in his. She could feel new calluses on his palm, right at the base of each finger, from all the hard labor he'd done this year. She wanted to kiss them all, one by one.

"Ready to go to sleep?" Atlas asked.

"We haven't finished the movie," Avery protested, though of course they hadn't really been watching. But Atlas didn't argue, knowing what she meant. She didn't want to go to bed because that meant the end of another day—which meant that they were one day closer to the return of reality. It had been so fun recently with their parents gone, playing house, not worrying about being caught. She glanced around at the blissful chaos that had taken over their apartment: discarded plates of food and pillows thrown off the couch and Atlas's shirt wadded in a corner.

Avery knew she was going to miss this, when her parents got back. She'd been trying to ignore the reality of their situation, but the ugly truth of it was always there, looming in the corners of her mind. Because no matter what she and Atlas did, their relationship couldn't amount to more than this—stolen, secret moments whenever they could manage it. They could never have a life together.

"What was your favorite place you went this year?" She sat up, trying to distract herself from those thoughts.

Atlas considered the question. "I went so many place, Aves. Pretty much anywhere I knew it would be hard to find me. Cuba, the Arctic, Budapest. I worked on a wilderness lodge in the Amazon and a ranch in New Zealand. I was a bartender in Africa for a while," he added, with a nod to her necklace.

"That sounds lonely," Avery whispered.

"It was. Especially since I was trying to forget about you," Atlas said, and there was a hurt in his voice she didn't like. She wondered how many girls Atlas had slept with in his quest to forget about her, then ushered that thought swiftly from her mind. It didn't matter, not anymore.

"But there was one place in particular that I really loved. An island in Indonesia that the rest of the world has pretty much forgotten about, with this insanely white sand and water so clear you can see straight through to the bottom. The town is small, with colored tiled roofs, and they eat nothing but fish and rice and rum. But they're all happy. I worked on a fishing boat there for a while."

"It sounds incredible." Avery smiled at the image of Atlas in rolled-up shirtsleeves and a big floppy hat, hauling fish into a boat in the middle of nowhere. It was a far cry from what he did now, working for their dad.

"It's tech-dark," Atlas was saying. "They don't ever have visitors. I had to specially rent a boat just to get there, and it took most of a day."

Avery was gripped by a sudden, wild, wonderful idea. "What if we went there?"

Atlas looked at her. She forged on, the idea gaining momentum. "You just said it, they're completely tech-dark. No one would ever find us. We could reinvent ourselves, start a new life."

"Avery," he said cautiously, but she didn't care, she could see it now: the little house she and Atlas would live in, with a porch and a hammock for hot summer nights; and steps leading down to the beach, where they'd walk hand in hand as the sun set over the water. Except—

"Mom and Dad," she said aloud, and the perfect image wavered a little.

"Exactly," Atlas agreed. "You'd be sad to leave them."

She nodded, her mind still racing over the plan—and realized that something about his wording had been odd. "We both would."

He seemed reluctant to speak. "Except they aren't my parents."

"Of course they are!"

"Avery," Atlas said levelly, "I wasn't born to this life the way you were. I was seven when they brought me up here. I remember what it was like before, how it felt to be hungry and scared. To not know whether you could trust anyone."

"Oh," she breathed, her heart aching. Atlas had never shared any of those memories. Whenever she asked questions about his life before, he would just shut down completely. She'd eventually stopped trying.

Atlas reached for her hands and squeezed them tight, looking straight into her eyes. "This life was never mine to lose. It *is* yours, though. I want you to think very hard before you say you want to give it all up."

Avery blinked back tears. But there wasn't a question. She would do anything, give up anything, to be with Atlas.

"Maybe we can visit them someday," she suggested. Atlas looked up, realizing the meaning of her words.

"You're serious," he said slowly, as if he couldn't quite believe it. "You actually want to go."

"Yes," Avery whispered, then said it again, louder. "Yes, yes, yes!" She kissed Atlas over and over, knowing that this was the right decision, the beginning of the rest of her life.

Atlas pulled her into a hug and held her close. She stayed there for a while, her head tucked into his shoulder, relishing the feel of him. It was so glorious being able to touch him. She would never take it for granted, she promised herself.

"How soon can we go?" she asked when they finally pulled apart.

Atlas raised an eyebrow. "How soon do you want to go?"

"This week?"

He laughed, but didn't seem shocked. "Okay. I think I can figure that out."

"Tomorrow night let's have a party," Avery decided impulsively. The moment she said it she knew it was a fantastic idea. They would bring everyone here, and act like it was just a normal Saturday night, but secretly it would be their going-away party. Someday when she and Atlas lived together on the other side of the world, they would look back and laugh at the memory of this—a silly high school party where everyone else got too drunk; and they stole furtive glances at each other the whole time, wildly in love; and said silent farewells to all their friends.

"Really?" Atlas asked.

"Yes! We haven't thrown a party here since before you left. It would be fun, hosting it together. Like our secret good-bye." Avery wavered for a moment, realizing that she'd never see Eris again, or Leda. But she couldn't think that way. She had to think about her and Atlas, and the fact that they were doing what had always seemed impossible. They were actually building a future together.

"Okay. You've convinced me." Atlas smiled.

Avery pulled out her tablet and composed a post, then uploaded it to the feeds. "That's perfect," he said, viewing the message on his contacts as it went live. "*You're* perfect." He leaned in to kiss her, but Avery pulled back.

"No one is perfect, least of all me," she countered, a little thrown by the statement. Atlas had always known not to say stuff like that to her. He was the one person she could count on not to.

"Sorry. I should have said that you're perfect for *me*," Atlas amended.

Satisfied, Avery scooted forward to kiss him. She was deeply content in a way she'd never felt before. "I'd go anywhere with you, you know," she told him, and Atlas smiled.

"Good," he said softly. "Let's go everywhere. Together."

And then the night really was over, and the holoscreen kept on playing its movie to an audience of none.

LEDA

LEDA STUMBLED FORWARD and fell to her knees behind the fountain, trying to keep out of sight of the restaurant. Though she wasn't the one who should feel ashamed here. *Eris and her father*. She briefly considered going home, but she was too desperate and her hands were shaking and she couldn't risk being caught by her mom. Her poor, clueless, cheated-on mom.

She fumbled with the bag Ross had given her. The drugs spilled out over the clover in front of her, her own little wellspring of fabricated happiness. Leda's eyes were immediately drawn to the small black Spokes envelope. Maybe it wasn't such a bad idea, getting into someone else's head—a screwed-up head, sure, but wasn't her own screwed up anyway?

Leda ripped the top of the envelope and popped the bright yellow Spokes pill into her mouth, swallowing it dry.

There was a brief, uncomfortable moment as her mind instinctively tried to push back. This didn't happen when the

Spokes were made for you, of course, but there was always a minute of adjustment when you took someone else's Spokes, as the needs of their consciousness forced themselves onto your brain. She held her breath, forcing her mind to quiet, and the Spokes slid smoothly over her awareness like a blanket.

Everything felt softer, more liquid. Time seemed to stretch like a rubber band. She blinked. Whoever these belonged to, it was clearly someone with anxiety—this was practically a relaxant. She could almost *feel* the other person, like a ghostly presence, as the drug began to make its way through her brain, searching for memories that weren't there, trying to elicit whatever emotional responses the person had needed.

Leda stretched her legs out in front of her and leaned back on her elbows, the rest of the drugs still scattered on the clover around her like brightly colored candy. The shadows were increasing, stretching longer over the fountain and across her legs. It wasn't cold out anymore. Eris and her dad, Leda thought again, with a dark, strangled laugh. She closed her eyes. Shadows of memories, half-formed thoughts, crouched hidden in her mind. *I know you*, she wanted to say, *but why?* How strange, it felt like déjà-vu, like this was all a song she'd heard before. Colors and shapes danced across her vision.

She recognized this high.

She knew it suddenly and instinctively, with a deep animal certainty brought on by the drug, the way she knew that she needed air to breathe. She'd done this before, experienced this particular blend of chemicals and neurostimuli. These were Cord's Spokes.

How strange, she wondered, digging her hands into the four-leaf clovers. She broke a nail. It hurt a little. Why were Cord's Spokes with *Ross*? Cord wasn't desperate for cash. These were probably stolen.

Cord should know! She needed to tell him!

Leda floated up to 969 like a balloon. "Cord!" She was banging on the door. Somehow she'd made it here, though she didn't remember taking an elevator, or a hover. *Thank god*, she thought, because her hands were starting to detach from her body and she was getting worried. She tucked them into her armpits. "Cord!" she repeated, louder.

The door swung open—but it wasn't Cord standing there; it was Brice.

"Leda? What's up?" Cord's older brother said slowly. He was dressed to go out, in dark-wash jeans and a collared shirt that had a lot of buttons undone. He looked so cool. She wished she could be more like him.

Leda blinked. She wasn't sure why she was here. Maybe Brice would know.

"Are you okay?" he asked, his eyes narrowing in concern. She was still standing weirdly, with her hands tucked into her arms. She lowered them self-consciously. It was more important that Brice like her. Even if her hands did float away.

"Why don't you come in," he said, taking her elbow and leading her gently inside. The walls seemed to be rippling toward her like waves in the ocean.

Brice led her to sit on the living room couch, pressing a cold glass of water in her hand. She drained it immediately. He said nothing, just refilled it. She drank the second glass more slowly.

"You're high as balls," he said, and she was happy because there was approval, or at least amusement, in his tone. "What did you take?"

Leda still had her red bag with her. She pulled out the empty Spokes envelope and handed it wordlessly to Brice. "Cord's," she remembered to say.

Brice's eyes narrowed. "You're telling me these are Cord's? Did he give them to you?"

She didn't answer. "Leda Marie Cole!" Brice said suddenly, reaching forward to grab her shoulders, and something about it—maybe the use of her full name, which she hadn't realized he knew—snapped her back into herself, at least partway. She shook her head.

"No," Leda croaked, and cleared her throat. "My dealer had them. That's why I wanted to . . . I mean, I got worried, for Cord. They're stolen, right?" She slid both hands under her quads and sat on them to keep from shaking.

Comprehension flashed in Brice's eyes. "Rylin," he said under his breath.

"What?" Leda asked. Brice looked at her through slitted eyes, then apparently decided that either she was too high to remember or it didn't matter.

"Our new maid. I think she and Cord have been getting a little . . . close," he explained.

"Fire her," Leda said automatically. "Knowing Cord, he's slept with her by now anyway."

"I love how ruthless you are." Brice laughed. "And, Leda, you should always ask me or Cord if you want Spokes. Don't go through your dealer again. You got lucky this time, honestly."

"I didn't even want Spokes, it's just what my dealer had. . . . I wanted xenperheidren."

"Wait a minute," Brice said. "Stay right there." As if she were going anywhere, she thought, dazed.

Moments later he reappeared. "Look what I've got." He dropped a full pack of pills into Leda's outstretched palm.

They were small and white and square, marked with a tiny X. "Oh, thank god," Leda half moaned, and took two of them at the same time.

Leda's thoughts, which had been sluggish and confused, immediately snapped back to life. Her whole body felt flooded with a new wave of energy. She looked at Brice, who was sitting there watching her, seeming deeply entertained. "Thank you," she said, her words already clearer than before. "Brice Anderton, human medicine cabinet. You're right, I should have come to you all along."

"There's the Leda Cole we all know and love," he said drily as Leda looked around the apartment with new eyes. She hadn't been here in years except for parties, when the space was loud and teeming with people. It was bigger than she remembered. Everything seemed sharper, drawn in starker detail, as though outlined with the fat black markers she used to draw with as a child. Her heart beat so hard she thought it would burst out of her chest.

"I actually have to go," Brice said after a moment, still watching her. "Though I wish I could stay. You're way more fun than Cord lately."

She reluctantly started to hand him back the packet of xenperheidren, but Brice shook his head. "Please, keep them. It's the least I can do, after what you told me."

Leda nodded gratefully. "Can I hang out for a minute before I head home?" she asked. Brice shrugged and headed out the front door.

A thousand scenes danced through Leda's accelerated brain. Eris and her father, kissing. Atlas. Avery. That guy Avery was dating now, Watt, laughing at her at the benefit. Atlas's eyes when he told her there was someone else. *You deserve the truth*, he'd told her. The truth will set you free, wasn't that the saying? She needed to tell Cord to fire that maid. She needed to know who Atlas liked more than he liked her. *As you wish*, Nadia had said, and promised to find out, but then nothing at all had gone as Leda wished, had it?

It all swirled in her mind, a kaleidoscope of blurring color, but where it had threatened to overwhelm her earlier, Leda now felt a deep focus and a pounding sense of urgency. God, she loved stimulants. And xenperheidren was the best of them. She took in a deep breath, letting the drug prickle pleasantly through her veins, all the way to her fingertips.

Nadia. She needed to ask Nadia about Eris and her father, find out how long it had been going on. *God*, she thought, disgusted, *it probably started right after Eris found out she was poor. Little gold digger.*

Halfway through the message Leda remembered she couldn't ask Nadia anymore. Nadia had quit on her.

There was something weird about Nadia, too, come to think of it.

And suddenly Leda knew. The answer was so elegant in its simplicity that she marveled she hadn't thought of it before.

She knew where she had to go, and what she had to do. Moving quickly, her eyes glassy and her breathing a little too fast, she swept her bag up onto her shoulder and started toward the express elevator.

WATT

WATT AND DERRICK were in the living room at Watt's house, sitting on the plastic yellow couch as they worked their way steadily through the cheap whiskey Derrick had brought over.

"It's been a while since you wanted to drink alone on a Friday night," Derrick said, though he didn't sound particularly bothered by the prospect.

"I'm not alone. You're here," Watt pointed out.

If it wasn't for Derrick, though, Watt would have been alone—Nadia was powered down. He'd been turning her off more lately, ever since the news she'd given him earlier that week. He wasn't sure why, except that he wanted some quiet in his own head. Besides, she was kind of annoying, even sanctimonious, whenever he set out to drink heavily like this; always reminding him of his blood alcohol content, and sending him headlines about the consequences of alcohol poisoning.

"Fair enough." Derrick glanced around the room, at the prints tacked on the walls, the twins' pile of discarded toys, foam blocks and a coloring wand and Zahra's tiara. "Is it Avery?" he asked.

Watt took another sip of the whiskey.

"What happened?"

"Let's talk about something else." Watt didn't exactly want to get into it, how the only girl he'd ever really liked was sleeping with her brother. He knew, of course, that they weren't technically related, that Atlas had been adopted when Avery was a toddler. But still.

"Want to go to Pulse?" Derrick suggested, but Watt shook his head. He knew Derrick was right, and he should bury all thoughts of Avery in the arms of some anonymous girl, whose face he wouldn't even remember the next day. But he kind of preferred the whiskey right now. At least it wasn't trying to talk to him.

Derrick opened his mouth to make another suggestion, but was interrupted by a vicious pounding on the front door.

"Watt?" *What the—* he thought, dazed. It was a voice Watt had never, ever expected to hear at his apartment, let alone anywhere downTower. "Watt, you'd better let me in!"

"You didn't tell me you had a girl coming over," Derrick laughed, reluctant admiration in his tone.

"I don't," Watt said shortly. His drunk reflexes kicking in—he hoped his parents hadn't heard—he ran to throw open the door.

Standing there in a rumpled school uniform, her ballet flat tapping impatiently against the worn surface of his family's front step, was Leda Cole.

"We need to talk." She spat the words at him.

Watt stood there dumb. He couldn't quite process her presence here. But Derrick seemed more self-possessed, or maybe he'd just had less to drink. "Hi. I'm Watt's friend Derrick," he said, stepping forward and holding out a hand. "Nice to meet you . . . ?"

Derrick trailed off, waiting for Leda to provide a name, which she failed to do. "We need to talk," she said again, looking at Watt. "In private. It's about Nadia."

The mention of Nadia was like a dash of cold water to Watt's face. "Derrick," he said slowly, turning to his friend. "I'm sorry. Can you . . ."

But Derrick was already on his way out, past Leda and out into the hallway, where the lights had lowered to a soft evening glow. He turned back and mouthed, *Who is Nadia?* but Watt ignored him, opening the door wider so Leda could step inside.

"Why don't you come in," he said, shuffling her to the living room, with a nervous glance back toward the darkened apartment. His parents would freak out if they knew he had a girl in here.

"Looks like I interrupted something," she said, wrinkling her nose at the whiskey bottle and disposable cups on the cheap coffee table. But there was something off about her usual haughtiness—a tremor in her voice, and a quick darting nervousness to her movements that Watt hadn't seen before. She looked wound so tight that the slightest touch would shatter her into a million pieces.

"Can I offer you a drink?" Watt asked. It was funny, really, the thought of Leda Cole drinking whiskey with him on the 240th floor. To his surprise she nodded, and sat down. He poured her a cup and refilled his own, settling on the couch as far from her as he could. She looked expectantly at him, but he gave a drunk little nod as if to say, *Ladies first.* He was too intoxicated to trust himself to speak right now. He needed her to make the first move so he could determine exactly how much she knew.

"I know you're Nadia."

Watt opened his mouth to protest, though he had no idea what he would say, but Leda kept talking over him. "I already figured it out, so don't bother denying it."

Nadia. He needed Nadia's help. *Quant on*, he thought, and felt reassured by the soft beep of Nadia waking up.

"What makes you think that?" he asked carefully, neither confirming nor denying anything.

"Please. I knew something was off about you the first time I saw you, at Eris's party."

"I didn't even talk to you that night!" Watt protested, but Leda just shrugged.

"You were acting funny, staring at everything just a little too long, slinking around like you didn't belong there. Which you didn't." She narrowed her eyes at him. "Plus, you wear contacts, but I never saw you giving them any verbal commands. It's kind of freaky, to be honest. Like you're not even using them."

Watt couldn't believe Leda had picked up on that. Of course he didn't talk to his contacts; he thought all his commands through Nadia. "But I still don't see how you knew that I was Nadia," he pressed.

Leda's red mouth curled up in a smile, and Watt realized he'd just inadvertently admitted it. "For a so-called 'information services expert,' you aren't very careful. You said 'As you wish'"—she raised her hands to make little quotation marks in the air—"all the time in your messages, and then again in person, at the gala. It just took me a little while to figure it out."

He couldn't believe he'd been so stupid. *If you hadn't turned me off whenever Avery was around, I could have warned you of this*, Nadia reminded him.

"How did you know where I lived?" Watt asked, ignoring Nadia's I-told-you-so.

"It wasn't hard to figure out. You'd already told me you went to Jefferson High. I just pinged your school and pretended to be a mom who'd lost the online directory link." She tossed her head impatiently. "Not every problem needs to be *hacked*, you know. Sometimes simply *talking* to people works just as well."

Her instincts weren't bad. "Sounds like you didn't even need to hire me in the first place," he said, stalling. *Get out of this situation. It's extremely unlikely to end well*, Nadia kept telling him, but Watt didn't listen.

"I wish I hadn't, since you suck at your job—"

"I'm the best on the market!" he said defensively. "Hacked all those flickers for you, found Atlas in the Amazon—"

"Not to mention that you're a completely terrible person," Leda went on, undeterred. "I can't believe you pretended to help me, took *money* from me, all so you could try to sleep with my friend." She rolled her eyes. "I mean, how stupidly clichéd is that? You know how many guys have tried to sleep with Avery? None of them get anywhere. She's a total prude."

"You call me a terrible person, but you talk about your best friend that way?"

"I have my reasons," Leda snapped, and knocked back her whiskey. She held the cup out for more, and Watt wordlessly refilled it.

"Just to be clear, I didn't even know Avery existed until after you hired me." He wasn't sure why he felt the need to defend himself, but he kept talking, fueled by the whiskey and some restless instinct. He hadn't been able to talk about Avery with anyone, or at least anyone who knew her. "And yeah, I thought she was pretty and tried to get to know her. So what? I didn't do anything wrong."

"Tried 'to get to know her.'" Leda snorted. "Tried to get into her pants, is what you mean."

"At least I'm not obsessed with a guy who's in love with someone else!"

Leda's eyes narrowed, and twin spots of color appeared high

on her cheeks. "You're pathetic," she snapped. "And incompetent. That was the *one* thing I asked you to figure out, and you couldn't even manage that. Some hacker you are."

Except that he had figured it out. Watt flinched, the thought of Avery and Atlas together making him ill. He drained the last of his whiskey to cover his uneasiness. The room started spinning disconcertingly.

Leda was watching him, her gaze strangely calculating. "She broke up with you, didn't she?" she said softly, scooting a little closer to him. Watt was confused—but also, a part of him found, not displeased—by her sudden nearness. He could smell her rose-scented perfume, dusky and rich.

"Yeah."

"I'm sorry. If it's any consolation, Atlas broke up with me too. But I'm sure you already know that, with all your hacking."

"Like I'd keep tabs on you anymore, now that I'm not paid for it," Watt said sarcastically.

Leda laughed, as if that were the funniest thing she'd ever heard. She searched through her bag a moment. "Want one?" she asked, holding out an array of pills in various shapes and colors.

Nadia sent alarm bells to ring in Watt's head. "No thanks," Watt said wearily. "I'm more of a booze guy, you know?"

Something flashed across Leda's face for a moment, and then it was gone. "Of course." She tucked the pills back into the bag and leaned over the table, busying herself refilling their drinks. When she pressed the cup of whiskey into his hand, Watt realized that a few of the pearl buttons of her school blouse had come undone. He could see through to her delicate white bra underneath.

"Here's to us," Leda said. "Both rejected by the Fuller siblings. But we'll survive it, won't we? Cheers."

She held out her cup expectantly. Watt clinked his to it and then drank the whiskey in a single gulp. The bottle was closer to empty than full.

"Thanks." Leda stretched her arms overhead and then leaned back on the couch, stretching out as if she'd always belonged there. "It's nice, not being alone right now," she murmured.

Watt sensed that Nadia was trying to get through to him. But even though she wasn't affected by alcohol, *he* was—the neurons of his brain firing at a much lower speed than normal, unable to fully process the messages she was sending through his synapses. "I know whashu mean," he said to Leda, and realized his words were slurring a little.

"Watt—" Leda's hand was on his thigh, and she was looking at him, a question in her eyes. She was so much prettier than he'd ever noticed: her luminous eyes and full mouth and the smooth richness of her skin.

This was a bad idea. She moved to sit on top of him, the pleats of her skirt fanning out over his legs like the plumes of a peacock tail, and lowered her mouth to his. He considered protesting for a moment, but then Leda's hands were under his shirt, and drifting lower, and it didn't seem to matter so much anymore.

RYLIN

SATURDAY EVENING, RYLIN walked up to Cord's apartment feeling lighter than she had in weeks. She'd met with V earlier to hand off the additional five Spokes packets—she'd been terrified that he might demand even *more*, and she wasn't sure what she would have said if he did—but he'd just given her a nod and an eerie smile, and transferred the fifteen thousand NDs to her at once. She'd submitted it to the police as Hiral's bail, but she hadn't heard anything yet about when he would be released. She wasn't exactly looking forward to it, after the way their last meeting had gone. What would he say when she told him they were over?

I'll cross that bridge when I come to it, she told herself. She'd gotten his bail money just as he'd demanded; he couldn't ask for anything else. Besides, all she wanted to think about right now was Cord. Every time she remembered their afternoon in Long Island—the waves pounding the beach below them, their bare feet digging into the sand as rain poured on the hovercover over their heads—she felt dizzy.

She stepped up to the front door, wearing a new sleeveless dress with shiny black zippers down one side and a scooped neck. Cord hadn't told her what they were doing tonight, but when he'd messaged her earlier it had sounded like he had something special in mind.

She held her eyes open for the retina scanner. But the door didn't open automatically, the way it had since Cord added her to the approved entry list weeks ago. Rylin frowned; Cord would have to call a tech to get that looked at. She pressed the bell for entry. "Cord?" she called out, knocking on the door the way lower-floor people did. Finally it swung open.

Rylin walked through the entryway and past the kitchen. The apartment felt strangely quiet: not a peaceful quiet, but an almost expectant hush, like in a holo theater before a movie was about to start. She walked a little faster.

"There you are," Brice said from the living room.

He was perched on a high, straight-backed chair; his feet firmly planted on the ground, his elbows resting on the chair's arms. Rylin was reminded of a king on his throne.

"Hi, Brice," she said, eager to get out of here. His staged, stiff posture was freaking her out.

"Have a seat." He nodded at the chair opposite him.

"Brice, I—"

"We need to talk about your little Spokes addiction," he said, smooth as silk, and held out an arm to block her path.

Rylin stayed standing. "What do you mean?" she said evenly. But a cold chill crept up her spine, raising the hairs on her arms.

"Rylin, we both know you stole from Cord, so quit pretending."

She didn't say anything, worried that any protest she made would only dig her in deeper. Her heart gave a dangerous lurch.

Brice's eyes grazed over Rylin in a bold, knowing way. "I knew there was something off the moment I met you. I tried to tell Cord, but he refused to listen. And look. I was right."

"Please. Let me explain," she said, leaning forward.

"No, let *me* explain. Here's what's going to happen right now: you're going to go in Cord's room, and break up with him, in a way that makes him never want to see you again."

"No," Rylin said automatically. She couldn't do that. She refused to.

"Let me make this clear. If you don't go break up with my brother, I'm telling him how you *used* him to steal his drugs, then I'm notifying the police. You'll go to jail. Are we clear?"

"I didn't use him," she whispered. Brice just looked at her. "You don't have any proof," she added, but her heart was sinking.

"It'll be my word against yours. Who do you think they'll believe?"

Brice was right. Rylin knew how these things worked. "Please," she whispered again.

"You have five minutes," Brice told her.

Rylin was surprised to feel tears running down her face. She was crying. She, the girl who never cried. She took a shaky breath and stood up, wiping at her tears, then started toward Cord's room.

"Hey," she said quietly, knocking at the door. "Are you busy?"

"Rylin! I thought you were coming over later." Cord opened the door, and the eager expression on his handsome face nearly broke her resolve.

"One of my friends is having a party tonight," Cord was saying as he stepped out into the hallway. Rylin followed helplessly. "I was hoping you'd come. You know, meet some of my friends." Cord kept going, telling her about his friend Avery and her amazing apartment, but Rylin wasn't really listening; she was looking up, to where Brice's shadowy form stood at the top of the stairs. He nodded imperceptibly.

"Cord," Rylin interrupted, her heart breaking a little, "we need to talk."

He paused. "Sure," he said after a moment, clearly trying to sound upbeat. "Let's sit down."

Rylin shook her head. She wanted to get this over with; it hurt enough as it was. "I can't see you anymore."

"What?" he said at once, stunned. "Rylin. Where is this coming from?"

"I just . . ." *Make him never want to see you again.* "I have a boyfriend," she said slowly.

"I don't understand." Cord sank into a chair as if he suddenly lacked the energy to stay upright.

"My friend Hiral, the one I told you was arrested for dealing? I've been dating him this whole time. I was just . . . pretending with you, because I liked this job. And then you took me to Paris, and . . ." She faltered, but it didn't matter; she'd made her point.

The worst part was, what she'd said was true. At least, it had been at the beginning. Rylin had never despised herself so much as she did in this moment.

"You didn't mean any of it?" Cord was looking at her like he'd never seen her before, like he couldn't believe the words coming from her mouth.

"No."

"Get the *hell* out of my house." His tone was ice cold.

"I'm sorry," Rylin whispered, looking through blurry, heavy-lashed eyes at Cord's face. She knew his features by heart, having traced them with her fingertips just the other afternoon in the enchanted half-light of the storm. But something had changed.

This was how he'd looked at the party, she realized, all those weeks ago: as if he didn't care about anything, or anyone. The way he'd looked when he was hiding how he felt, when Rylin hadn't known what he was like underneath it all.

"I'll say it one more time," he snarled, vicious now. "Get the hell out, and don't come back."

Rylin stumbled backward, shocked at the emptiness in Cord's eyes. He was staring straight through her, as if she weren't even there. The afternoon they'd spent on the beach together suddenly felt like it had happened to a different girl.

"Good-bye." Rylin turned toward the door. Regret gathered in her chest, raking at her with tiny sharp claws.

She was in the entrance hall, about to walk out of Cord's apartment for what was surely the last time, when she heard Brice clatter down the stairs. "I'm sorry, Cord," he was saying. There was a clink of ice in a tumbler, and she realized furiously that they were drinking. "But honestly, she's from the thirty-second floor. What else can you expect from a girl like that?"

ERIS

"ERIS?" MARIEL WAS knocking on the front door.

"Coming!" Eris called out, balancing on one red-soled heel as she pulled the other on, then running to let Mariel inside. She'd never realized how convenient the instant-access list was until she had to start answering her own door.

"Sorry, I just need a few more minutes, to curl my hair . . ." she said, stepping back into her bedroom. Her mom was out somewhere—probably apartment shopping; she'd been talking of nothing else since she got the transfer from Mr. Cole.

Mariel sailed calmly through the clutter of Eris's room. "I should have known we'd be on Eris time," she said, not unkindly. "Do you always have this much trouble making decisions?" She nodded at Eris's narrow bed, invisible under the mountain of clothes piled atop it.

"I like options," Eris replied, feeling an inexplicable stab of guilt. Most of those clothes had been purchased on the shopping spree she and her mom had gone on this morning, funded by Mr. Cole.

The hair curler beeped, and Eris reached up to attack the long layers around her face, her lower lip pulled under her teeth. Seeing her expression, Mariel sighed. "Here, let me," she said, stepping to the corner where Eris stood. As she turned, Eris caught a glimpse of her plain black dress from behind. It was shockingly low-cut. Normally Eris wouldn't have cared; god knows she was all for showing more skin. But the dress swooped so far that it revealed part of one of Mariel's inktats, a line of script in Spanish. Eris cringed at the sight. The half-revealed inktat looked completely tacky.

"What does that say?" she couldn't help asking.

"Oh, the tat?" Mariel arched her neck to look over her shoulder. "Don't you know how to look things up, Eris?" She laughed and began using the curler to wind pieces of Eris's hair tight, letting them fall again in wide tousled waves. "See? I have the hang of it way better than you."

"Thanks." She met Mariel's eyes in the mirror. Mariel was smiling. Eris smiled automatically in return.

"Tell me more about this party," Mariel went on. "I'm excited to meet your friends."

Avery was having a party tonight—the first real party she and Atlas had thrown since he came back from abroad. It would be huge.

"Do you want to borrow one of my dresses?" Eris heard herself say.

Mariel paused. The lock of Eris's hair in the curler sizzled, and she let it go. "What's wrong with my dress?" she asked.

Eris opened her mouth to answer, but no sound came out. How could you tell your girlfriend that she looked bad? That next to your glamorous classmates with their custom-made clothes and perfectly applied makeup, she seemed almost pitiable?

The thought of what they would all say about Mariel—and about *her*, walking with Mariel into the party—made her flush a sudden bright red.

"Nothing. Forget I said it," she amended quickly. After a beat of pained silence, she kept going, answering Mariel's question as if nothing had happened. "Anyway, yes, you're going to love Avery. She's been my best friend since we were kids. She and her brother, Atlas, are throwing the party—and Jess and Risha will be there too, I'm sure, and all the girls I used to play field hockey with. . . ." She was babbling, she knew it. Mariel kept working on Eris's hair, her motions tight, her back stiff with wounded pride.

"What about Leda?"

"I'm sure she'll be there."

"Does she know yet, about her dad?"

Eris hesitated a moment. "He isn't going to tell her."

"What!" Mariel set down the curler and moved around to look Eris square in the eyes. "Eris, why didn't you mention this sooner? I thought you said the dinner went well! What do you mean, he isn't going to tell her?" She sounded upset.

Eris took a deep breath and related the whole story, about the restaurant and the scarf and all the questions Mr. Cole had asked about how she and her mom were doing. How he'd mentioned that it probably wasn't a great idea to be publicly related—that it would cause too many issues with his job and his family. "He's transferred a ton of money to us," Eris said finally. "We'll be able to move back upstairs, as soon as we can find an apartment."

"Wait. Let me get this straight." Mariel had taken a step back from Eris, and was looking at her with something akin to disgust. "He's *paying you off* to keep quiet about the fact that you're his daughter?"

"That's a harsh way of phrasing it."

"I'm sorry, how would you phrase it? Eris, this man is buying your silence with a new apartment full of shiny things. Don't you see? It's hush money!"

"I'm taking it." Eris squared her shoulders stubbornly. "I've already decided. Hell, I've already spent some of it." She gestured to the heap of clothes on the bed, all new and expensive, still on their velvet boutique hangers.

"It doesn't bother you that your father is bribing you to stay quiet? Because your existence is *inconvenient* for him?" Mariel had raised her voice.

"Why are you getting so upset about this?" Eris shot back. "I can't force him to spend time with me if he doesn't want to. At least with money I can do something."

"Do what? Buy yourself more worthless crap?" Mariel grabbed a handful of necklaces from the dresser and let them slide through her fingers. "Does this really make you *happy*, Eris?"

"Yes, it does!"

Mariel blinked at her, horrified. Eris sighed and lowered her voice. "That's not what I meant. It's just . . . don't you see? I can *do* things with money, real things that matter. I could help you and your family!" Misreading Mariel's expression, Eris forged on. "You could move to a higher floor. You wouldn't have to work at Altitude after school anymore—you could focus on school, spend more time with your mom."

"God, Eris. You don't get it, do you? I don't want your damn charity."

"It's not—"

"I thought you'd changed," Mariel went on, and the disappointment on her face hit Eris like a physical blow. "I thought you were different. But I was wrong. You're just the same spoiled bitch you were back when you waltzed into Altitude every day and saw straight through me like I wasn't even there."

"*I* haven't changed?" Eris felt her temper rising. "You're as stubborn and arrogant as you were the first day I met you!"

"Guess what, Eris? Money won't solve your problems for you."

"At least it'll get me out of this shithole!" Eris shouted.

She knew right away she'd gone too far.

"This *shithole* is where I grew up," Mariel said coldly, punctuating every word.

"I'm sorry," Eris began, but Mariel was already taking another step back, the distance between them gaping ever wider.

"Forget it, Eris. God forbid I come to the party and embarrass you, in this dress you apparently hate so much." She turned and left the room. A moment later Eris heard the front door close behind her.

She thought of running after Mariel, but her feet were rooted in place. Eris felt as if something were shattering inside her. Maybe it was her pride breaking, she thought; her stupid, foolish, stubborn pride. Or maybe it was her heart.

She stepped closer to the mirror, taking a shaky breath, trying to hold it together. There was no denying that she looked fantastic in her new vermilion dress. Fortunately she owned the perfect accessory for it.

Eris tied the scarf Mr. Cole had given her in a tight loop around her neck, Parisian-style, and set out for Avery's alone.

WATT

"LIGHT OFF," WATT moaned, rolling over.

Everything hurt. His throat felt dry, his tongue fuzzy, and his head was pounding worse than the day he'd had Nadia installed. He wasn't sure why the damned light wouldn't turn off, but he kept his eyes shut tight in a valiant attempt to block it out. He wanted to curse, except that it seemed like too much effort.

"Watzahn," Nadia spoke into his eartennas.

"Ow! Too loud!" He winced, hands over ears. He rolled himself over and realized, dimly, that he was still in his clothes from last night. What had happened?

"Drink," Nadia commanded. There was a pitcher of water on the tiny table next to his bed, and a bottle of painkillers. Watt managed to sit up and grabbed the pitcher with both hands.

"Wow," he said, shaking his head, after drinking almost half of it. "What time is it?"

"Eight p.m. on Saturday."

"What the hell!" Watt started to stand, but sank back down again, his legs unsteady. "My parents—"

"Think you're sick. I snuck into the local medical mainframe and hacked a check-in bot, made it report that you have the flu. I even got a messenger bot to clear away the whiskey before they woke up, to hide the evidence," Nadia told him, almost proud. "Your dad carried you to bed this morning. And your mom was taking care of you earlier, before she had to leave for work. I made the med-bot tell her to bring you all this," she added, referencing the water and the painkiller.

"Thanks," he murmured. Nadia's crisis mode was kind of impressive.

"I did warn you about the potential side effects of illegal substances."

"What?" He took another sip of the water and rubbed at his eyes, exhausted. "God. I've never been so hungover before."

"You aren't hungover. You were drugged," Nadia insisted. "By Leda. How much do you remember?"

Leda. He'd forgotten she came over. Watt struggled to put the events of the previous night in order, but it all felt like a blur. He remembered being with Derrick, and then Leda showing up on his doorstep . . . her questions about Atlas . . . and their kiss, which had tasted like whiskey. . . .

He didn't remember anything after that.

"What happened?" he whispered, hoarse.

"I'll play you the feedback," Nadia replied. Even when Watt was too intoxicated for Nadia to get through to him—too far gone to record his own memories—Nadia was there to log all of it. It was both a blessing and a curse.

She played it directly onto his contacts, like an immersion vid. Watt relived last night from his own drunken perspective as Leda barged in, talked to him about Avery, offered him the drugs. He watched himself refuse—that part he remembered—and then she shrugged and started to pour them both whiskeys instead.

"There." Nadia paused the vid and zoomed in on Leda's hands, replaying it in slow motion. "Do you see? She slipped something into your drink."

"Why the hell would she do that?" he cried out.

Nadia kept playing. Watt watched, dismayed, as Leda straddled him and kissed him. How stupid he'd been, he thought. The kiss went on, longer than was comfortable for him to watch. "You can fast-forward, Nadia," he said, and she did.

Eventually Watt's eyelids began to close—he assumed that was the drug at work—just as Leda sat back, her shrewd gaze on him.

"Watt." Her tone was light and coaxing, syrupy sweet. "How are you feeling?"

"Great," he murmured.

"You've been very bad, you know." Watt's eyes blinked open for an instant, and he saw her reach up toward his head. He guessed she was playing with his hair. Thankfully Nadia's playback included only audio and visual stimuli, not touch.

"No," Watt protested. His eyes fluttered closed and didn't open again.

"You lied to me earlier, when you acted like you could never figure out who Atlas was seeing behind my back."

"I don't . . ."

"You do know, don't you?" Her voice was soft, like a feather bed. The kind of voice you might use on a sick child.

"Yes." *Shit*, he thought, hearing it all now, his stomach twisted in dread.

"Who is it?" The sweetness was gone, replaced by urgency.

"Avery . . ."

"Focus, Watt! I asked you who *Atlas* is seeing. Forget about Avery!"

"No, Avery and Atlas, they're together. . . ."

There was a long silence. Watt was suddenly glad his eyes had been closed this entire time. He didn't want to imagine the look on Leda's face as she processed this news.

"You're sure?" she said quietly, finally. He could hear the shock in her tone. "Atlas and Avery Fuller? You know they're brother and sister," she said, but it sounded at this point as if she were reminding herself as much as him.

"Nadia hacked it! I heard them in bed. . . ."

There were the sounds of pill bottles shaking, of rustling and rearranging, and then Leda's voice came from farther away, by the door. "Thank you, Watt," she said. "You've been so very helpful. Sweet dreams."

Watt heard the door close, and then the replay ended.

What have I done? Watt thought, horrified.

"Don't blame yourself," Nadia was saying. "I did a scan on your vitals this morning, and she'd given you an extremely high dose of vertolomine, mixed with some sedatives. It's an inhibition-reducing drug, known for slowing the thought processes so much that people find it difficult to lie."

"I mentioned *you*!" Watt added, with growing alarm.

"Yes, but Nadia was the name you used with her. She probably thought it was just a drunken slip."

"You're forgetting that Leda is completely insane." And now she knew about Avery and Atlas.

Watt couldn't explain the sense of responsibility he felt for Avery. He didn't technically owe her anything—she'd kicked him out in order to hook up with her own *brother*, he reminded himself. Yet he hated the way he'd handled all this. He remembered how sad she'd seemed, that very first day he met her at the ARena, when she'd said wistfully that no one could really know anyone else, because everyone was hiding something big.

He'd taken her greatest secret and delivered it straight into the hands of her crazy ex–best friend, who had no line she wasn't willing to cross.

"Has Leda already blasted it out, about Avery and Atlas?" Watt sat up, suddenly panicked.

"No," Nadia assured him. "I've followed all their movements today, and it doesn't seem like Leda has done anything, yet. As far as I can tell, she hasn't even seen Avery."

"Where are they?"

"Avery is having a party," Nadia said, and pulled up Avery's feed on his contacts. "Leda's headed there now."

"Then I need to get up there!" Watt started for the door, still in his stale, rumpled clothes from last night. He wasn't sure why, but he had a bad feeling, almost like a premonition, that something terrible was going to happen. This was all too tangled and screwed up not to end in disaster.

RYLIN

RYLIN SAT IN her bed, not seeing anything, barely thinking. The room was dark. She knew Chrissa was worried about her, that she should go say something to her sister, but she couldn't move right now. She just kept blinking up into the darkness, her mind a whirlpool of dark, spinning thoughts. She wished she could go back and do things differently.

A pounding sounded on the front door.

"Ry," Chrissa called from the entryway, her voice quavering, "it's Hiral."

Rylin stood up and ran a hand through her matted curls. She was still wearing the dress with zippers she'd so naively put on earlier.

"I'll get it. Don't worry," she said to Chrissa, and went to open the door.

There he was, standing on their front doorstep as if nothing between them had changed, wearing the sweatpants he'd been in when he was arrested—they must have returned his clothes when they released him, which meant that he'd come straight here. That didn't bode well.

"Hiral," she said carefully, making no move toward him. "I'm so glad you're out."

"Thanks to you, babe." He looked her over and gave a strange smile. "Ready to go celebrate?"

"Why don't you come in," she said instead, opening the door.

"What, no welcome-back kiss?"

"Hiral, have a seat. We need to talk," she said, using the same words she'd used on Cord earlier, though this time she meant them. The bitter irony of it wasn't lost on her.

He slid into one of their plastic chairs, his fingers drumming on the table. He looked even more muscular than when he'd left, as if the contours of his body had been shaded with a pencil, though Rylin had no idea how he'd managed to bulk up in prison. "You're still upset that I asked you to help with my bail sale," he guessed, watching her.

That was part of it. "I don't like V, yes."

"It's because of V that I was able to get out. You should be grateful to him!"

"He made me steal again!"

Hiral's brows lowered. "You just don't like doing the dirty work. God, Ry, if I didn't know any better I'd say you weren't happy to see me."

She couldn't have asked for a better opening. "I want to break up."

The words hung there between them. She tensed up, waiting for a sudden outburst, violence—

Hiral gave a harsh, joyless laugh. "Can't say I'm surprised, after the way you acted when you visited me in jail. Like you felt forced to see me." His eyes narrowed. "At first I thought you were just scared about everything, but then you didn't even want to touch me. When I kissed you good-bye, you flinched."

"You threatened me!"

"And it *worked*! We both know you wouldn't have handled the sale otherwise."

When Rylin didn't answer, he leaned forward, his face twisted into an ugly snarl. "It's Anderton, isn't it," he accused. "You're seeing that highlier asshole."

"Hiral, you and I have been over for a long time. We both know it," she said, as gently as she could.

"Holy shit," Hiral said, and the fury in his voice was unmistakable. "You slept with him."

Rylin said nothing. She didn't trust herself to lie. But the truth must have been written there on her face, because suddenly Hiral made an angry, guttural sound and knocked the entire table onto its side.

"What the hell?" Rylin breathed, in the wake of the crash. A leg had broken off the table, glasses clattering across the floor. Hiral was red-faced, taking great, heaving breaths.

"I trusted you, Rylin!"

"Clearly you didn't, or you wouldn't have been forced to *blackmail* me!" she yelled.

In the sudden stillness, an eerie calm settled over Hiral's face. "Maybe I still will," he said. "Maybe now that I know how you cheated on me, I'll tell the cops all about you, and your little illegal activities."

"No, you won't," Rylin said, more bravely than she felt. "Because even though you act like it sometimes, you aren't hateful. You're still the person I fell in love with, even if we've gone our separate ways." Her voice lowered, a little wistful. "I know you told V that you were the one who stole the Spokes. Thank you. For protecting me."

Hiral looked at her for a moment. "You disgust me," he said at last, and walked out, slamming the door behind him.

"Rylin?" Chrissa appeared from the bedroom. She was very pale.

"Did you hear everything?"

"Yeah. What's going on?"

Rylin's head was spinning. She couldn't think. She'd wanted to protect Chrissa, to keep her out of all of this, and yet she was failing at every turn.

"Okay," she said. "Just . . . promise to hear me out before you get upset." She took a deep breath, and told Chrissa everything. From the first night she'd worked at Cord's, to stealing, to Hiral's arrest and subsequent threat, and everything that had happened since. She left out only the private moments, like the beach.

Chrissa said nothing as she talked, just listened wide-eyed. Together they lifted the table back upright—it wobbled on three legs, but managed to hold—and restacked the fallen cups. Finally, when Rylin was out of words, she sat down and put her head in her hands, closing her eyes.

"You love him," Chrissa said softly.

Rylin nodded, not looking up.

"So go tell him!"

"I can't! His brother threatened me!"

"If he loves you the way you love him, you'll figure it out! He'll stop his brother from going to the cops. Or he'll say that he *gave* you the Spokes. It'll work out somehow!"

Rylin hesitated at something in Chrissa's voice. It was *hope*, she realized: a stupid, naive, romantic hope that love could conquer all. Rylin felt silly for believing in it, but Chrissa was right.

She had to at least try.

"Go up there!" Chrissa said eagerly, gaining momentum. "Go tell him the truth, exactly the way you told me!"

Rylin shook her head. "He's at a party right now, on the thousandth floor. Thrown by some girl named Avery." The last thing she wanted was to crash a party, and make a big scene.

"Seriously, Ry? When has a party ever stopped you before?"

Rylin laughed, shaking her head. "This must be a first, you convincing me to go to a party."

"So do it!"

Rylin nodded at her sister's words, gripped by a sudden sense of urgency. She should go up there, tell Cord the truth, and try to fix what she'd so terribly broken. Maybe Cord could find it in himself to forgive her.

LEDA

LEDA PAUSED AT the door to Avery and Atlas's party, looking around the room with a strange smile on her face. God, it was good to be back. She felt fully awake for the first time in months. Every cell in her body was on high alert, thrumming with anger and xenperheidren.

What a wild ride the last twenty-four hours have been, she mused, thinking over everything that had happened—and all the secrets she'd accumulated, which her hyped-up mind was weighing and assessing and hoarding carefully away. Eris and her dad. Leda shuddered at that one, still disgusted. Figuring out that Cord's Spokes had been stolen, and telling Brice. Confronting Watt, to learn the truth about Avery and Atlas. What he'd said was awful and incomprehensible and shocked Leda into silence—but she'd realized that as utterly fucked up as it was, it made a twisted kind of sense. It explained so many things about both of the Fullers, from the moment Leda had hooked up with

Atlas in Catyan. Hell, from the moment she and Avery had first become friends.

No wonder she needed drugs, Leda thought, a little crazed. All along she'd been playing the role of third wheel in the Fuller siblings' twisted love story, and she hadn't even known.

Well, tonight that was all going to change.

Leda had barely slept after learning about Avery and Atlas. She'd spent all day huddled at home, popping various pills from her little bag, her mind chasing down one rabbit hole and then another as she concocted ever more elaborate scenarios for revenge. She'd come to the party tonight in order to do just that. She wanted to destroy Avery and Atlas, publicly and painfully.

She made her way through the crowd toward the living room windows, where she knew she would find Avery. She plucked an atomic shot off a passing tray and knocked it back. The alcohol flared hot and fast through her overstimulated system.

Her contacts lit up with an incoming flick-link request— from none other than "Nadia." Watt. He needed to re-add her, after permanently disconnecting them before. Seized by a dark, warped amusement, she accepted the request.

"Hey there," she said as he immediately pinged her. "How are you feeling?"

"What are you going to do to Avery?"

She sighed dramatically. "Quit trying to play the white knight, Watt. You've already lost."

"Leda, please—"

"You have enough to worry about yourself right now, you know," she warned him, and hung up.

Watt's secret had been the most surprising of all. After she'd drugged him up and gotten him to confess about Avery and Atlas, Leda hadn't been able to resist snooping around his family's apartment. The door to Watt's bedroom was open; it was all too easy for her to slip inside and take a quick look around. She wasn't sure what she was searching for, exactly. She just wanted to know how he was such a good hacker—how a seventeen-year-old downTower kid had infiltrated the Fullers' home security, and the State Department.

In one of the drawers of Watt's desk she'd found a flat box of silicon optic processors. She looked them up online, and what she discovered had stunned her. They were only used in the construction of quantum computers.

Watt Bakradi had an illegal quant.

Nadia hacked it. Funny, she realized, Nadia must be what he called his little illegal toy.

She snooped around his room for a while longer, looking for the computer itself, so she could steal it; but after a half hour of searching she gave up. It didn't really matter whether or not she had the actual computer. She had the ultimate blackmail card over Watt, and could play it indefinitely—because if she told on him, he'd go to jail for life.

It would be kind of fun, really, having Watt under her thumb. And with Watt's quant hacking for her, no one would ever be able to surprise Leda again.

They were liars, all of them, she thought, Atlas and Avery, Eris, her parents—they'd all been hiding something from her. It was hurtful, and yet the knowledge was also strangely reassuring, as if she'd known it on some level all along, and now had the satisfaction of seeing her suspicions proven correct.

She couldn't trust anyone in the world but herself, but then again, Leda never really had.

ERIS

BY THE TIME Eris arrived, Avery's party was even more crowded than she'd expected. Every junior and senior from Berkeley was here, as well as the more daring underclassmen, and some kids who Eris was sure didn't go to Berkeley at all.

She moved slowly along the tide of the party, pausing constantly to say hello, tell a story, accept compliments. Tonight should be a celebration, she reminded herself. Finally, after weeks of torment, she was about to get her old life back.

Yet for some stupid reason, tonight felt false—her friends' designer clothes looked garish, their words seemed meaningless. Eris couldn't stop thinking about what Mariel had said. Compared to the time she spent with Mariel, this felt like a bizarre whirlwind that moved too fast. Why did she care about it all anyway?

She wondered what Mariel was doing right now. She wished Mariel were here, wished she could apologize. *Why not?* she decided, she couldn't make things worse than she already had.

Swallowing her pride, Eris composed a message to Mariel. *I'm sorry. I didn't mean what I said. It was stupid and hurtful, and I regret it. Can I make it up to you?* She nodded, and it sent.

Eris looked up to see Leda staring at her from across the room.

Out of habit she forced a smile—though it came out more like a grimace—and gave a little half wave. But Leda didn't return the gesture. She just stared at Eris, unblinking, with such raw hate in her gaze that Eris took an involuntary step back. She felt powerless to move as Leda's eyes scraped slowly over her, finally landing on the scarf tied around her shoulders. Her face was as flat and unyielding as the blade of a knife.

Leda knows, Eris thought wildly, in a sudden panic. She had to, to be looking at Eris like that.

Eris faltered and broke eye contact, wondering what she should say. It wasn't fair for Leda to hate her—none of this was her fault. Eris hadn't *asked* to be related to her. She looked back up, ready to return Leda's glare, or even walk over and confront her. But Leda had disappeared into the crowd.

"Hey." She felt a touch on her arm and turned to see Avery. "You okay?"

"I guess." Eris was shaking a little, thoroughly unsettled by the whole scene. Her head had started pounding. She wondered if Leda had somehow forced the pain onto her through sheer malice.

"What's going on?"

Eris didn't really want to talk about it. "It's nothing. You look amazing, by the way." Avery seemed so happy these days, Eris noted. You could practically feel the joy radiating off her, like shimmering waves of heat.

"So do you," Avery gushed. "Where's your date?" She started to look around, but Eris shook her head.

"She didn't come. We had a fight. A bad one."

"Oh, Eris." Avery squeezed her hand in sympathy. "I'm sorry to hear that. But you'll make up, right?"

"I hope so." This time Eris wasn't so sure.

She shivered, suddenly feeling the weight of another gaze on her. She had a moment of blind terror that it was Leda again, and wondered if she shouldn't have come—but it wasn't Leda.

It was Cord, staring at her. He was at the window, drinking alone, and Eris knew instinctively that something was wrong.

"I'm gonna go . . ." she heard herself tell Avery.

Avery followed the direction of her gaze and sighed. "Just be careful," she said in warning. But Eris was already crossing the room toward the only boy who had ever broken up with her.

"What happened?" she said in greeting.

"Nice to see you too, as always." Cord was affecting his old sarcasm, but Eris could sense a deep layer of pain underneath. His eyes looked red-rimmed. She wondered if he was high.

"I'm having a sucky day too, if it makes you feel better," she told him. They drifted into a corner, behind one of the giant sculptures Avery's mom collected. It was so loud in here that no one conversation could really be distinguished from any other. This was as much privacy as they would get, unless they went into a bedroom. Or a closet.

"Oh yeah?" Cord gave a mirthless laugh. "I guarantee mine's more fucked up. Unless your new boyfriend pretended to fall in love with you for your money. Sorry," he added, seeming to remember that she didn't have money anymore.

"It's a new girlfriend this time," Eris said evenly, "and no, she didn't. But I did fuck things up with her pretty royally." Cord started to pass her his drink, but she shook her head. "It's okay, I'm not in the mood," she told him.

He shrugged and finished it himself. "Someone really pretended to fall in love with you?" Eris pressed, a little disbelieving.

"Yeah. She was my maid, if you can believe it. I know, I'm an idiot." He gave Eris a sidelong glance. "Although, now that I know how strapped you were for cash at the start of the year, I guess you were doing the same thing."

"I'm going to forgive that comment based on how excruciatingly drunk you are."

Cord shrugged. "Catch up," he said, and handed her a shot glass off a passing tray.

Eris shook her head. "To be fair, though," she went on, "I never pretended to fall in love with you. Just hooked up with you."

"And you're damned good at it too," Cord said, sliding his hand lower over her ass.

Eris swatted at it nonchalantly. "The sad thing is," she said, "I really liked this girl."

"Do you love her?" Cord asked.

"I don't know."

"If you aren't sure, then you definitely aren't in love," Cord told her.

Eris laughed. "Like you're such an expert." *Unless* ... "Wait, do you love this girl?"

"I don't believe in love," Cord announced.

"That's terrible," Eris said automatically, though she wasn't so sure either. "Everyone believes in love."

"I believe in happiness," Cord said, and there was a look in his eyes that told her he was far away right now, from her, the party, the entire Tower. "I'm just not sure love will actually get you there."

Eris didn't know what to say, but she didn't feel like Cord really needed her to answer. It was strange: being with him wasn't anything like being with Mariel. It was easier, somehow. As though Cord were Eris's dark mirror. He didn't expect anything more of Eris than he did of himself—which was to say, not much at all.

Eris leaned forward, letting her chest rise a little more prominently in its push-up bra, trying to catch that familiar rush of flirtation. It seemed like no time at all had passed, like it was summer again and she and Cord were playing their games—and yet everything was different. It was like an echo of that time, a little less sharp, a little less thrilling. They had both changed too much.

"I've missed you, Eris." Cord laughed again, the sound hollow. "You and me, we kind of deserve each other, don't we?"

There was a time when Eris would have thrilled to hear him say that, yet now the words shot her with a pang of loneliness. She looked up at him and sighed imperceptibly. "Yeah. Maybe we do."

AVERY

"THIS IS THE craziest party we've ever thrown," Avery whispered to Atlas, their bodies pressed together in the tiny linen closet. She'd been aching for this moment since the night began. It had been exquisite torture: meeting Atlas's eyes across the room, letting their hands graze as they walked past each other, but unable to do anything more until they snuck away just now.

"Ending on a high note," he answered, and kissed her.

Avery marveled at the illicit thrill of it, of being wrapped up in the boy she loved—the boy she planned on running away with, in just a few days—when their classmates were just meters away down the hall. It was insane.

She leaned into Atlas, wanting to rip his shirt off button by button and pull him down onto the fluffy towels, but instead she accidentally knocked his head back into the shelf. He cursed, wincing.

"I'm sorry!" Avery exclaimed, stepping back.

"No, *I'm* sorry." Atlas laughed ruefully. "I would have brought us to my room, but it was already occupied."

"Mine too!" Normally Avery would have been furious that some couple was in her bedroom. But standing here with Atlas, her hair disheveled and her blue dress covered in fluffs of white bath mat, she didn't care about any of it. "I guess that's the sign of a great party," she added.

"Like I said, we're going out with a bang." Atlas leaned over to drop one more kiss on her lips. "See you out there," he murmured, and slipped into the hallway. Avery counted to twenty before heading the other direction, unable to wipe the grin from her face.

It *was* a great party. Avery tried to savor every detail so she could recount them all someday when she and Atlas were old and gray together, living happily ever after. Earlier this afternoon they'd directed the bots to push the living room furniture against the walls, clearing a dance floor in the middle. Now the room was crushed with people, all of them laughing and drinking and having a good time. Gleaming bottles of booze were arrayed on the counter, constantly being replaced from the order she'd placed earlier. Music blasted from the speakers, the volume adjusting to match the voice level. And so far, at least, no one had done anything stupid.

But Avery would have remembered this party forever even if it had turned out to be a total disaster. She treasured every single moment of her time with Atlas, especially now that they'd finally discovered their love for each other.

She wandered toward the dance floor, seeing Risha there with Scott Bandier—that was a new development—and Jess with Patrick, as always. If only she could dance for even a minute with Atlas. Then again, she reminded herself with another irrepressible smile, they had the rest of their lives to dance together.

A hand clamped on her arm like a vise. "I've been looking for you."

Avery gasped. Leda looked terrible. Her hair was pulled back in a tight bun, highlighting the severe architecture of her face. Her features were drawn and tired, her mouth a thin line. She seemed frail, somehow, in her geometric-printed dress, as if her body were running on nothing but sheer willpower—and drugs.

Avery knew this look; it was the way Leda used to be before exams sometimes, when she'd popped one too many xenperheidren. She would be amped up all day, take the test, then go home and sleep it off. Avery had never really approved, but every time she mentioned it Leda would clam up and get defensive.

Leda let go of her arm. She was shaking with agitation. "I can't believe you. You're a terrible friend, you know that? Not to mention, you're disgusting," she spat.

"Leda. What did you take?" Avery asked, gently pulling her friend to the side of the room.

"Back off!" Leda raised her voice, clearly not caring whether she made a scene. A few people glanced their way, eyebrows raised. "I *know*," Leda said. "So don't *mess* with me, okay?"

Avery felt a nervous rush of apprehension. She didn't dare speak. She was trying to read Leda's eyes, which were darting wildly all over the party. A sick instinct told her that Leda was searching for Atlas.

"Where is he?" Leda hissed.

"Who?" Avery asked, as innocently as she could.

"Your brother! Or should I say your *lover*?"

Avery felt sick, as if the world were tilting dangerously. Leda had spoken the words almost at a whisper, and the roar of the room had risen so high that Avery was pretty sure no one had heard—yet. She couldn't afford to take any chances.

"Can we talk about this in private?" she asked, with all the dignity she could. She looked directly into Leda's eyes. "Please. For the sake of all our years of friendship. Please don't do this, not here."

Something of the old Leda flashed in her eyes, and she sagged a little, as if she'd been strumming along through sheer outrage and now lacked the propulsion to keep herself upright. "Fine," she conceded. "For a couple of minutes."

Avery nodded. It was the best she was going to get right now. "Follow me," she said, pasting a wooden smile on her face, nodding to everyone they passed as if all were well. As if she and her best friend were off to refresh their makeup together and exchange bits of gossip, not threaten each other with their darkest, most private secrets.

But everywhere she went there were people. Her and Atlas's bedrooms, the library, the greenhouse: the party had sent its tendrils throughout the apartment. Every room had someone in it, passed out or making out or a combination thereof. Avery felt Leda growing restless next to her, a silent time bomb ticking down.

Then Avery got the idea that would change everything, forever.

"Here," she said, pushing open the door to the pantry and reaching for the hidden handle. "No one will be up here. We can talk in total privacy."

She grabbed the ladder and it retracted down, revealing a tiny square of midnight-blue sky above them. It was a sign of how upset Leda was that she didn't even react to the existence of a hidden rooftop above Avery's apartment. She just inclined her head a little and said, her voice cold as ice, "You first."

Her Italian leather stilettos slipping a little on the rungs of the ladder, Avery started the climb up into the darkness.

LEDA

LEDA STEPPED FORWARD unsteadily into the wind. Her instincts should have been screaming at her to go back down the ladder, but those instincts were muffled under a powerful cocktail of xenperheidren and several other pills whose names she'd forgotten. Right now the xenperheidren was keeping her in check, if a little glazed over and tightly wound. But already there were starting to be strange distortions in her vision, shapes elongating and shadows brightening. It was all pleasant and bright, like a children's carnival holo.

"Hooking up with your brother, a hidden rooftop." She turned around to face Avery. "How many other secrets is perfect Avery Fuller hiding?"

"There's no need to be cruel." Avery stood there unmoving. The moonlight glimmered on the silver-blue of her dress, making her look like some ancient Greek statue of a goddess.

"There's a need for whatever I say there is," Leda said

viciously. Up here on the roof, so close to the stars, she felt young and alive and hateful. "So, you and Atlas. What do you think your parents will say when they find out?"

"How did *you* find out?" Avery asked quietly.

"I have my ways." Like hell Leda was going to tell Avery about Watt. Although there was a beautiful poetic justice to it: that the boy who'd fallen hopelessly for Avery was the one to spill her darkest secret.

She'd come to the party tonight for revenge, she reminded herself. What were they doing up here on the roof, *talking*? Leda gave her head a shake, trying to focus. She wasn't on her game. Maybe she'd taken too many pills.

"Leda," Avery said haltingly, "I've loved him forever. Since we were kids. But I never thought until now that we could possibly . . ." She trailed off. "I never meant for you to be hurt. I'm so sorry for everything that happened to you."

"Is that why you've been a bitch to me all year? Because I liked Atlas?"

"I'm sorry," Avery started to say, but Leda was talking over her, her voice straining.

"You made me apologize, at Eris's party! You made me *beg* you for forgiveness! I assumed you didn't think I was *good* enough for him!"

"Leda! Of course you're good en—"

"And the whole time you just wanted him *for yourself*!"

Avery blanched. "I'm so sorry. It was really hard for me, seeing you two together."

"You don't think it was hard on *me*, losing the only guy I ever cared about and my best friend all at once, right when my family is falling apart?" Leda nearly shouted. She reached up to wipe angrily at the single tear that had escaped the corner of her eye. Stupid pills, making her lose her grip on her emotions. Hadn't Leda promised herself never to let anyone see her cry?

Avery noticed the gesture and stepped forward—but Leda's hand darted out, warning her to stay back. "Leda, what's happening with your family?" Avery asked.

Leda didn't answer. Fuck Avery and her false sympathy. She didn't want to talk about it. Even high, she could only handle one crisis at a time.

Avery's voice was gentle. "Why don't we go back downstairs. We can get you help, whatever you're on, and—"

"Just back *off*!" Leda shouted. Her entire body quivered with tension.

Avery fell silent. "What are you going to do?" she said carefully.

"I don't know!"

Why was she on the rooftop anyway? It was all Avery's fault—Avery had tricked her into coming, "for the sake of our friendship." *What friendship?* Leda should have asked. She needed to get back to her plan—although what it was, she was struggling to remember. . . . All she knew was that she wanted Avery to suffer as much as she had. Atlas too, though for some reason most of her anger was focused on Avery. But that made sense. It was a much greater betrayal.

"I don't know," she said again, staring at her former friend, as a cloud drifted to cover the moon.

RYLIN

RYLIN STEPPED THROUGH the doorway to the thousandth floor, and into another world.

Not even working at Cord's apartment—not even the trip to Paris he'd taken her on—had prepared her for this level of grandeur. Everything, from the sweeping two-story entryway to the enormous living room with floor-to-ceiling windows, had all been designed down to the smallest detail, to emphasize the taste and wealth of the Fuller family.

And crammed into this absurdly expensive apartment were hundreds of teenagers, loud and bright-eyed with booze and dancing. Rylin pushed her way forward, trying her best to look out for Cord.

People were looking at her. Most of them noted her off-the-rack dress and cheap shoes and dismissed her negligently; but a few of the glances were more interested. Rylin kept her eyes straight ahead, daring anyone to talk to her. She needed to find

Cord. She didn't like this, the crushing crowds or blaring music or the way everyone's eyes dilated in their contacts.

This was Cord's world, she reminded herself. It didn't feel that way when they spent time together—it felt like they'd created their own world, just the two of them—but these were his friends. He'd wanted to bring her here tonight, before she ruined everything.

Her tablet buzzed with a message from Lux. *I'm at the steel forest, and Hiral is here, upset. Where are you? Is everything okay?*

I'm okay. I'll explain later, she shot back. The kids around her noticed her typing with her fingers on a cheap tablet. They looked at her eyes, noticed her lack of contacts, directed even more curious stares in her direction.

Ignoring them all, Rylin methodically made a lap of the party in search of Cord, trying to plan what she would say when she saw him. She grabbed a drink from a passing tray, hoping it would settle her nerves. She shouldn't have done this; it was a mistake to come. Where on earth was he? She'd looped through the entire party, twice, with no sign of him. Maybe he'd already left.

And then she saw him.

He was in the corner of the library by the living room, talking to a girl with red-gold hair. Rylin caught her breath at the sight of them. The way their bodies were curled toward each other, her hand resting on his arm, their hips just slightly touching—she knew, without being told, that Cord had slept with her.

Rylin stood there for a moment, watching as the girl laughed at something Cord said. She was gorgeous, Rylin thought bitterly, all soft curves and wide eyes and that riotous mane of hair. Cord laughed with her, his gaze traveling over her body appreciatively, his hand falling lower on her waist. The sight of them together was like a blow to the stomach.

Feeling the weight of her gaze, Cord looked up. "Rylin?" he

said stupidly, as if he wasn't quite sure he could believe his own eyes. And really, why should he? What reason did Rylin Myers have to be on the thousandth floor?

They stood there for a moment, the two of them looking at each other, like they were actors in some bad movie and the vid-screen had frozen. "Oh," the girl breathed, turning to look at Rylin, her strange amber eyes lighting up in recognition. "Is this her? Your maid?"

Those words—the realization that Cord had talked about her with this stranger—unlocked something in Rylin, and she whirled blindly around, suddenly desperate to escape.

"Wait, Rylin!" she thought she heard Cord say behind her, but she wasn't sure if she'd really heard it over the din of the crowd, and it was too late—she was already running away.

ERIS

"THAT'S HER?" ERIS said again, turning to Cord. "Your maid?" She was pretty enough, Eris had to admit, with her pale oval of a face and sparkling almond-shaped eyes.

"Yeah." Cord was looking after the girl, his voice thoughtful.

"Why'd she run off like that?" It seemed like odd behavior to Eris. If she'd seen a boy she liked talking to someone else, she would have barged over and forced her way into the conversation and generally made a scene until she got what she wanted.

Cord glanced at her sidelong. "You're kind of intimidating to other girls. You know that, right?"

"Me?" Eris laughed. She'd been called many things in her eighteen years, sexy and selfish and flighty, but intimidating had never been one of them.

She started to say something else teasing, but as she studied Cord's face, she realized the atmosphere had shifted. Their easy banter was gone. Cord's thoughts were turned inward, his mind seeming undecided about something.

"Oh my god," Eris murmured. "You love her."

Cord didn't reply, and that in itself was her answer.

"You love her, even though she used you," she went on, wondering. "After all your big statements about not believing in love, you're as much of a sucker as anyone."

"Love and trust aren't the same thing," he shot back, just as Eris's contacts lit up with an incoming message.

Did you mean that, or were you just drunk?

Eris turned aside, waving her hand at Cord to indicate that she was making a call, and pinged Mariel. She answered after the fourth ring.

"I mean all of it. I'm not even drinking tonight! And I'm sorry," Eris hurried to say, all in one breath. "I'm so, so very sorry. I should never have said that."

Mariel was quiet. Eris knew she needed to do something more. "It was wrong of me, and insensitive. I just lashed out. I felt defensive, after the way you reacted when I told you I was taking the money."

"I don't want to fight with you, Eris," Mariel said after a beat. She sounded tired. "I'm sorry too. I know I provoked you. I just . . . worry, for you."

"I worry for you too," Eris said softly.

"Are you really not drinking?" Mariel asked. She sounded incredulous.

"Yeah. I just wasn't in the mood, after our fight." She sighed. "I've been thinking about it all night, trying to figure out how to make it right. I don't want to lose you," she added, a little quieter.

Mariel inhaled. "Why don't you come over, and we can talk about it."

"Yes!" Eris said. "I'm on my way!"

A sudden warmth spread from the center of her chest, and she burst out laughing; a joyful, bubbling laugh that came from her unthinkingly. Mariel forgave her. As long as Mariel forgave her, everything else would work out.

She started to walk away, but the wounded confusion in Cord's eyes stopped her. Well, why shouldn't Cord's romance with that girl work out too? If she and Mariel could figure it out, there was no reason Cord and his maid shouldn't be able to do the same.

"If you love her, go talk to her," she insisted. But Cord just shook his head, stubborn and stupid the way boys always were. Eris felt torn. She couldn't just leave him like this, not when she'd gotten back the thing she'd been most terrified of losing. She felt expansive, glowing with a wild, furious joy.

I can fix it for him! The thought rang out sharp and clear in her mind, like the bells in Mariel's church.

I need to do one small thing for a friend. It's important. I'm sorry! Be there in half an hour, she replied to Mariel, and looked up at Cord. "I'm getting her for you," she announced.

"What?" Cord looked lost. "Where are you—"

"I'm bringing her back to you, and then I'm going home to Mariel!" Eris called out over her shoulder, delighted. She took off running in the direction of the lower-floor girl, laughing again at the strangeness of the universe.

RYLIN

RYLIN WAS RUNNING headlong through the party, no longer caring who laughed at her. All she wanted was to get out, but she'd gotten lost in this stupidly huge apartment, and somehow ended up in the kitchen. There were people here, other kids just around the corner; she could hear their voices. She turned a circle, wondering which way was the exit—and saw a flash of red-gold hair in the hallway just outside. *Holy shit*, Rylin thought wildly, was that girl *following* her?

She grabbed a door that looked like it led to a pantry, and ducked inside.

Her eyes widened at what she saw, and in her shock, she left the door open. In the middle of this tiny pantry was a ladder—leading up to a square of deep blue that could only be the velvet of the sky, scattered with stars.

This was a ladder with roof access.

She heard voices up there, girls' voices, but they were too far away and the wind too loud for her to distinguish their words. Rylin hesitated, curiosity momentarily outweighing all other emotions. Why shouldn't she climb up this ladder and see where it led? Out there in the party were Cord and the red-haired girl and the sharp pain of disappointment. And farther down were Chrissa, and Hiral and Lux and everyone else Rylin had managed to hurt. This whole damn Tower was filled with her mistakes. But up there on the roof, who knew?

She grabbed the edges of the ladder, her black-painted nails holding tight, and climbed up.

Moments later she was pulling herself out of the trapdoor. She almost couldn't believe her own eyes. She was standing on the roof of the entire *Tower*. Everyone in the steel forest was literally two and a half miles below her. The thought made her light-headed.

She was standing on a central platform, probably big enough to accommodate thirty or so people standing close together, with a railing on one of its sides. On the other ends it fell away at a drastic slope, disappearing far into the shadows. Overhead Rylin could see the Tower's spire, arcing up into the heavens. She shivered, rubbing her bare arms. She hadn't counted on the wind up here.

They were fighting, the people across the platform. Rylin could hear it in their voices. There were two of them: a black girl whose thin wrists were raised in angry gesticulations, and a blonde who was probably the most beautiful girl Rylin had ever seen. They hadn't noticed her yet.

"I don't know!" the smaller girl snapped, taking a step away from the blonde. There was something so wounded and dangerous in her voice, it scared Rylin a little. She wouldn't want that girl as an enemy.

She should go back down. This wasn't something she needed to be part of. But before she could get back, she heard footsteps coming up the ladder.

LEDA

LEDA THOUGHT SHE heard a noise, and looked sharply over toward the trapdoor. There was a *girl* standing there, she realized in bewilderment. "Who are you?" she snapped.

"Rylin Myers," the girl stammered, and Leda thought she recognized the name. "I'm sorry, I didn't mean to—"

"You should go," Avery said urgently.

Another set of footsteps clattered on the ladder, and a moment later, Eris's golden-strawberry head appeared. Great. The last person on earth Leda wanted to see right now, and here she was.

"There you are!" Eris exclaimed, unfolding herself from the ladder. She was looking at the Rylin girl. "Listen, I just want to talk to you. Cord is looking for—"

"What the hell is your problem?" Leda hissed, venomous. Her anger had swerved wildly from Avery to Eris, sharpened to a single white-hot point.

Eris raised an eyebrow. "Calm down, Leda. I'm sure she didn't mean to come up here."

"I'm not talking to her, I'm talking to *you*!" The moonlight gleamed on the cream Calvadour scarf—the scarf that Leda's *dad* had given Eris—and Leda lost whatever self-control she had left. "How dare you even look at me right now?"

"Eris!" Avery cried out. "Go back down, okay?"

Eris glanced at the other girl—the one she'd followed upstairs—and then back to Leda. For some crazy reason, she stood her ground. "I'm guessing that you found out," she said steadily, looking right at Leda. "Did your dad tell you?"

"I don't want to talk to you!" Leda backed away frantically, approaching the edge of the roof.

Avery came to stand next to Eris, and the two of them exchanged a worried glance. "Leda," Avery said, and Leda could hear the fear in her tone, "please come down from there, and we'll talk about it."

But Leda looked only at Eris, her eyes glued to the scarf. How could she go around wearing that in public, a gift from a married man? Wasn't she ashamed? "What's wrong with you?" she shrieked. "Why can't you just leave my family alone?"

She took another step back, feeling desperate. They were literally backing her into a corner, these two girls who were supposed to be her *friends*. But one of them was having an affair with her dad and the other had stolen the only boy she ever cared about. The joke was on her, she thought frantically, for having such shitty friends. She fumbled in the pocket sewn into the side of her dress, looking for another xenperheidren. She just needed to *think* a little more clearly; then she could figure out how to handle all this. But her hand came up empty.

"I know you're upset!" Now Eris's voice was raised too. "I'm sorry, okay? I know it's weird! But I won't tell anyone. And I'm never going to s-see"—she stammered a little—"see your dad, ever again. I promise."

"Take your stupid scarf and just *go*!" Leda wanted to cry, or scream, or tear Eris apart limb from limb—anything except stand here another second, hearing Eris talk about seeing her father. As if she hadn't had enough to deal with tonight.

By now Eris was standing next to her, close enough for Leda to pull the scarf right off her neck. Her heart pounded with the razor-sharp clarity brought on by the stimulant. They were both dangerously close to the edge. Avery kept shouting at them to get back. "This has all been weird for me too, okay?" Eris murmured, looking right into Leda's eyes. "Please," she said, and reached out to touch Leda's arm. That was the final straw.

"I told you, don't *touch* me!" Leda cried, pushing Eris blindly away. Dimly she thought she heard another set of footsteps coming up the ladder.

Eris stumbled backward, almost in slow-motion, her sky-high heels folding underneath her.

For a moment it seemed like she would recover her balance, and Leda was reaching for her—but it was too late, Eris had already fallen backward. Her beautiful face was wide-eyed with shock. Leda watched as she hurtled toward the earth, the folds of her scarlet dress fluttering around her, the scarf whipping up like a useless white flag of surrender. She looked strangely beautiful, Leda thought with an eerie sort of detachment, the way her tiny form was slipping away into the darkness of the city below.

Leda stood there watching long after Eris had disappeared from view.

An unknowable eternity later, the horror of what had happened finally sank into Leda's mind. She buried her face in her hands and began to scream.

In the distance the sun was edging over the horizon, stretching bold red fingers into the retreating night sky.

When she looked at it, all Leda could see was the sickening red of freshly splattered blood.

WATT

WATT COULDN'T BELIEVE what he just saw.

He'd gotten to the party and started pushing wildly through the crowds, asking if anyone had seen Avery, or Leda. Eventually a pair of scared-looking freshman girls had pointed him in the direction of the kitchen. He'd seen the open pantry door, and a ladder stretching up into the darkness, and his stomach had twisted in distress even as Nadia said urgently, "Get up there. Now."

At the top of the ladder, Watt found Leda and Eris yelling at each other. Eris had reached for Leda, and Leda had recoiled, pushing her back. And then Eris *fell*, just slipped off the side of the Tower and out into the void. He thought of her hurtling toward the ground, her arms stretching upward helplessly. If she were lucky, she would die of shock before the impact.

He felt nauseated at the thought of what her body—whatever was left of it—must look like now, on the ground.

Leda was still standing there, looking out over the edge, her eyes vacant, her mouth opened in a shrill, endless scream. There were other girls up here on the rooftop too: Avery, and a girl with bright green eyes and dark hair whom he didn't recognize. Both were staring in utter shock at the spot where Eris had disappeared.

Watt couldn't take it anymore. He reached forward with rough hands and pulled Leda back, hard, so that her head snapped a little and that unearthly scream finally came to an end.

They stood looking at one another for a moment, he and Avery and the other girl. They had all seen what happened. Avery's face was white, her shoulders shaking, and Watt realized she was silently crying, the moonlight turning her tears a shimmering silver. Of course, Eris had been Avery's oldest friend. He wanted to fold her in his arms and hold her while she sobbed, but he didn't move.

Leda was hunched over, trembling. Her eyes twitched under their closed lids, and her face was twisted in pain. God, was she still high from last night? Watt couldn't believe that it was only yesterday that he'd been drinking whiskey with Derrick in the living room. Everything since then felt like a blur—Leda seducing him and drugging him, and him waking up only to rush up here, frantic with worry for Avery.

But Eris was the one he'd been too late to save.

The unfamiliar girl broke the silence. "We need to call the police," she said, and her voice quavered only a little. Watt asked Nadia who she was, and Nadia cross-checked her features with the Tower's master facial recognition. *Rylin Myers, thirty-second floor.* Watt wondered how she'd ended up here.

Avery blinked, dazed. "I'll do it," she said, but she was still crying. Watt couldn't bear the sight of it. There was very little he could do to help right now, but at the very least he could give her the chance to grieve properly.

"Let me," he said. Avery nodded gratefully.

It was as if the words were a spell, ripping Leda from whatever living nightmare she'd been trapped in. She straightened her back and lifted her head, her eyes blazing. "Oh no you won't," she said, frighteningly calm. "You don't want to do that."

"Leda, Eris is *dead*," Avery said. "We have to get help!"

"No one can help her if she's dead," Leda pointed out ruthlessly.

"It's your fault she died!" Avery screamed.

"Really?" Leda took a deep breath. The more the rest of them panicked, the more she seemed to be regaining a measure of calm. "As I seem to remember, you're the one who brought us all up here."

"You *pushed* her!"

"Did I?" In the wake of Avery's shouting, Leda's voice was low and quiet. "I don't think I did. I think Eris had too much to drink, at *your* party." She leveled her gaze at Avery again, her eyes unblinking, as if she were a Gorgon and could turn her friend to stone. "And then she slipped."

Rylin chimed in. "I *saw* you push her. I'll tell the police that's what I saw."

Leda glanced around, her eyes darting from person to person as if she were a cornered animal plotting a way out. Her mind seemed to be turning over various possibilities. "Rylin, right?" she said, turning to the lower-floor girl. "You're the last person who should be going to the police right now, and you know why."

Rylin hesitated, and in the silence Leda drew her shoulders up, gaining momentum. "None of you are going to the police until we have our story straight. Eris got drunk; she slipped and fell. If anyone says otherwise, then I can't promise to protect *your* secrets." She laughed wildly, a bright hard glitter in her eyes.

Watt bristled as he understood her meaning. She was trying

to threaten him with his hacking. *Screw that*, he thought; he and Nadia were careful, too professional, to leave any kind of trace. "You think you can threaten me about my side jobs?" he snarled, not caring that Avery and the other girl heard. "You'll never be able to prove it. You've got nothing on me."

"Oh, Watt," Leda said. Her voice lowered conspiratorially. "Like I said, I have so much worse on you. Don't push me."

He stared at her, confused.

"Sorry about the pill," Leda added, in an almost cheerful tone. "But you forced my hand. If you'd been a little more *fun*, I wouldn't have needed to resort to it."

Avery glanced from Watt to Leda, struggling to keep up. Watt was livid. "I'm calling the police and telling them everything!" he exclaimed.

"As you wish," Leda said, with a tight, mirthless smile. "Please put them on with me, afterward, so I can tell them who Nadia really is."

Silence fell over the roof. Leda looked at Watt. *Could she really know?* he thought wildly. But how?

"Oh yes," Leda said, following the direction of his thoughts. "I'm so eager to meet Nadia, you know. Unquantifiably eager." She put just the slightest emphasis on *quant*, so slight that only he would hear it.

Watt felt sick. He was powerless to say anything.

"As for you," Leda said, turning to Rylin, "I'll tell the police what you've been doing to Cord. You'll serve at least ten years for that. Maybe life."

Rylin blanched. Watt wondered what Leda had on her. *Nadia, try to find out*, he commanded. Maybe there was some way he could help. If only one of them could get out from under Leda's thumb.

"I'm not covering for you, Leda, not after—" Avery began, but Leda whirled on her.

"Don't even *think* about opening your mouth, Avery. Your dirty little secret is the worst of all."

Avery fell silent. Watt's heart went out to her. Of course he knew what Leda had on Avery, because he'd handed it to her on a silver platter.

"So," Leda went on, and for the first time her voice was a little unsteady, a nervous, hysterical edge to it. "We're all in agreement? Eris got drunk, slipped, and fell. Okay?"

She stared at each of them in turn. Rylin nodded, slowly, and then Avery joined her, like the helpless puppets that they were. Watt stared at Leda for a moment, his mind racing, desperate to think of a solution.

But there was no foreseeable way out. He was going to lie about an innocent girl's death.

Watt finally nodded, inevitably, as Leda had known he would.

AVERY

AVERY HAD NEVER seen the Church of St. Martin, on the 947th floor, so completely packed as it was the morning of Eris's funeral.

Eris's funeral. It was almost impossible to believe, even for Avery, who had seen her die.

The church was dimly lit and draped all in black, filled with somberly dressed mourners. The only bright spot was a profusion of white flowers around the burnished wood casket up front, and the view screen propped up next to it, flashing pictures of Eris— all of them stuffy posed portraits that her mom must have forced her to take, not the spontaneous selfies Eris filled her feeds with.

Eris would have hated this, Avery thought, with a sob that was half laugh. It was somber and far too traditional. Not at all like Eris herself had been, expansive and eager for life.

She had so many memories of Eris. Playing dress-up together when they were kids, fighting over the princess dress that changed color when you waved the matching wand. The time they'd gotten those awful bowl haircuts together in seventh grade, the night they first drank beer, how Eris had snuck Avery back to her place and held back that same haircut while Avery was sick all night. Giggling in Latin class because all the words in their translations sounded dirty. That time they'd run away to London for a weekend, just because Eris professed herself "bored of New York."

Eris had been going through a rough time lately, though, and Avery suddenly wished that she'd been more supportive. Eris had really needed her, yet Avery had been too wrapped up in her own Atlas and Leda and Watt drama to do more than throw her a birthday party. Even that had ended in disaster.

At least Eris had been happy the last couple of weeks with that lower-floor girl she was seeing. Avery wondered where that girl was, if she was here this afternoon. She wished she'd been able to meet her. Eris had never even told Avery her name.

Avery glanced around from her vantage point at the front of the church. It seemed like everyone who had ever met Eris was here, all their classmates and teachers, their friends' parents and parents' friends. Avery had seen Watt toward the back, his eyes just as shadowed as hers, though she hadn't spoken to him since that night. Eris's other friends sat in the row behind her: Jess, Risha, even Ming—and Leda, of course, whose eyes were boring into Avery's back the whole time. Eris's family was arrayed in the front pew: her mom, wearing a black crepe dress that wasn't quite funeral appropriate, though no one would dare tell her; Eris's aunt Layne, flown in from California; and to Avery's surprise, Everett Radson and his elderly mom. Grandma Radson stared forward, her eyes unreadable. She was draped in more diamonds than Avery had ever seen on a single person, as if she could make up for in carats what she lacked in youth. Next to her, Mr. Radson sobbed into a monogrammed handkerchief.

Avery wanted to be upset with him on Eris's behalf. It didn't seem right that he'd abandoned Eris in life, only to act so grieved upon her death. Yet she couldn't be mad, not at a man who looked broken with sorrow.

Avery and her family were in the second pew, behind the Dodd-Radsons, a surprising place of honor given that Eris had died at Avery's party. But Eris's parents didn't seem to blame her for what had happened. She couldn't say the same for her own parents, who could barely bring themselves to look at her. Their faces were still white with shock. Next to Avery stood Atlas, looking handsome as ever in his dark suit. He kept trying to catch her eye, but she stared determinedly forward at the screen, flickering with stiffly posed portraits of her dead friend.

"For we brought nothing into this world, and it is certain that we can carry nothing out . . ."

Nothing, nothing, nothing, the word echoed hollowly in her mind. Avery knew about nothing, because it was exactly what she had done for Eris. She hadn't told anyone the truth about her friend's death. Not even Atlas.

The truth wouldn't change things, she'd tried to rationalize to herself. It wouldn't bring Eris back to life. But Avery knew those thoughts were cowardly and self-interested, and she despised herself for harboring them.

After Eris's fall—just three nights ago, though it felt like a lifetime—Avery had abruptly broken up the party and called the cops. They'd arrived on the scene almost instantly. Avery led them to the roof and explained in a shaky voice how she'd found it, how she brought a few friends up here to show them the view. The four of them had gone in for police questioning. As they'd agreed, they all stuck to Leda's story: Eris was drunk, and had slipped.

Avery was a little shocked at how easily their lie was accepted.

No one asked for any proof, or pressed any charges. Avery knew she should probably be held accountable for opening the roof in the first place, but the only consequence was a maintenance crew coming to seal it off forever. And all the stares that followed her now, even worse than they'd been before. *How shocking that Avery Fuller exhibited such poor judgment,* they all whispered, *letting her intoxicated friend onto the roof like that. What a tragic accident.*

The enormous church organ struck up, and everyone stood to sing a funeral hymn. Avery reached for the old-fashioned songbook—this wasn't the kind of church that projected the words onto your contacts, like hers did—and tried to follow along, her voice hoarse. She was holding the book with her right hand, but her left, the one next to Atlas, was hanging by her side. He brushed his pinky finger against hers, ever so carefully, in a gesture of silent support.

Avery ignored it. She could feel Leda staring at her from the row behind, just daring Avery to test her limits.

Avery didn't know what to do about Atlas. She loved him so much that it hurt, with a love that saturated every fiber of her being. But her love was complicated now, underpinned as it was by tragedy, and grief.

They couldn't run away, not with Leda knowing the truth the way she did. It would have been all right before—their parents would have figured out some story, a way to spin it the way they'd done last year when Atlas went missing. But if they left now, Avery knew Leda would expose their secret the moment they were gone. She refused to subject her parents to that. She and Atlas had to stay, at least until they figured out how to handle Leda.

A secret for a secret, she thought caustically. Yes, she had a secret on Leda, to counteract what Leda knew about her and Atlas. But how long could this tenuous balancing act really last?

Everything was different now. The time before Eris's death felt like another lifetime, another world. That Avery was gone. That Avery had broken, and a new Avery—harder, more brittle—had stepped out of the shards.

As she stood there, unable to even cry in grief over her friend, it seemed to Avery that she would never feel safe again as long as Leda was around.

MARIEL

MARIEL STOOD AT the back of the church, half hidden in the shadows, almost a shadow herself. She was wearing the dress that Eris had hated so much—she didn't own any other black dresses—but she'd thrown a sweater over it; paired with her black flats and fake pearl studs, it didn't look so terrible. She'd even left off her normal red lipstick, only dusting a little powder around her red-rimmed eyes, raw from crying. She wanted to look nice as she said her final good-bye to Eris. The only girl she'd ever really loved, though she hadn't told Eris, at least not in so many words.

She clutched the rosary in her pocket so tight that her hand turned white, and looked around.

The church was packed with hordes of people in black couture, clutching their quilted patent-leather bags and sniffling into monogrammed handkerchiefs. Were they all really Eris's friends? They couldn't have known her as intimately as Mariel had. Certainly they didn't *miss* Eris the way she did, with a howling grief that roared up from inside her, threatened to drown her. Every morning for the past three days, Mariel had woken up and thought of something she wanted to tell Eris—only to remember. And then the grief would hit her all over again.

Mingled with the grief was a terrible gnawing guilt, about the cruel things she'd said the night Eris died. She hadn't meant any of them; she'd just been upset in the moment, afraid that once Eris moved upTower, Mariel would lose her to that world. When Eris went to the party alone, Mariel had been nearly frantic.

She knew she loved Eris more than Eris loved her—that Eris might not even love her at all. That knowledge terrified her.

She'd loved Eris from the beginning, almost. She couldn't say why, but she'd felt inexorably pulled in from the very first moment. Eris was bright and careless, sure; but she was also luminous and magnetic, with an energy that made Mariel feel suddenly alive. She'd tried to fight it, for a while, but in the end Mariel had never really had a choice. She couldn't help loving Eris.

When Eris called her that night from the party, Mariel was overcome with relief. They were going to make up. Eris said she would be there soon. Mariel had stayed up all night and half the morning waiting, but Eris never came.

In the end, she lost Eris to this upper-floor world after all.

Mariel's gaze traveled to the casket at the front of the church. She couldn't believe that Eris was really in that thing. It wasn't big enough to hold her, with her deep, rich laugh and her exaggerated gestures and her larger-than-life emotions. This entire church—no, this entire *Tower*—wasn't big enough to hold her. Eris was more than all of it.

As the priest droned on, Mariel kept thinking about the way Eris had died. They said she'd followed her stupid friends up a ladder, onto part of the Tower's roof that should have been closed off. That she'd had too much to drink, and slipped and fell—a terrible, tragic, avoidable accident.

Mariel knew it wasn't true. Eris had *told* her she wasn't drinking. And then she'd sent that strange text, about how she needed to do something for a friend first. What was it that Eris had needed to do? What kind of friend would send Eris up onto the roof? Something didn't add up, and it was tormenting Mariel.

These highliers thought they were immune to real-life problems, that they were safe up here, ensconced miles above the ground with their money and their connections. But they were wrong. Mariel was going to find out the truth about Eris's death. If anyone was responsible—if anyone had anything to hide—she would make them pay.

She stayed in the back of the church for the rest of the funeral service, uninvited and ignored. But anyone who looked would have noticed the candelabra casting shadows on her dramatic cheekbones, illuminating the tears that streamed down her face.

ACKNOWLEDGMENTS

WRITING A NOVEL has always been my dream, and yet at times it felt like a near impossible task. I'm grateful to have had an incredible amount of support and assistance throughout this process.

First of all, huge thanks to the entire team at Alloy Entertainment. Joelle Hobeika, my intrepid, tireless, fearless editor: thank you for being my partner in crime from the very beginning. This book has benefitted from your encouragement and ideas in more ways than I could ever count. Josh Bank, the first person to hear my pitch on *The Thousandth Floor*: thank you for falling in love with it the way I did, and the countless hours you spent hammering out story beats with me. Sara Shandler, thank you for your energy, your encouragement, and your editorial insights. Les Morgenstein, Gina Girolamo, Maggie Cahill, and everyone else at the Alloy LA office, thanks for all your constant and enthusiastic support of *The Thousandth Floor*. Thanks also to Theo Guliadis, for your social media genius; Elaine Damasco, for your incredible vision and design work; Liz Dresner, for all your design talents; Romy Golan, for keeping us on schedule; Stephanie Abrams and Matt Bloomgarden, for managing more financial and deal spreadsheets than there are pages in this book; and Heather David, for somehow making the whole operation run smoothly despite all our efforts to the contrary.

I am so grateful to the wonderful team at HarperCollins, without whom this book would never have been possible. Emilia Rhodes: we've come a long way from the days when you and I edited vampire novels together. There is no one I would rather work on this project with. Thank you for believing in it, and in me. Jen Klonsky: thank you, thank you, thank you for your boundless enthusiasm and support throughout this process. Alice Jerman: I know firsthand what a difficult job it is assisting the editorial process, and I am so appreciative of all your help (especially all the last-minute edits you so patiently entered for me by hand!). Jenna Stempel: thank you for this lush, gorgeous, utterly perfect cover. Sarah Kaufman, Alison Klapthor, Alison Donalty, and the rest of the Harper design team: thank you for making this book look as beautiful as it does. Huge thanks as well to Elizabeth Ward and the rest of the Harper marketing team, and to Gina Rizzo and the publicity team, for your tireless and insanely creative efforts getting the word out about *The Thousandth Floor*.

To everyone at Rights People—Alexandra Devlin, Allison Hellegers, Caroline Hill-Trevor, Rachel Richardson, Alex Webb, Harim Yim, and Charles Nettleton—thank you for bringing *The Thousandth Floor* to so many places in the world. I couldn't ask for a more generous, gracious, and truly wonderful team of foreign rights agents. I am lucky to have you, and don't I know it!

To my friends and family, thank you all for your contributions to this work, and for putting up with me during its creation.

Mom and Dad—I would never have gotten here without your unwavering support and confidence in me. John Ed and Lizzy, you have always been my inspiration, my cheerleaders, and my earliest fans. Thank you to my grandparents, especially Snake, for teaching me to read many years ago. You are dearly missed, and always will be.

Thanks also to the Field family, for housing me during more than one long writing weekend, with a special shout-out to Kiki, for driving me eight hours home from a wedding while I wrote the whole way in your front seat. And finally, of course, to Alex: thank you for your patience, your guacamole incentives, for talking about fictional teenagers far more than you ever bargained on, and for reading this novel every step of the way.

READ ON FOR A PEEK
AT THE NEXT BOOK IN THE SERIES

the dazzling heights

PROLOGUE

IT WOULD BE several hours before the girl's body was found.

It was late now; so late that it could once again be called early—that surreal, enchanted, twilight hour between the end of a party and the unfurling of a new day. The hour when reality grows dim and hazy at the edges, when nearly anything seems possible.

The girl floated facedown in the water. Above her stretched a towering city, dotted with light like fireflies, each pinprick an individual person, a fragile speck of life. The moon gazed over it all impassively, like the eye of an ancient god.

There was something deceptively peaceful about the scene. Water flowed around the girl in a serene dark sheet, making it seem that she were merely resting. The tendrils of her hair framed her face in a soft cloud. The folds of her dress clung determinedly to her legs, as if to protect her from the predawn chill. But the girl would never feel cold again.

Her arm was outstretched, as though she were reaching toward someone she loved, or maybe to ward off some unspoken danger, or maybe even in regret over something she had done. The girl had certainly made enough mistakes in her too-short lifetime. But she couldn't have known that they would all come crashing down around her tonight.

After all, no one goes to a party expecting to die.

MARIEL

Two months earlier

MARIEL VALCONSUELO SAT cross-legged on her quilted bedspread in her cramped bedroom on the Tower's 103rd floor. There were countless people in every direction, separated from her by nothing but a few meters and a steel wall or two: her mother in the kitchen, the group of children running down the hallway, her neighbors next door, their voices low and heated as they fought yet again. But Mariel might as well have been alone in Manhattan right now, for all the attention she gave them.

She leaned forward, clutching her old stuffed bunny tight to her chest. The watery light of a poorly transmitted holo played across her face, illuminating her sloping nose and prominent jaw, and her dark eyes, now brimming with tears.

Before her flickered the image of a girl with red-gold hair and a piercing, gold-flecked gaze. A smile played around her lips, as if she knew a million secrets that no one could ever guess, which she probably did. In the corner of the image, a tiny white logo spelled out INTERNATIONAL TIMES OBITUARIES.

"Today we mourn the loss of Eris Dodd-Radson," began the obituary's voice-over—narrated by Eris's favorite young actress. Mariel wondered what absurd sum Mr. Radson had paid for *that*. The actress's tone was far too perky for the subject matter; she could just as easily have been discussing her favorite workout routine. "Eris was taken from us in a tragic accident. She was only seventeen."

Tragic accident. That's all you have to say when a young woman falls from a roof under suspicious circumstances? Eris's parents probably just wanted people to know that Eris hadn't jumped. As if anyone who'd met her could possibly think that.

Mariel had watched this obit video countless times since it came out last month. By now she knew the words by heart. Oh, she still hated it—the video was too slick, too carefully produced, and she knew most of it was a lie—but she had little else by which to remember Eris. So Mariel hugged her ratty old toy to her chest and kept on torturing herself, watching the video of her girlfriend who had died too young.

The holo shifted to video clips of Eris at different ages: a toddler dancing in a magnalectric tutu that lit up a bright neon; a little girl on bright yellow skis, cutting down a mountain; a teenager on vacation with her parents at a fabulous sun-drenched beach.

No one had ever given Mariel a tutu. The only times she'd been in snow were when she ventured out to the boroughs, or the public terraces down here on the lower floors. Her life was so drastically different from Eris's, yet when they'd been together, none of that had seemed to matter at all.

"Eris is survived by her two beloved parents, Caroline Dodd and Everett Radson; as well as her aunt, Layne Arnold; uncle,

Ted Arnold; cousins Matt and Sasha Arnold; and her paternal grandmother, Peggy Radson." No mention of her girlfriend, Mariel Valconsuelo. And Mariel was the only one of that whole sorry lot—aside from Eris's mom—who had truly loved her.

"The memorial service will be held this Tuesday, November first, at St. Martin's Episcopal Church, on floor 947," the holo actress went on, finally managing a slightly more somber tone.

Mariel had attended that service. She'd stood in the back of the church, holding a rosary, trying not to break out into a scream at the sight of the coffin near the altar. It was so unforgivingly final.

The vid swept to a candid shot of Eris on a bench at school, her legs crossed neatly under her plaid uniform skirt, her head tipped back in laughter. "Contributions in memory of Eris can be made to the Berkeley Preparatory Academy's new scholarship fund, the Eris Dodd-Radson Memorial Award, for underprivileged students with special qualifying circumstances."

Qualifying circumstances. Mariel wondered if being in love with the dead scholarship honoree counted as a qualifying circumstance. God, she had half a mind to apply for the scholarship herself, just to prove how screwed up these people were beneath the gloss of their money and privilege. Eris would have found the scholarship laughable, given that she'd never shown even a slight interest in school. A prom drive would have been much more her style. There was nothing Eris loved more than a fun, sparkly dress, except maybe the shoes to match.

Mariel leaned forward and reached out a hand as if to touch the holo. The final few seconds of the obit were more footage of Eris laughing with her friends, that blonde named Avery and a few other girls whose names Mariel couldn't remember. She loved this part of the vid because Eris seemed so happy, yet she resented it because she wasn't part of it.

The production company's logo scrolled quickly across the final image, and then the holo dimmed.

There it was, the official story of Eris's life, stamped with a damned *International Times* seal of approval, and Mariel was nowhere to be seen. She'd been quietly erased from the narrative, as if Eris had never even met her at all. A silent tear slid down her cheek at the thought.

Mariel was terrified of forgetting the only girl she'd ever loved. Already she'd woken up in the middle of the night, panicked that she could no longer visualize the exact way Eris's mouth used to lift in a smile, or the eager snap of her fingers when she'd just thought of some new idea. It was why Mariel kept watching this vid. She couldn't let go of her last link to Eris, forever.

She sank back into her pillows and began to recite a prayer.

Normally praying calmed Mariel, soothed the frayed edges of her mind. But today she felt scattered. Her thoughts kept jumping every which way, slippery and quick like hovers moving down an expressway, and she couldn't pin down a single one of them.

Maybe she would read the Bible instead. She reached for her tablet and opened the text, clicking the blue wheel that would open a randomized verse—and blinked in shock at the location it spun her to. The Book of Deuteronomy.

You shall not show pity: but rather demand an eye for an eye, a tooth for a tooth, burn for burn, wound for wound . . . for this is the vengeance of the Lord . . .

Mariel leaned forward, her hands closing tight around the edges of the tablet.

Eris's death wasn't a drunken accident. She knew it with a primal, visceral certainty. Eris hadn't even been drinking that night—she'd told Mariel that she needed to do something "to help out a friend," as she'd put it—and then, for some inexplicable reason, she'd gone up to the roof above Avery Fuller's apartment.

And Mariel never saw her again.

What had really happened in that cold, thin air, so impossibly high? Mariel knew there were ostensibly eyewitnesses, corroborating the official story that Eris was drunk and slipped off the edge to her death. But who were these eyewitnesses, anyway? One was surely Avery, but how many others were there?

An eye for an eye, a tooth for a tooth. The phrase kept echoing in her mind like cymbals.

A fall for a fall, a voice inside her added.

LEDA

"WHAT ROOM SETTING would you prefer today, Leda?"

Leda Cole knew better than to roll her eyes. She just perched there, ramrod-straight on the taupe psychology couch, which she refused to lie back on no matter how many times Dr. Vanderstein invited her to. He was deluded if he thought reclining would encourage her to open up to him.

"This is fine." Leda flicked her wrist to close the holographic window that had opened before her, displaying dozens of décor options for the color-shifting walls—a British rose garden, a hot Saharan desert, a cozy library—leaving the room in this bland base setting, with beige walls and a vomit-colored carpet. She knew this was probably a test she kept on failing, but she derived a sick joy from forcing the doctor to spend an hour in this depressing space with her. If she had to suffer through this appointment, then so did he.

As usual, he didn't comment on her decision. "How are you

feeling?" he asked instead.

You want to know how I'm feeling? Leda thought furiously. For starters, she'd been betrayed by her best friend and the only boy she'd ever really cared about, the boy she'd lost her virginity to. Now the two of them were *together* even though they were adopted siblings. On top of that, she'd caught her dad cheating on her mom with one of her classmates—Leda couldn't bring herself to call Eris a friend. Oh, and then Eris had *died* because Leda had accidentally pushed her from the roof of the Tower.

"I'm fine," she said briskly.

She knew she'd have to offer up something more expansive than "fine" if she wanted to get out of this session easily. Leda had been to rehab; she'd learned the scripts. She took a deep breath and tried again. "What I mean is, I'm recovering, given the circumstances. It's not easy, but I'm grateful to have the support of my friends." Not that Leda actually cared about any of her friends right now. She'd learned the hard way that none of them could be trusted.

"Have you and Avery spoken about what happened? I know she was up there with you when Eris fell—"

"Yes, Avery and I talk about it," Leda interrupted quickly. *Like hell we do.* Avery Fuller, her so-called best friend, had proven to be the worst of them all. But Leda didn't like hearing it spoken aloud, what had happened to Eris.

"And that helps?"

"It does." Leda waited for Dr. Vanderstein to ask another question, but he was frowning, his eyes focused on the near distance as he studied some projection that only he could see. She felt a sudden twist of nausea. What if the doctor was using a lie detector on her? Just because she couldn't see them didn't mean this room wasn't equipped with countless vitals scanners. Even now he might be tracking her heart rate or blood pressure, which were probably spiking like crazy.

The doctor gave a weary sigh. "Leda, I've been seeing you ever since your friend died, and we haven't gotten anywhere. What do you think it will take for you to feel better?"

"I *do* feel better!" Leda protested. "All thanks to you." She gave Vanderstein a weak smile, but he wasn't buying it.

"I see you aren't taking your meds," he said, changing tack.

Leda bit her lip. She hadn't taken anything in the last month, not a single xenperheidren or mood stabilizer, not even a sleeping pill. She didn't trust herself on anything artificial after what had happened on the roof. Eris might have been a gold-digging, home-wrecking whore, but Leda had never meant to—

No, she reminded herself, clenching her hands into fists at her sides. *I didn't kill her. It was an accident. It's not my fault. It's not my fault.* She kept repeating the phrase over and over, like the yoga mantras she used to chant at Silver Cove.

If she repeated it enough, maybe it would become true.

"I'm trying to recover on my own. Given my history and everything." Leda hated bringing up rehab, but she was starting to feel cornered and didn't know what else to say.

Vanderstein nodded with something that seemed like respect. "I understand. But it's a big year for you, with college on the horizon, and I don't want this . . . situation to adversely affect your academics."

It's more than a situation, Leda thought bitterly.

"According to your room comp, you aren't sleeping well. I'm growing concerned," Vanderstein added.

"Since when are you monitoring my room comp?" Leda cried out, momentarily forgetting her calm, unfazed tone.

The doctor had the grace to look embarrassed. "Just your sleep records," he said quickly. "Your parents signed off on it—I thought they had informed you . . ."

Leda nodded curtly. She'd deal with her parents later. Just because she was still a minor didn't mean they could keep invading her privacy. "I promise, I'm fine."

Vanderstein was silent again. Leda waited. What else could he do, authorize her toilet to start tracking her urine the way the ones in rehab did? Well, he was welcome to it; he wouldn't find a damned thing.

The doctor tapped a dispenser in the wall, and it spit out two small pills. They were a cheerful pink—the color of children's toys, or Leda's favorite cherry ice whip. "This is an over-the-counter sleeping pill, lowest dose. Why don't you try it tonight if you can't fall asleep?" He frowned, probably taking in the hollow circles around her eyes, the sharp angles of her face, even thinner than usual.

He was right, of course. Leda *wasn't* sleeping well. She dreaded falling asleep, tried to stay awake as long as she could, because she knew the horrific nightmares that awaited her. Whenever she did drift off, she woke almost instantly in a cold sweat, tormented by memories of that night—of what she'd hidden from everyone—

"Sure." She snatched the pills and shoved them into her bag.

"I'd love for you to consider some of our other options—our light-recognition treatment, or perhaps trauma re-immersion therapy."

"I highly doubt reliving the trauma will help, given what my trauma was," Leda snapped. She'd never bought into the theory that reliving your painful moments in virtual reality would help you move past them. And she didn't exactly want any machines creeping into her brain right now, in case they could somehow read the memory that lay buried there.

"What about your Dreamweaver?" the doctor persisted. "We could preload it with a few trigger memories of that night and see how your subconscious responds. You know that dreams are simply your deep brain matter making sense of everything that has happened to you, both joyful and painful . . ."

He was saying something else, calling dreams the brain's "safe space," but Leda was no longer listening. She'd flashed to a memory of Eris in ninth grade, bragging that she'd broken through the Dreamweaver's parental controls to access the full suite of "adult content" dreams. "There's even a celebrity setting," Eris had announced to her rapt audience, with a knowing smirk. Leda remembered how inadequate she'd felt, hearing that Eris was immersed in steamy dreams about holo-stars while Leda couldn't even *imagine* sex.

She stood up abruptly. "We need to end this session early. I just remembered something I have to go take care of. See you next time."

She stepped quickly out the frosted flexiglass door of the Lyons Clinic, perched high on the east side of the 833rd floor, just as her eartennas began to chime a loud, brassy ringtone. Her mom. She shook her head to decline the incoming ping. Ilara would want to hear how the session had gone, would check that she was on her way home for dinner. But Leda wasn't ready for that kind of forced, upbeat normalcy right now. She needed a moment to herself, to quiet the thoughts and regrets chasing one another in a wild tumult through her head.

She stepped onto the local C lift and disembarked a few stops upTower. Soon she was standing before an enormous stone archway, which had been transported stone by stone from some old British university, carved with enormous block letters that read THE BERKELEY SCHOOL.

Leda breathed a sigh of relief as she walked through the arch and her contacts automatically shut off. Before Eris's death, she'd never realized how grateful she might feel for her high school's tech-net.

Her footsteps echoed in the silent halls. It was sort of eerie here at night, everything cast in dim, bluish-gray shadows. She moved faster, past the lily pond and athletic complex, all the way to the blue door at the edge of campus. Normally this room was locked after hours, but Leda had schoolwide access thanks to her position on student council. She stepped forward, letting the security system register her retinas, and the door swung obediently inward.

She hadn't been in the Observatory since her astronomy elective last spring. Yet it looked exactly as she remembered: a vast circular room lined with telescopes, high-resolution screens, and cluttered data processors Leda had never learned to use. A geodesic dome soared overhead. And in the center of the floor lay the pièce de résistance: a glittering patch of night.

The Observatory was one of the few places in the Tower that protruded out *past* the floor below it. Leda had never understood how the school had gotten the zoning permits for it, but she was glad now that they had, because it meant they could build the Oval Eye: a concave oval in the floor, about three meters long and two meters wide, made of triple-reinforced flexiglass. A glimpse of how high they really were, up here near the top of the Tower.

Leda edged closer to the Oval Eye. It was dark down there, nothing but shadows, and a few stray lights bobbing in what she thought were the public gardens on the fiftieth floor. *What the hell*, she thought wildly, and stepped out onto the flexiglass.

This sort of behavior was definitely off-limits, but Leda knew the structure would support her. She glanced down. Between her ballet flats was nothing but empty air, the impossible, endless space between her and the laminous darkness far below. *This is what Eris saw when I pushed her,* Leda thought, and despised herself.

She sank down, not caring that there was nothing protecting her from a two-mile fall except a few layers of fused carbon. Pulling her knees to her chest, she lowered her forehead and closed her eyes.

A shaft of light sliced into the room. Leda's head shot up in panic. No one else had access to the Observatory except the rest of the student council and the astronomy professors. What would she say to explain herself?

"Leda?"

Her heart sank as she realized who it was. "What are you doing here, Avery?"

"Same thing as you, I guess."

Leda felt caught off guard. She hadn't been alone with Avery since that night—when Leda confronted Avery about being with Atlas, and Avery led her up onto the roof, and everything spun violently out of control. She wanted desperately to say something, but her mind had strangely frozen. What *could* she say, with all the secrets she and Avery had made together, buried together?

After a moment, Leda was shocked to hear footsteps approaching, as Avery walked over to sit on the opposite edge of the Oval.

"How did you get in?" she couldn't help asking. She wondered if Avery was still talking to Watt, the lower-floor hacker who'd helped Leda find out Avery's secret in the first place—Leda hadn't spoken to him since that night, either. But with the quantum computer he was hiding, Watt could hack basically anything.

Avery shrugged. "I asked the principal if I could have access to this room. It helps me, being here."

Of course, Leda thought bitterly, she should have known it was as simple as that. Nothing was off-limits to the perfect Avery Fuller.

"I miss her too, you know," Avery said quietly.

Leda looked down into the silent vastness of the night to protect herself from what she saw in Avery's eyes.

"What happened that night, Leda?" Avery whispered. "What were you *on*?"

Leda thought of all the various pills she'd popped that day as she'd sunk ever deeper into a hot, angry maelstrom of regret. "It was a rough day for me. I learned the truth about a lot of people that day—people I had trusted. People who *used* me," she said at last, and was perversely pleased to see Avery wince.

"I'm sorry," Avery told her. "But, Leda, please. Talk to me."

More than anything, Leda wanted to tell Avery all of it: how Leda had caught her cheating scumbag of a father having an affair with Eris; and how awful she'd felt, realizing that Atlas had only ever slept with her in a fucked-up attempt to forget Avery. How she'd had to drug Watt to uncover that particular grain of truth.

But the thing about the truth was that once you learned it, it became impossible to unlearn. No matter how many pills Leda popped, it was still there, lurking in the corners of her mind like an unwanted guest. There weren't enough pills in the world to make it go away. So Leda had confronted Avery—screamed at her atop the roof without fully knowing what she was saying; feeling disoriented and dizzy in the oxygen-thin air. Then Eris had come up the stairs and told Leda she was *sorry*, as if a fucking apology would fix the damage she'd done to Leda's family. Why had Eris kept walking toward her even when Leda told her to stop? It wasn't Leda's fault that she'd tried to push Eris away.

She had just pushed too hard.

All Leda wanted now was to confess everything to her best friend, to let herself cry about it like a child.

But stubborn, sticky pride muffled the words in her throat, kept her eyes narrowed and her head held high. "You wouldn't understand," she said wearily. What did it matter, anyway? Eris was already gone.

"Then help me understand. We don't have to be this way, Leda—threatening each other like this. Why won't you just tell everyone it was an accident? I know you never meant to hurt her."

They were the same words she'd thought to herself so many times, yet hearing them spoken by Avery wakened a cold panic that grasped at Leda like a fist.

Avery didn't *get* it, because everything came so easily to her. But Leda knew what would happen if she tried to tell the truth. There would probably be an investigation and a trial, all made worse by the fact that Leda had tried to cover it up—and the fact that Eris had been sleeping with Leda's dad would inevitably come to light. It would put Leda's family, her *mom*, through hell; and Leda wasn't stupid. She knew that looked like a damned convincing motive for pushing Eris to her death.

What right did Avery think she had, anyway, gliding in here and granting absolution like some kind of goddess?

"Don't you dare tell anyone. If you tell, I swear you'll be sorry." The threat fell angrily into the silence. It seemed to Leda that the room had grown several degrees colder.

She scrambled to her feet, suddenly desperate to leave. As she stepped from the Oval Eye onto the carpet, Leda felt something fall out of her bag. The two bright pink sleeping pills.

"Glad to see some things haven't changed." Avery's voice was utterly flat.

Leda didn't bother telling her how wrong she was. Avery would always see the world the way she wanted to.

At the doorway she paused to glance back. Avery had slid to kneel in the middle of the Oval Eye, her hands pressed against the flexiglass surface, her gaze focused on some point far below. There was something morbid and futile about it, as if she were kneeling there in prayer, trying to bring Eris back to life.

It took Leda a moment to realize that Avery was crying. She had to be the only girl in the world who somehow became *more* beautiful when she cried; her eyes turned an even brighter blue; the tears on her cheeks magnified the startling perfection of her face. And just like that, Leda remembered all the reasons she resented Avery.

She turned away, leaving her former best friend to weep alone on a tiny fragment of sky.

Dear readers,

In the summer of 2014, when I first started working on a book about a group of teenagers in futuristic New York, there were six main narrators: Avery, Leda, Eris, Rylin, Watt . . . and Cord.

The story eventually developed in a different way, and I decided to cut Cord's point of view. But I wanted to share some of those deleted scenes now, just for fun. I hope you love getting a peek inside Cord's head!

Katharine

CORD

"INCREDIBLE," MUTTERED CORD Anderton, letting his hand skim lightly over the hood of the convertible. The antique, driver-run car was black—so inscrutably black that in the shadowed half-light of the garage, it almost seemed purple. He glanced at Travis. "Where did you say you found that last part again?"

"Tokyo. Don't worry, I routed it through Sydney and then San Diego first," Travis assured him, though Cord wasn't really listening. He'd opened the car door and slid into the driver's seat, an eager nervousness prickling over his skin. Finally. Here he was, about to drive the convertible after six years of searching for those final few pieces.

Like it, Dad? he thought, as if his father were here right now, leaning back in the passenger seat with a grin.

Like always, the silent question remained unanswered.

Driving the convertible had been his dad's dream, not Cord's.

Before he died, Jeff Anderton had collected these driver-run cars, and hired Travis to get them running again. Owning cars like this was definitely illegal, and as for driving them—to most people it would have been unthinkable. Far too dangerous, and crazy.

Cord's dad had driven them. A lot.

Not that Cord had known any of this the day his parents' will was read. He still remembered walking into the lawyer's office that afternoon: everything had felt cold and muffled and just a little bit distorted, like a dream. Or maybe that was just the Spokes he'd been prescribed.

He'd stood in the stuffy conference room, wearing that awful dark suit, surrounded by distant family members, while the executor divided up his parents' estate in clipped, businesslike tones. The whole time, Cord kept thinking that this couldn't be happening, that his parents weren't gone, not really.

When the lawyer rattled off the Andertons' various vacation properties, Cord registered a moment of surprise at the "home in West Hampton, and all its contents," bequeathed to him and Brice. He hadn't even *known* about a property in West Hampton. "We should sell that," Brice had muttered, and then they'd moved on to the London flat, and the moment was forgotten.

Later, Cord would never understand why he'd gone out to the Hamptons one January afternoon. Maybe on some level he'd known that it was more than just another line item in his parents' will. Whatever the reason, he'd gone—and saw the garage.

"If you want to sell, I can line up some buyers," Travis had explained as Cord glanced around at the cars lined up in neat, orderly rows. "It might take some time, but I'll ask around, and—"

"No," Cord said automatically. "I want to drive them."

Travis had lifted a skeptical eyebrow. "Are you sure? This shit's pretty illegal, and you're . . . how old are you, exactly?"

Cord had insisted. If his dad had done this, then he was determined to do it too.

Now, five years later, he leaned forward to adjust the mirrors of the 2032 convertible. At a glance, Travis tossed him the keys.

Cord's gaze drifted to the fuel gauge, and he frowned. "You only got a quarter tank?"

Travis reached down to manually lift the garage door. It wasn't on loop with the electricity in the rest of the house: too risky, in case anyone came looking. "My usual guy got arrested, and I haven't found someone new. At this point I might just learn to home-brew it myself," Travis quipped, but Cord heard a distinct note of fear beneath the sarcasm. It was easy to forget how dangerous this was.

"Just don't burn down the garage," he called out over the engine as he pulled into the residential street.

Most houses were sleeping till next summer, but Cord saw lights on in a few of them—a family watching a holo, a porch streaming with floodlights. He hummed toward the turnoff. The highway extended silently before him, a dark ribbon leading in one direction toward the ocean and in the other back toward the Tower. Cord paused only an instant before turning east and slamming the accelerator.

The world seemed to fall silent, or maybe it was impossibly loud; everything blurred into a roar of adrenaline and rubber and metal, the wind whipping fast around the windshield of the car. The convertible felt like a living thing, responding to Cord's thoughts almost before he knew them himself. The road curved slightly, and he barely even leaned before the car was turning with him, smooth and certain.

His eyes flicked to the speed, lit up in glowing yellow numbers on the dashboard. It was getting high. Still he pressed on the accelerator. He was going so fast that the wind brought tears to his eyes, or maybe they'd been there already. Cord wiped at them angrily.

This was the very last car his dad had been trying to reconstruct before he died.

Cord knew it was selfish, but he'd never told Brice about any of this. He'd meant to after the very first visit, except . . . Brice never asked about the Hamptons house, never followed up to see what had happened to it. And after the reading of the will, he'd just left town without warning. "I had to go," he later explained to Cord. As if the loss was Brice's burden alone, as if they weren't both struggling under the impossible weight of it.

The garage had acquired an almost sacred aspect in Cord's mind. He *needed* to drive, now, needed that numbing feeling of going so fast that everything else in the world shrank down to nothing. It was better than any drug, which Cord could say with some authority, given that he'd tried most drugs at least once.

What had his father been chasing when he went out driving like this? Or maybe the better question was, what had he been running from?

Cord had spent years trying to finish this convertible. He'd become convinced that if he could finally drive it—could do what his dad had intended to do but never got the chance—he might finally understand him.

The road curved sharply up ahead. He braced himself, his grip tightening on the steering wheel, but it seemed to fight against him. Something was suddenly clawing at his throat, something bitter and disappointed.

He'd been reaching so eagerly for a flicker of connection, for just a brief flash of insight about his father. But his dad wasn't here.

Belatedly Cord realized that his turn was wrong—he was swerving too far to the side, the wheels skidding angrily on the smooth, conductive pavement—

He pulled sharply on the wheel, trying to turn into the spin somehow, but it was too late—momentum had snared the car and thrown it violently out of control. The world outside was reduced to ribbons of variegated darkness. Cord braced himself for the impact, throwing his arm above his head. The edge of the old-fashioned seatbelt sliced into his stomach.

Then everything jolted to a sudden, loud, brutal stop.

Cord opened his eyes and saw that the convertible had smashed into a tree. The entire right half of the car was gloriously shattered. The passenger door was folded in on itself, fragments of metal and glass scattered over the ground in gleaming shards.

He fumbled for the door and released it, only to fall painfully to the ground with a yell. His palms were cut up with tiny shards of windshield. He looked down at them and realized they were shaking.

I had an accident, he flickered to Travis, and dropped a pin for his location.

What happened? Did anyone see? Travis replied. Cord didn't answer.

No one had seen because the road was empty. There was no one here but Cord. No matter how hard he tried—no matter how many cars he rebuilt, how fast he drove—he wasn't going to bring back his dad. Nothing he did would change the fact that he was still alone.

He glanced at the clock in the corner of his vision and sighed.

Fourteen whole minutes he'd lasted, with the car he'd spent years trying to build. Somehow he wasn't shocked. He was always breaking things, wasn't he?

He leaned his head back against the smashed car and closed his eyes.

CORD

"NO!" THE IMAGE of Cord's mom exclaimed, illuminated on the Holoden wall in vibrant 3D. "Don't you dare!"

Holographic four-year-old Cord clutched at the garden hose in the yard at his grandparents' house in Rhode Island. "Oops," he proclaimed without an ounce of contrition as he turned the hose on his mom. She laughed, her eyelet sundress drenched, her dark hair streaming with water down her back.

Cord swirled the watery remains of his drink as he watched. He knew it was weird, and probably melancholy, to sit here with old family holos after a party. But he was moody and drunk, and no one else was here to see, and who was to say what he could or couldn't do, anyway? He smiled a little as his dad began chasing a squealing Cord around the yard. God, even Brice looked happy back then, his arms outstretched as he played some kind of VR flying game.

Just as his dad scooped Cord into his arms, the door to the Holoden swung inward.

Cord looked up sharply, ready to let loose at whoever had broken the illusion—and paused.

There was something familiar about the girl standing there, though Cord couldn't exactly remember why. She was startlingly pretty, with delicate half-Asian features and bright green eyes. He wondered what she was dressed as, with her messy ponytail and low-slung jeans and her multicolored kaleidoscope of rubber bracelets.

"I'm sorry," she mumbled. "I just wanted to let you know that I'm finished. So I'm heading out."

Shit, Cord realized belatedly, she wasn't wearing a costume at all. This girl was the maid. Mrs. Myers's daughter. What was her name again? He nodded slowly.

"I didn't have time to go home and change. You didn't give me much notice," the girl added, her voice stiff, and her name came to him in one of those rare drunken flashes of brilliance.

"Rylin Myers," he said slowly, almost conversationally. "How the hell are you?" For some surprising reason, he gestured to the chair next to him.

For some other, equally surprising reason, Rylin took it.

"Aside from being groped by your friends, just great," she snapped, tucking her legs up to cross them beneath her. "Sorry," she added with an exhale. "It's been a long night."

"Well, most of them aren't my friends." Even though he'd forgotten about her existence until five minutes ago, Cord felt newly angry at the thought of people harassing Rylin. God, he really *was* drunk and moody.

Rylin glanced around the Holoden, taking in its dark carpeting and oversize armchairs, the massive bar along the back wall, currently covered with snack-pack wrappers. After their parents died, Brice had installed a bar in almost every room of the apartment. *Always have a drink within arm's reach*, he'd joked. Cord had thought it was funny—but now, seeing it through Rylin's eyes, it seemed juvenile. He wondered why he even cared.

Rylin leaned back, her shirt slipping up to reveal the pale ribbon of her midriff. Cord forced himself to look higher, to where she was playing with something on a chain around her neck.

"What is that?" he asked.

Rylin seemed caught off guard. She quickly dropped the necklace. "It was my mom's."

"Why the Eiffel Tower?" he asked, because it seemed like a safe enough question.

Rylin bit her lip. "It was an inside joke of ours. We used to always say that if we ever had the money, we would take the train to Paris, eat at a fancy Café Paris."

"Did you ever end up going?"

"I've barely left the Tower." Rylin spoke the words matter-of-factly, not looking for sympathy. Definitely her mother's daughter.

Cries of laughter flooded the room as the holo lit back up. Cord quickly muttered a few commands, and the room sank back into darkness.

For a moment they both just stared at the empty screen. Cord didn't know what to say. He hadn't meant to share that footage with anyone; it was *private*—but when he glanced over and saw Rylin's expression, his resentment faltered.

"It's nice that you have those vids. I wish we had more of my mom," she said, breaking the silence.

"I'm sorry," Cord told her, though he'd always hated when people told him they were sorry; he knew the words were useless and ineffective. But sometimes he didn't know what else to say.

"It's fine," Rylin told him.

Cord knew she was lying. He'd told the same lie plenty of times. It wasn't fine, not at all.

A sudden growl came from Rylin's stomach. Cord glanced at the time: 3:21 a.m. "You hungry?" he asked unnecessarily. "We could dig into the leftovers, if you want."

"Yes." Rylin practically jumped up from her seat, then followed him along the hallway and back down the enormous glass staircase.

"Next time you should eat the catering. Sorry, I should have told you that."

Rylin nodded distractedly. Beneath the swoop of her ponytail, Cord saw a small, vicious red mark on her neck. It looked almost like a bite. His hands clenched imperceptibly as he wondered what—or rather, who—it was from.

It was only after he tried to open the refrigerator that Cord remembered he'd set it on output-restriction mode.

"Per the instructions of Muscle Regime 2118, your daily nutritional intake has been capped. Calorie count will reset after the conclusion of REM cycle," the fridge's automated voice informed him.

"Muscle regime," Rylin repeated, her eyes dancing. She was clearly struggling not to laugh. "I should get one of those."

"Guest override," Cord mumbled, the blood rising to his face. What was *wrong* with him? Maybe he'd had more to drink than he realized. Or maybe he was still experiencing the aftershocks of wrecking that convertible. "Can you just put your hand on the fridge, to prove you're here?"

Rylin placed her palm to the refrigerator door, and he pulled the door open to grab takeout containers at random. Rylin took a box of pizza cones from his hand and tore into one. "Mmm," she exclaimed through a mouthful of the cheesy fried crust. She had dribbled pizza sauce on her mouth but was eating too ravenously to notice.

She was nothing like the other girls Cord knew.

"Oh my god! Are those Gummy Buddies?" Rylin burst out, looking over his shoulder at the box. "Do they actually move when you bite off their heads, like they do in the adverts?"

"You've never had a Gummy Buddy?" He and Atlas used to eat them all the time when they were kids. It was fun in a mindless, hilarious way; biting off half a gummy and watching the other half squirm. Even more fun when you were high.

"No." Rylin took an abrupt step forward, her eyes lit up with eagerness. She really was pretty. Not the way Avery was, all symmetrical and flawless, or flashy and sultry like Eris. No, she was different. He would have called it softer, except that he sensed a steely determination underlying Rylin's every move.

"Come on. Try one." He handed her the bag, wondering why he was doing this, what he really thought was going to happen.

Rylin selected a gummy and popped it whole into her mouth. She frowned in disappointment when nothing happened.

Cord barely held back a laugh. "You didn't do it right. You have to bite off the head, or the legs. You can't just eat it all at once."

Rylin narrowed her eyes as if she wasn't quite sure whether to believe him. Then she took a cherry-red gummy and bit off the bottom half, revealing her row of small white teeth. The RFID chip in the remaining top part of the gummy abruptly let out a high-pitched scream.

"Crap!" Rylin exclaimed, dropping the gummy on the floor. It kept twitching near her feet. She sidled backward, watching the gummy with wide, terrified eyes, as if it were an animal that might dart out and bite her ankles.

Cord burst out laughing. It was all too much: the gummy thrashing about on the floor; the fact that he was here with the daughter of his family's former maid, a girl he didn't know and didn't understand. He felt oddly proud to have surprised Rylin. For some reason, he suspected she wasn't surprised that often.

"Here, try again," he suggested, holding out the bag of Gummy Buddies. "If you bite off the head, they don't scream, just move around."

Rylin crossed her arms. Cord found himself watching her, his eyes drawn to the tiny stitches along the neckline of her shirt. They were fraying a little at the back. That red mark on her neck had grown even brighter with her flush of excitement.

"I'm good, thanks," she said, and Cord heard the finality in her tone. She was about to leave. He realized to his surprise that he didn't want her to.

Before he could think twice, he closed the distance between them and lowered his mouth to hers.

The kiss was hot and sweet and tasted like lightning. It was as disorienting as the car crash out on Long Island, as if all Cord's senses had been set on fire at once. He pulled Rylin closer, bending her backward—

Dimly he realized that her hands were on his chest and she was shoving him away.

He stumbled back. His pulse beat erratically under the surface of his skin.

Rylin took a shaky, careful breath. Then she raised her arm and slapped Cord across the face.

"I'm sorry." Cord felt suddenly like the worst kind of ass. He'd thought— He'd been so certain that there was something between them—

"I clearly misread the situation," he added, stumbling over his words in his confusion.

Rylin's expression was closed off. "I—um, I should get going."

At first Cord couldn't think how to react, from the lateness and the bourbon and the swirling aftermath of that kiss. But before she reached the door, he'd realized that he had to say something, anything that would end the night on a better note than this.

"Hey, Myers. Catch."

He tossed the bag of Gummy Buddies toward her. She startled but caught them in both hands. A sugary peace offering.

"Thanks," she mumbled as the door shut behind her.

Cord stood there awhile after she left, leaning back against the refrigerator. Its cool surface felt pleasant on his overheated skin. What would he say to Rylin Myers when he saw her next?

Because he *would* see her, even if he wasn't yet sure when.

CORD

IT HAD STOPPED raining.

That was Cord's first realization as he swam slowly up to awakeness—that the rain had fallen silent. He kept his eyes closed, letting the events of the afternoon cascade over him: bringing Rylin to West Hampton, the breathless car ride, the storm on the beach. The way Rylin had turned to him with such calm surety and kissed him in the tiny square of shelter beneath their hovercover. Cord smiled indolently and reached across the warm sand toward her.

She wasn't there.

He sat up, running a hand through his hair as he glanced around, his heart calming an instant later when he saw her. She was sitting at the edge of the water, her legs tucked to one side, meticulously building a house of sand. In the watery light of the overcast sky, against the gray backdrop of the sea, her cranberry sweater was a vibrant splash of color. The wind lifted tendrils of hair off her shoulders.

She glanced up at his approach. Cord watched as she repeatedly scooped a palm of sand from beneath the waterline, drizzled it over the walls, then scooped another handful. Her pale features were somehow delicate and fierce at once.

"Nice sand Tower," he remarked, taking a seat next to her.

"It's a sand castle," Rylin corrected. "People used to build them, you know, before all the self-generating sand Tower kits."

Cord and Brice used to have a kit like that. You poured the attractant liquid on the ground, and it caused the sand to self-form into cohesive bricks marked with tiny colored labels so that you could stack them into a model Tower in a matter of minutes. Cord decided not to tell Rylin about that. He just reached for a handful of sand and began to copy her movements.

For a few minutes they worked in silence. Cord kept glancing at Rylin's wrists, her movements deft and quick. She would catch him looking and their eyes would meet and they would both smile. Then Rylin would flush and let her gaze drop quickly back to the sand.

She was nervous around him—even, or maybe especially, after what had just happened.

Cord was suddenly hyperaware of everything—the cool breeze on his skin, the graininess of the sand in his fingers. Everything felt sharply drawn, like when he'd first seen the Tower from a helicopter or drove a car for the first time.

"You do know that this will be destroyed in less than an hour, when the tide rises," he said, just to break the silence.

"I know. But the best things in life never last as long as we want them to." Rylin sat back on her heels. The hem of her jeans was dark with salt water.

"Is that a famous quote?" For some reason Cord felt like he'd heard it before.

Rylin blinked, startled. "Brice said it, in his speech at your parents' funeral."

What? "You were at the funeral?"

"My sister and I went with our mom. It's okay, we didn't come say hi to you or anything," Rylin said quickly.

Cord tried to shake off the sudden sticky, guilty feeling. But he and Brice definitely hadn't gone to Rylin's mom's funeral. He wondered if they'd even sent flowers.

"Thank you for today," she added. "I had a lot of fun."

"You weren't scared?" he asked. Rylin looked up in surprise, and catching her expression, Cord hurried to clarify. "Of the car ride, that is."

"I loved it. All of it." Rylin's smile was bright and wicked with meaning.

At that, Cord put a hand around her waist and pulled her close, kissing her.

Rylin's breath caught, and she shifted toward him, her hands snaking up around his neck as she kissed him back. She tasted like cherry lip balm and rainwater.

When they pulled away, she was beaming. Cord couldn't help smiling too. He thought fleetingly of all the other girls he'd kissed—girls who didn't even know him, who were only interested in him because of his last name—rushed and alcohol-fueled and careless, at parties.

But with Rylin, everything was just . . . easy, simple and uncomplicated and honest out here in the clean salt air.

"You really should stop working for me," he thought aloud, not for the first time. She was far too good to be working as a maid.

Rylin looked out over the water, her expression shuttered, and Cord knew at once that he'd said something wrong. "Maybe soon. I have a lot going on."

"I could always fire you," he suggested. He meant it as a joke, but Rylin didn't even smile. He ventured another try. "Rylin, I just want to help. And this—working for me—is so much less than you deserve." *You deserve to take on the whole world on your terms*, he thought but didn't say.

"Trust me, being with you is more than I deserve." She pulled her knees up to her chest and looped her arms around them.

He hated when she got all closed off like this. "I wish you would—"

"Don't," Rylin interrupted, and now she sounded angry. "Don't offer me money again, okay?"

Cord nodded jerkily, though he didn't understand. God knows he had more than enough money, and she could use the help. But he knew better than to push her and ruin what had been an incredible day.

He muttered at his contacts to call up the clock, and was startled to see how late it was. "Should we get going?" he asked, holding out a hand to help Rylin to her feet.

Rylin brushed the sand off her jeans as she stood, fiddling anxiously with something in her back pocket. She glanced down at the castle below them.

Then, in a single deliberate motion, she jumped on it. Its ramparts crumbled beneath her bare feet.

"Whoa, okay," Cord said, startled.

Rylin turned back, her dark hair spilling wildly over one shoulder. "Like you said, the tide will ruin it anyway. And if something of mine is going to be destroyed, I would rather end it myself."

There was a cynical ruthlessness to her logic that for some reason frightened him. But then she jumped again, kicking the sand in an exaggerated motion, and the odd foreboding in Cord's chest loosened. "Come on!" She gestured impatiently for him to join.

Cord gave up and stomped on the castle. They both began laughing at the silliness of it. "I feel like a ten-year-old," he admitted, but didn't stop because he wanted to preserve that light in Rylin's eyes.

When there was nothing left of the castle, he took her hand and led her back toward the car, her grip warm and certain in his. He wondered if the leather seats had been ruined by the rainstorm, then decided he didn't really care. His dad would've wanted him to *use* the car, not leave it pristine and untouched in the garage. And Cord knew for certain that his dad wouldn't have told Cord to drive it alone.

He would have wanted Cord to share it with someone special.

CORD

NO ONE BUT Eris ever looked at him in quite this way, Cord thought with a drunken, detached amusement. She stood before him now—both of them tucked away in the corner of Avery's party, beneath an abstract sculpture—a hand on one hip, her smile flirtatious and challenging. She looked as sexy as ever in her crimson dress and bold makeup, a designer scarf tied jauntily around her neck. But Cord wasn't fooled; he knew her too well. He could tell her heart wasn't in it.

Well, his wasn't in it, either.

"I've missed you, Eris. You and me, we kind of deserve each other, don't we?" He'd meant it to sound teasing, but it didn't come out right.

Eris deflated a little, tucking her hair behind her ears in a surprisingly vulnerable gesture. "Yeah. Maybe we do."

They were silent for a moment. Cord wished he had another drink. He wished he could shut up his stupid brain, make it stop thinking about Rylin. He wasn't going to see her again, anyway—

Except for some reason she was here. She stood there right now in the entrance to the library, looking at him and Eris, her expression raw with some painful emotion.

All night Cord had been thinking about what he would say to her, if he ever got the chance. That he'd cared about her, more than he'd admitted, and maybe not telling her that was a failure of his; but then, she was the one who'd stomped on his heart with the same casual violence that she'd unleashed on that sand castle.

He was hurt and pissed off, and yet all he could say was "Rylin?"

"Oh," Eris said breathlessly. "Is this her? Your maid?"

A wounded comprehension flickered over Rylin's face. Her eyes darted rapidly from Cord to Eris and back again, and then she spun around and fled back to the party.

For an instant Cord started forward as if to chase after her, only to falter in his steps. Let Rylin assume he was with Eris now. He didn't owe her anything.

"Yeah," he murmured in answer to Eris's question.

Eris tilted her head. Her earrings glimmered in the dancing shadows of the library, sparkling against her fiery curtain of hair. "Why'd she run off like that?" Typical Eris. She had a habit of saying exactly what she thought in the very instant she thought it, and somehow, because she was Eris, it came off as cute rather than rude. He could only imagine what Rylin had made of her.

"You're kind of intimidating to other girls. You know that, right?" Cord said wearily.

"Me?"

His gaze flicked around the party again but found no sign of Rylin. *Stop looking for her.* He glanced back at Eris. After Rylin's simple black dress, her face so naked with emotion, Eris's beauty felt aggressive and overdone.

"Oh my god," Eris pronounced slowly. "You *love* her. You love her even though she used you. After all your big statements about not believing in love, you're as much a sucker as anyone." She said it a little sarcastically, as if she wasn't quite sure whether she meant it.

"Love and trust aren't the same thing," Cord pointed out.

Eris raised an eyebrow. He wondered suddenly if he'd wronged her, the way he cut things off with her so abruptly all those months ago. He knew Eris hadn't loved him, but she *had* trusted him, and he hadn't exactly proven worthy of that trust. He shifted in discomfort. Maybe he owed her an apology?

Eris's expensive amber-flecked eyes narrowed as she read a flicker, and she turned away, giving a little toss of her head to indicate that she was making a ping.

It had to be that new girl she was dating. Cord shifted in mild discomfort, a little embarrassed that he'd been about to apologize—how self-centered of him to think that he mattered to Eris anymore at all.

"I mean all of it," he heard her say before her voice dropped lower.

Cord was vaguely aware of other people moving into the library, the hum of the party growing louder and wilder as the night wore on, but he tuned them out. He was strangely curious about what would happen with Eris and the new girl. He knew it was bad form to eavesdrop, but what the hell.

He caught the moment when Eris's whole face lit up at something her girlfriend had said. She transformed, relief strumming visibly through her system, as if she were illuminated by some private, personal sunbeam.

Cord leaned back and reached for a passing drink. He was

happy for Eris, he told himself. God, at least one of them should have a good night. And yet some terrible corner of his mind felt *jealous* of her joy, which was so shameful and base that he tried firmly to shove it aside; but it was still there. He was jealous that Eris and her girlfriend could work things out, that their fight was the kind that could be fixed with an *I'm sorry* ping.

What Rylin had done . . . he didn't know how to begin repairing that kind of damage.

Eris ended her ping and turned back to him, and Cord knew she was leaving, going back to her lower-floor girlfriend and happily ever after. He started to make a joke, something about how it wasn't a party if you didn't even have a single drink, but the words died on his lips.

Eris paused, looking Cord up and down as if considering something. He found himself strangely quiet under her stare. He realized that she'd changed recently—she was as incandescent and electric as ever, but that intensity was focused now, no longer impulsive and scattered.

"If you love her, go talk to her," Eris declared, as if it were obvious.

Cord's hand tightened around his drink, so tight that the shape of his fingerprints molded into the flexiglass. *We did talk,* he wanted to say, *this afternoon, when I learned the truth about who she really was.* But the words stuck, painful and blocky in his throat. He didn't want to relive that moment, even with Eris.

Eris sighed and shook her head. "I'm getting her for you," she informed him.

"What? Where are you—"

"I'm getting her for you!" Eris repeated, her words snapping with a new excitement, and Cord knew there was no stopping her. There never was, not until Eris either got what she wanted or failed dramatically in the attempt.

Of course she wanted to help, in her own, Eris-like way—but more than anything, he knew, she wanted to get Rylin here to prove him wrong. Eris never could resist the prospect of a good *I told you so.*

"Stop, Eris, you can't," he argued, except she'd already vanished into the crowd; the party melted amorphously back over her. Cord started off in pursuit, searching for a glimpse of her telltale red-gold hair, but eventually his steps slowed. What good did he really think he could do? Whether or not Eris found Rylin, it would end poorly for him.

He circled the party for a few minutes in a stunned haze, saying hello to people without realizing who they were. He picked up a shot off a passing tray and started to raise it to his lips, then caught sight of himself in one of this apartment's ubiquitous mirrors—his eyes red-rimmed, his hair disheveled and not fashionably so. No wonder Eris had felt worried for him.

"Cord! Have you seen Avery?" It was Atlas, wearing a boring blue button-down and an expression of concern.

"No, why?" Cord asked lazily, and set the shot down on some random antique. Why did Atlas always have to be such a buzzkill?

Atlas let out a breath. "I can't find her, and I have this feeling that something's going on . . ."

"Lighten up, Fuller. She's at a *party.*" Cord didn't bother hiding his sarcasm. "Probably she's off hooking up with someone."

Atlas flinched at that, in a way that seemed strange to Cord—but the thought was wiped brutally from his mind an instant later as the kitchen erupted in screams.

He and Atlas glanced at each other for only an instant before they both turned and started running toward that awful sound.

The crowds were thicker than ever, all the drunk and curious people congealing uselessly around the kitchen.

Cord pushed forward in Atlas's wake. The screams had grown louder, making him want to clap his hands over his ears. He felt a sickening sense of foreboding—there was something so *final* about the sound, something that lifted the hairs on the back of his neck and made him want to turn and run in the opposite direction.

"What's going on?" he shouted to no one in particular. There was a loud roaring in his ears, and at first he thought it was the roar of the party, but the party had gone silent as the screams grew even shriller. No one moved.

"Shit, *shit*." Atlas looked pale and wide-eyed. The screams were cracking now, rising and falling like an otherworldly orchestra. "Someone's on the roof."

"The *roof*?" Cord repeated, because it couldn't be possible.

He didn't believe it even when Atlas pushed open the door to the pantry and he saw the ladder with his own eyes, stretching up toward a tiny square of midnight.

He watched as Atlas stumbled forward, his face a mask of pain, but someone was already coming down the ladder. The crowds backed up, the terrible magnitude of the situation finally settling over them. Someone had turned off the music, and now they were all murmuring in low tones, pulling together in stupid, drunk curiosity. Cord wanted to shout at them to leave, but he couldn't find the words.

Avery came down first. She was crying in a way that terrified him, bent over and shaking with silent, broken sobs. Even now she looked so beautiful, like some ancient goddess of grief and sorrow. Cord wondered if those raw screams had come from her.

"We called the police," she whispered, and Atlas pulled her

into a brusque hug before stepping back. Cord saw his own fear reflected there in Atlas's eyes.

"Police?" Cord asked, since no one else seemed able to. "What? Why?"

Avery looked at him, and the anguish in her impossibly blue eyes, brimming with tears, made Cord feel sick. "She fell."

Cord wanted to ask what she meant, but his brain seemed to have broken, the entire world frozen and muffled. *Please not Rylin,* he thought wildly, incoherently. He knew it was irrational to assume that Rylin had gone up to the roof at all, but hell, the *existence* of the roof was irrational. And he hadn't seen Rylin anywhere in the apartment—and she was so maddeningly unpredictable, who could say whether she had seen this ladder and gone on up—

More footsteps clattered on the rungs.

Leda appeared next, tears streaking down her face. But she seemed somehow controlled beneath her grief, as if she'd taken a deep breath and buried all her feelings beneath the tightly wound surface.

Cord's heart gave a strange lurch. *Please no,* he thought again, *it can't be her, don't let it be—*

Rylin appeared, looking shaken and stricken and pale, and he let out an audible sigh of relief. He was still furious, still wounded, but now he wanted to yell and scream at her for going up on that damned roof on top of everything else.

"What do you mean, Aves? Who fell?" Atlas's question dropped gratingly into the silence.

And then Cord knew, with a terrible sinking realization. He craned his neck and looked around, hoping—wishing—he was wrong, but he didn't see her red-gold hair anywhere.

He wasn't surprised when Avery lifted her head and met his

eyes with a small, pained nod. And it felt like she was speaking to only him, that it was just the two of them in this crowded space together, alone with their shared grief.

"Eris."

Cord knew in that moment that nothing would ever be the same.

THE
TOWER [10,560 FEET]

THE EIFFEL TOWER
[984 FEET]

THE EMPIRE STATE BUILDING
[1,454 FEET]

PETRONAS TOWERS
[1,483 FEET]

ONE WORLD TRADE CENTER
[1,776 FEET]

SHANGHAI TOWER
[2,073 FEET]

BURJ KHALIFA
[2,717 FEET]

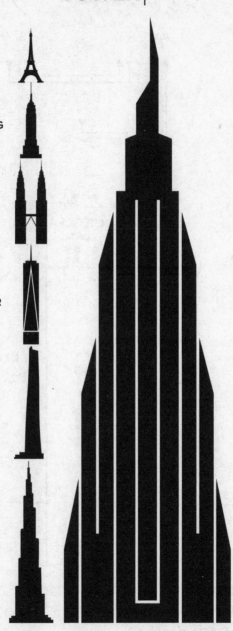

WHO'S WHO IN THE
the thousandth floor

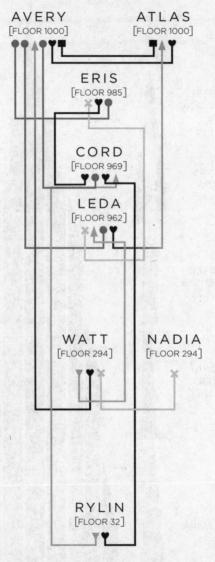

AVERY
[FLOOR 1000]

ATLAS
[FLOOR 1000]

ERIS
[FLOOR 985]

CORD
[FLOOR 969]

LEDA
[FLOOR 962]

WATT
[FLOOR 294]

NADIA
[FLOOR 294]

RYLIN
[FLOOR 32]

♥▶ LOVE   ▶ WORKS FOR
■▶ FAMILY   ✕▶ IT'S COMPLICATED
●▶ FRIEND